Trimmed with Murder

OTHER SEASIDE KNITTERS MYSTERIES

BY SALLY GOLDENBAUM

Death by Cashmere

Patterns in the Sand

Moon Spinners

A Holiday Yarn

The Wedding Shawl

A Fatal Fleece

Angora Alibi

Murder in Merino

A Finely Knit Murder

Trimmed with Murder

A SEASIDE KNITTERS MYSTERY

Sally Goldenbaum

AN OBSIDIAN MYSTERY

OBSIDIAN
Published by New American Library,
an imprint of Penguin Random House LLC
375 Hudson Street, New York, New York 10014

This book is an original publication of New American Library.

First Printing, November 2015

For more information about Penguin Random House, visit penguin.com.

LIBRARY OF CONGRESS CATALOGING-IN-PUBLICATION DATA:

Goldenbaum, Sally.
Trimmed with murder: a seaside knitters mystery / Sally Goldenbaum.
pages cm.—(Seaside knitters mystery; 10)
"An Obsidian mystery."
ISBN 978-0-451-47162-8 (hardback)
1. Knitters (Persons)—Fiction. I. Title.
PS3557.O35937T75 2015
813'.54—dc23 2015030573

Printed in the United States of America
10 9 8 7 6 5 4 3 2 1

Penguin
Random
House

For my family

Cast of Characters

THE SEASIDE KNITTERS

Nell Endicott: Former Boston nonprofit director, lives in Sea Harbor with her husband, Ben

Izzy (Isabel Chambers Perry): Boston attorney, now owner of the Seaside Knitting Studio; Nell and Ben Endicott's niece; married to Sam Perry

Cass (Catherine Mary Theresa Halloran): Lobster fisherwoman

Birdie (Bernadette Favazza): Sea Harbor's wealthy, wise, and generous silver-haired grand dame

THE MEN IN THEIR LIVES

Ben Endicott: Nell's husband

Sam Perry: Award-winning photojournalist, married to Izzy

Danny Brandley: Mystery novelist and son of bookstore owners

Sonny Favazza: Birdie's first husband

CLOSE FRIENDS AND FAMILY

Charlie Chambers: Izzy's younger brother

Andy Risso: Drummer in Pete Halloran's band; son of the Gull Tavern owner

Don and Rachel Wooten: Owner of the Ocean's Edge restaurant (Don) and city attorney (Rachel)

Ella and Harold Sampson: Birdie's housekeeper and groundsman/driver

Gracie Santos: Owner of Gracie's Lazy Lobster Café

Jane and Ham Brewster: Artists and cofounders of the Canary Cove Art Colony

Mary Halloran: Pete and Cass's mother; secretary of Our Lady of Safe Seas Church

Pete Halloran: Cass's younger brother and lead guitarist in the Fractured Fish band

Willow Adams: Fiber artist, Fishtail Gallery; Pete Halloran's girlfriend

TOWNSFOLK

Alan Hamilton, MD: Family doctor

Alphonso Santos: Owner of construction company; chamber of commerce cochair; married to Liz Palazola Santos

Amber Harper: Hitchhiker whom Charlie Chambers picks up and drives to Sea Harbor

Annabelle Palazola: Owner of the Sweet Petunia Restaurant

Archie and Harriet Brandley: Owners of the Sea Harbor Bookstore

Barbara Cummings: Co-owner of Cummings Northshore Nurseries

Beatrice Scaglia: Mayor of Sea Harbor

Carly Schultz: Nurse at Ocean View

Ellie Harper: Amber Harper's deceased mother

Esther Gibson: Police dispatcher (and Mrs. Santa Claus in season)

Father Lawrence Northcutt: Pastor of Our Lady of Safe Seas Church

Garrett O'Neal: Accountant at Cummings Northshore Nurseries

Harry and Margaret Garozzo: Owners of Garozzo's Deli

Helen Cummings: Wife of co-owner of Cummings Northshore Nurseries

Henrietta O'Neal: Longtime resident; Garrett O'Neal's aunt

Janie Levin: Nurse practitioner in the Sea Harbor Free Health Clinic; Tommy Porter's girlfriend

Jerry Thompson: Police chief

Laura Danvers: Young socialite and philanthropist, mother of three; married to banker Elliot Danvers

Lydia Cummings: Owner of Cummings Northshore Nurseries

Mae Anderson: Izzy's shop manager; twin teenage nieces, Jillian and Rose

Mary Pisano: Middle-aged newspaper columnist; owner of Ravenswood-by-the-Sea B&B

Merry Jackson: Owner of the Artist's Palate Bar and Grill; keyboard/singer in the Fractured Fish

Polly Farrell: Owner of Polly's Tea Shoppe

Richard Gibson: Esther's retired husband

Stella Palazola: Realtor in Sea Harbor; Annabelle's daughter

Stuart Cummings: Co-owner of Cummings Northshore Nurseries

Tommy Porter: Policeman

Trimmed with Murder

Chapter 1

Charlie hadn't yet reached the bridge that crossed over onto Cape Ann proper when he decided it was all a terrible mistake. A cruel joke his conscience had played on him, punishing him for all the wrongs in his life.

But it was too late to turn back. He'd vowed that in this grown-up chapter of his life he'd keep promises, honor commitments. Even if the truth was that it might not matter to anyone. No one was expecting him, not tonight, at least. And maybe the doctor had exaggerated the need in her clinic. But the fact was that he had said he would come. So he would.

Gripping the steering wheel until his fingers hurt, he squinted into the black wintry night. The highway was narrow and full of curves, unfamiliar to him.

And there was the rain that had begun about the time he'd passed a big mall at the Danvers exit. It was coming down harder now, fat sloppy drops that splattered on the windshield and spread across the glass. An angry wind pulled and pushed the car across the road, and the wild trees, swaying with weather's elemental force, seemed to reach out toward him until he found himself hugging the center line, avoiding their touch.

He approached another curve, his eyes stinging, focusing on the yellow line, the bend ahead.

He slowed slightly, pulling the wheel to the right. The shadows beside the road grew thicker here, the trees dense. At first he thought it was a sapling, a bare, slender tree bending along with its taller peers like naked dancers in the frigid, icy night.

But suddenly the road straightened and his headlights sliced through the darkness—catching the swaying figure as it stepped directly into the car's path.

Charlie slammed his foot on the pedal, the repeated pulsing of the ABS brakes sending vibrations through his body. His body shook, his mind ragged with fear. He'd almost hit someone, or maybe an animal. It couldn't be happening . . . not again . . . not . . .

His thoughts froze in the air. With white fingers clutching the steering wheel, he leaned forward, staring through the windshield, his eyes straining to see beyond the flapping wipers.

But there was no time to process what he was seeing. Seconds later the passenger door flew open. A rush of wind and rain filled the heated car, followed in seconds by a hooded body that slid onto the passenger seat.

The door slammed shut.

At first he felt confusion, a ringing in his ears so loud it blocked out the wind that rocked the small car. He pushed against his door, staring at the stranger.

Finally facial features appeared under the folds of the hood and he saw that it was a woman—sopping wet and disheveled—her face barely visible, but striking gray eyes luminous as they stared at him.

He glanced down at the slushy pools of water collecting on the leather car seats and dripping onto the floor of his BMW. An old backpack fell onto the floor, landing in a sea of leaves and frozen rain.

She followed his look and he thought he heard the trace of a laugh. Then she looked at him again, her eyes going up and down his body. "I thought big guys like you drove trucks."

He ignored the comment. Instead he concentrated on the girl herself, and his medical training kicked in. He couldn't see blood, just a wet, nondescript woman staring back at him. Was she hurt? Mentally ill?

She pushed back the hood of her parka, revealing a narrow, pale face and brown hair touching her shoulders in damp, limp strands.

But it was her eyes that stunned him, staring, challenging him. They reminded him of a piece of granite he had in his old stone collection. Granite with a touch of mica. A touch of glitter.

"Well?" she asked. "What are you waiting for?"

"Waiting for? Who the hell are you?" A foolish question—but the words came out of nowhere.

The smell of freezing rain and wet leather filled the car.

She laughed.

It was a strong laugh, but youthful. She was younger than he was, but not much. Late twenties, maybe. Lean, pretty, if she'd let herself be.

"What's your name?" Charlie asked.

"Jane Doe," she snapped, then buckled her seat belt and looked through the windshield at the road ahead. "Come on. Let's go. It's freezing."

Charlie's hands were on the wheel, but he kept staring at this peculiar woman who had somehow taken over his car. He forked one hand through thick, slightly curly hair. "Go where?"

Her face contorted into a frown. Then she released it, and spoke slowly, as if to a child. "From the signs along this road and the exit sign back there, I'd say we were headed for Sea Harbor."

Charlie shifted the car into first and pulled slowly back onto the road, his head turning now and then to get a better look at his passenger. Or maybe to be sure she wasn't slipping his phone or wallet, sitting on the console between them, into her pocket or backpack.

"You shouldn't be hitchhiking," he said finally. His voice was tight, with an unexpected paternalistic tone. "It's dangerous."

She laughed, mocking him, then said in a low tone, matching his, "You shouldn't be picking up hitchhikers. It's dangerous, young man."

He glanced over, unsure if she was joking or ridiculing him.

She pulled off her soggy gloves and dropped them on the floor, then slipped one hand into the pocket of her parka while she warmed the other in front of a heat vent. She twisted in the seat, her body turning toward his.

The movement pulled Charlie's eyes from the road again. He watched the bulge beneath the jacket grow as her fingers curled beneath the fabric.

"How do you know I'm not about to off you?" she said, her hand still in her pocket. "Maybe I'll take your money and your Bimmer and leave you by the side of the road."

Her look was focused and direct. It was so concentrated and sharp that Charlie squirmed in the seat. She was crazy. He was twice her bulk, a football player's body visible even beneath his heavy jacket—but she made him nervous. He wondered briefly if she'd wandered off the grounds of a mental health place somewhere along the highway.

"Or maybe worse—maybe I'll ravage you first," she said. She pulled her hand out of her pocket and walked her fingers across the console, over to his leg, crawling up his thigh.

"Cut it out," Charlie said through clenched teeth. His foot pushed down on the gas pedal, and the car skidded across the road. He held tight to the wheel and brought it back under control.

The girl pulled her hand away.

Charlie could feel the smile on her face and it irritated him.

"No gun," she said. "No nothing. Just me."

He swallowed a sudden swell of anger and drove across the bridge in silence. The rain was letting up slightly and on both sides of the river houses sparkled with holiday lights, cheerful and alive, defying the weather. Charlie glanced at the GPS and drove along the river road for a way, then followed the signs that welcomed him into Sea Harbor, home of the fighting Cool Cods.

The girl read the sign out loud. "I remember that. High school mascot."

"You're from Sea Harbor?"

"No. Well, sorta." She kept her eyes glued to the passing neighborhoods, houses lit up for the holidays. "I haven't been here since I was a kid. It looks different. You?"

Charlie shook his head. He felt as if he'd been there, though. All those pictures from his mother. Guilt pictures. He *should* have come over those many years. But he hadn't visited. Not once. Not when his whole family came to Boston for his sister's graduation. Not when she married their older brother's best friend—and his good friend, too.

He couldn't come, not then. Those were dark times for Charlie. His wandering years. Flings, morose moods. Anger. There was no room for darkness at a wedding. He'd done everyone a favor by staying away, or at least that was how he justified it in his head.

"So, why are you here?" Her voice had softened slightly and was almost friendly. He looked over. Her face had softened, too—her eyes brighter, her cheeks slightly flushed from the cold. A long straight nose. Her features fit together more pleasingly, as if the car heater had warmed more than her skin, bringing her face to life.

He looked back at the road and said, "A job."

She nodded and repeated his words. "A job. Okay. What kind of job?"

Charlie was quiet.

"Cat got your tongue?"

"I guess it does." He made a right turn, following signs that routed traffic to the harbor. COMMERCIAL AREA, one read. He pressed his foot on the gas and picked up some speed.

He hadn't intended to arrive in town so late, but the rain and an accident on 95 had slowed traffic to a crawl. Since no one was expecting him, it didn't really matter when he showed up, he supposed. The doctor had said she'd help him get settled when he arrived, but he hadn't told her exactly when he was coming—sometime around mid-December was as close as he came to nailing it down. A cowardly act. What he was really doing was giving himself time to change his mind.

But no matter, he couldn't show up on her doorstep unannounced, not to mention that he had no idea where her doorstep was. The only address on her card had been that of a community center. He'd find a place in town to spend the night.

Charlie looked out the side window, as if to hide his thoughts from the woman sitting inches away. There were other people living in Sea Harbor whom he could call to put him up for a night or two until he got organized. But he wouldn't. He couldn't. He pushed the discomforting thought to the back of his head.

"Amber," the woman said, pulling his attention back into the car. "You can call me Amber."

He nodded. "Charlie," he said, and took a curve faster than necessary. "Okay, Amber. It looks like we're in Sea Harbor. So, where can I drop you?"

She didn't answer. She was nibbling on her bottom lip, her eyes scanning the streets as if trying to match them to a memory.

"You okay?" Charlie asked.

"I hate this place," she said.

"But you're here."

"Briefly." Her look told Charlie to stop asking questions.

Charlie nodded. Briefly. It might be the same for him. No plans beyond the month he'd promised the clinic.

The houses were starting to give way to small shops. Straight ahead, beyond the harbor lights and spread out as far as Charlie could see, lay the ocean, its only definition a series of whitecaps that repeated themselves, over and over. He pulled to the left, turning onto Harbor Road, a street lined with old-fashioned lampposts fronting bars and cafés and retail shops. Sparkling white lights wound around the posts and up and down the street, giant red bows and boughs of evergreen-decorated storefronts, restaurants, and signs.

It was a scene from a Disney movie with one exception: the streets were nearly empty of people.

. . .

Tommy Porter, his uniform jacket smelling of wet polyester, stood in front of Jake Risso's Gull Tavern, just beneath the green awning. The rain had turned into a freezing drizzle and he pulled up his collar against the wet cold. *Snow,* Tommy predicted.

He thought about his fiancée, Janie, helping out at the big community center party in Anya Angelina Park, and he wished for the umpteenth time that night that he was with her. But then, he always wished that. And the wish made him smile. It was okay—Janie'd be ultrabusy tonight, helping run the darn thing, too busy to pay attention to him. She'd pulled her brother, Zack, into helping tonight, too—trying as always to keep the college kid on the straight and narrow path.

He couldn't complain about not being there anyway—he had volunteered to take the Harbor Road shift tonight, knowing no one else wanted it. It'd be a cinch, there'd be no crime. The weather was too bad for bar fights. Too cold for thieves or derelicts passing through. Too close to the holidays for people to entertain ill will.

He half listened to the canned music escaping from the bar as a few fishermen straggled out. Tommy waved and watched them lumber across the street, then spotted an unfamiliar car out of the corner of his eye. It was driving toward him on Harbor Road. Not that Tommy knew every car that came in and out of Sea Harbor, but this one didn't look homegrown. A red BMW, not new but well cared for, stood out.

And it was going too fast for the slick streets, was his second thought.

He took a few steps from beneath the awning, but before he could register anything, the car pulled over to the curb and came to a sudden stop, water spitting up around the wheels and sloshing over the curb.

Drunk driver? Probably not. Unless he was so drunk it didn't register to him that he was pulling up in front of a policeman in full uniform.

The driver left the car running, but opened the door, stepped out, and pressed his gloved hands on the roof, calling over to the policeman, "Hey—where is everyone? It's like a ghost town around here."

Tommy hunched up his shoulders against the drizzle and walked over to the car, his eyes not leaving the driver. He was a decent-sized guy, shoulders wide and with a thick head of hair that blew in all directions as the wind picked up. A little older than himself, he thought. Nice-looking in a collegiate sort of way—strong cheekbones and chin, a straight nose, inquisitive blue eyes set wide apart—features that probably got him carded in a bar now and then.

Not that thieves or killers or lowlifes had a certain look, but Tommy suspected this guy wasn't one of them.

Just then the passenger door opened and a woman climbed out, boots and jeaned legs coming first, then followed by a parka-clad figure that seemed to unfold with a certain grace from the car. Her hood was pushed back and she swept away strands of brown hair from her cheeks and eyes as she looked around, her gaze settling finally on the policeman.

She nodded, a brief and silent greeting.

Tommy held out an umbrella, but she shook her head, looking up into the black sky and letting the icy rain fall onto her cheeks.

The driver still stood on the other side of the car. Tommy looked back at him. "There's a big event at our community center. Most everyone's there. What do you guys need? Who are you looking for?"

It was the woman who spoke up. "Esther Gibson."

Tommy's eyebrows lifted. He looked more closely at her. She was attractive in a rough-around-the-edges way, maybe a little too skinny. "Esther?" He'd worked with the longtime police dispatcher since joining the force as a rookie ten years before—and he knew Esther's granddaughter. Nieces. This woman wasn't any of them.

"She'd be at the party." He pointed a finger toward the far end of

Harbor Road, where signs pointed out to a spit of forested land that held the center, a park, hiking trails, and picnic spots along the shore.

"Party?" Amber said.

"Yeah. It marks the beginning of the holiday season. Everyone's there, out at the community center."

"Is that where the free clinic is?" Charlie asked.

Tommy nodded. "Yep. Why? Are you sick?" *Silly question. The dude's driving a BMW and looks healthy as a horse.*

"No. Just wondering."

"The community center sits at the edge of a park—close to the water. They have all kinds of programs out there, parties, a great place for cross-country skiers to get warm. But the big to-do tonight is to make money for the free health clinic. It's a great program Doc Virgilio brought to town. I guess you've heard of it?"

Tommy nodded. *Dr. Virgilio.* That was Charlie's contact, the doctor who had spoken to his nursing school class and passed out her card. She could always use volunteers for her free clinic, she'd said. The clinic was in Massachusetts, a little town right on the water. *Sea Harbor.* That was when he had raised his head that day—at the words *Sea Harbor.*

So Charlie had taken a card when she passed them out and stuck it in his wallet. He looked out toward the water, remembering. But right now, at this very moment, he had no idea why he'd finally pulled out the card when he did all those months later. And even less why he had given the doctor a call. He must have been crazy.

He shook away the thoughts and concentrated on the man standing on the curb. The cop had answered one question anyway. He wouldn't be able to reach the doc tonight even if he wanted to. She'd most certainly be at the benefit. "So, is there a motel around here?" he asked. He glanced over at Amber. She had pulled her backpack out of the car and was standing on the sidewalk, taking in the gaslights along the street, the sheets of rain changing the glow into panels of light. He wondered what her plans were. She seemed unconcerned about where she would be spending the night.

"Yes and no," Tommy said. "There's a great B and B not far from here. Ravenswood-by-the-Sea. But it's booked solid, probably until after the New Year. There're some places in Rockport and Gloucester, but my bet is they're filled, too—there is some convention going on over in Gloucester, plus, people came in for our benefit here."

Charlie looked up and down the street, thinking. It wouldn't be the first time he had spent the night in a car. Maybe not in this weather, but it wouldn't kill him. He'd find a parking lot somewhere, pull out the blanket in the backseat that his dog used to use.

"Hop back in your car and follow me," Tommy said. "The community center has a few cabins that might not be full—they're rustic, bare-bones, but they have heat and beat the sidewalk or beach. Or I can find someone at the party who can put you up. Not usually a problem."

Amber shrugged, but Charlie didn't move. "Yeah, well, thanks, but there's no need for that," he said. "Maybe you can take the girl there to find Eloise or whoever she's looking for. I'll be fine—"

"Call me Tommy," he said, "and let's go. Neither of you should be wandering around in this weather. Besides, you were driving too fast and it's my bet you don't have a clue where you're going."

Before Charlie could argue, Tommy turned and headed over to a police car parked in a narrow drive beside the bar. In the next minute he had backed out, and was waiting in the middle of the empty street for Charlie to follow.

Charlie glanced inside the car, then looked over the roof to the curb.

Amber was gone.

Chapter 2

Amber Harper stood against the side of McClucken's hardware store in the narrow alley that ran alongside the stone building. It wasn't more than a slice of gravel, wide enough for a Dumpster, leaving just enough room for a skinny kid or two to hide with a pack of stolen cigarettes.

A skinny kid with wild hair who didn't quite fit in Sea Harbor.

Amber's thoughts slid uneasily back to those years of feeling lost and angry. A gangly teenager, mad at the world. Her once-edgy hormones were more level now, her mind clear, her anger under control. And she didn't smoke any longer; she'd grown up. But the feelings seemed to lurk in the shadows, sneaking up on her and reminding her that it's difficult to revisit one's past. And maybe not even a good thing.

She rummaged through her pockets for gloves but came up empty. *The car,* she remembered now. She had pulled them off to warm her hands on the car vent. *Good gloves, too.*

She stepped out from behind the metal refuse can, rubbed her hands together, and looked through the sleet and wind, watching the taillights of the police car and BMW driving away from where she stood. The cop drove slowly, carefully, probably looking for her, until both cars finally disappeared around the bend in the road.

She wasn't sure why she'd walked away. The cop was friendly enough and wanting to help. But facing a mass of people celebrating good cheer in a community center that hadn't existed in her other life wasn't where she wanted to be tonight. Not to mention the possibility of seeing people she had worked at avoiding nearly her whole life, even when she lived under their roofs. Tonight was definitely not the night to break her pattern.

She needed time to adjust, to figure out why she'd even come.

She shivered, hunched her shoulders up to her ears, and walked into the wind, her backpack moving slightly back and forth.

Harbor Road was the same—but different, she thought.

The old bookstore across the street was still there. Her gray eyes lingered on the familiar sign and took her back to the hours and hours that she had spent sitting on the floor on the store's upper level, her legs folded like a pretzel. She'd lose herself in Nancy Drew, *Anne of Green Gables, A Secret Garden,* and every Judy Blume she could get her hands on.

There were new stores, too—a yarn shop across the street where a beat-up bait shop once stood. Amber stared at it, thinking about Esther Gibson and her piles of yarn, the fat needles she'd used to teach Amber to knit as they sat side by side in the nursing home.

Amber shook off the memory and concentrated instead on a brightly decorated sign with a giant scooper. It was outlined in lights—an ice-cream shop. SCOOPERS, it read. Nice. And it didn't close for the winter as some on Cape Ann did. That was nice, too. A coffee shop with a patio was nearby. Apparently life hadn't stood still since the night that she packed the North Face backpack Esther Gibson had given her and hitchhiked her way out of Sea Harbor and into a new life.

Her hometown had grown up some.

Amber pulled up her hood and tucked a handful of wet hair beneath it, then shoved her hands into her pockets and began walking again, down Harbor Road toward the Gull Tavern. It would be warm at least. And unlike the many times she'd snuck up to the bar's rooftop patio, this time she'd be legit. Photo ID and all. Not that anyone would card check an almost thirty-year-old who looked every bit her age and then some.

Maybe she should have gotten back into the car with the Charlie guy. He was nice enough, even in the face of her rude behavior. Lack of sleep had a habit of bringing out the worst in her. At first she hadn't been able to gauge his age easily—something she was usually good at. The few freckles sprinkled across his nose didn't fit well with the worried look in his blue eyes or the concerned wrinkle in his forehead. So she'd flipped open his wallet when he was concentrating on the highway signs. Half a dozen years older than she was, if she'd read it right.

The cop reminded her of some of the nice people she'd known in Sea Harbor. He'd have found Esther for her, probably, and Esther would have hugged her close against her big ample breasts, the light flowery scent of her lavender lotion bringing a strange comfort. She would have insisted on giving her the wide bed in the back of the house—and probably a glass of warm milk.

It was an easy answer to the freezing rain and no place to sleep.

But she'd be fine, she'd find a place to sleep somewhere. And she would stay in town long enough to do what she had to do—to meet with the lawyer Esther had mentioned in the e-mail, and the priest her grandmother prayed with and confessed to, and all those other things church people did.

Father Northcutt. His name came to her suddenly. He was the only person in Amber's recollection that Lydia Cummings ever deferred to. And he was probably the reason Amber hadn't ended up in an orphanage.

So she'd see them, sign some papers, collect whatever it was that her grandmother had left her—a toothbrush, maybe, if she was lucky.

But mostly she'd say a final good-bye to her mother.

And then she'd be on her way.

The door to the Gull Tavern opened and a noisy group of kids younger than she exited into the night. Amber slipped in as the door closed behind them, cutting off the harsh wind.

She paused just inside the door, sinking back against the wall as her eyes adjusted to the dim light. Small groups sat around the tall round tables scattered throughout the room. The long shelf that ran along the window wall was partly full, couples passing baskets of calamari and fried clams between them and washing it down with beer. Others stood or sat at the bar, elbows rubbing against elbows as they drank beer and screamed at a football game playing out on the big-screen TV above the bar. The smell of grilled burgers and fried onions filled the air.

Some were college kids home for the winter break, feeling their oats with the relief of finished exams behind them, Amber guessed. The older guys in slickers had probably come right off the lobster, cod, and tuna boats, now moored in the choppy waters near the harbor. It was a good crowd—one that wouldn't have any idea who she was: the college kids would be too young, the fishermen too old and unconcerned.

She made her way to the bar and ordered a beer.

But Amber hadn't considered the person behind the bar. A sudden jolt shot through her and she held back a gasp. The bartender's shoulders bent forward as he pulled down on the tap handle, filling a mug with beer. His hair was white, thin, and straggly, his profile etched with age. He turned around slowly and set the beer in front of her, its froth curling over the mug and running down the sides.

Amber waited for him to look up.

Finally he did, his eyes scanning her face, his large nose filling a ruddy, weathered face. He kept his head still and then his eyes locked in to hers, holding her there as his face softened in recognition. His lips pulled up into a wry, lopsided smile, deep wrinkles spreading out in all directions. His voice was raspy, more weary than Amber remembered.

"So," he finally said, "you still trying to sneak your way into my bar, you skinny rascal? Got your ID ready?"

In the next breath he leaned over the sticky bar, pushed the beer and a bucket of peanuts to the side, and wrapped Amber in a hug.

Jake Risso never forgot a face.

Chapter 3

No matter that winds howled through the pine trees and freezing rain continued to pelt Sea Harbor, inside the lodgelike community center, a winter fairyland warmed the welcoming lobby.

"Oh, the weather outside is frightful," sang Birdie Favazza, her small, veined hands keeping rhythm with the band playing in the distance. She smiled up at Ben Endicott and coaxed him into joining her as she wound her way through the crowd, a slight jig shaking her body.

"Holiday fever or holiday punch?" Ben said, his words warm with affection for the woman at his side, her white cap of hair barely reaching his shoulder.

"Maybe a bit of each, Ben, dear." She moved toward an elaborate display a few feet in front of them. "How could you not feel good holiday vibes looking at this magical sight?"

A low round platform was set up in the middle of the foyer. But looking at it, one didn't see a platform; instead a magical scene hovered directly above the wooden floor. It was a replica of the parklike space near the town pier—the Harbor Green, as locals called it. But tonight the miniature scene wasn't green, it was wintry white, created from soft yards of snowy fleece. A gazebo stood in the center, its gables bright with tiny lights. Doll-sized park benches and picnic tables sat in the snowy folds, and narrow pathways meandered through the park, lit by black lampposts casting shadows across the snow. The entire scene evoked memories from every single person who had ever walked the Harbor Green, the well-loved wide-open space that hosted Fourth of July fireworks, summer picnics, seafood fests, open markets, and winter carnivals. It was where children would gather in a few weeks to cheer Santa on as he approached Sea Harbor in a lobster boat filled with cheery elves. Scattered throughout the snowy park, around the gazebo and among the benches and tables, were miniature Christmas trees, no more than ten inches high. They mirrored the recently planted trees down on the harbor, waiting to enter into the field of battle—waiting to be trimmed. A small white card rested at the base of each miniature tree, bearing names of the decorating teams.

Magical. Sea Harbor. Christmas.

"Well, what do you think?" Laura Danvers walked up to Ben and Birdie just as Sam Perry and Nell inched their way in to see the display. "The Canary Cove artists built the whole thing. It's amazing. And thanks to Cummings Northshore Nurseries, each of those tiny trees has a real counterpart planted over at the harbor." She stopped for a breath, her excitement coloring her cheeks, and looked at the faces of the crowd as people gathered for a glimpse of the scene.

"It's beautiful," Nell Endicott said. "You have such a gift for tugging on people's memories, their emotions, and their purse strings, all at the same time—and you do it in such a charming way, Laura."

Laura laughed, pleased. She worked ferociously hard on events like these, pulling in family and friends and anyone else who might make the events more successful. The young mother and civic leader was the consummate fund-raiser. She pointed across the crowded lobby to where Janie Levin was directing people to the coatroom and passed the accolade along. Janie's red curls bounced as she greeted group after group. "Janie gets tons of credit for this. She was a huge help. She even talked her brother into helping."

"Janie's a gem," Lily Virgilio said, leaning into the conversation. "The best nurse I ever had. You two are a dynamic duo, Laura, but I forbid you to steal her away from me."

Laura brushed off the compliments. "The free clinic is essential to this town." She looked over at a group standing near the bar and nodded their way. "I think having civic leaders like Alphonso Santos and Stuart Cummings come on board so quickly is proof of how highly people regard it."

It was especially generous of Stuart, Nell thought. In spite of his jovial, good-fellow manner, there was a sadness on his face that reflected the family's recent loss. Lydia Cummings's death had been expected, following a lingering illness, but nevertheless the family matriarch's passing had been a blow to her two grown children and to the entire north shore.

"I hesitated to approach Stuart so soon after his mother's death," Laura said, "but then he approached me and insisted Cummings Nurseries support it. He said his mother was completely behind the free clinic and she'd want her family involved."

"That's true," Birdie said. "Lydia was nothing if not generous with her money." She waved Laura off as she was called to another group.

"Where's Iz?" Sam asked, looking over the heads of the women. "She was with me a minute ago. Then she disappeared."

"She's probably in the ladies' room or caught up with friends," Nell said. "If you can't find her, come back and help Ben and me 'work the crowd,' as Laura put it. A handsome man on each arm makes it ever so much easier."

Izzy Perry stood at the edge of the crowd, far enough away to be swallowed up in the groups of people swarming about the lobby. She saw Sam looking for her and ducked around the corner, her cell phone in her hand.

"Our daughter is fine," Sam had insisted a few minutes earlier. *"She's in good hands. Trust me. Trust the sitter. Relax and enjoy yourself, m'love."*

He was right. Of course he was right. But between the community center and her home on the other side of town, a storm raged. And suddenly that placed a whole menacing world between her and her small daughter.

She cupped a hand over one ear and pressed her cell phone against the other, listening carefully to what she knew she'd hear when the ringing stopped and Stella Palazola picked up the phone. And it was exactly what she heard.

She ended the conversation and slipped the phone back into her purse. Abby was fine, ate a whole bowl of Izzy's homemade brown rice with carrots, and Stella was in heaven playing blocks with the toddler.

Why was she being such a worrywart? It was the weather, she told herself. The rain was turning to sleet and the sound of pellets beating against the large windows was disconcerting. Each time the door opened to welcome more guests, the sleet pounded louder, more persistent. Determined to be heard.

She stepped into the crowded lobby and looked around for her aunt and uncle, but it was Sam she spotted first, his sandy hair still wet and glistening. He must have gone briefly outside, wondering if that was where she was. She felt a twinge of guilt, but he was happily listening to something her aunt Nell was saying now, his head held low and his warm brown eyes looking up every now and then, scanning the tops of heads.

Sam. Her Sam.

Sam Perry had been in and out of Izzy's life for as long as she could remember—a friend of her older brother, Jack, he'd spent many summers with the Chambers family. An only child adopted by an older couple, Sam loved the chaotic family life of the Chambers brood. He was the one who sometimes stood up for her when her older and younger brothers teased her mercilessly. Sometimes he teased her right back. But he was always there, it seemed. Always a part of the pack.

But back then he was inconsequential to her life. And when she had headed east to college and law school—and finally abandoned her law practice for a new life in Sea Harbor—he was removed from it almost completely, except for a few random encounters over the years and mentions now and then from her mother or her brother Jack. And then, even those mentions became fewer.

Inconsequential. That was what he had been. Until that summer day when he'd come to Sea Harbor as a guest of the Canary Cove Art Colony. He'd been invited to be a guest lecturer for a photography class—and he had never left.

Izzy took a deep breath as the memories swirled around her. And then the door to the community center opened again, people hurried in, and the frigid night air gusted into the room, pressing against her heart and pushing her memories back into their pockets.

More people joined Sam and the others now as the crowd swelled, with Birdie waving to friends and neighbors she'd known for decades, making people feel at home, talking up the benefit as they praised Lily Virgilio's free health clinic.

Holiday cheer—they were scattering it everywhere, like rose petals at a wedding.

Izzy waited for it to touch her, to wrap her up in its warmth. Instead she felt the cold, the freezing rain.

And she wasn't sure why.

"Come on, Scrooge," Cass Halloran whispered near her shoulder. "Let's party." She wrapped one arm around Izzy's waist and spun her around. "Who can resist dancing to 'Frosty the Snowman'?"

Izzy laughed in spite of herself. Cass knew her inside and out. She knew not to pry, not to scold. *It's just an Izzy mood,* she'd be telling herself and anyone else who might ask. She'd shake it off soon.

And Cass also knew that sometimes, every now and then, Izzy's mood portended something unexpected. Sometimes something good, sometimes not so good.

"So, did you see our Seaside Knitters' name on one of those miniature trees? The real ones are going to be more of a challenge to decorate."

"Yep," Cass said. She grabbed two glasses of punch from a

passing waiter and handed one to Izzy. "But I'm going to be between the devil and the raging sea on this one. Some of the Halloran crew members have bought a tree and they're threatening to win the whole competition."

"Pete and that motley crew of fishermen? Decorating a tree? Nah, not a chance. It'll be trimmed with clumps of seaweed." Izzy spotted Pete Halloran across the way, his blond head thrown back and laughing heartily at something tiny Willow Adams had said. *Oh, my.* She hadn't considered Willow. The artist had Pete wrapped around her little finger, and as different as the two were, they were madly in love with each other, as least as far as anyone could tell. "Argh," Izzy said. "I forgot those lugs have partners and friends and wives in their life who might actually be creative. Like Willow. Surely it's not fair to let artists into this competition, is it?"

"Absolutely fair," Laura Danvers said, passing by. The event coordinator was waving her hands in the air, encouraging the crowd to move into the wooden-beamed room off the lobby. "All's fair in love and war and winning our first annual tree decorating contest," she said with a grin.

In minutes Laura had all but a few groups of stragglers crowding into the large room, its floor-to-ceiling windows aglow with hanging stars and snowflakes. Ropes of greenery hung from one beam to the next, and candles in thick-glassed lanterns decorated the tables and seating areas scattered across the room.

Laura climbed the steps to a narrow stage at one end of the room and tapped on the microphone to quiet everyone.

Cass and Izzy made their way through the wide doors, trailing after the others. Sam took a step back and pulled Izzy into a hug, then leaned low and whispered in her ear, "So . . . how's the sitter? Has the house burned down? Has our toddler whipped Stella at poker again?"

Izzy wrinkled her nose at him. Was she that transparent that she couldn't make a phone call without Sam knowing it? "Shush," she said, pointing to the other side of the room, where Laura was introducing Dr. Lily Virgilio and explaining the tree decorating project that was going to bring in sleighs full of money for the clinic. Laura's excitement was contagious and the crowd cheered wildly as each team was announced—from the Altar Society ladies at Our Lady of Safe Seas Church to the Portuguese fishermen poker club to a local running club—and everything in between. The competition grew more boisterous and voices traveled all the way up to the high ceilings as burly fishermen and tiny white-haired women and a well-conditioned running club stood and waved and urged people to pledge to their team—the *winning* team.

Finally Laura tapped on the microphone and hushed everyone to silence again so she could introduce and thank the people behind the holiday competition—the Sea Harbor Chamber of Commerce, cochaired by Alphonso Santos and Stuart Cummings.

"Two generous men who have thrown themselves into this project wholeheartedly and completely," Laura said in her polished voice.

The crowd cheered as the two men took the stage, the distinguished heads of Santos Construction Company and Cummings Northshore Nurseries.

Alphonso took the microphone first. "You've all seen the Cummings guys at work along the Harbor Green these past couple weeks? Not an easy task with this weather. They've been mulching and feeding and whatever else you do to the dozens of young trees that have been planted over there. If you haven't seen them, they'll be ready to admire in a week or so. So come on down, then, bring the kids. The Cummingses not only planted each of those trees; they donated every last one." He paused for the applause, then continued.

"We'll have name cards ready next week, a fine weatherproof holder for them in front of each tree. You'll have a chance to pick your tree, and that's the tree you'll turn into a work of art. The chamber challenges each of you to make your tree the best lit, the best decorated—and, of course, the best funded—" He looked out over the audience, his eyebrows lifting. "Stu and I are thinking every last one of you can't wait to scribble your name on a team's pledge card, right?" He waited for the cheering to die down and handed the phone over to Stuart Cummings, who along with his wife and sister, Barbara, owned a fleet of successful nurseries up and down the north shore.

"We only have a few weeks, my friends," Stuart intoned, his voice too loud for a microphone and his belly nearly touching the stand. "We're keeping the rules simple. Those trees we planted down at the harbor are young and small—so treat them with care. No real lobster traps on these trees—that'll have to wait till next year. But pick a theme and go with it." He peered around the group, his eyebrows pulled together in fake severity. Finally he settled on a burly fisherman known to everyone in town as Cod and said with a scolding grin, "But we'll keep it all in wicked good taste, you got that, Cod?"

The crowd laughed heartily as friends pounded on the fisherman's broad back.

Laura came back to the mic next and finally quieted the crowd. She took a few questions and gave the dates for the final decorating event along with a reminder to show up a week from Saturday to pick out a tree.

"Now enjoy this delicious food being passed around along with the best eggnog on Cape Ann—or so the bartender tells me. And last but definitely not least, please welcome our very own Fractured Fish band." The crowd erupted in applause as Pete Halloran, Merry Jackson, and drummer Andy Risso began tuning up in a corner of the room. "Take it away, Pete," Laura said with a wave of her hands, and moved off the stage with the chamber cochairs following behind her.

In minutes, holiday music filled the air and waiters circled the room with steaming bowls of chowder, plates piled high with lobster rolls, and a dessert table groaning beneath chocolate pies and cakes and puddings.

Nell and Birdie found a spot near the fireplace and happily

accepted bowls of chowder a waiter set down in front of them. Nell waved at Zack Levin, working as a server tonight. He was conscientiously picking up empty bowls of chili and taking them off to the kitchen. She remembered the days when she had witnessed the young man being reamed by a restaurant owner for not being so responsible. This new Zack made her smile.

Rachel Wooten wandered by and Nell waved the city attorney over.

"If you're looking for your husband, he headed over to the bar with Sam and Ben," Birdie said. "Sit with us. It's much cozier here and we have a marvelous view of all the goings-on."

Nell pulled up a chair for Rachel. She frowned as her friend sat down beside her. "You've been working too hard, Rachel. I see it in your eyes. Is everything all right?"

Rachel managed a smile. "I'm fine," she said, sinking back into the chair. "Things at the courthouse actually slow down around the holidays. It's another matter I'm caught up in that's putting extra wrinkles on my face—" She stopped talking as several neighbors walked by.

"Ben mentioned you were executor of Lydia Cummings's estate."

Rachel nodded. "Yes. Ben's been a help to me. I don't often take on private clients, but I've helped Lydia over the years with legal matters. Trusts and wills. That sort of thing. Somehow details that seemed simple when someone is alive can become more complicated once they're gone."

"I'm sure the family is relieved Lydia's affairs are in good hands." Nell looked over at Stuart Cummings, standing next to his sister. His head was lowered as he listened intently to whatever Barbara was saying. She seemed to have something other than decorating trees on her mind.

Rachel followed Nell's look. "I hope so. They knew I handled legal matters for their mother. But they'd like the estate settled soon. I don't blame them. But sometimes there are complications, especially with all the properties Cummings Northshore Nurseries now has."

A waitress approached with a tray of eggnog and set three glasses down on the small table in front of them.

"To the holidays," Birdie said, lifting her glass. "And to the town we love." She nodded across the room to the band area, where the Fractured Fish had begun playing a medley of holiday favorites. Her eyes crinkled with laughter as she watched Henrietta O'Neal, as wide as she was tall, balancing her portly frame on her nephew Garrett's arm, moving slowly in a semblance of a dance. Garrett was looking down at his feet, as if counting the steps to a dance. The glass in his tortoiseshell frames caught the light from the ceiling and turned them transparent.

Soon Esther and Richard Gibson joined the couple, moving into the small cleared space in front of the band and dancing very slowly to "I'll Be Home for Christmas," their gray heads touching and eyes nearly closed.

"Esther needed a break tonight," Rachel said, watching them over the rim of her eggnog glass.

"Lydia's death has been difficult for her," Birdie said.

"And then some. She seems to know the most about Lydia's life—intimate things that Lydia didn't share with her children. She's been wonderful helping me sort through things. That, in addition to helping Father Northcutt with that massive funeral."

"And grieving her friend at the same time," Birdie added.

Rachel nodded, her eyes tired.

"But you'll figure it all out, Rachel. You always do," Nell said.

From their spot near a giant wreath, Izzy and Cass were also watching the dancing couples. Henrietta had finally hobbled over to a chair and insisted Barbara Cummings take her place on the dance floor. She seemed relieved to sit, and watched briefly while her fifty-year-old nephew, Garrett, stumbled through a dance with Barbara.

Barbara and Garrett's names were often tossed about in Izzy's shop as customers gathered in the back room to knit and purl and discuss the town's secrets and transgressions. The sturdy businesswoman and the quiet accountant, at least ten years her junior, were an odd couple. It almost sounded like the stuff of cinema, someone had said. Not in terms of romantic movies, but in terms of "not real." Pretend. But they were nearly always together, whether discussing successful financial reports or things more intimate was anyone's guess. They both seemed comfortable with the arrangement, whatever it was.

The couple danced briefly before Garrett trailed Barbara off the dance floor and to the bar, leaving Esther and Richard dancing alone in the shadow of a giant Christmas tree.

Izzy looked over at the Christmas tree, so high it nearly touched the beams crisscrossing the vaulted cedar ceiling. "That tree makes me think of the one my dad cut down every year and helped us decorate. Then he'd wire up speakers outside and play Christmas songs for the whole neighborhood to hear, like it or not. My ornery brothers would try to switch the music, put on Pink Floyd or Michael Jackson."

Cass laughed. "Your brothers were brats. So was mine. Are your parents coming for Christmas?"

"Dad is taking Mom to Hawaii this year. Escape the Kansas cold. Maybe that's why I'm melancholy tonight—not having family here for the holidays."

A flash of light beyond the Christmas tree interrupted the memories. They glanced out the tall windows. A police car was pulling up to the front door.

"I hope no one's sick," Cass said, looking around. But the music was still playing, people were laughing and moving around, and the small dance floor was now crowded with people swirling and dipping along with Esther and Richard.

Janie Levin had seen the car pull up, too, and smiled a secret smile as she paused near Cass and Izzy. Her green eyes were bright. "It's probably Tommy," she whispered. "He's on duty tonight and said he'd try to stop by if things were slow."

"Hmm," Cass said, her eyebrows lifting. "So, do I have this right? Our hard-earned taxes are supporting a lovers' tryst, is that what's going on here?"

"Oh, Cass," Janie laughed, her cheeks turning as red as her hair. "Come say hi."

Cass and Izzy followed her into the lobby where people were milling about in the less-crowded area, drinking wine and eggnog, and taking selfies in front of the miniature harbor display.

They were steps from the door when it opened, bringing in a wild rush of wind and freezing rain.

Izzy stepped back, her eyes watering, blurring her vision. She blinked against the cold and then watched Tommy Porter walk in, pulling the heavy door closed behind him.

Janie hurried over, unconcerned with the cold and wet that saturated Tommy's uniform. She hugged him tightly. "Boring night on Harbor Road?" she asked, her face just an inch away from his. "Or is it that you simply can't stay away from me?"

Behind her, Cass laughed, about to tease the police officer fiercely. Babysitting Tommy Porter before he grew into one of Sea Harbor's finest brought with it some rights, she always told him. Besides, their early start had grown a deep friendship between the two, and Tommy always teased her right back.

But Cass stopped short of embarrassing the policeman when he stepped aside and revealed that he hadn't walked in alone. Following him through the door was a man equally wet and shivering, his hands shoved into the pockets of a heavy jacket, his cheeks red, and his head bare. Wet hair fell across his forehead.

He was taller than Tommy, with broad football-player shoulders. He stood a few steps behind the policeman, an uncomfortable look on his face, as if he was unsure of why he was there or what was going to happen next.

What happened next was totally unexpected.

A noise from Izzy pulled attention away from the stranger and focused it all on the yarn shop owner. Her arms were wrapped tightly around herself, as if holding unhinged parts of her body together. Her eyes were round, and thick eyebrows were lifted up into a scattering of bangs. She gasped, a ragged, unfamiliar sound.

"Iz?" Cass said. "You okay?"

But Izzy seemed incapable of answering the simple question. Instead it was the man standing with Tommy who looked over at Izzy and answered it.

"Hey, sis," he said. "Long time no see."

Chapter 4

Saturday loomed sunny and cold, the storm leaving behind glistening frozen lawns, the blades of grass catching the sunlight like tiny icicles. Nell stood at the kitchen window, a cup of coffee cradled in her hands. Her eyes were focused beyond the frozen tops of the fir trees, on the blinding blue of the ocean in the distance.

On the floor above, Ben's footsteps moved from bath to bedroom to closet. It was nearly nine o'clock, a late Saturday morning start for both of them, but the evening before had stretched out far longer than any of them had anticipated.

It had definitely been a night filled with surprises.

Her long-lost nephew. At least that was how she'd come to think about Charlie—long lost. And now here he was, in the most unlikely of places. Cape Ann. Her home. Izzy's home. A place he had been invited to many times. But had never come.

Once they had arrived back at the Endicotts' the night before, a weary Charlie briefly explained how he'd gotten a nursing degree a year ago and had worked for an NGO doing medical work in Ghana. When political factions destroyed the hospital, the organization had sent the staff home to their headquarters in Arizona.

It was there he came across Dr. Lily Virgilio's card. He remembered her needing volunteers at her health clinic. Christmas didn't seem like Christmas in the desert, he'd said. And a call to Dr. Virgilio had encouraged his decision.

Nell wondered briefly how Charlie could afford a volunteer job. Most nongovernment organizations certainly didn't pay well. But then she remembered that Izzy had used a small inheritance she'd received from a relative of her father's to buy a house and open the yarn shop. Charlie was probably living off his.

But personal things like money didn't factor into Charlie's explanation the night before.

Nor did he allude to the fact that he had removed himself from his family for more than a dozen years, that he'd missed holidays and weddings and births. That his own siblings didn't know where he was most of the time, and it was only the occasional e-mails to his mother that told any of them he was still alive.

And if he had noticed the resentment that had been so blatantly clear in his only sister's eyes—he didn't mention that, either.

Nell knew bits and pieces of Charlie's adventures from Caroline, although *adventure* wasn't exactly the word her sister had used. Once the most easygoing of the Chambers children, Charlie had deviated considerably from the path that his parents had anticipated he'd follow, and Caroline didn't talk about it often. He'd dropped out of college—and seemingly out of his family as well.

A bird fluttered in front of the kitchen window, then settled on the narrow bird feeder on the deck. Nell watched it for a minute, then looked down the sloping yard to the cottage on the edge of the woods.

Maybe she was wrong about Charlie. Maybe he had considered that he might not get a prodigal son's welcome . . . And maybe that was why he had kept his arrival secret.

The rattling of the front door scattered Nell's thoughts and announced the arrival of Birdie, followed closely by the Perrys: Izzy, Sam, and Abby and their aged golden retriever, Red.

Sam closed the door behind them and set Abby down to toddle her way through the family room and into the kitchen, where she gleefully wrapped her arms around Nell's knees.

Nell lifted her up and cuddled her grandniece close, unzipping her jacket. "This is the way every day should begin." She felt Abby's sweet breath against her cheek and breathed in the intoxicating smell of baby shampoo.

Ben bounded down the back steps and greeted everyone, giving Birdie a quick peck on the cheek. "Hey, glad you're all here." He looked at Izzy and Sam. "But I'm surprised to see you two. I thought you'd sleep till noon."

Sam looked down at Abby, now set free and rummaging through a toy box Nell kept in a corner of the family room. Red sat at her side. "I guess my Abigail forgot to read the memo. She didn't seem to give a hoot that her old mom and dad were up *way* past their bedtime last night."

Izzy poured herself a cup of coffee and leaned against the sink. "Big night. What a surprise, huh?" She looked at Nell. Her voice was a monotone.

A surprise? An understatement. Nell had been headed for the community center restroom when Sam waved her over the night before. Her eyes had gone immediately to her niece, her thoughts on Abby, thinking something might be wrong at home. Izzy read her stricken look and shook her head.

Only then had Nell looked at the silent giant of a man standing a few feet from Izzy. Even with the sleet turning his hair dark and a puffy jacket hiding his shape—and years intervening since she'd last seen him—Nell had recognized Charlie in an instant.

And in the next minute, she had wrapped her arms around her nephew, releasing him only when Ben walked over, wondering what was going on.

A surprise, yes. "He is embarrassed, I think. Unsure of how we all feel . . ."

"He should be," Izzy asked. "Where is he?"

Birdie repeated the question, insisting she had had no more than a fleeting introduction the night before, certainly not enough to assuage her curiosity.

"He's in the guest cottage. Probably wondering how he got there,"

Nell said. She looked at Sam. "Whatever you plied him with last night did a job on him. He went off to bed as soon as you left our house. But thank you. You were gracious to lead him over, Sam. Your being here made Charlie more comfortable, I'm sure."

Sam shrugged. "I spent a lot of time around Charlie when he was a kid. The Chambers boys were my buddies. Charlie spent the better part of his summers tagging after Jack and me."

Izzy hadn't objected the night before when Sam dropped her at home to relieve the babysitter, then headed back to Ben and Nell's to check on things.

Nor had she made any move to invite Charlie to stay at their own home.

Izzy ignored the conversation and walked to the sink. She cradled her cup between her hands, looking out the window, beyond the deck and flagstone pathway, to the cottage. The Endicott guesthouse held some of her most cherished Sea Harbor memories—a special retreat she called her own.

And today it held her brother, who'd effectively removed himself from her life. He didn't deserve it, she thought. Not her special place.

Ben handed Sam a cup of coffee, then put a cast-iron skillet on the stove and turned it on. "The poor guy was frozen stiff. A little scotch does wonders for that—it was a good antidote."

Sam looked over at Izzy. She was still looking out the window, but seemed to be a million miles away. He turned back to Nell and Ben. "It was nice of you to suggest Charlie stay here. It wasn't just the cold that was freezing poor Charlie out."

Nell knew what he was saying. Izzy carried resentment, sure, but she'd come around. "No need for thanks," Nell said. "That's what that cottage is for. He'll have some privacy. And I'm looking forward to getting to know Charlie all over again. He looks good."

Izzy turned around. "He'd have looked good at our wedding, too, at our family reunion, at—"

Sam stopped her. "Sure, those are sore spots. He should have been here for our wedding. And it hurt your parents as much as anyone. They worried about him a lot. But life hasn't always been easy for Charlie."

Izzy glared at him, unable to let go of her feelings. She turned back to the window.

"He looks well, don't you think?" Nell repeated to Sam.

"He's skinny," Sam said.

"Skinny? I wouldn't have used that word. He was a big baby who grew into a big man," Nell said. She began cracking eggs into a bowl as Ben rinsed spinach and tomatoes at the sink.

"Yeah. But he's skinnier than he used to be. I haven't seen him in a long time, but the guy was a linebacker in college and had all the bulk that goes along with it. The bulk is definitely gone. I wonder . . ." But Sam's voice drifted off, as if whatever came into his mind was better left unsaid.

Izzy turned away from the window and walked to the end of the island, sitting on one of the stools. "From linebacker to nurse. How did that happen? I wonder. Charlie used to get sick at the sight of blood."

"Perhaps it's in the genes," Nell said. "From linebacker to nurse—from lawyer to yarn shop owner. My niece and nephew don't close the door on life's vast possibilities. I like that."

Izzy didn't answer. Instead she looked over at Abby. Her tone immediately softened and she turned back to her aunt. "You're right. But it's an odd choice. It surprised my mother. He was attending that small college in Colorado and then that fall, he just left." She frowned, trying to piece her brother's life together. "That's when he started—"

The French doors on the deck had opened and footsteps interrupted Izzy midsentence.

Charlie Chambers walked in, his hair damp from a shower, his jeans clean and a fleece jacket covering his flannel shirt. "That's when I started being a jerk?"

Izzy looked over, still startled at the sight of her brother.

"Nah," Sam said. "You were always a jerk."

Charlie laughed. Then, surprised, he stared down at the little girl sitting on the floor. She was looking up at him with enormous blue eyes not unlike his own. He crouched down beside her and spoke in a gentle, quiet voice. "Hi. So you must be Abby. I'm Uncle Charlie."

Abby answered with a giggle and then Charlie was laughing with her, his fingers crawling up her lap like a spider and making her giggles grow.

From her perch on the stool, watching her daughter, Izzy took a quick breath, her eyes fixed on Abby.

Nell watched Izzy taking in the scene. She saw the lines of her face soften and a bit of hardness fall from her eyes.

The power of a child.

Charlie looked up. His voice held a huskiness that hadn't been there before. "She's beautiful, Iz." He shrugged off his emotion and offered a half smile. "She looks like me, right?"

That brought shouts of laughter as the broad-shouldered Charlie brought his face down beside the sweet, round, curly-haired toddler. Sam joined his brother-in-law on the floor, vying for his daughter's attention and teasing Charlie about his football face and nearly red hair. "Like you? No way, ugly man," he said. "My Abby is gorgeous, just like her mother."

Ben interrupted the banter a short while later with a call to eat, ushering people with a wave of his hand to the kitchen island, now filled with spinach and goat cheese omelets, bagels and lox, and fresh fruit. And orders to help themselves.

They filled their plates and sat on oversize chairs and sofas near the family room fireplace, Abby happily strapped into her own tiny chair at the coffee table. Ben passed around Bloody Marys and refilled coffee mugs.

Charlie had filled his plate to overflowing, then settled down on the couch, close enough to Abby's chair to entertain her with strange airplane noises as he flew a piece of a bagel to her waiting mouth.

Sam was on Abby's other side. In the distance, Izzy sat apart, watching her brother effortlessly ease himself into her daughter's life.

On the other side of the table, Birdie had opened her knitting bag and pulled out her needles, attached to the beginnings of a sea blue angora sweater. A small cardigan with cables up the back that drew attention, even from Abby. "Yes," Birdie said, smiling at the toddler. "It's for you, my love."

When Nell's cell phone rang, she almost ignored it, not wanting to move away from the comfort of the scene—the sound of Birdie's needles, the look on Charlie's face as Abby responded to him. But scene or not, she found it enormously difficult to let a phone go unanswered, in spite of the teasing Izzy and Cass gave her. Phones rang for a reason, she insisted.

She walked to the kitchen counter and picked it up.

The number on the screen was out of state. A sales call, probably. Her "hello" led to a long silence as Nell listened to the caller. Ben started to get up, wondering if there was a problem.

Nell motioned that it was okay, and allowed a slight smile. She nodded as if the caller could see it, then finally said, "Yes, you've called the right place. I'm sure he'll want to thank you himself. Just a second please." She stretched out her arm, the phone cupped in her palm. "Charlie, this is for you. It's your phone calling you."

He stood up, puzzled. "Impossible. My phone. . ." He dug into his pocket as if to prove her wrong, then glowered as he came up empty.

"What the . . . ?" But his expression was washed away almost immediately with a glimmer of amusement.

Nell watched the play of emotion with a sense of déjà vu. Charlie was so like his father—with that sudden hair-trigger temper that rose out of nowhere, but just a thin layer beneath it was a sweetness that scattered anger into nothing. The Charlie who had always been their gentle giant.

Charlie held the phone to his ear, listening, while the others in the room tried not to, a task that proved relatively easy, since Charlie seemed to be saying little.

He listened some more, then forked his fingers through his hair, his back turned just enough to hide whatever expression was playing out on his face.

He leaned against the kitchen island, his wide shoulders slightly stooped, tousled hair falling over his forehead. "Okay," he finally said, loud enough for the others to hear. "So we've established you're a thief. What else will I find missing?"

Chapter 5

Charlie hung up and stayed at the counter for a minute, as if wondering what to do next. Finally he walked back to the group near the fireplace and sat down in front of his uneaten omelet. He looked up, almost apologetically. "Do any of you know someone named Esther Gibson?"

Without waiting for an answer, he dug into Ben's moist omelet and closed his eyes with a look of pure pleasure.

Nell looked at Ben, then Izzy. Why was he asking about the police dispatcher?

"Of course we know Esther," Izzy said. "Everyone in town knows her. Why? She's the police dispatcher. Are you in trouble?"

Charlie shook his head, his mouth full of eggs. Finally he talked around them. "I guess she's bringing my phone over. And apparently there's a pair of gloves in my car she needs."

"Esther needs your gloves?" Ben leaned forward, his elbows on his knees.

"Hey, sorry, I'm not making a lot of sense."

Finally he looked up and tried to explain about the hitchhiker he'd picked up on the way into town. "It was a frigging mess out there," he said. "And this girl—woman, I guess—appeared on the side of the road. She was thumbing her way into Sea Harbor.

"I let her off—and apparently my cell phone, too—in town. Seems she left her gloves in my car and wants them back in exchange for the phone."

The short explanation brought a bevy of questions—who was the woman? Why was she coming to Sea Harbor? Where had she gone when he dropped her off?

And Charlie hadn't touched on Esther Gibson at all—and how she figured into his hitchhiker story.

Before they could pin him down, the doorbell rang.

Nell walked to the front hall to let Esther in. She loved her nephew, but suspected that the police dispatcher would be able to explain the cell phone and gloves and hitchhiker in a far more coherent way than Charlie was doing.

But the woman Nell led back into the family room was definitely not Esther Gibson.

Even Abby turned her blond curls to look at the stranger walking up behind her.

"Charlie, your friend is here. Everyone, this is Amber Harper."

"Esther dropped me off," Amber said to Nell, as if somehow it explained everything. "She's a crazy driver."

The others filled in the awkwardness with hellos, their greetings coming in a rush, with furtive glances flitting from Amber to Charlie and back again.

Ben pulled up another chair and insisted she sit. "I make the best Bloody Mary in Sea Harbor. It's a great antidote after a ride in Esther's truck."

Amber allowed a slight smile, then nodded to the others self-consciously. Finally her look settled more comfortably on the one familiar face in the room. "Hey," she said, her bravado of the day before muted by the circle of strangers. She held out a cell phone. "I guess this is yours."

Charlie leaned forward and took it from her. He examined it, shaking his head. "Yep, you're right, it's mine. Did you take anything else?" he asked.

"Nope. Sorry about that. And I want my gloves back. This town is cold."

"Fair exchange, I guess."

She laughed, a kind of nervous laugh, and the others joined in, trying to put the slender woman at ease.

Birdie was sitting closest to the fireplace, her glasses perched on her nose. She looked intently at the woman with the pale complexion and long brown hair. It was swept back into a ponytail, but several strands had tugged free and she hooked them back behind one ear. She had high cheekbones that gave some definition to her face. Her nose was straight and slightly angled at the end, but not in an unpleasing way. There was a promise of beauty there, but one disguised behind suspicious eyes and the set of her narrow jaw.

Nell glanced at Birdie, wondering what was going on inside her head. She was usually the first to make a newcomer feel welcome. But today she was noticeably quiet, as if examining the woman before she spoke.

"Are you a relative of Esther's?" Izzy asked, breaking the uncomfortable lull.

Nell had wondered the same thing. Esther had given Amber her phone number—and she had dropped her off. There was a connection there.

Amber murmured something about passing through town but not staying long. Then she shook her head, as if scolding herself for being rude, and explained that she was staying at Esther's. "Esther used to . . ."

The thought dangled, unfinished. Finally Amber said, "Esther said she thought Charlie might be here." She laughed self-consciously. "I'd forgotten how people in this place know everyone else's business. And how everyone seems to tell Esther everything."

It might have been the mention of Esther again, or the familiarity with which Amber said it, that pushed Birdie forward in her chair, then to rise from it to get a closer look at the visitor.

"Amber Harper," she said, repeating the name, infusing life into it.

She walked around the couch to where Amber sat. Then she touched her lightly on the shoulder and Amber looked up into her face. "I should have recognized your name, Amber. I'm Birdie Favazza. How nice to see you."

A blush crawled up Amber's neck to her cheeks. She smiled at Birdie, but the expression on her face made it clear that she wasn't sure who she was.

Birdie patted Amber on the shoulder again and smiled. "It's all right, dear, you can't be expected to remember someone from all those years ago. Besides, we probably only met a few times. But Esther Gibson is a dear friend of mine."

The puzzlement began to disappear and Amber's face softened. "Birdie," she said softly. "Sure, Birdie, Esther's friend. I sort of remember."

"And you've come to see Esther? I'm sure she's thrilled."

"She asked me to come to sign some papers. To pick up some things. I'm just here for a day or so."

The others sat up straighter, listening, curious, but it was Charlie who was the most intent. He leaned forward on the couch, his elbows on his knees, and his attention completely focused on Amber and Birdie's conversation.

"Hey, you all need to eat," Amber said, shaking loose of Birdie's look. She stood up so quickly her coffee spilled onto the napkin Ben had given her. "Oh, I'm so sorry." Quickly she wiped the few drops that had made it to the coffee table. "I really need to go." She looked over at Charlie. "I need my gloves—it's freezing out there. I left them in your Bimmer."

Without waiting for an answer, she offered another thank-you to Nell and Ben, nodded toward the others, and headed toward the door.

Ben looked over at his nephew. "Charlie, she's right. It's freezing. If she needs a ride somewhere—" he began.

But Charlie had already gotten off the couch, eyes lingering briefly on the remains of his omelet. He nodded to Ben, then looked over at

Izzy and Sam and Nell and Ben and Birdie, as if he'd brought yet another interruption into their lives. "Hey—I'm sorry about this—"

"Go, Charlie," Nell said. "We'll have days to catch up." *Days to make up for years. Days to heal old wounds.* She felt Izzy's eyes on her as she spoke.

Charlie nodded, his eyes on Izzy.

"Go," Izzy said.

"It's . . ." He looked flustered, as if whatever he might say would require more than a few words.

Finally he grabbed his jacket, pulled his car keys from the pocket, and hurried out the door after his fleeing hitchhiker.

Chapter 6

"There's nothing like a little excitement to get our juices flowing on a Saturday morning," Birdie said as the sound of Charlie's BMW finally disappeared into the cold Saturday air. She picked up her knitting again and smoothed out the cable stitches.

Sam got up and began refilling coffee cups. "You seem to be the only one in the loop, Birdie. Who is that gal?"

Birdie was still looking toward the door, her fingers moving the needles as she worked to place Amber Harper exactly in the right pocket of her memory. Finally she rested her knitting in her lap and stirred cream into her coffee. "Amber Harper is the late Lydia Cummings's granddaughter." She waited while the news settled in, and then set down her cup and held up her Bloody Mary glass, suggesting Ben refresh it a bit. It might make Amber's story flow more easily.

"The Cummings Nurseries," Ben said out loud, his mind trying to piece the puzzle together.

"Yes. Amber was born out of wedlock, as some folks referred to it back then. Her mother was a waitress at Jake Risso's Gull. Jake had a soft spot for the girl and his wife, Marie, took her under her wing, Esther said."

Ben was frowning. "Stuart Cummings had a child?"

Birdie shook her head. "No, no. Patrick Cummings was Amber's father—the youngest of Lydia Cummings's children."

Recollection flooded Ben's face. "Oh, sure. Patrick. My parents talked about him, about what happened to him—"

"Esther was Patrick's godmother. He was a surprise baby, enough younger than Barbara and Stu to almost be an only child. He was the joy of his mother's life—handsome, brilliant. A Rhodes scholar. He was just on the brink of beginning his adult life when he died in a terrible accident."

"So the waitress—Ellie Harper—was Patrick's girlfriend?" Nell asked.

Birdie said yes. "When she got pregnant, she hid it from everyone, even Patrick for a while. Finally the two of them went to tell Lydia about the pregnancy, knowing they wanted to get married. Lydia was shocked. She knew nothing about his relationship with Ellie until that night—I think Stu and the Rissos were the only ones Patrick and Ellie confided in."

"Lydia must have been happy at the thought of a grandchild." Nell looked over at Abby.

"No. She was furious. She had so many plans for Patrick, and none of them included a waitress from the Gull. Of course Patrick was distraught over his mother's reaction, and drowned his emotion in a few too many beers. So Ellie drove when they left the bar that night. They were out on 128. A pickup truck crossed over the line, and Patrick was killed instantly."

The story settled around the room as if it were fresh and poignant, bearing relevance a thirty-year-old news story wouldn't have.

"Ellie was hurt badly, but she survived. The baby was delivered prematurely and she also survived."

"Amber." Izzy's word escaped on a hushed breath. She picked up a sleepy Abby and cuddled her close, as if to shield her from life's tragedies. Then she carried her upstairs for a nap.

"Lydia's husband had died a year or two earlier."

"And then the accident ripped her youngest son from her life," Sam said.

"How awful." Nell sat back against the chair cushions. "I never suspected Lydia had suffered such tragedy in her life. She always seemed to be in charge, in control."

"Oh, I think she was in control. Always," Birdie said. "But Patrick's death changed her. I even noticed it, though I wasn't aware of all the reasons. She refused the compassion people offered, preferring to handle it all in her own way. One of the few people she let in besides Esther was Father Northcutt—he helped her tremendously."

"So Ellie recovered?" Izzy asked.

Birdie leaned back in the chair and pulled at the threads of her memory. "Ellie wasn't even thought about much during those difficult days. No one asked about her. It was as if Patrick had been in the car alone. The town's attention was on the grieving Cummings family—on Lydia, Barbara, Stuart, and his young wife, Helen—not on Ellie, much less a baby. Both of them were taken to a hospital in Boston and there were rumors that Ellie was recovering, her broken bones healing. But then weeks or maybe it was months later, she had a setback—an embolism or something, I believe—and she ended up in a persistent vegetative state. She never recovered from it."

"What became of the baby?" Izzy asked.

Birdie looked out the window, trying to remember. The story was still slightly muddled in her head, a story that had been buried, then slowly resurrected, but appearing now with broken parts—or perhaps parts that had remained shielded from the public. "Lydia assumed responsibility," she said finally. "Ellie had no family."

Nell thought about the stately Cummings matriarch, already a powerful figure in Sea Harbor when Ben and Nell moved there to make it their permanent home. She was tall, always dressed elegantly but simply—black cashmere sweaters, tailored slacks. She was a pillar of society, and also a pillar of Our Lady of Safe Seas Church, deeply generous to all of Father Northcutt's causes. Her recent funeral had been one of the biggest he had ever presided over, the parish priest had admitted. It was planned by her children. Very showy. Something he himself thought Lydia would have hated.

But the thing Nell remembered most about the times she had

been in the presence of Lydia Cummings was the sadness that darkened her eyes, never completely hidden behind her powerful demeanor. And now she knew why.

The impact of Ellie Harper's story came gradually to those in the room, like a lazy wave on the shores of the beach, etching in the sand a realization of lives irrevocably changed by young love, a pregnancy, a death.

"Lydia's granddaughter," Ben said, mulling over the information. He put a palm to his forehead, as if patting the facts in place.

Prominent families in Sea Harbor were usually open books as far as their lineage went, especially when a family business was integral to the unit. Ben and Nell knew the Cummingses. Until her illness, Lydia had been highly visible in the community. Formidable, but generous, as were Barbara and Stuart, her adult children. The only grandchild they knew about was a son of Stu's, now a banker in Boston.

But Lydia having another, little-known grandchild was a surprise.

"What happened to Amber's mother?" Sam asked.

"Ellie Harper lived, and died, at the Ocean View Nursing Home. Not too long ago, in fact. Two or three years ago, I believe."

"Ocean View is a beautiful place," Nell said.

"And expensive," Izzy added.

"It's very upscale—with wonderful care in the assisted-living section. And charming homes for those who are able but choose to live in a community with its own gardeners and maintenance men. My husband, Sonny, was on the board in the early days," Birdie said.

It was Abby who was able to change the serious mood of the morning in an instant. Her cheerful wake-up giggles echoed through the house from the small speaker on the counter and in short order she was sitting on the floor, front and center, gleefully knocking down colorful blocks and insisting with a wave of her pudgy hands that they be restacked immediately.

Nell watched her from the kitchen sink as she and Danny rinsed plates and mugs and filled up the dishwasher.

"A child has such power," Danny said, following her look. "It makes me wonder about Amber Harper's childhood. Did she have any power like our Abby? Was she ever the child who sat in the middle of a circle of attentive, loving adults?"

The question hung there in the air without an answer, a question that would be revisited often in the days to come.

It was much later that day, long after Birdie's driver, Harold, had picked her up for a dentist appointment, after Sam and Izzy had taken Red and Abby home, that the real reason Amber Harper had come back to town began to make sense.

"This is the perfect getaway," Don Wooten said, pulling out his wife Rachel's chair as they settled into a small seaside restaurant in Gloucester.

"Is that what we're celebrating?" Nell asked, taking the inside chair near the bank of windows. Don and Rachel had invited them to dinner weeks before to celebrate something or another, though Nell had confessed to Ben on the way over that she couldn't remember what it was. But it didn't matter—Duckworth's Bistrot was one of their favorite restaurants and they needed no nudging or excuse to say yes. It was where they'd dined the night Ben had proposed to Nell, where they'd taken Izzy to celebrate the opening of the Seaside Knitting Studio, where they had toasted Izzy and Sam's engagement.

"Getting away is a fine thing to celebrate," Rachel said, her tiredness of the evening before gone.

"And sometimes that means getting out of Dodge," Don said, and they all agreed.

Although the drive from Sea Harbor to Gloucester wasn't a long one, the cozy restaurant was filled with holiday cheer and felt far removed from mundane concerns. And, as Don said, the chances of his wife running into a disgruntled city employee or someone wanting legal advice were far less likely than if they were dining at the Ocean's Edge, his own Sea Harbor restaurant.

"I'm going to assume by the relaxed look on your face that you're also making headway on the Cummings estate," Ben said. He settled down next to Nell and put on his reading glasses, looking over at Rachel before glancing down at the menu.

"Yes," she answered. She smiled up at the friendly waitress as Don ordered a bottle of wine for the table. "I have Esther Gibson to thank for some of that. She is a miracle worker."

"Esther?"

"Lydia's will wasn't as complicated as you'd expect, considering the size of it, mostly because Cummings Nurseries is a family business and Lydia wanted to keep it that way. There were some little things—well, not so little. To no one's surprise, she made a sizable endowment to Our Lady of Safe Seas. Their food pantry and other causes will be in fine shape for the rest of their life. She asked, though, that the family section of her will be held back until I could get the family together—like they used to do in the old days. And I had some trouble locating everyone."

Nell looked up, startled, a piece suddenly falling in place. "You must mean Amber Harper," she said.

Rachel laughed. "No secrets in a small town. Do you know Amber?"

"No," Ben said. "But we've met her, thanks to Izzy's brother, Charlie. Amber was hitchhiking out on 128 last night and he gave her a lift into town."

"I didn't know Izzy had a younger brother," Don said. He sat back while the waitress uncorked the bottle of wine and offered him a taste.

Nell stopped short of saying that there were times Izzy wasn't sure she had a younger brother, either, at least not one who communicated with her. Instead she said, "Charlie is an interesting guy.

Man, actually, though I sometimes have difficulty realizing my niece and nephews are amazing grown-ups. He's here to work at Lily Virgilio's free clinic. They're ramping up their vaccination program and Charlie is putting his nursing degree to good use by helping out."

"We haven't seen Charlie in a while. Having him here for the holidays is a welcome surprise," Ben added. "He'll stay at least through the new year."

"Amber was the second surprise," Nell said. "She left something in Charlie's car last night and showed up at our house this morning to claim it."

"Small world," Don said, lifting his glass. "Here's to yuletide finds and surprises. Rachel has found the long-lost Amber and you've found a nephew."

The others lifted their glasses, candlelight reflecting off the crystal.

Outside, a beastly wind howled in the black night. Nell glanced through the tall windows that fronted East Main Street. Scattered snowflakes and bits of paper danced across the street, glinting in the headlights of passing cars. Horns honked. But inside, all was warm and softly lit. She brought her attention back to the table. "To discoveries," she repeated. "May they bring us joy."

The catch in her voice was followed by a flutter deep inside her chest, unexpected, and for a moment, startling. Nell took a sip of wine and swallowed it slowly, only then realizing that the feeling had not been a pleasant one but one touched with a deep frisson of foreboding.

None of the others seemed to notice Nell's discomfort. The taste of the fine Cabernet Don had ordered was a far more pleasant focus. She half listened as Ben expanded on their brief encounter with Amber and the bit of history Birdie had supplied.

"You're a step ahead of me," Rachel said when Ben had finished. "I have yet to meet her in person, although I talked to her briefly today."

"But you knew she existed," Don said.

They paused while the waitress wrote down their dinner choices and disappeared.

"I did, although Lydia rarely talked about her granddaughter," Rachel said, "and when she did, it was with a coldness that surprised me."

"It's interesting that Amber carries her mother's name," Ben said.

"Father Northcutt told me that Amber's mother had named her daughter and filed her birth certificate from the hospital, before she became incapacitated. I suppose Lydia could have changed the last name if she had wanted to, once she had confirmed the baby's paternity, but she didn't. She said if I had any questions when settling the will, Esther or Father Larry might have the answers. Esther apparently kept in touch with Amber—or at least tried to—after she left Sea Harbor."

"There's something very sad about it all," Nell said. "This is such a small town and the Cummings family is so well known. And yet Amber appears almost as a ghost, an outsider." She thought about the woman with the angry eyes, but someone who softened almost immediately by simple acts of kindness, a cup of coffee. Birdie's gentle touch on her shoulder.

"What about Barbara and Stuart?" Ben asked. "Are they involved in Amber's life at all?"

"I don't know anything about that. Amber was already gone when I met Lydia and got to know the family. And as I said, she wasn't talked about much. I'm finally meeting with all of them tomorrow to go over that part of Lydia's will, including Amber. Lydia insisted on that, even though this kind of dramatic 'reading of the will' is usually only done in the movies. She also wanted Father Northcutt involved. Maybe to calm any ill will. Keep peace. Though I don't think any of them will have a problem with it."

The arrival of quail and lobster risotto, monkfish and duck breast silenced them while they breathed in the intoxicating aromas.

The candlelight flickering on the table, the succulent fish and meat, and the warm ambience of the small room brought peace and contentment to the couples, and the next two hours went by in a comfortable haze of friendship. It was only after pushing out his chair, declaring that the homemade banana cake had made the added space physically necessary, that Don Wooten suggested they call it a night. "It's that or I have to get rid of this belt," he said. "Besides, Rachel has a full day tomorrow. Not a restful Sunday, for sure."

Don and Ben went to retrieve coats and scarves, pay the check, and bring the car around, while Rachel excused herself to use the ladies' room. Momentarily alone, Nell let the pleasantness of the evening settle around her. She looked through the bay window into the black night, savoring the quiet. Passersby were infrequent, and she watched a couple coming toward her, their shoulders touching as if to share bodily warmth. Their heads were close together, hands shoved in pockets.

The couple was almost beyond the windows before Nell realized whom she was watching. She half stood, lifting a hand to catch their attention, but before she could wave, they had moved on and only the backs of Amber Harper and Charlie Chambers were visible through the last pane of windows, her nephew's hand now out of his pocket, his arm wrapped protectively around his companion's hooded jacket.

"They looked chummy," Nell said to Ben as they prepared for bed.

"Hmm," Ben responded, his eyes already drooping as he sat on the side of the bed and slipped off his watch.

Nell plumped the pillows. "And where do you think he's been all day?" Charlie hadn't come back to the Endicott's guesthouse since walking out that morning, following Amber through the door. The space in the driveway where they had suggested he park, noticeably vacant.

"Maybe he's meeting with Lily Virgilio. Finding out what he's supposed to be doing at the clinic. The fellow has a job that probably starts Monday. It'd be a wise move to find out exactly where and when."

"Of course," Nell murmured. She had vowed, with Ben's enthusiastic encouragement, not to hover. Charlie was in his mid-thirties, certainly able to plan his day without her help.

But she was hovering; she knew it, and Ben knew it, too.

"You're right," she said, forcing conviction into her voice as she crawled in beside Ben, wrapping one arm across his chest. "Of course you're right."

"Hmm," he said, reaching up with one hand and clicking off the light.

But what had Charlie been doing in Gloucester? With a woman he didn't know, someone he'd called a thief.

Nell's thoughts became more tangled as Ben drifted off, his breathing gradually slowing down.

She turned onto her back, her eyes tracing the night shadows on the ceiling and her thoughts on a nephew who had had a much harder time navigating adulthood than his brother and sister had—even though outwardly Charlie Chambers had it all going for him: brains, looks, personality.

But somewhere along the road, he'd stumbled.

And now that she had this unexpected chance to be in her nephew's life, Nell felt a compulsion to make sure no one threw pitfalls into the road he wanted to travel.

Chapter 7

It was Father Lawrence Northcutt who brought Ben into the fray the next day. But even important matters like wills had to wait until after breakfast. He spotted Ben at the Sweet Petunia Restaurant, sidled up to him, and suggested he'd like to have a word. But only after breakfast.

Ben wholeheartedly agreed on that. So it wasn't until after both men were filled to the gills with the chef's creamy spinach omelet that Father Larry had his time with Ben. They walked to the window and talked in private for a few minutes, and then, while Ben left to get the car, Father Larry came over to Nell.

"I'm stealing him away for a bit later this afternoon, Nell," the priest said with a bow of his head. "But never you fear, darlin', I promise he'll be back home in time for dinner and in fine shape. No worse for wear—at least that's my honest hope."

"I second that hope," Nell said. She studied the look on the priest's face. "But you're looking a bit worried. I'm assuming that means you aren't inviting Ben to the rectory for a taste of your finest Irish whiskey."

"No, not this time. But it's nothing to worry about. We're meeting with the Cummings family, is all," he said. He paused for a moment and looked off into the distance, as if imagining the scene, seeing the family sitting around his rectory, waiting, listening—all of them together, including the niece they'd never claimed. Then he concentrated back on Nell. "I always tell my parishioners to mentally prepare themselves before they go to family weddings or funerals—and all the things that surround those events—like who gets Mama's favorite chair, Papa's pipe. And bigger things, of course—property, wills. Those events have an insidious way of sometimes bringing out the worst in people. I've known Lydia Cummings for a long time, helped her bury her husband. And then a son.

"It's a decent family and certainly a successful one, very generous to the church. But there can always be emotional complications after a mother or father dies, one who has held the reins. And I've found it never hurts to have Ben's calm presence at my side on such occasions." He pulled back Nell's chair, helped her with her coat, and walked her toward the entrance.

Calm presence. . . along with a dose of legal expertise, Nell suspected. And just maybe, in this case, so Amber Harper had someone in her court.

Father Northcutt had called upon Ben frequently in recent years, employing him, as he told Nell, as his unofficial consultant. "Especially in family matters," he said. "Ben is the voice of calm and logic in those cases."

Nell touched the priest's arm and reassured him with a smile and squeeze, but added that she wanted Ben back in one piece.

Father Northcutt agreed with a smile, then released Nell to hurry out the door and into the warmth of the car waiting at the restaurant steps.

Father Northcutt stayed true to his word—and more so. Ben came home, but even sooner than Nell had anticipated. The beginnings of a fire in the stone fireplace had just begun to warm the room, and she'd yet to pull the chowder out of the refrigerator to heat up.

At the sound of the garage door opening, she pressed a button on the controller and Laila Biali's husky voice filled the room.

A glass of wine together in front of the fire. Mood music and spicy chowder. Sunday with Ben. Her favorite time of the week.

But Father Northcutt had failed to mention that Ben's return would not bring with it the promise of a quiet Sunday evening.

"She never showed up," Ben said as he walked through the back door. He glanced at the fire, then strode across the room to the kitchen island and gave Nell a hug. "Fire feels good."

"Who didn't show up?"

"Amber Harper."

Nell frowned. "Really? That's strange. Rachel had given her all the information, and it's just a short walk from the Gibsons'. Esther would surely have told her how to get to the church if she'd forgotten."

"Rachel called Esther from the rectory after we rescheduled the meeting. She and Richard had talked to Amber this morning—the first time they'd really seen her. Esther said she'd gotten in very late last night."

Nell nodded. They hadn't heard Charlie drive in, but assumed it was late.

"They talked about the meeting, where it was, what time. Amber said she had a couple of things to do first but she'd be there. Esther made sure she had a heavy scarf and hat and off she went, asking briefly where a good doughnut shop was.

"Esther felt awkward with all her mothering, she said—she didn't want to overwhelm Amber. But apparently Amber didn't take offense. She listened, even tapped the time into her phone. Esther did say that she didn't show much interest in the reason for the meeting, though. She told Esther that if Lydia left her anything, it wouldn't be much. She was cynical, Esther said."

"But that doesn't explain why she wasn't at the meeting," Nell said. "She came all this way—and wasn't that why? For the will? Do you think her inheritance was insignificant?"

"I don't know. I haven't read the will, just the directives that

Lydia had insisted on. Often now, wills are mailed out to people, but Lydia wanted the will read to all the beneficiaries at the same time."

Ben took a beer out of the refrigerator and snapped off the cap. He looked out the window toward the cottage. "Charlie's car wasn't in the drive when I drove in, but there's a light on in the cottage. Any idea what's going on?"

Nell walked over to the sink and looked out. "That's strange. Maybe we should check—"

Ben nodded. "Okay. Let me do it, Nell."

Nell knew what he was thinking. It wouldn't seem like hovering if he did it. The man's way.

Without grabbing a jacket, he pulled up the collar of his flannel shirt and opened the deck doors, walking quickly into the impending darkness.

Nell watched him walk down the steps and across the yard to the guesthouse. Its front door faced the woods, a design she and Ben had purposely implemented to give their guests privacy and not feel their front door was being watched from the kitchen window. Easier to come and go without being detected.

Nell turned away from the window and took the chowder and loaf of French bread out of the refrigerator. She had made too much, as usual. But it didn't matter, she could freeze the rest. It was too early for dinner, but being busy calmed the anxious feeling inside her that something in her world wasn't quite right.

The ringing of the phone was a welcome distraction, not intrusive as it sometimes was. Nell rummaged around on the counter until she found her cell. Izzy's name appeared, and Nell picked it up quickly.

"What are you and Ben up to?" Izzy wondered. And, "Is Charlie there?" She told Nell he had been floating around in her head all day. "He's right here in Sea Harbor, Aunt Nell, and the only words I've spoken to him have been about as intimate as what I exchanged with the sacker at Shaw's today."

"I'm not sure if he's here." Nell glanced out the window. Two figures were walking up the flagstone path. "I take that back. He's here. He and Ben are coming in right now. I'm putting on some chowder—"

"Chowder? My favorite. I made that apple crisp you like this afternoon . . ."

It was settled, then. Sunday night dinner, a family affair. They'd collect Abby and be over shortly.

If that was all right, of course.

Ben stoked the fire, then began mixing a shaker of martinis while Nell explained to Charlie that Amber hadn't shown up for an important meeting that afternoon. The others were worried. Did he know where she was?

Charlie, frowned, concern shadowing his face. "She didn't show? She has my car."

The sound of a car in the drive interrupted and they all looked toward the door, half expecting Amber to walk in.

But it was the Chambers clan, Red leading the way, immediately rubbing up against Charlie's jeans.

Charlie kneaded his ears while Izzy put the still-warm apple crisp on the counter and Sam climbed the back stairs to settle Abby down for an early bedtime.

Ben repeated briefly to all of them what little he knew about the meeting that was cut short. "Basically nothing happened. We rescheduled," he said.

The creases in Charlie's forehead deepened.

"So you loaned her your car?" Ben asked.

Why? Nell thought, and realized suddenly that while she'd felt some compassion for the young woman, she had also felt a slight distrust, something she wasn't proud of. She tried now to push it aside. The concern on Charlie's face was easy to see—but whether it was for his missing car or for the missing woman, she wasn't sure.

"I told her last night that I was still camping out in your guesthouse, just in case she needed anything. And I guess she did. She showed up this morning, pounding on the door with doughnuts and coffee. She had walked up from Harbor Road, bundled up like an Eskimo. The doughnuts were a ploy so I'd let her use my car. She needed one today and had never driven a stick, which is what the lady she's staying with has."

"Why did she need a car?" Nell asked.

Charlie didn't answer for a minute, as if it was a most logical question, but one he himself hadn't thought to ask. Finally he said, "She mentioned the meeting at the rectory around four."

"She came for your car this morning?" Ben said. The implication was clear. He passed around martinis while he talked.

"She said there was something else she needed to do first." This time there was a hint of defensiveness in Charlie's voice that he tempered with a swallow of martini.

Nell watched the shadow across Charlie's face. It wasn't really their business. They all knew that. But somehow it seemed as though it was. Amber had taken Charlie's car. Somewhere.

Everyone was quiet.

Izzy busied herself by unwrapping a circle of Camembert. She tugged off the last piece of paper and set the cheese on a board next to the crackers.

Nell stirred cream into the chowder.

Charlie stared into the martini glass as if the answer were there in the clear liquid. He took another swallow, then fingered the toothpick, swirling the olive around the sides. Finally he looked at Ben. "Hell, Uncle Ben, I don't have a clue where she is or why she needed my car. All I know is wherever she was headed was too far to walk. For someone who likes to walk and is used to hitchhiking, I suppose that means some distance." His voice had an edge to it, but his eyes held concern.

The popping and crackling of the cheery fire at the other end of the room belied the grim silence that settled over them.

Sam spoke first, his words tentative. "Hey, man, what do you think? We're here to help. Do we need to call the police? The chief's a friend of ours. He'd be discreet. Could Amber have taken off, gone back to wherever she came from?"

And taken your BMW with her?

Chapter 8

And the silent answer was *Of course she could have.*

The rattle of the deck doors rescued the moment. It saved them from saying what was on all their minds, words they'd regret—a stolen car, Charlie's poor judgment. A missing girl.

Amber stood on the deck, her breath fogging the glass and one gloved hand tapping insistently.

The sigh of relief was audible.

Nell reached the French door first and ushered Amber in out of the cold. They walked together into the steamy kitchen, the chowder now warming on the stove, the oven readying to crisp the French bread.

Amber brushed a strand of hair from her eyes and looked around until she spotted Charlie on the other side of the kitchen. She dangled his keys in her hand. "I didn't want to leave these on the doorstep back there. It's so windy. But your car's in the drive." She dropped the key chain on the island and looked around at the others. Then looked slightly awkward. "Thanks," she added.

The relief on Charlie's face was clear, his anger dissolving in an instant as his eyes met hers. He looked down at the keys in her hand.

Amber glanced at the others. "You must think I make a habit of barging in on you—like a bad penny." Her words came out slowly, with a slight catch to her voice.

At first Nell thought it was because she was truly embarrassed about coming in the way she did. But when she suggested to Amber that she warm up with a glass of wine and walked over to take her jacket, she realized it wasn't embarrassment that was causing the catch in her voice—at least not because she had barged in on them.

Amber had been crying.

Her narrow face was swollen with leftover tears, their tracks still visible on her cheeks. Her eyes were red and puffy. In the bright overhead lights of the kitchen, she looked sad—and as vulnerable as a small child.

"May I use the restroom?" she asked Nell, allowing her hostess to take control, first by helping Amber with her jacket, then by leading her out of the limelight and down the shadowed hallway to the bathroom at its end.

Ben looked over at Charlie, but Sam had already recruited him into refilling martini glasses and Charlie seemed relieved to have a job. They were laughing together, an unspoken relief coloring their mood.

It was a muted celebration for the safe return of Charlie's car. But they could tell that to Charlie it was something more.

By the time Amber and Nell returned, the music had been turned up a notch, an old Beatles medley filling up the room. In the background, a lively fire crackled as if keeping time with "Hey Jude."

Amber drifted over to Charlie's side, her slender frame smaller in the shadow of Charlie's broad shoulders. She had washed her face and was more composed, though her mind was clearly elsewhere. She looked over at Ben.

"Esther told me you were going to be at the meeting today. I'm sorry I missed it. I didn't intend to mess anything up. I . . ." She stopped, as if her explanation wouldn't matter, then said softly, "I hope it went okay."

"We canceled it. It's been rescheduled," Ben said.

Amber looked surprised. "Why?" She accepted a glass of wine from Sam and sipped it, color slowly returning to her face.

"Lydia Cummings attached a stipulation to the will that all those mentioned in it be present when it's read. That's one of the reasons the lawyer—Rachel Wooten—was so anxious to find you." His voice was level and kind, nonjudgmental. "Usually wills can be handled by mail, but not this time. Anyway, no problem, we've rescheduled the reading for tomorrow morning, same place. I'd be happy to give you a ride."

"They need you there to finalize it," Charlie said.

Amber stared hard at him, the vulnerability that she'd shown when she walked in earlier fading. "I get that now. Maybe we both have a knack for inconveniencing people, Charlie boy," she said softly.

Amber reached over and picked up the bottle of wine, refilling her own glass. She looked at Ben. "I'm sorry."

Ben smiled. "It's okay. No one had to travel far."

Charlie took a sip of his martini. "How about I give you a ride in the morning?"

"You want to make sure I get there?"

"Maybe."

Amber's voice lost its edge. "It's okay, Charlie. I'll be there, I promise. Maybe we can get together after. I may need a hand to hold."

"Sure," he said. "And Uncle Ben will make sure they don't beat you up."

Amber laughed and asked Ben who else she should expect to be in the firing line.

He named off the list, including Garrett O'Neal. "He's their financial guy, and is included in most family meetings. Stu will bring his wife, Helen, and he'll probably bring along a couple of his own lawyers."

"Of course," Amber said, more to herself than the others.

"I'm curious about one thing, Amber," Nell said. She lined up napkins and silverware on the island. When Amber didn't answer, she went on. "You came all this way because Esther told you there'd be a will and some papers to sign. But you didn't go to the meeting . . ."

Amber was quiet, thinking. Finally she took a deep breath, then said, "I came back for other reasons, too. More personal. I had to come back. At least once. So I didn't come because of the will, not really."

"Aren't you curious about it?" Izzy asked.

"Not in the slightest." Amber drained the glass of wine and set it down on the island with more force than she intended.

"But Lydia provided for you while you were growing up. She must have cared about you." *Provided for. Must have . . .*

The words sounded hollow, even to Nell as she listened to Izzy.

"She provided for me, yes, because she felt she had to. But inheritances are for family. I was never family, not really. I don't expect anything from the Cummingses."

Nell automatically opened her mouth to assure Amber that that wasn't true; surely Lydia considered her grandchild family. But she shut her mouth quickly. She had no idea what Lydia had thought.

"Lydia Cummings cared for me because her religion told her to. Esther Gibson liked me, not Lydia. But anyway, religion doesn't dictate wills or control feelings. Lydia's feelings for me would have prevented her from giving me anything."

"Why do you say that?" Charlie asked. He sat on a bench right next to her, leaning in until their shoulders touched.

"Because it's true." Amber touched her fingers to her cheek and rubbed it lightly in a nervous way. "I don't remember clearly what my early years were like. But as I got older and began to look exactly like my mother, Lydia Cummings could barely look at me; she had trouble meeting my eyes. Ever."

The quiet that followed could only be broken by remarks that were without substance. Shallow assurances that she was wrong. But none of them knew that to be true and Amber was a no-nonsense person. So the quiet remained, until Amber herself broke it.

"It all made logical sense, you see. If not for me and my mother, she'd still have her son. We killed him."

Chapter 9

It was Charlie who suggested the hike the next morning. Dr. Virgilio wouldn't be at the clinic Monday. She was busy in her own obstetrics practice and suggested he take another day to get acclimated to the town.

A hike sounded like a perfect place to do it and he'd talked to both Izzy and Nell, suggesting all three of them get some fresh air together. *A family hike,* he said.

Nell resisted. He and Izzy should go alone, have time to talk. Time to clean out the cobwebs, to reconnect without others around. She didn't spell it out quite like that, of course. Instead she explained that it was a busy day. But Izzy loved to hike and sometimes could get away on Mondays . . .

But a subsequent phone call from Izzy rattling off a dozen reasons why it would be much, much better if Nell came along, too—*don't forget you're his favorite aunt, after all!*—wore her down. At least Charlie and Izzy were getting together without an entire bevy of friends and relatives around. And Nell certainly walked more slowly than Izzy. Being the lingerer on a Ravenswood trail was perfectly acceptable.

She and Charlie drove to Harbor Road to pick Izzy up at the yarn shop. Her day off never meant she didn't check in, although her manager, Mae, protested and practically pushed her out the door. Mae waved to Nell and Charlie, whose car was idling at the curb, and suggested they keep Izzy out for hours. She was sorely in need of exercise, according to Mae. Izzy walked to the car with Red trailing close behind. "He needs exercise, too," she explained as the golden retriever leapt into the backseat. "I couldn't say no to him."

Nell had suggested they hike Ravenswood Park. It would add a bit of distance from Sea Harbor—a slight nod to privacy. And the glacial moraine was one of her very favorite places on all of Cape Ann. Each season held its own special magic, and winter was no exception. The oaks and maples and swamp magnolias were eerily beautiful and it took little more than a light snowfall to turn the glacial erratics into giant snowballs.

The drive out of Sea Harbor to Gloucester was quiet, but revealed one good piece of news.

"Amber is at the meeting with the Cummingses' lawyer," Charlie said. "I took her there myself."

"That's a good thing," Nell said.

He'd also taken Amber home the night before, and although both Izzy and Nell had watched Charlie and Amber's interactions with interest, it was difficult to figure out what, if anything, was going on between them. Amber's moods seemed more erratic than Cape Ann weather, and Charlie went back and forth from displaying a tender side toward this woman, who had seemingly inserted herself into his life, to pulling away in irritation. Or maybe frustration. Nell realized she hadn't been around Charlie enough to be able to interpret his moods. As a youngster he'd been pleasant and amiable. A teddy bear, as his mother had sometimes described him, and Nell agreed.

When his father's trait of quick eruptive anger appeared in his youngest son, it was tamped down so quickly it made those around him laugh. And it was seen as a good thing; it made Charlie more competitive, maybe a little better at playing sports.

How Amber figured in this man's life after so few hours of their knowing each other was curious.

They drove toward Ravenswood Park, traffic almost nonexistent in the quiet, wooded neighborhood. In the backseat Izzy played with Red's coat, then leaned forward and said, "Was Amber in better shape this morning?" Her eyes were on Red, his head resting on her knees. She clenched her jaw, unhappy with her choice of words. "I mean, is she okay? She seemed to have a lot on her mind last night."

Charlie shrugged. "I guess she's okay. We talked for a while after we left Aunt Nell's. Maybe it was Ben's martinis, but she needed to unload on someone. I was handy, I guess. We drove around for a while, along the shore, over to Gloucester, all the way up to Manchester-by-the-Sea. There was a small bar up there still open, so we sat and drank coffee. Talked some more. I found out some surprising things about her. She put herself through business school down in Florida while waiting tables. She had just finished when Esther contacted her about the will. She's got a head for math. Honors student, top of her class, the whole shebang. Who would have thought that from looking at her?"

"Looking at her?" Izzy said. Red's ears perked up at the tone in Izzy's voice. "That's a sexist thing to say, don't you think?" she said.

Charlie kept his eyes on the road but lifted one hand in the air to put a stop to his sister's chide. "Hey, Iz, I didn't mean anything by it, nada. Okay? Maybe I shouldn't stereotype. But you have to admit she looks more like a starving artist than an accountant or economist."

"Maybe." Izzy paused for a moment, then said softly, her words barely audible in the front seat, "But you don't look much like a nurse, either."

Why did you become a nurse, Charlie? The unspoken question hung there in silence.

Red flopped his furry tail against the door and Nell shifted in her seat. Her thoughts slid back to the dozens of Kansas visits she'd made when Jack, Izzy, and Charlie were growing up. Being a part of her sister's family was an adventure and one she cherished. They had had a good childhood, the kind Nell would have wanted for her own children, and she never forgot for a moment the gift her sister had given her in making her an integral part of her family.

But as she listened now to Izzy and Charlie, what she heard in their voices wasn't the teenage teasing or bickering she'd so often witnessed in the Chamberses' kitchen. It wasn't something that would be easily forgotten after a game of touch football in the backyard or galloping through the ranch woods on their favorite horses.

It was something else—something still held hostage in those years that had been pushed into the shadows. Undefined years, a void in the middle of a family's life. The unknown—a mighty, sometimes destructive, force.

The Chambers children were all so different, their parents' genes mixing and matching in that mysterious way that created fascinating children.

Charlie was the athlete. How many football games had Nell flown back to Kansas to watch? A handsome high school linebacker and the same in the small college he attended. She remembered the night he told his parents that his dream was to play football professionally.

But somewhere along the path, Charlie had unexpectedly dropped out of his dreams and landed in a different world, one in which he traveled around like a wanderer in a desert. A careless and aimless life, or so it seemed to those who loved him and never knew exactly where he was.

And then, one day, they'd learned that Charlie had gone to nursing school. And no one knew why.

The parking lot was nearly deserted on the cold Monday morning, and Charlie found a place easily, grabbing his backpack and water bottles from the trunk and heading toward the trailhead. "Hey, this is great. Who'd have thought there'd be something like this around here?"

"'Around here' is a pretty great place, Charlie," Izzy said. She looped a wool scarf around her neck and pulled a hat down around her ears. "Come on. You'll see."

Nell smiled at the lack of sarcasm in Izzy's voice. Ravenswood Park wouldn't allow it—and neither would she.

She opened the door and released a barely contained Red, who bounded over to Charlie's side.

They hiked up the path, with Red, Izzy, and Charlie in the lead and heading north on Ledge Hill Trail. The crisp air and crunch of the snow beneath her boots filled Nell's senses and she happily held back, letting her nephew and niece gain some distance and allowing her to savor the scenery in private. Although some of the park's features, like kettle ponds and vernal pools, disappeared beneath the snow, stands of eastern hemlock and birch, sweetbay magnolia and beech trees were majestic in their winter coats.

When she didn't see Izzy's bright yellow jacket ahead, she quickened her pace and finally spotted them again. "Sorry for being a poke," she huffed, coming up alongside them.

From the lookout, Izzy was looking down toward the steep white banks of the harbor, the fishing boats making their way in and out of slips. It was as if the views and the water and the exertion of hiking up a trail were a magical leveling force—the mystery of nature somehow putting things into perspective.

"I'm glad you're happy here, Iz," Charlie said, looking out to sea. His eyes searched for the horizon, but the sky and the water merged seamlessly at some distant point. Only an occasional whitecap added definition to the water. "Sam seems happy, too. Who'd have thought you two would end up together?"

"Serendipity, I guess," Izzy said. "Once I got to know him away from my bratty brothers, I realized he wasn't all that bad."

Charlie laughed. "Amber says Sam reminds her of a guy who used to take care of her mother. Same smile."

"She talked about her mother?" Nell asked. "It sounds like you have had good talks. That's good."

"She's unique, that's for sure. Sometimes it's hard to know what's true and what she says to get a rise out of you, especially after she smoked some pot she got ahold of somewhere. She's complicated. And young. But in some ways she seems old, jaded. I get that, though. Life can do that to you. Maybe that's why we gravitated toward one another." He paused and looked up at the clear sky, his eyes tracing a long weaving contrail as a plane flew over. Then he looked down, focusing on his hands, as if trying to figure Amber Harper out while he talked.

"She's moody as hell. Hot and cold. She comes on to me like we've known each other in another life, all affectionate, and then in the next instant she's making fun, a harsh teasing that isn't really funny and it roils me. You know?"

"Like you and Jack used to do to me?" Izzy asked, her eyebrows lifting into her bangs.

Her teasing brought a grin to Charlie's face. "Nah. That was our way of saving face since you usually got the best of us."

"Always," Izzy corrected. "Always got the best of you."

"So Amber isn't even-tempered, you're saying," Nell said, pulling them back.

"Nope. Not so you'd notice. But, hey, I've known her for what, three days?"

"Is she still planning on leaving as soon as the estate is taken care of?"

"Far as I know. She never liked this place. And it never liked her, she said. She wants to leave, but then she asks me out. Can you believe it? Like we need to get to know each other better. She wants to be with me. She needs a friend, she said. We're meeting for coffee after the meeting with Uncle Ben and the lawyer today. See what I mean? She's unpredictable. Why does she need to get to know me better?"

Charlie's words were barely strung together when a louder, more distinctive sound filled the crystal air.

A coyote's howl.

Charlie grimaced. "Oh, jeez. No worry. It's my cell." He dug into his parka pocket.

"Are you crazy?" Izzy said.

"When someone steals your phone it can come back to you with strange sounds on it. This was Amber's way of identifying her texts to me. She said it's the howl of a coyote seeking a mate. Weird woman." Charlie pulled out his phone. "I guess she's telling me it's time for coffee. Maybe she wants to tell me what kind of toothbrush her grandmother left her in her will."

Charlie looked at the screen, and then read the text out loud. "Hey, Charlie boy. Put the coffee on hold. I have promises to keep and miles to go before I sleep. B4N."

Chapter 10

Ben came home midafternoon, the meeting over. He brought a yellow pad filled with notes, and he was starving, he said.

By the time Izzy, Nell, and Charlie walked through the back door, he had filled the island with leftovers.

"I can see you've heard the news," Ben said, scanning their faces as he swallowed a forkful of tuna salad. He wiped Nell's homemade mayonnaise from the corners of his mouth.

"Not really. Charlie got a text from Amber. But it was vague." Nell pulled off her jacket and boots and left them in the mudroom off the kitchen.

"Vague is putting it mildly," Charlie said. "So, was she right? Was her trip back here just a farce?"

"No, not exactly." Ben put his glasses on and looked down at a yellow pad on which he'd scribbled some notes. "I've been going over my notes, but it's pretty clear how Lydia wanted all this to play out. Her reasons for what she did are not so clear. It turns out she gave Amber the original tree nursery, the one here in Sea Harbor. The other seven or eight nurseries, the house, all that, go to Barbara and Stu."

"Good grief," Izzy said, her eyebrows shooting up. She looked over at Charlie. His eyes were wide.

Ben nodded. "Yes. Those aren't exactly the words Stu used, but it gets to the point. Needless to say, it was a surprise, and not a happy one for some. I'm not even sure how Amber felt about it. All the nurseries are part of one company, so they're tied together from a financial and legal standpoint, at least until they can figure it all out. If one does badly, it affects the whole. Garrett O'Neal—I'm not sure what his title is, but he keeps tabs on all of them. I've never heard him say much, but he was clearly concerned."

"I don't understand," Nell said. She took some plates from the cupboard and brought out a bowl of fruit. "What are Amber's choices here?"

"That's something that has to be figured out. Rachel asked me to meet with Stu, Barbara, and Garrett to go over some of the fine points. Garrett has been working with the company's books a long time and he's good at what he does. Lydia trusted him. But I suppose the real answer to your question depends on what Amber *wants* to do about it."

Izzy heaped some tuna salad on a sandwich roll and cut it in half. "So, what really happened at the meeting?" she asked. "I mean the drama, the emotion. Were Barbara and Stu friendly to Amber? Stu's wife, Helen? Were they upset? Surprised?"

Ben laughed. "Sorry to disappoint you, Iz, but there wasn't a whole lot of drama, although Stu had some choice words to say later. He calmed down when Father Larry reminded him that this was his mother's will, not some stranger's. But there may be drama yet to come. There are decisions to make."

"Did they all talk? Hug? I mean, Amber is related to these people. Their brother was her father. Surely they acknowledged that."

Nell knew what Izzy wanted to hear Ben say. She wanted to hear that Stu and Barbara hugged their niece, pulled her into the family fold, and cast aside any memories or bad feelings that might have festered in their family over the years. She wondered if her own niece realized she hadn't done a very good job of that herself just a couple of days ago.

But today had been a better day for the Chambers family, and hopefully a harbinger of things to come. She wished the same for the Cummings family.

Ben handed a distracted Charlie a beer and helped himself to one. "There wasn't much interaction between the Cummingses and Amber. They sat on opposite sides of the room, Amber next to Father Northcutt and me, and no one talked much before Rachel started in. There were others there, too—another company lawyer, Garrett O'Neal, and Stu's wife—Helen can be a leveling force if Stu gets excited. Rachel Wooten had brought an assistant. Once the will was read and Rachel had passed out copies, she asked them to bring signed copies to her office, and she'd be available to answer any questions once they'd digested all the information in the will. All I could read on Amber's face was curiosity, a touch of surprise, and that bit of sadness that seems to appear when there's any mention of her mother."

"That's it?" Charlie said. "She must have been happy about this. It could have life-changing consequences for her."

"She could give up hitchhiking," Izzy suggested.

Charlie frowned at her.

Ben thought back to Amber's reaction. "She didn't seem happy or unhappy. She listened intently; it wasn't as if she didn't understand what was going on. Amber impresses me as being very smart."

"What did she say afterwards?" Charlie asked. He fingered his phone, glancing down as if expecting a message to appear at any second.

"As it turns out, she didn't say anything. Rachel ended the meeting and people got up, moved around, like they do. There was lots of chatter going on, questions, shuffling of chairs, checking of phones. I went up to talk to Rachel for a minute, then looked back to make sure Amber was all right—everyone else seemed to have someone at their side—but she was gone."

Charlie frowned again. "Gone?"

"Gone. Mary Halloran was sitting in the back of the room during the meeting and she said Amber rushed out like she had a train to catch."

Gone. Again. They'd tried to bring some meaning to Amber's text on the drive home from Ravenswood Park, but they couldn't make sense of it. *Promises to keep? To whom?* "She probably texted you right after the meeting, Charlie," she said.

He nodded, trying to make sense of the words.

"She quoted part of that Frost poem about the snowy evening, dark and lonely woods," Izzy said. "I imagine Amber has been in and out of those woods often during her life. Maybe she just meant she had some things to figure out."

"Miles to go before she sleeps . . ." Nell looked at Ben this time. "I hope she hasn't left Sea Harbor."

Charlie listened in silence, his eyebrows pulled together. The frown finally loosened up and he took a deep breath, then drained the bottle of beer. He looked relieved. "The night I picked her up on the highway, she mumbled something about hating it here. And then she said she had made a promise. I think it's why she came back when Esther contacted her. And I think I know where she went. She went to see her mother."

The fact that Amber's mother had been dead for three years was a given, and it wasn't a surprise that Amber would want to visit her grave—assuming there was one.

"Charlie might be right," Ben said. He washed down the last of his salad with a final swig of beer. "There aren't that many cemeteries around here. If the grave is here, it shouldn't be hard to find it. The Cummingses should know."

Nell knew a more comfortable way. She called Esther Gibson, who was on duty at the police station. She knew exactly where Amber's mother was buried. It was a small cemetery, adjacent to Ocean View, the place where Ellie Harper had spent the better part of her life. It was a lovely place, Esther said, owned and maintained by Ocean View. She had visited Ellie's grave frequently, and had made sure the granite vase she'd put there was always filled with flowers. Sometimes she'd find blooms she herself hadn't put there. "A secret friend," she guessed.

"Ellie Harper's death caused barely a ripple in our small town—I don't think it even made Mary Pisano's 'About Town' column. It was almost as if she'd never existed. Father Northcutt buried her with Richard and me at his side. Jake. And her doctor. Lydia, of course, righteously paid for the plot."

"And Amber?"

"Amber wasn't here. There were times when I didn't know where she was, and the year Ellie died was one of them. I couldn't locate her in time."

Although she hadn't yet heard, Esther wasn't surprised when Nell told her about the will. Lydia was difficult to read, she said. But it was a terrible shame she hadn't given the child more of what she really needed—a warm and nurturing home—when she was growing up. Far better than a plant nursery, in Esther's opinion. "She was my friend, but her son's death froze a part of her heart," Esther said before hanging up and getting back to work.

Ben left soon after for a late-afternoon meeting.

The others piled in Nell's car. The Ocean View campus was out near the quarries, at the end of a hilly road. With the sun slipping behind heavy gray clouds, a ride back would surely be welcomed by Amber, even though their presence might not be.

They drove slowly along the lightly traveled road, aware of icy patches and a few dedicated bikers braving the cold. Around a slight bend, the tall wrought-iron fence and carved sign that read OCEAN VIEW came into sight. From a distance, it looked like a New England college campus, with small, tasteful structures, each one different and each one welcoming, protected from the outer world by a stone gatehouse standing alongside the closed electric gate.

"Esther said to drive by the gate, then follow the road that goes back alongside the property and we'd come to the cemetery. Ellie is buried beneath a hawthorn tree. The cemetery is separate; there's no need to go through security."

"Security?" Charlie said.

"There's a community of wealthy people from all over the north shore who bought houses on the Ocean View campus," Nell said. "The assisted-care section is just one part of it. I remember being turned away once because the person I was visiting had forgotten to put me on the list. I imagine it helps keep theft at a minimum and makes everyone feel safe—families as well as those who live here."

It took less than a few minutes for Izzy to spot the area they were looking for. She pointed to a large tree in the distance, its spreading branches bare. In better weather they could imagine the cool shadows that would fall over the grave from the white-blossomed branches.

Nell pulled over to the side of the road and they got out of the car, heading for a winding pathway.

At first they didn't see her. But when they circled the low-hanging branches, Nell spotted the curved shape of Amber's back as she leaned over a lightly frosted mound. It was no different from dozens of others lining the treed lanes in the small cemetery. A small monument marked the spot, and next to it was Esther's granite vase, filled with white pine and fir tree branches, pinecones, and bright red berries adding a cheery color to the mix.

Finally Amber looked up, as if she had known they were there all along. Her face was grave. Without a hello, she got up and brushed the frost off her jeans. She spoke to Charlie, her voice clipped. "I was about to text you for a ride."

She looked down at the slight mound. "Well, there she is. Meet my mother, Ellie Harper."

Nell walked over to Amber's side, but sensed immediately that a hug wouldn't be welcome.

"I don't much like cemeteries," Amber said. "It's just a place to bury dead bodies. But I came out here yesterday . . . it's where I lost track of time, I guess, and why I missed the meeting."

And why you showed up at our home, with tears staining your face, Nell thought.

"I wasn't sure I'd come back. But I needed a place to think today. It's quiet and peaceful here—"

They nodded.

"Do you need more time?" Izzy asked.

She shook her head. "Not today. It's odd, isn't it?"

They waited, not understanding where her thought was going.

When she looked up, her eyes were moist. "When I was little and would visit her with Esther, there was nothing there. Just a still body. There wasn't any connection. But now that she's no longer trapped in that body, she's real to me. We talk. We make promises to each other." Amber took a deep breath and stood up, brushing away the sentiment that had softened her voice.

Once in the car, she turned to Charlie. "I suppose you've heard that she gave me one of the Sea Harbor nurseries."

"We all heard," he said.

She pointed to her backpack. "I have a copy of the will. I read it again while I was sitting there with my mother. All the nurseries the Cummingses own are connected. So the health of one affects the health of the others. If I ran mine into the ground, there'd be a domino effect. What do you think she was thinking?"

Her voice was filled with such emotion that for a minute Nell thought she might break down—but not over grief.

Nell idled the car as they reached the stop sign at the end of the cemetery road while a line of cars passed by. She looked back at Amber. "You know we're here to help if you need it," she said, not even knowing what the words meant. But at that moment, her passenger looked lost.

Charlie reached over and put one hand on her knee.

Amber smiled, then turned away and looked out the window as if the answer to her future were out there somewhere.

Along the road ran the tall wrought-iron fence and beyond it, the carefully manicured lawns of Ocean View Nursing Home. The sound of an engine revving up on the other side of the fence drew their attention to a man climbing onto a motorcycle near the service entrance. Tangled blond hair escaped from the edge of a helmet. He waved to the uniformed guard at the gate, and the man nodded, smiling.

Amber watched the cyclist, her fingers playing lightly on the fogged glass. He spotted the car, and then the face peering out at him. He seemed to peer closer through the dark goggles, then grinned and lifted a gloved hand in greeting. Amber waved back.

Nell watched through the front window, curious at the interaction, but the man, hidden behind his helmet and goggles, had revved the engine again and driven out, turning in the opposite direction. She watched the bike disappear in a plume of smoke.

Izzy shifted against the seat belt and looked into the backseat. "Do you have plans, Amber?" she asked. "You probably haven't had much time to think about it."

The question hung in the heated air of the car.

"I don't know," Amber said simply. "The inheritance is kind of a blur. But I know what I'm going to do for my mother."

Nell glanced at her face in the mirror. It held little emotion, and her voice was eerily calm.

Amber looked out the window, her breath clouding the glass as she spoke into it. "For the first time in forever, I feel some control over this family. They've controlled me, my mother. But no longer. I have no idea what I will do with this inheritance, but I'll use it in whatever way I need to. You can bet on it."

Chapter 11

It was tacitly agreed that Charlie would stay on in the guesthouse. Ben and Nell had assumed from the start that he would stay there as long as he chose. And Charlie simply didn't leave. They added a microwave to the small galley kitchen in the back of the cottage and told him the laundry in the main house was his to use and their meals his to enjoy whenever the spirit moved him.

Dr. Lily Virgilio was thrilled to have Charlie helping at the free health clinic—Janie Levin was going to show him the ropes and as far as all of them were concerned, they would keep him as long as he could stay.

"I can see already that he's an excellent nurse," Lily had told Nell when she saw her in the checkout lane at the Market Basket on Tuesday. "He met a group of kids this morning and they love him. He's kind and gentle and very smart—just as I'd expect Izzy's brother would be."

Kind and gentle and smart. Nell repeated the adjectives to Ben and Sam later that day. They all agreed that he was those things. And more.

Sam had scratched his head. "There's something else going on in that head of his that he needs to get rid of. It's as if he's locked up ten years of his life and thrown away the key. He might be better-looking now, but that young pimply kid I used to know when he was young had a spirit that seems to have dimmed along the way."

Nell questioned him on what he meant, but Sam just shook his head. "Izzy talks about it, too, about those years. The lost years, she calls them. Though he wasn't really lost. Just not available, I'd guess you'd say. He doesn't ask Izzy much about her life, law school, why she moved here, marrying me. It's as if he's afraid to go there—to open that conversation—because then he'd have to reciprocate. But if you ask me he and his sister are never going to completely mend the sibling bond Charlie has done his best to sever unless he gives Izzy the key to those years."

On Wednesday night, Charlie pulled his car into the driveway just as Ben and Nell were leaving.

"We haven't seen much of you the past couple days," Ben said, and insisted Charlie join them at the yacht club for a drink and food. "It's the best winter buffet you'll ever find anywhere, anytime. Sam and Izzy will probably show up, too. Sometimes Birdie. You just never know."

Charlie checked his watch, then his phone for messages, then finally agreed. But he'd follow them over in his own car. He was whipped and might call it an early night.

Izzy, Birdie, and Sam were already at the club, greeting the hostess and waving to friends across the room. "Danny and Cass are on their way," Izzy said. She turned toward Charlie.

"This is a middle-of-the-week pickup for us," she said, then without thought looped her arm in his and followed the hostess to a table near windows.

Nell looked into the lounge just as Barbara Cummings and Garrett O'Neal walked out.

Barbara spotted Nell, waved, and walked their way. Her greeting was firm and pleasant, as was her way. She always looked the same, Nell thought, her short cropped hair perfectly groomed, her pantsuit dark colored and well made. Her expression businesslike, even in social settings. Ben saw it differently. She was difficult to read, he said—lots went on behind that composed expression, which probably fared her well in business. Who knew what was behind the smile and set jaw, the intelligent greeting?

Garrett O'Neal stood next to Barbara. He was about the same height but seemed smaller in stature when standing with the nursery owner. He nodded politely to Ben and Nell and said a few words but seemed anxious to move on. He touched the rim of his glasses nervously, his eyes behind them seeming tired.

"Are you here for dinner?" Ben asked.

"Garrett and my brother, Stu, love this buffet," Barbara said. "They insist on coming, even after grueling days at the office. Sometimes I escape—there are things I enjoy doing with my time off—but tonight Garrett insisted."

Nell suspected the last few days might have been especially grueling for all of them as they absorbed Lydia's will and any changes it might mean for the company.

Garrett's attention had already drifted away from them as he looked around the room.

Nell spotted the rest of Garrett's party at the same time that he did. Stuart Cummings sat in quiet conversation with his wife, Helen. Beatrice Scaglia, Sea Harbor's mayor and a good friend of the couple, sat across the table from them, listening attentively.

Beatrice looked across the room and met Nell's eyes one second before Nell could look away. The mayor was a formidable force, and sometimes avoiding conversations with her made for a more peaceful evening, in Nell's opinion.

But it was too late. With an enthusiastic wave, Beatrice gestured them over.

"Two of my favorite people," the mayor said, standing up on her signature three-inch heels, smoothing her silk suit, then kissing Ben on each cheek. She turned from Ben and gave Nell a hug.

"Always the politician, Beatrice," Ben laughed. "You've perfected the gracious hello."

Stuart stood and shook hands all around. "That's our mayor.

But we love her just the same, even though she makes us look puny and poorly dressed sometimes."

Beatrice ignored him and looked beyond Ben and over to a nearby table where Izzy, Charlie, and the others had already emptied one basket of calamari. "That's Izzy's brother, correct? I haven't had the pleasure of meeting him yet. Helen and Stu tell me he's been hanging out at the company business office."

"Charlie?" Nell said, puzzled. "I don't think so . . ." She glanced over at Charlie.

"Amber Harper has practically moved in over there," Beatrice said. "She's doing everything but sleeping on the desk. Garrett can barely get to his files, or so I've heard."

Garrett looked annoyed, but more at the mayor and what she was saying than being inconvenienced. He was about to say something when Barbara discreetly touched Beatrice's arm and said firmly, "Bea, it's all right. Let's not drag the whole town into this."

But Beatrice was known for protecting her political supporters, and the Cummings family was among the most lucrative and generous of them. She looked at Barbara, then Stu. "I'm sure you'll be able to control the situation. But if City Hall can be of assistance, I want you to know that you have my help and support."

Ben frowned. "City Hall?"

But Beatrice wasn't quite through. "Barbara and Stuart are trying to protect the amazing and successful company their mother and father worked so hard to build. Cummings Northshore Nurseries does wonderful things for our town. Having a stranger come in and poke around isn't appropriate now, is it?" She tossed the question out indiscriminately, to anyone who might want to answer it. Her black eyes flashed.

Her voice level, her face expressionless, Barbara answered, "She's doing it because she now owns part of the company, Beatrice. You know that. She'll lose interest soon."

"I just wonder what she hopes to find over there," Helen said, speaking up for the first time. She looked around at the others, her shyness lessened by a sip of martini.

Helen was the opposite of her sister-in-law, Nell thought, watching her now. She wondered if they were friends—or simply thrown together by marriage, polite sisters-in-law. As always, Helen's attire was impeccable and more feminine than Barbara's—a tasteful green wool dress, a gold necklace circling her long neck, and an elegant brooch near the scooped neckline. Helen clearly cared for herself, making the most of what otherwise might have been nondescript features, a long and narrow nose and chin, graying hair covered expertly with dark brown highlights. Nell imagined the two women's contrasting days: Helen's at a salon or gym and doing whatever she could to make her husband's life more comfortable; Barbara's in an office crowded with files and books and computers, her keen mind playing with figures and financial reports.

Stu glanced down at his wife and answered her question, his face not as cheery as normal, but his voice calm and reasonable. "It's not rocket science what she's looking for—Miss Harper is trying to get her arms around what she inherited. Barbara's right—she'll soon figure out that running a company is complicated—business always is—and she'll do the right thing and move on with her life. It's what my good mother intended. I'm putting together a package for her right now. She doesn't know anything about business—she's been a waitress in Florida from what my sources tell me." Stu smiled and huffed at their foolish worry. The cigar in his shirt pocket wobbled against his wide chest. "Problem resolved," he said.

His intentions were clear—to change the subject and move to the buffet where steaming containers of boiled lobster and crab and piles of oysters were waiting.

Nell looked over at Ben, who was as uncomfortable as she was at being privy to the Cummingses' private family and business affairs—and equally appreciative of Stu's cordial and valiant attempt to end the discussion.

But his reasoning wasn't very sound, a fact that didn't escape either of the Endicotts. If Lydia Cummings intended for Amber to sell the Sea Harbor Nursery back to her children, why didn't she just give her granddaughter a monetary inheritance and avoid this kind of consternation?

Nell was even more curious about what Charlie's role was in the whole affair. She looked over at him now, his head back, laughing at something. "Is Charlie helping Amber in some way?" she asked Garrett and Barbara. "Why is he at the office?"

Barbara looked at Garrett, who seemed hesitant to answer. Finally he said, "Miss Harper seems to have her friend Charlie on speed dial. She was at the office until nearly midnight one night—I stayed too, not wanting to leave her alone. She said Charlie was picking her up and I didn't need to stick around, but I felt I should."

"That was nice of you," Nell said, although she wasn't sure that was what it was. Garrett looked nervous, and she had the distinct impression that leaving Amber alone in the office would be like leaving a stranger alone in his house. Especially one he didn't trust.

When no one else spoke, Garrett seemed to feel the need to fill the silence with more information. "I offered to answer any questions she had, but she doesn't seem to want that kind of help from me," he said. "We have an intern, Zack Levin. She goes to him, but he's there to help with the computers, that's all. He doesn't know anything. Mostly Amber pokes around on her own, reading company history, files, computer files, whatever she can get her hands on, using my printer. My worry is that something might get misplaced or lost. I keep careful track of everything. I suggested she might stick to regular company hours, but, well, she made it clear our office wasn't the only thing on her agenda. She'd fit it in when she could."

"All right, then." Stu smiled broadly and pulled out a chair for his sister. "On a more festive note, we'll see all of you Saturday, no?"

"Saturday?" Nell said, and then she remembered. It was the evening the decorating teams laid claim to their tree. "Of course we'll be there. Let's hope for decent weather."

"It doesn't matter. Stu has thought of everything," Helen said, reaching up and touching her husband's arm, smiling at him. "Northshore Nurseries is putting up a heated tent on the Harbor Green. It will be a winter wonderland event."

When Nell and Ben finally reached their table, Danny assured them their drinks were on their way and that he'd ordered more appetizers for the table. "I thought for a minute you'd ditched us to be seen with the mayor, maybe get your picture taken?"

Everyone laughed. They all liked Beatrice well enough, and to the surprise of some, she was doing a decent job as mayor. But spending an evening with the very opinionated and talkative mayor would not be on Ben Endicott's bucket list, not in a million years.

"The Cummingses look a little worse for wear," Izzy said. She glanced over, then quickly back when she noticed Helen Cummings staring at their table.

Nell glanced back, too. Garrett looked worn out, and she realized she had never heard him string so many words together. And to do it in front of all the Cummingses plus the mayor had to have added stress to his effort.

Charlie followed her look. "I met that guy last night," he said. "He doesn't talk much, but I don't think he's crazy about Amber coming in like she owns the place."

"But she does," Sam said. "At least part of it."

"What's she going to do with it?" Cass asked.

"Are you asking me?" Charlie asked, poking a thumb into his chest. "Amber keeps things pretty close to her chest." He changed the topic. Finally Ben roused them by rising from his chair and suggesting they head for the buffet table and show Charlie what living in Sea Harbor was all about.

Plates were filled with baked potatoes, lobster and crab, coleslaw, and cheesy corn. The waitress had left baskets of rolls and Irish butter on the tables, along with bowls of sauces and dips.

"Why don't all of you weigh seven hundred pounds?" Charlie finally asked. He pushed his chair back a few inches and stared at his plate that had been wiped clean more than once.

"Because we've learned not to go back for seconds and thirds," Izzy said sweetly.

Even Charlie laughed, then heartily seconded Ben's suggestion that they finish off the meal with baked apple and cinnamon ice cream. Then he backed out of the conversation and let the talk circle around him, looking down at his lap as his thumb tapped on his phone, checking for messages.

From the other side of the table, Danny brought the conversation back to the reluctant guest. "So you played football in college, Charlie?"

"High school," he said.

"But . . . ," Izzy began to correct him. But the memory was vague. She was in law school on the East Coast when Charlie went off to college half a country away. She looked over at Nell, who seemed to be picking at her own memories as well.

"He played in college, too," Sam said.

Charlie nodded. "Oh, yeah, for a while." He got up then and excused himself, heading for the restrooms.

"That's one way to avoid being the center of attention," Izzy said.

Nell watched her nephew disappear. Yes, that was one way. Easier, for sure, than the other way Charlie had tried—quitting college, disappearing into his own world.

Sam watched Charlie, too. His eyebrows pulled together as his mind crawled back into time. He remembered how strong the youthful Charlie was, powerful. On and off the field. He didn't see it now, not in his stature, his manner. Not good or bad. But different. Charlie was different.

The memory slipped away as Charlie returned to the table. His demeanor was lighter, back on an even keel. Ben suggested more coffee or after-dinner drinks.

His offer was suddenly interrupted by the howl of a coyote.

Charlie grimaced, a blush coloring his chiseled profile. "Got to change that text tone," he mumbled, and dug his cell phone out of his pocket.

He read the message, then looked up, shaking his head. "Looks like my princess needs a chariot or whatever."

Before questions intervened, he grabbed his jacket, gave Nell a hug, and thanked Ben for the dinner. Then, with an athlete's grace, he moved across the crowded dining room to the parking lot exit.

Ben watched him walk away. "So much for an early night."

"It's the 'whatever' in his comment that bothers me," Izzy said.

"He barely knows her," Cass said. "What, five, six days? Is that how long since they met?"

"I fell in love with Sonny the day I met him," Birdie said. Her head tilted to one side, her eyes bright and thoughtful as she spoke of a love that had lasted fifty years and was still going strong, untarnished by her husband's death years before.

"You did, too, Cass—come on, admit it," Danny teased.

They all laughed at the unexpected blush that crept up Cass's cheeks.

"See?" Ben said. "Love doesn't wear a watch."

Nell studied Ben's face and knew he had more to say. He wanted to take the attention off Charlie. Ben felt strongly that the last thing their nephew needed was interference in his life. He'd disappeared from them once. They didn't want it to happen again.

Chapter 12

Nell turned the wheel and rounded the corner onto Harbor Road too quickly, hoping one of Tommy Porter's squad wasn't around. She scolded herself mentally and slowed down as she neared Harry Garozzo's deli. She had planned her day carefully, allowing just enough time after a meeting at the museum to pick up a loaf of bread, then was going home to finish off the casserole for the evening knitting session.

Every Thursday knitting session was important, but when emotional clouds as heavy and ponderous as a nor'easter weighed over all of them, the gatherings took on even more urgency. They were utterly necessary.

A parking place opened up a few steps down from Harry's deli and Nell maneuvered her car into the space. She had gathered up her bag and her keys, and started walking toward the deli, when she stopped suddenly.

The wide display windows of the Italian deli were filled today with elves and reindeer and baskets of Italian bread, but what caused Nell's slowdown was the unlikely couple exiting through the glass door.

Helen Cummings moved through the door, then looked briefly at the younger woman directly behind her, who was holding the door open for the older woman. Helen was walking straight and stiff, as if she'd injured her back. But when she turned and Nell glimpsed her face, she knew it wasn't her back that was bothering her.

It was the woman holding the door.

Amber stood still, her face impassive, her eyes locked in to Helen's.

Helen raised one arm, her gloved hand spreading open, her fingers tight together, as if she wanted to slap someone.

The younger woman didn't move, although her expression changed slightly, a look of defiance settling in.

Finally Helen dropped her arm and spun around, then walked away so quickly that her boots nearly slipped out from beneath her. She regained her composure quickly and without a backward glance hurried down the street, oblivious of Nell's presence.

Amber let the door close behind her and stood on the sidewalk briefly, looking at Harry's imaginative display window. Then she shifted the deli bag from one arm to the other and took off in the opposite direction, a slight spring to her step.

Nell leaned back against her car, processing what she'd seen. Finally she remembered her schedule, hastily got out of the car, and walked into the deli.

As always, the aromas alone awakened her senses. Sweet and pungent odors of garlicky tomato sauce, pickles and peppers, freshly baked bread.

"Nellie, my love," Harry greeted her from behind the counter, stretching his beefy hand across the glass case to grab her hand. "And what can I tempt you with today—Margaret's saltimbocca? Her mother's own recipe." He kissed his fingers and lifted them into the air. *"Magnifico."*

Nell laughed and pointed to a plump loaf of rustic Italian bread. "Thursday night at Izzy's yarn shop," she explained.

Harry slapped the side of his balding head. "I shoulda known. You don't need Harry's specials tonight."

"Not tonight," Nell said with a smile. She paused for a moment, wondering if she should mind her own business. But anything connected to Amber these days seemed a family matter, fair game, somehow. "Harry, I just saw Amber Harper walking out of here with Helen Cummings—"

Harry wrapped the bread quickly and then walked around the counter to the steamy window, rubbing it clear with stubby fingers.

When assured the women were no longer in sight, he sidled up close to Nell and lowered his head, his voice as quiet as Harry could get it. "Okay, now, what gives with those two?" he asked Nell. "Amber comes in for one of my wicked-good paninis today—she got an extra one for Izzy's brother, she said. She's in the money now, you know, with the Cummings inheritance."

Nell nodded, always amazed at how quickly private matters became public in a small town. "So Amber and Helen weren't here together?"

Harry guffawed. "Not till hell freezes over. It was a chance encounter, I suppose you'd say. Helen comes in here often, late lunches with a friend after a tennis game or what have you, has a glass of wine—she loves my lambrusco—then she heads for early drinks down the street at the Ocean's Edge or wherever. Or so I hear." He shrugged. "Today she was alone, just sat there at her favorite table, chatting with my wife, enjoying the lambrusco."

"It looked like she and Amber left together."

"That they did. Amber was at the counter, waiting while I packed up her sandwiches. That's when Helen walks up front, wrapping her scarf around her neck, heading for the door."

Nell held her breath, feeling suddenly protective of Amber and hoping she hadn't said something awful to Helen Cummings. Insulting a quiet, genteel woman who was the wife of the Cummingses' CEO wouldn't fare well as it traveled around town. "I hope Amber didn't say anything. I know she has a temper, but this has been a trying week for her—"

"Amber? Oh, no, Nellie, you got it wrong. I don't think Amber even noticed Helen. But Helen noticed *her*, right away. Bam, just like that. And that usually nice face hardened like granite. She walked over to her—scared Amber, she did—and began scolding her. Like a schoolmarm, at first. Accused her of causing unnecessary problems for the company. She needed to leave them alone, to leave town, something like that. And then she mentioned something about Ocean View."

"Ocean View?" Nell said.

"Don't know what that was about. She said Amber should be grateful for all Lydia Cummings did for her and her mother instead of minding other people's business."

"That's odd."

"Well, Nellie, the whole exchange was odd, if you ask me."

"What did Amber do?"

"She ignored her at first, and that made Helen mad. So she poked at Amber with her finger to get her attention. Surprised my wife, who came around the corner and walked over to Helen, trying to calm her down. Margaret and Helen are friends. But neither of us had seen her like this. Poor lady was shaking. She just wants things to be good for Stu, I think, but Margaret thought maybe it was the lambrusco.

"I handed Amber her bag of sandwiches and she had turned to go when Helen followed her, telling her that she had to stop meddling or she'd be very sorry. The Cummingses weren't people who wanted interference," she said. "She was warning her for her own good. 'Stay away or else,' she said.

"Amber was at the door by then, holding it open, and Helen walked right on through, her head high, without even a good-bye to Margaret and me. Just like that. And I suppose that's what you saw—them coming through the door together."

Harry took a deep breath, feeling the exertion of his monologue. He wiped his forehead and shook his head. "Damnedest thing I ever saw. That young woman held herself tight, though. Never a bad word said back to Helen. Not one word."

Esther Gibson and Nell happened to arrive at the Seaside Knitting Studio at exactly the same moment. Seeing that Nell's hands were full, Esther held open the door with her hip, using her cane as a stopper. Nell thanked her and walked through, carefully balancing a foil-wrapped casserole dish.

"Crab?" Esther asked, the wrinkles around her eyes deepening as thcy fanned back into thinning white hair.

Nell laughed. "Is it that smelly?" Nell set it down for a minute on a nearby display table.

"Smelly is not the appropriate word," Esther said, wrapping Nell in a soft plump hug. "Not by a long shot."

It was a stronger hug than usual. Something was on Esther's mind. Nell looked over at Mae, standing behind the computer tabulating the day's receipts. Mae shrugged. She didn't know why Esther was there, either. She already had enough yarn in her house to start her own shop. "Tell Izzy I'm locking up in a few," Mae said. "Birdie's here and Cass is on the way."

Nell picked up the casserole dish as Esther relieved her of the bag hanging from her arm.

"Come, dearie," Esther said. "Let me help you carry it to the back room."

The Thursday night knitting group—along with the meals Nell brought to the gatherings—was known to anyone who shopped in Izzy's yarn shop, or who happened by the shop on warmer days, when the smells of garlic and wine and fresh herbs would float through the front door and out onto the street. The store always closed early on Thursdays, another clue.

It was that special sacrosanct time each week that Izzy and Birdie, Nell and Cass shared food and friendship, laughter, and sometimes tears, all while bamboo needles worked soft luscious yarns into spirit-soothing hats and sweaters.

But sometimes, like tonight, someone happened by, whether by design or accident or some mysterious force, that led them through the bright blue door on Harbor Road. And no one was ever turned away. There was always enough food—and plenty of shoulders to lean on, and listening ears, if that be the need.

Tonight Esther made no move to leave. She settled herself in the comfortable couch near the fireplace and gratefully took the glass of wine Birdie offered her. "Thank you, Bernadette," she said.

"It'll take the chill off, Esther. Enjoy," Birdie said, and continued filling the remaining glasses.

Nell looked over. The use of Birdie's given name portended something serious on the police dispatcher's mind.

Cass bounded down the three steps to the back room, carrying a recently baked rhubarb pie.

"Cass, you shouldn't have," Izzy said. "Bet you worked all day on that."

Cass glanced at Esther on the couch and Birdie sitting across from her. She gave them a wave, then simply wrinkled her nose at Izzy instead of words she might otherwise have said to counter her friend's teasing. Birdie had a way of stopping Cass's more colorful retorts.

The pie, of course, came from Danny Brandley, who found cooking and knitting therapeutic when his mystery plots needed airing out. It was a happy day for the knitters when he finally moved back into Cass's house, up on the hill above Canary Cove, along with his cookbooks and a presence they had missed.

"Hey, Esther," Cass called over. "How did you know you were exactly the person I wanted to see tonight?"

Esther's laugh was sweet and loud at once. "I love you, Cass. Now come sit beside me, right here." She patted the cushion next to her.

Cass did as Esther directed, slipping off her tennis shoes and sitting down, legs folded up beneath her. Purl purred her way between the two women. "So, what's going on with you, Esther?"

"Here's what's going on," Esther said, sipping her wine. "You're all aware that my Amber is back."

"*Your* Amber?" Izzy looked over.

"Yes. Lydia Cummings did what she was capable of for the girl, but that didn't include love. She left that to me."

Izzy filled plates for everyone, adding a sprinkling of fresh

Parmesan cheese to the creamy, wine-laced crab. She and Nell carried them over to the group around the fireplace.

"Lydia was my dear friend," Esther went on. "God knows why. She could be a pain in the sweet patootie sometimes. But I loved her the way we women do, in spite of one another's faults.

"She loved her son Patrick more than life itself. He was so like his father, and when Lydia's husband died, all her dreams, every single one, were poured into that boy, whether he wanted them there or not."

"Stu and Barbara aren't exactly the dregs," Cass said.

"No, of course not. And I think Stu was a decent older brother to Patrick, though Barbara never gave Patrick the time of day. But Patrick was special to his mother—maybe because he came along so late—who knows? But it was clear to everyone that Patrick was the prince."

"And then he was gone," Izzy said softly.

"Yes. And Lydia was never the same." Esther balanced her plate on her lap and began eating again, deliberately and quietly, as if the food was somehow the reinforcement she needed to go on.

For a while the only sounds were the wine being sipped, the scrape of forks spearing remaining chunks of chunky crab, and the soppy sound of bread soaking up the last remnants of Nell's savory sauce.

Finally Birdie broke the silence. "Esther, why are you here?" she asked.

Esther looked up. Her usual smile was gone as she handed her empty plate to Nell. "Of course you would call me out, Birdie dear. I can never put one over on you. You don't think it's simply to enjoy this magnificent crab casserole?"

She settled back into the cushions as if she was suddenly very tired. "You women have been kind to Amber. She said as much, something she doesn't admit to easily. She's a harsh young woman. I've excused it because she had no role models, at least not consistent ones. Amber was never really a part of that family, not in the way you and I think of family anyway. Richard and I wanted to take her in, relieve Lydia of a baby who only deepened her grief. But she wouldn't have it. Lydia was quite religious, and she tried to keep her commandments intact. Giving away a blood relative would surely be against one of them. But as Amber grew and started looking more like her mom, Lydia allowed me to help, sometimes taking the toddler, and then young child, to see her mother at Ocean View. But as soon as Amber was old enough, Lydia sent her off to boarding school and I only saw her on vacations."

"That was cool of you, Esther. Did Lydia visit Ellie, too?" Cass asked.

"No, never. Someone told me Stu went over, probably the only family member, though when I mentioned it to him, he said no. But Lydia, for her part, made sure Ellie Harper was in the best facility, got the best care, and she paid for it all. Ellie was a terrible reminder of what she'd lost. In her mind, Ellie shouldn't have been the one who lived. But she did, no matter how limited a life it was."

"It doesn't make sense," Izzy said. "Why did she include Amber in her will if she felt that way about her?"

"Well, I've thought about it long and hard and I think I know why. The one thing Lydia paid attention to were her children's minds, their learning—and in this case, her grandchild's. Achievement was important, so she always read school reports. Amber's reports and testing showed that she had her father Patrick's keen intellect. The girl is a genius at numbers, extremely intelligent. Off the charts, as they say, just like her father was. Lydia knew that. I think she bequeathed her the business because she knew Amber would be an asset to the company's growth once she was gone."

"That's interesting," Nell said.

"And perverted," Cass said.

But Esther seemed not to hear and continued on with what she came to say.

"Once Patrick died, the success of the Cummings Northshore Nurseries became the most important thing in her life. Almost like another child. Amber has the capability to continue that. Lydia didn't need Amber while she was living. But in death, she did. And she wouldn't have to be around to look at her, to be reminded of that awful day Patrick died. So maybe that's why she did it. Stu is a wonderful front man and visionary, but maybe she thought Barbara and that Garrett fellow could use some looking after." Her voice seemed to drop off then, her face drawn.

Birdie handed her a piece of pie. "But this all seems to worry you, dear. Am I right?"

Esther nodded. "I'm not sure Lydia took into account that everyone might not automatically do what she wanted. And that would be especially true once she wasn't around. How could she possibly think Amber, of all people, would cater to her wishes? And that's my worry, sort of. Not that Amber won't do what Lydia intended, but what she might do instead." Esther took a bite of pie and continued.

"I ran into Helen Cummings and Beatrice Scaglia having lunch at the Ocean's Edge yesterday. Helen mentioned that Amber was spending time with their financial records and that it's causing stress on the family and it worries her. By family she means Stu, of course. Stu's heart isn't what it used to be, she told me."

Nell listened, although the story was becoming repetitive.

"Therefore, Amber is harming Stu's heart?" Izzy said.

"Oh, I know, Izzy. I suggested Stu stop with the cream tarts and steak. But the thing is, the Cummingses are strong, powerful people and don't take kindly to meddlers. And Amber? She's this skinny young woman finally grieving her mother. And that's why I worry. I worry about Amber.

"I have this awful fear that she's out for revenge."

Esther got ready to leave shortly after finishing her pie. She was weary, and Richard would be waiting for her.

"Amber is staying with you, right?" Birdie asked as she handed Esther her cane and prepared to walk her to the door.

"She has a key to the house. A warm bed. And she knows we're there for her." She looked over at Izzy. "She's also leaning on your brother. Amber is moody and can cover up emotions by lashing out—she's always been that way, even when she was little—and she probably does that with Charlie. She's done it to me, so I know. But she cares for him."

Esther took a sip of water. "Amber keeps things bottled up. I'd like to talk with her, find out what she's thinking. But she is on a bit of a quest right now. She doesn't seem to have a sensible ounce of fear in that body of hers. I'm worried where it might take her."

It was what they expected to hear, but somehow it left a chill in the room as Birdie helped Esther up the steps and to the door of the yarn shop.

Izzy got up and stoked the embers in the grate, bringing them back to life. She curled back up in a chair and pulled a skein of wool from her knitting bag. Somehow fingering the easy fibers brought warmth into her body.

In the distance, they listened for the roar of Esther's old truck rumbling down Harbor Road, going a few miles an hour too fast and knowing no one on the police force would ever consider stopping her for it.

"Esther's worry brings a reality to all this," Birdie said. "She knows Amber better than any of us, certainly better than her relatives."

"Amber may be fearless and even angry about things in her past, but she's smart." Nell had cleaned up all the dishes and returned with fresh coffee. "I don't think she'd do anything foolish." She told them about the encounter at the deli—and the restraint Amber had showed.

"Did Harry think Helen was seriously threatening Amber?" Birdie asked. "It sounds to me like she was just trying to protect Stu. Sometimes I think that is her goal in life. She worries about his blood pressure, his heart, like Esther said. I heard her worrying about his cavities one day. She used to pour out her worries on her mother-in-law, Lydia. Now I think it's anyone who will listen."

"A threat is a threat, whether you mean it or not. Amber was the grown-up it sounds like," Cass said. "I might have been a tad more vocal in her shoes."

Izzy agreed, but still looked worried. "I'm not crazy about Amber. I guess it's Charlie I'm really worried about. Amber seems to have some weird power over him—and even though Esther thinks it might be a good thing, I'm not so sure."

Birdie tucked a lap blanket over her legs to ward off the draft. She fingered the soft angora snowflakes Izzy had knit into the pattern and thought about the designer's brother. "Izzy, I don't think you need to worry. Charlie's attraction to Amber is tempered with common sense. She has common sense, too, judging from what we just heard. And if she lashes out now and then, Charlie gets that, too. He doesn't like it—but the girl hasn't had an easy life, and he's sensitive to that. He told me so himself. He feels some responsibility for her because he rescued her that night on the highway. Misplaced or not, it's like rescuing a bird. You can't simply throw the robin into a snowbank and walk away, now, can you?"

Birdie stopped talking for a minute. She sipped her wine and let the words settle wherever they might. Then she wiggled the tightness out of her fingers and with a quick change of tone, said, "Speaking of snowbanks, that might be where we'll land if we don't commit to knitting up some of these ornaments for our tree."

Izzy laughed. "Good segue, Birdie. You're right. Here's the deal. Anything goes, as long as it's hand-knit and reflects Sea Harbor life—on land or sea. Some of my customers will knit up a few ornaments if we need them."

She slid several patterns across the table: a sailboat, a snowman with an anchor on its hat, starfish and lobsters, whales and surfboards. They sorted through them and sank their fingers into the pile of yarn Izzy and Nell had chosen. In minutes the patterns were selected and bright green, red, blue, and multicolored yarns were claimed by fingers eager to begin.

And just like that, the needles began clicking.

A lovely familiar sound.

A new project had been born.

And along with it, blood pressures lowered, worry slipped aside, and the warmth of a fire held four friends close.

Birdie decided she'd knit a whole school of fish and sea life, and quickly began casting on for a jolly fat whale that she'd brighten up with a red Santa hat. Izzy picked a snowman with an anchor on its scarf, Cass a bright red lobster, and Nell began the moss-stitched hull for a sailboat named *Mistletoe.*

They set to work casting on, coming up now and then for talk or coffee or simply to lean back with needles in hand and listen to the gentle voice of Tori Amos singing about promises and sunshine.

Cass finished a claw on her tiny lobster and set down her knitting to concentrate on Purl, the shop's calico cat, gently rubbing her belly. "Willow has taken over the Halloran fishing crew's tree decorations," she said. "Good thing he has a girlfriend."

"Willow will do him proud. Imagine, those scruffy guys having a beautiful tree," Izzy said.

"While we're on the subject of my family," Cass said, "Pete and I had breakfast with Ma this morning. It's dinner at her place or Sugar Magnolia's, that great restaurant over in Gloucester—once a week, like clockwork."

"And she pummels you with questions about when you're going to marry Danny?" Izzy asked. "All before the Sugar Mag special arrives at your table?"

Cass laughed. "Oh, sure. Pete gets some of it, too. Subtle inquiries as to when he and Willow will reproduce the amazing Halloran genes. But mostly she takes care of that with the candles she lights at Our Lady of Safe Seas. She even has Father Northcutt lighting a few."

"So, what else do you talk about? The scandalous rumors in the Ladies' Altar Society?" Izzy asked.

"Like Ma would ever tell their sordid secrets?"

Birdie held up her whale. Its yarn belly was already taking shape as she began the process of short rows. "I imagine Mary has other things on her mind these days, like helping Father Larry with funerals and wills and trusts. Your mother is a dear soul and I know she's the real power behind that church."

"Yes, she is," Cass said. "She's a worrier, too. And these days she's more worried about Father Northcutt's pressures than when her kids will get married and give her grandbabies. I guess that takes the pressure off—but I'm not sure her new worries are so good for her." She slipped her knitting into a backpack, finished for the evening.

"What do you mean?" Izzy asked. She looked down at the beginnings of the small knit snowman and smoothed out a stitch around what would be his belly.

"I'm not sure what I mean. Let's talk about something else, like what I should get Danny for Christmas."

"How about an engagement ring?" Izzy said, lifting her head. "Why should it always be up to the man to decide if and when? You could lure him out to the Harbor Green, kneel down beside our tree filled with exquisitely knit ornaments, ask for his hand—"

"He wouldn't give me his hand. He needs that for writing," Cass said.

But no matter her retort, they all enjoyed the image of Danny Brandley sporting a diamond on his large hand. And even more, they enjoyed the fact that Cass hadn't immediately told them they were crazy, that she'd never get married, that everyone didn't have to, you know?

Izzy stuck the end of her needles into a ball of yarn and moved it to a basket on the table. "So, why are you concerned about Mary?" she persisted. "We all love her. She shouldn't have worry in her life." She reached for a bottle of Baileys and added a final splash to their coffee mugs.

"She thinks Father Larry is under too much stress. He was close to Lydia."

"Her funeral took a lot of his energy," Birdie said. She folded the lap blanket and stood up, dropping her whale in the knitting bag. "Maybe it's that, but I think it's more the burdens that a priest bears that are weighing on him, at least according to Ma. Normal people have more outlets, like I'll never get high blood pressure because I have you guys to dump on." Her voice softened and she added with a touch of awkwardness, "And I have to admit, Brandley isn't half-bad in that department, either. He's . . . he's cool. Has a good shoulder."

Izzy raised her eyebrows and Nell looked over at Cass with interest. Birdie smiled in that way she had and patted Cass's knee. But no one spoke, knowing it sometimes fared better with Cass to accept silently what hints of her love life she offered—and simply to savor the joy that, at the least, Cass was not running away from a dear mystery writer who belonged in her life, whether she knew it or not.

Cass coughed, then added brusquely, "Ma says Lydia Cummings—especially after she got sick—called on Father Larry a lot. Constantly, actually. Helen usually brought her, but she always wanted to be alone with Father Larry. Then when she got too sick, she'd beckon him to her home. He and Esther might have been the only people she allowed into her life those last couple months. Priests have to keep secrets—I think they go to a special school for that. Probably one that includes lots of Irish whiskey. Anyway, Ma thinks whatever secrets Lydia shared with Father Larry burdened him."

They listened to Cass as they finished knitting rows and packing up their knitting, then stood and walked around the room, cleaning up crumbs as Izzy worked on tamping out the fire.

Outside, the wind rattled shutters and a group of shivering carolers made their way down Harbor Road.

The lights in the yarn studio went out, one by one, as the knitters carried their thoughts of a priest's burdens to the front door.

Nell took out her keys and looked into the night.

"Father Larry shared a similar thought with Ben recently," she said, one hand on the front doorknob.

"'Sometimes the dead are more difficult to protect than the living,' he said."

Chapter 13

By Saturday Nell's weather wish was granted. During the night the northern winds had loosened their icy grip, moving out over the ocean and leaving the skies blue and the sunshine welcome and plentiful. It would warm the air and the Harbor Green, and infuse the town with a short respite before winter gripped Sea Harbor for good.

Best of all, it would make the evening festivity pleasant as teams gathered to claim their trees for the decorating competition, children danced to the music of Pete, Merry, and Andy's band, and the fragrant aroma of spicy drinks and hot chili rose and filled the heated tent.

Nell and Ben walked past the gazebo and called out a greeting to the Fractured Fish band members as they tuned their instruments. Willow was helping with the extension cords and Andy Risso, idle for a minute, jumped off the stage and gave Nell a huge hug. "Haven't seen you folks in forever."

"But I don't get a hug like that?" Ben joked.

"Nope." Andy grinned. "I've always had a special thing for your wife. You know that."

Nell felt the same. She liked all of Pete's friends, but was especially fond of the long-haired drummer who would often ignore his bartending duties at the Gull Tavern—a place he practically ran for his dad these days—to talk English literature or existential philosophy with Nell. Andy was a true Renaissance man, just like her Ben.

"Jake tells me you're trying to take over his bar from him," Ben said.

Andy laughed, pushing long strands of blond hair back from his face. Finally he pulled a rubber band from his wrist, bunched it into a ponytail, and secured it tightly. "The old man's getting up there," he said. "He'd be the last to admit it, but he should be spending more time catching cod and less on that hard concrete floor."

Nell agreed. Andy was a good son. She sometimes thought if she and Ben had had a son, she would have wanted him to be just like Andy Risso. Easygoing, smart. And very kind. He had sacrificed an Ivy League scholarship to help when his mother was dying—and then he stayed in Sea Harbor when she went into nursing care, helping his dad and picking up classes at a community college. And he never seemed to regret a minute of it.

"Hey, Risso," Pete called from the gazebo. "'Frosty the Snowman' has a heck of a time resonating without a drummer."

"Everyone does, Halloran. You're just finding that out?" He saluted Nell and Ben and in one bounding leap, hefted himself back onto the gazebo floor. With one finger, he trilled Merry Jackson's keyboard before settling in behind his drums.

Ben and Nell turned away from the gazebo and almost immediately spotted Birdie. She was standing with Tommy Porter, his girlfriend, Janie, and her brother, Zack.

Freshly painted gaslights bordered the pathways on which they stood. Newly planted trees, well mulched and well fed, filled the air with the scent of holidays. In front of each tree was an iron placeholder, staked into the ground. Some of the markers already had the name of a decorating team slipped into the holder. By evening's end they'd all be claimed.

"It's intoxicating," Nell said, breathing deeply.

Then she spotted a waving Izzy just a short distance down the path. Izzy was shouting over the heads of some customers from her shop, pointing to a Colorado blue spruce, "How does this one look for our knitting tree, Aunt Nell?"

Nell craned her neck to see it. All around her it looked like woods, with the Northshore Nurseries fir trees taking center stage among the old-timers, the black pines and hemlocks and oak trees that had graced the park forever.

"It's perfect," Nell replied. She held back her thought that all the trees looked equally beautiful. Cummings Nurseries had wisely planted varieties: Austrian and eastern pines, blue spruce, and white and Douglas fir—but they were all perfect, all standing proud, waiting to hold ornaments and lights. It would be even more magical than the miniature display at the community center.

"This whole thing is a terrific idea," Ben said, greeting Stu Cummings and Alphonso Santos, both on hand for the festivities. Their wives were chatting a short distance away.

The chamber representatives agreed, pointing to groups of people still streaming down the hill to the Harbor Green proper. "We have thirty trees and every single one will be accounted for by evening's end," Stu boasted. "Thirty, thirty-two trees . . ." He lifted his head as if multiplying numbers in the air. "Let's say each team has two or three thousand in pledges . . ."

"Not bad, old man," Ben said. He clapped Stu on the back. "And you can bet the clinic will put it all to good use."

Alphonso directed their attention through the trees to an area closest to the shoreline where a group of burly cod fishermen were engaged in an argument with Sea Harbor's fit and all-woman running club. Both groups argued that the slightly taller Douglas fir was their team's to decorate. Much playful jostling accompanied the feud. Alphonso laughed. "Competition breeds success," he said.

"My money's on the women," Stu said, his robust laugh traveling on the crisp air and his bright red jacket puffing in and out. Helen walked up beside him and slid her arm through his, greeting

Ben and Nell. "Stu's in demand tonight," she said as she ushered him away to greet and welcome other teams.

Nell watched them walk off, intrigued by the two sides to Helen Cummings she was beginning to see. The quiet, sedate, corporate wife Helen. And the woman who seemed to shed that image after a drink or two, becoming more talkative. In a way, Nell thought, more free. She turned back to see Izzy coming toward her, her cell phone held to her ear.

Izzy spotted Nell looking at her and hung up. "Okay. It was just one call to the babysitter," she said. "I'm weaning myself." She slipped the phone into her pocket and waved to Birdie, who was scurrying up the path toward the tent, one arm tucked into that of Harold Sampson, her driver and groundsman.

"Good," Izzy said, watching her disappear. "Birdie thinks she's Paul Bunyan, but it's wicked cold out here. She needs to be near those heaters." She looked around. "Where's Charlie?"

"He was home when we left," Nell said. "He's enjoying that job, by the way. Even more than he thought he would. Maybe he's finally found his niche."

"Is he coming tonight?"

"He's picking Amber up and said he'd look for us when they got here."

"Amber again," Izzy said.

Nell gave her niece a hug. "Charlie's all grown up," she whispered to Izzy, then looped her arm through her niece's as they walked up to the tent, the tall heaters and the hot food waiting to warm them.

Danny had claimed a table and waved them over.

Henrietta O'Neal, Birdie's neighbor, was leaning on her cane, sharing her outspoken view of the world with anyone within earshot. Behind her, half listening to the exchange, was her nephew, Garrett.

"My aunt is filling us in on the next election," he said.

"Mayoral?" Ben asked.

"Presidential. Congressional. County commissioner. Boston mayor."

They laughed, even though his comment held more truth than fiction. The eighty-plus-year-old activist would be a common sight marching in protests as soon as the opportunity presented itself.

"The trees are beautiful," Nell said. "Your company has done an amazing job."

"It's not my company, but thank you. It was a generous decision made by civic-minded people." He looked over at Barbara, standing in the center of another group, explaining the type of mulch they had used to protect the trees against the weather. Her face was serious, her formidable voice commanding attention like a strict schoolmarm's. Garrett watched her, his usually unreadable face softening. "Barbie isn't one for small talk. She can tell you every worm that lives in Cummings Nurseries compost." He took off his glasses and wiped them clean with a handkerchief.

The nickname struck Nell as fanciful, very unlike the serious accountant speaking it. Garrett spoke with a mixture of admiration and affection—and Nell found the idea that Barbara might have a softer, private side pleasing.

Minutes later, Henrietta poked Garrett with her cane, then ushered her nephew off to the pizza booth.

"You made it," Nell called out to Charlie and Amber. They were walking toward them with plastic bowls of chili cupped in their hands. Charlie looked happy.

"Janie Levin signed us up—docs and nurses and staff," he said. "We're going to decorate a tree. I now have a stake in this, as it were." He grinned.

Cass whooped. "I won't even begin to guess what will be on it. You medical types have raunchy senses of humor."

"How about you, Amber?" Nell asked, attempting to engage her with the group. She was far more sedate than when she'd seen her the previous day. "Are you helping with the tree?"

"It's not exactly my thing," Amber said, her tone indicating that decorating a tree was the furthest thing from her mind tonight. And whatever was there instead was weighing on her heavily.

"I understand," Nell said kindly. "It's been a long week for you." Probably an overwhelming one. Finally facing the death of her mother. Facing the Cummings family. Dealing with an inheritance that she seemed to treat with suspicion. It was difficult to imagine handling all that without the support of a friend or a partner—or family.

From the looks of things, Charlie was filling that role for Amber as best he could. And if the shadows she had seen in the guesthouse the night before were an indication, perhaps he was filling a larger role as well.

Amber then turned slightly, concentrating on the chili, and looking out over the crowd just as Stu and Barbara Cummings circled around the side of the tent.

Amber stopped eating, her spoon held in midair. Her eyes focused on the brother and sister. Not far away, Helen Cummings stood with Garrett O'Neal.

As if frozen by the stare, Stu stopped walking and turned, meeting Amber's eyes.

His expression was odd, Nell thought, though at that distance, perhaps she was reading it wrong. Barbara turned, too, but her expression for once was easier to read. It was cold and chilly. *Get out of our life,* it seemed to say.

Then Stu raised his hand as if to wave, and Nell imagined a white cloth billowing from his fingers, a sign of peace. But then the moment passed, and he looked away, welcoming instead a smiling Helen, who was coming forward to claim her husband.

Nell watched the scene play out.

Amber had a fierce look on her face and took a few steps in their direction, until Charlie blocked her way.

"Hey, what's up?" he said. "Amber? Are you okay? Let it go—"

She took a deep breath, then faced him as if he had accused her of a crime. "Am I okay? Of course not."

Charlie frowned, unsure of her tone. He set his chili on a serving tray and wrapped an arm around her shoulders, trying to draw her in.

But Amber pulled away, sloshing chili on the front of her parka. She stared at the stain running down her jacket. "It looks like blood," she said. "An omen." Her voice was hard.

Charlie rushed over to the table and returned with a fistful of paper napkins. But when he tried to help, she shook her head and brushed him off. "No, leave it. You'll mess it up."

Nell watched, surprised at Amber's behavior, her sudden shift, her distance, but most of all her treatment of Charlie. She looked to the side and saw that Birdie was watching, too.

Charlie's face was blazing with embarrassment, yet he tried again, once more, smiling slightly and trying to shake off the emotion flooding his face. "Hey, Amber, it'll be okay. We'll figure it out." His voice was soft, soothing.

But his words met with ice. "I'll settle it myself. Tonight. They're evil people."

Her voice was steely. She spun away from Charlie and distanced herself, alone in the darkening night, as if surrounding herself with an invisible field, one that Charlie Chambers couldn't pass through, no matter how hard he tried.

Janie Levin walked over and latched onto Charlie. "We've been looking all over for you," she said. She insisted Charlie come with her to see "their" tree. "It will just take a sec." She spotted Amber and called over to her, "Want to come with us, Amber?"

But her words fell on deaf ears. Amber ignored the gesture, walking farther away instead, finally stopping beneath a tall portable heater. Her eyes stared vacantly into the crowd of people milling about, their holiday spirit frozen before they could reach her.

Charlie looked uncertain, then shoved his gloved hands in his pocket, glanced once more at Amber, and turned and followed Janie down the path.

Nell started walking toward Amber, not sure why or what she

would say. She was irritated at the mood Amber seemed to have pulled out of thin air—and how it had been used to embarrass her nephew. It was as if she couldn't help herself. As if her emotions were raw.

Birdie came up beside Nell and motioned that it was okay. It was her turn. Nell nodded; Birdie read her emotions sometimes before she felt them herself. She walked back inside the tent and watched Birdie approach Amber, smiling, looking up into her eyes. Birdie would smooth it over, bring Amber back to a better place. It was a gift she had.

"You've found a warm spot, Amber," Birdie said. "I'll join you if I may."

Amber turned toward her. At first she looked surprised, unsure of who was behind the gentle voice coming out of a bundle of scarves and a knit hat pulled nearly down to her eyes.

It took just a minute to recognize the smile on the small lined face. Amber didn't smile back, but her shoulders relaxed and the look in her eyes didn't send Birdie away.

"You seem a million miles away, my dear. I hope it's a nice place you're visiting, one worth the trip."

Amber nodded, a gesture Birdie couldn't interpret easily. But one thing was clear, wherever Amber had been in her mind, it had troubled her greatly.

Finally Amber asked, "Have you ever been to Ocean View?"

"Yes. It's a beautiful place. A few of my first husband's family members lived there," Birdie said. "The Favazza family donated money for some of the buildings."

Amber nodded. "I thought so. Your name is on that elaborate plaque in the lobby."

Birdie chuckled. "You have a good memory."

"Memory? No, not so good, not really. Some things are better not remembered. Best buried." A sadness seemed to overwhelm her as she spoke, one that traveled from her face down into her whole body. She took a deep breath. "Ocean View is like a resort." But the tone in her voice indicated it might not be one in which she'd like to spend time. "When I was little it scared me. Sometimes I had nightmares after I'd been there."

"Yes," Birdie agreed. "I can see it would be a bit overwhelming to a small child."

"My mother lived there. Did you know that?"

"Yes, I did."

"And then she died there."

Birdie was quiet, watching the emotions play out on the young woman's face. Sadness. But edged with an anger Birdie couldn't put into context. She wasn't sure if it was directed at herself or someone else—or at Ocean View.

"You've lived in this place a long time, haven't you?" Amber said suddenly. "Esther says you represent the heart and soul of Sea Harbor. In her words, you are 'infinitely wise.'"

Birdie chuckled. "I don't know about that. We all do the best we can with the life we have, now, don't we? But yes, I have lived here a long time, that's absolutely true. Sometimes I think it has been hundreds of years."

Amber was quiet for a minute, her eyes wandering over the crowd until they settled again on the Cummingses, standing now with the mayor and a group of dignitaries. Without turning back to Birdie, she said quietly, almost as if to herself, "Bad things have happened in this town. I need to do something about it. I promised her—"

Birdie was silent, waiting for Amber to say more.

She turned back to Birdie, her voice now thick with emotion. "I need wisdom. Esther says you have that."

Birdie waited. She held back from suggesting Amber talk to Father Northcutt, thinking this might be more up his alley.

"Could I talk to you about all the awful stuff? Maybe it will help me see it clearly, help me make decisions. I've talked to my mother, but—" Again her voice dropped, the end of her thoughts lying on the frozen ground.

"Of course you may. Anger is a poisonous thing and I think you have more of it stored up than one body can bear. Sometimes hearing your thoughts spoken out loud brings clarity to them—and hopefully will relieve that anger and send it off. Would you like to talk now? We could take a walk among the new trees. And it's quiet there."

Amber turned and looked toward the winding pathways. She shifted her gaze to the giant tent where crowds of people mingled and speakers carried the music from the gazebo into their revelry. For a moment she seemed to be listening to the music and the voices that poured out into the cold night.

Finally she pushed up the cuff of her jacket and checked her watch. She looked at Birdie. "I'm sorry. I can't tonight. I've already—" She looked off again, then focused back. "I have to talk with someone tonight. It'd be better to talk after that. Later—"

Amber fiddled with the edge of her glove, then asked, "Maybe tomorrow? Maybe things will be more clear to me then."

"Tomorrow would be lovely."

They set the time and place, and Amber smiled a thank-you, a smile that seemed to take great effort. It was weighed down by a burden that was too heavy for one woman to carry, Birdie thought. Whatever it was, she would do what she could to share it, to lessen it and ease Amber's distress.

Amber started to turn away, then suddenly turned back and to Birdie's surprise, wrapped her arms around her and hugged her tightly.

Before Birdie could respond, Amber turned and walked briskly away from the tall heater, the darkening night folding in around her.

Birdie watched her for a minute, wondering about the emotion that enveloped her. It was in her eyes, her tone, her entire body. Slowly she pulled herself loose from the disconcerting feeling and walked over to the tent, looking around for Nell.

The crowd had grown, people milling around, families feeling the effects of hot dogs, chili, and the huge pizza slices offered at the stand just beyond the tent. When the old-fashioned lamplights turned on, parents began collecting wayward children and headed toward their cars. Birdie spotted Ben's tall head, and worked her way back to friends.

Ben handed her a hot mug of cider and suggested that they leave soon.

"There you are," Charlie said, working his way over to them. "I almost couldn't find you in this crowd. Janie couldn't find the right tree, so it took us a while." He looked around. "Hey, where's Amber?"

"I was talking with her for a bit," Birdie said. "But I think she wanted to be alone. That happens to all of us, Charlie. It's the way of women." She tried to ease his concern with a smile.

But Charlie didn't seem convinced. He headed out of the tent and toward the heater, looking over the tops of heads and peering into the darkening night. Nell followed him, scanning the crowd.

Large groups of college-aged kids were moving into the tent, filling in the spaces vacated by families and children. On the frosty lawns, beer was passed around, music pulsed from iPads, and laughter rolled down toward the harbor lights.

A festive night.

"Could she have gone home?" Nell asked. "I'm not sure she was in a party mood, Charlie. That happens to all of us at times."

Charlie shook his head, his concern growing. "No, she wasn't. Amber is moody, but tonight it was something else. Even if she says otherwise, I don't think she should be alone."

A crowd was gathering near the gazebo where the Fractured Fish had given the stage over to a lively singing group accompanied by several electric guitarists beating out an upbeat collection of holiday music. The crowd was loving it, swaying to the beat, their movement adding protection against the cold.

"I think I see her. There she is," Nell said, pointing toward the back of the white bandstand. Charlie took a few steps forward, looking beyond the fan of spotlights on the gazebo to a cleared, darkened space beside the structure where Andy Risso's drums were piled in cases on a dolly, ready to move to his truck.

Nell frowned, suddenly not sure if it was really Amber she was seeing.

The woman she thought was Amber was standing with Andy Risso, whose ponytailed profile was unmistakable even in the shadowy light. One arm was wrapped around the slender woman, his blond head bent and his fingers caressing her tangled mass of hair, then patting it affectionately.

Amber's face was buried in his chest.

Beside Nell, Charlie froze. He took a deep breath and his voice dropped. "Yeah, you're right. That's her."

His fingers curled into a tight fist.

Then, without another word, he turned his back on Nell and strode resolutely into the tent and toward a cooler filled to the brim with beer.

Nell stood still, wishing away the look she had seen in Charlie's eyes. She took a deep breath and commanded the uncomfortable swell inside her to go away. It must have been the slice of pizza Ben had put in front of her, reminding her they hadn't had dinner.

When she looked up again, Andy Risso and Amber were gone.

She looked back inside the tent.

And so was Charlie.

It was a short time later that Ben whispered in her ear. He was ready to go, ready to build his own fire at home. Izzy and Sam had left, heading to the Gull Tavern with Danny and Cass and friends for a nightcap.

They walked toward the parking lot, away from the sound of the waves and wind that was whipping up off the water. Ben's arm looped around Nell's shoulder, pulling her into the protective shield of his body.

"Nice evening?" he asked.

Nell pressed closer to his side, one arm sliding around his waist. The uncomfortable feeling hadn't gone away, but instead of the sharper sensation she had felt earlier, it had settled into a dull feeling more easily identified.

It wasn't indigestion.

It was dread.

Chapter 14

Cass was up early Sunday morning, her concern over a broken lock pulling her from her disturbed dreams and from bed while the sky was still dark.

Danny found her in the kitchen cradling a giant mug of coffee between her palms. He forked his fingers through his thick head of sleep-tousled hair, trying unsuccessfully to tame it. He squinted at her. "That *is* you, right, Cass?"

Cass laughed and Danny put his glasses on, then walked across the chilly kitchen, wrapping her in a morning hug. "Yeah, it's you."

"I could rent you out," Cass said. "Best bear hugs on Cape Ann."

"Or anywhere," he said, nuzzling her neck. "So, what's up? It's practically the middle of the night. Did you forget it's Sunday—the day of no work, no writing, no fishing, no lobsters, no office work? Just lazy lolling around and letting me pay inordinate amounts of attention to you. Or . . . or perchance . . . you to me?"

Cass took a drink of coffee. Then she took a step away so she wouldn't give in and let Danny lure her back to bed. "Here's the thing. I want to lollygag and frolic and loll around with you, but I need to go check on something down at the dock."

"Now? On Sunday?" Danny looked at the clock. "It's still dark out."

"It'll be light by the time I get dressed. I noticed last night when we were walking up to the harbor parking lot that the lock on that cage where we keep the lobster traps was broken off."

"Why didn't you say something then?"

"We were headed to the Gull to have fun. And I figured it could wait until morning. But you know how that goes. I wasn't worried until it woke me up, then bounced around in my head until it became way more important than it really is. But it'll stay there, irritating me, until I go check it out and replace the lock."

"Geesh, Cass," Danny began. Then he forced away his disappointment, turned, and started back toward the bedrooms.

"What?" Cass said. "You're going back to sleep?"

"No." He tossed the word back over his shoulder without turning around. "I'm getting my jeans on. You think I'm letting you go down to the harbor alone? Who knows? One of those night watchmen might have the hots for you. Know it or not, you're one hot lobsterwoman, Cass Halloran."

When they walked outside, they were both surprised to discover it had snowed during the night, a light blanket that quieted the world. A few snowflakes were still falling, just enough to turn the almost dawn into a magical moment.

"Currier and Ives," Danny said, turning the key in the ignition.

"Currier and Ives," Cass echoed, looking through the window in awe, as if she had never seen snowflakes before. Or at least, not ones quite like this. And not with this strange feeling swelling her heart, happy that she wasn't sitting alone in the cab of the truck. Happy that a sleepy, bespectacled writer was next to her.

Without a thought, she suddenly leaned across the seat and kissed him, a lingering kind of kiss. Then she pulled away and said, "I love you, Danny Brandley. Now drive."

The slip where the Halloran lobster boats were moored was on the far side of the harbor, the opposite side of the main harbor parking lot that just the night before had held SUVs and families, couples and visitors, shop owners and fishermen, all there for a good time on a chilly winter evening.

But at this hour, with the sun just beginning its ascent, the lot was empty, the lights casting eerie shadows across the freshly fallen snow.

"Come on, let's get this done," Danny said, reaching over and opening the passenger door for Cass. "You realize, don't you, that this is one of those favors that demand a huge payback? Huge." He jumped out his side and together they headed to the commercial side of the pier. It was the side where rusty fenced-in bins held lobster traps and buoys and odds and ends. Where instead of the holiday scent of pine trees, they breathed in the strong odor of fish, oil, and dank, ocean-logged equipment.

Danny had brought a flashlight and shone it on the broken lock. Cass pulled it off and opened the bin, looking around. The traps were piled high, covered with snow. The white blanket was untouched by human footsteps or a thief's fingerprints.

"Okay, then," Cass said, tossing the old padlock on top of a lobster cage and quickly snapping the new one in place. "Job well done, partner."

Danny was standing a few feet away, closer to the water, and looking across to where gaslights still lit the newly planted trees in Harbor Park. The tent hadn't been taken down yet, and its white peaks were stark against the sky that was just beginning to lighten above the water.

"Let's go for a walk," he said when Cass came up beside him.

She looked at him quizzically.

He took her gloved hand in his. "It's eerily beautiful." Then he looked down at her with mock sternness. "And you're in no position to say no, young lady. No arguments. This is the kind of thing writers like to do when they can't be lollygagging."

"As long as you don't start singing Christmas carols," Cass said, and matched her step to his.

They walked around the pier, over to the Harbor Green. The

gazebo was a white castle against the sky, its low security lights making it seem twice its size. They walked around the mountain-peaked tent, then slowly down a path that meandered along the ocean side of the newly planted trees. They walked past the copses of evergreens, imagining them lit up, their branches heavy with handmade ornaments.

Still holding Danny's hand, Cass led him into the thick of the trees, a pathway so narrow you could touch trees on either side, with an occasional bench breaking the space.

Danny breathed in the crisp air, tilting his head back as snowflakes landed lazily on his face.

But while Danny was looking up, Cass was looking down—at the winding pathway, the shadows the fir trees were casting on the fresh blanket of snow, startling in its purity.

And in the precise moment that Danny Brandley was catching a snowflake on the tip of his tongue, Cass Halloran screamed, a blood-curdling and terrifying sound.

Even to a man who made a living writing murder mysteries.

Chapter 15

Tommy Porter was the first policeman to arrive, his droopy eyelids and disheveled look indicating he'd had his police radio on, but had been dreaming of something other than what met him in the forest of Christmas trees.

Danny held a shaking Cass close to his side and did the talking, explaining about their walk.

About how a thin red line—like a ribbon dropped by a gull or a wind-flung strip of silky yarn—had marred the pure snow, forcing Cass to look closer. It was beautiful—artistic, a Calder slice of color on a stark white canvas.

Until it became human.

The body was facedown, covered with the same layer of pure snow that had enchanted them just a short time before.

No, they hadn't touched anything, done anything, moved anywhere, they told Tommy as he walked them away from the body.

Tommy glanced up as Chief Jerry Thompson appeared, looking as haggard as his first in charge. "Sorry to get you up, Chief," Tommy said, words that meant little in the light of finding a body.

Jerry nodded. He looked at Cass and Danny, people he knew, cared about, and considered friends. His look said he wanted to apologize, wishing he could have saved them from this. And then he motioned for Tommy to walk with him off the path to the body.

The two men leaned over, their backs to the couple on the trail. Shadows fell across their backs.

Cass and Danny heard the chief's sharp intake of breath from where they stood, a few feet away.

When Tommy got up and walked back to them, they saw that the blood had drained from his face. The friendly grin they were used to seeing was replaced by the sadness of seeing someone you know, someone you recognize.

Someone who was now lifeless.

The chief walked back to the path a few seconds later. Hearing the screech of brakes and a door slamming, he looked back to the parking lot, where he spotted a woman from the local paper pulling out a camera.

The chief punched in a number on his phone, spoke quietly into it, then hung up. He slipped the cell phone into his pocket and looked regrettably at the couple standing in front of him on the path.

"Danny and Cass—I'm very sorry you had to be the ones to find this. It's awful, plain and simple. I think the best thing is for you to leave now—but I'll catch up with you and we'll talk later." He glanced back at the parking lot. "I know you probably wouldn't do this anyway, but please don't talk to those media mongers up there when you go to your car. I've sent for more men and we'll keep them at bay. The town will know soon enough—at least they'll know the little we know right now—but there's no need to feed the reporters' frenzy."

His expression matched Tommy's. Sadness. Maybe shock. Even after all these years, the Sea Harbor police chief didn't take death easily. Nor did he look on it without emotion. Finally he looked at them again, as if wishing he could change his words around. Or the day. Certainly the results.

"Amber Harper is dead," he said.

Chapter 16

The sun had finally come out; the day had begun. Was it really hours since Danny had found Cass at the kitchen island, drinking coffee? Or was it a lifetime?

They held gloved hands and walked slowly around the parking lot, insistent on each other's touch. The warmth of each other's body. They were reluctant, somehow, to get in the truck, as if leaving made it real. Staying might miraculously change it.

When an ambulance arrived, Danny led Cass away from the harbor—across the street and up a hill, where they walked around the neighborhood that edged the shops. Inside the small homes people were getting ready for their Sunday, making breakfast, venturing out for a cold morning run. Others bundling up for an early church service.

Finally Cass and Danny headed back to their car and, in silent agreement, drove to a place where there'd be good coffee. But even more important, good friends.

Thanks to a call from Jerry Thompson to Ben, his close friend, their arrival was anticipated.

Nell ushered them inside and, without many words, poured coffee and motioned toward the comfortable sofas. Ben had brought a morning fire to life, and its warmth and crackle immediately began to thaw Cass's blood.

Nell looked at her younger friend with great compassion. She, too, had been in that position—finding a dead body—and knew firsthand the nightmares that Cass and Danny would be plagued with in the days to come.

"Sam and Izzy are coming over," Nell said. She walked around the island and pulled out more coffee mugs, her thoughts going through the last twenty-four hours, bit by bit. An irrational sliver of guilt moved through her. She should have known somehow. She should have heeded the uncomfortable feeling inside her the night before, the sensation that something was entering their lives that she wanted desperately not to be there.

And then, just as quickly, she rid herself of the discomforting thought. What could she have done? Nothing . . . nothing but be anxious, something she was trying very hard not to be.

Her thoughts were interrupted by the sound of brakes, then Izzy rushing in, leaving Sam and their daughter trailing after her. She pulled Cass into a hug so tight her friend could barely breathe. "I'm so sorry you had to see that, Cass," she whispered into her hair. "It's so horrible. So awful." She finally released Cass and looked around the room, her eyes as round as little Abby's. They rested on Nell.

"Aunt Nell, where is he? Where's Charlie?" Her voice was frantic, as if Charlie might be with Amber, lying lifeless in a blanket of snow. Or worse.

Charlie.

He'd been the first person the chief mentioned after telling Ben about the night's tragedy. Charlie had come with Amber last night, hadn't he? Jerry had asked. Tommy had said as much. That was all he'd said, telling Ben something he already knew. They had all been with Amber last night. Hundreds of people. But Charlie more so.

"His car is here," Ben said. "I checked the guesthouse and the shades are drawn. We decided not to wake him."

"So he doesn't know about Amber?"

Nell shook her head. "He'll know soon enough and he'll need the additional sleep."

Izzy was only half listening to her aunt's rationale. She turned to Ben. "Uncle Ben, I watched him last night. Charlie really likes her."

Nell and Ben had watched him, too. Yes, somehow Charlie had fallen for Amber, a woman who made him crazy. But it didn't seem to matter; as Izzy said, he really liked Amber.

Birdie appeared at the door, as if by some mysterious telepathy. But it wasn't that. Birdie usually showed up in the Endicotts' kitchen on Sunday morning, sometimes because they were headed to Sweet Petunia's for brunch. And if not that, it was the day Ella deep-cleaned Birdie's elaborate home and she didn't want Birdie around. But Birdie also came because Sundays meant being with Ben and Nell. No matter where they ended up.

This morning Birdie knew there would be no Sweet Petunia's, but she had brought some coffee cakes and banana bread her housekeeper had baked. She handed Nell the box.

No one, however, not even Cass, felt like eating.

"I think we should wake Charlie," Birdie said without preamble. She had heard the news from Harold, who had a police scanner on his bedside table. A phone call to Esther Gibson confirmed what they hoped would be denied. Esther, who had so recently mourned her friend, would now be mourning her friend's granddaughter.

Cass and Danny got up and crossed into the kitchen. "Charlie doesn't know," Cass said. It wasn't a question or even a statement, it was an expression of sadness for the realization that if there was one among them who would be more affected by this than the others, it was Charlie.

Ben grabbed his jacket. "Birdie's right. If Charlie doesn't hear it from us, it'll be from some stranger." But as he reached the door, a bedraggled Charlie was walking across the deck, holding an empty coffee mug in his hand.

"He looks like death warmed over," Birdie said softly, the irony of her statement not escaping anyone.

Ben opened the door and Charlie walked in. He wore the same

clothes he'd had on the night before, disheveled and reeking of beer. His unshaven face spoke to a night he wanted to forget.

But it was more than the hangover, they could see that almost immediately. His entire body spoke louder than a headline; Charlie already knew that Amber Harper was dead.

Nell headed toward him as he fumbled with the zipper on his coat.

She stopped, staring at his hand. "Charlie, you're hurt." An injury was much easier to deal with than the reality they faced. She took his hand in hers. The hair was matted down, scraped, and bloody.

Charlie stared at it through blurred eyes as if it belonged to someone else.

He pulled away. "It's nothing," he said, and took a few steps back. He looked around the room, surprised that others were there.

"Charlie," Izzy began, but he stopped her with a vigorous shake of his head "Amber is dead . . . ," he said. His voice was husky and raw. "I got a phone call, a reporter," he said, and then he rubbed his bloodshot eyes and waited for someone to deny what he had said.

Ben took his mug and put it in the sink. He poured a fresh cup and handed it to him. "It's awful news about Amber. We're so sorry, Charlie," he said.

Charlie's eyes were focused on the black coffee, his face changing expressions from sadness to anger, belief to disbelief, as his mind seemed to be assembling and disassembling whatever he knew and didn't know about death.

Finally he pulled out words and said, "There're tweets out there, crazy things about Amber. She fell? Someone attacked her?" His voice was thick, his face immeasurably sad. "What happened to her?"

Izzy took a deep breath. "No one knows much, Charlie. We know she's dead. We know it's a terrible, terrible thing. And we know this is so sad for you." She touched him then, gently, without the estrangement of the past days and years. Those feelings melted away, at least for the moment.

Nell could see the effort it took Charlie to hold himself together, especially when he felt Izzy's fingers on his sleeve.

She moved from the sink to the island and stood across from him. "Whatever you're hearing is mostly rumor. People trying to make sense of someone dying in their midst, maybe while they danced or partied just yards away. People become desperate for instant answers so they make them up. But it's foolish to listen to them."

"When he called earlier, Jerry said she died of an injury," Ben said. "They're working on the assumption that the wound was inflicted by someone else. It probably happened sometime last night. Possibly while people were still at the party. The college crowd had taken over the tent, and the music was loud—"

So if Amber had tried to scream, had called for help, no one would have heard her. The thought registered with all of them. Chilling and vivid.

Charlie looked as though he was going to be sick. "I should have been there. I should have protected her," he said.

But it was his eyes, not what he said, that were filled with a terrible grief.

Izzy leaned lightly into him. "That thinking's not helpful, Charlie," she said. "And it's probably not valid. If someone wanted Amber dead and you had been with her, it would have happened at another time."

But maybe not, Nell thought. Maybe Charlie was right. Maybe it was a random killing, someone wandering through the trees, someone who had had too much to drink. And if so, if Charlie had been there, he might have been able to stop it.

She stopped herself then, unwilling to give legs to her next thought. Charlie had brought Amber to the event last night. They should have left together . . . Why hadn't he been with her?

Ben pulled out a frying pan and began breaking eggs into a bowl.

Nell watched him, knowing exactly what he was doing. Izzy began taking the coffee cakes out of the box, slicing them, and putting them on a plate, and Sam followed suit, pulling a stack of plates from the cupboard, cream and sugar, forks and knives. Put some routine into the day. Breakfast. Life.

"Charlie, come with me," Nell said, and while the others were busy with acts they could understand, she took him into the guest bathroom and wet a washcloth, gently dabbing at the wound on his hand, forcing her mind clear of questions. *How did you get this, Charlie? Tell me you fell out of bed. Or you slammed it in your car door or . . .*

But her fingers felt the tiny traces of debris, a stone as small as a pinprick on the edge of his fist.

In minutes she had washed away the blood and the dirt and covered the wound with antibiotic cream. "It's not a bad cut and I don't think you've broken anything on your hand. But you're going to have a bad bruise, Charlie."

Charlie listened dumbly, then followed Nell back through the hall.

The family room and busy kitchen now smelled of eggs and spices and bacon. Of sourdough toast and strawberry jam. The ordinariness of it all was startling. But beneath the ordinariness was a sea of uncertainty.

They all had questions, each one of them, about the terrible fact of Amber's death. Cass and Danny had seen blood. A wound, the chief had said. Not self-inflicted.

There were other unspoken questions, too, that swelled around the quiet breakfast, nearly blocking out the ordinary conversation going on around the room: questions about the evening, about people, about Amber's frame of mind, her actions, her walking back into the woods.

About the bruise on Charlie Chambers's hand.

And if anyone had answers to those questions—even partial, unimportant answers—it would be Charlie.

But in the presence of the grief that had caused his body to slump and his face to sag, they couldn't go there.

Even Birdie, her heart and head filled with the last conversation she'd had with Amber.

Not now.

But later.

"The sooner we start the process, the sooner we'll find answers, and the sooner we'll find the person who did this," Jerry Thompson explained as he accepted the coffee mug Nell had filled for him. He looked at each of them—Sam, Ben, and Nell—but his eyes lingered the longest on Charlie. "And one part of the process is talking to everyone who had contact with Amber last night and since her arrival in Sea Harbor. You all fit that description, I presume, so having all four of you together is making my life easier."

It was late afternoon and the sun was setting, casting long shadows across the room.

"Tommy is talking to some folks down at the station. I thought I might as well make a couple house calls," Jerry said. "No law says I can't do that."

But they all knew another reason he did it was that he was a good friend, and he knew this was a hard time for Ben and Nell's nephew, the person who knew Amber Harper best and who might have the answers the police were seeking.

After the others had left earlier that day, Charlie had admitted to Nell what had been obvious: that he'd gotten wasted the night before, "awful stinking drunk," he said. He had finally made it to the guest cottage, where he passed out on his bed.

From the smell and sight of him, Nell believed every word of it. Even though he was functioning now, he was definitely hungover and didn't seem to be in any position to explain why he'd done it.

But Nell certainly could guess. She'd been standing next to him, she'd felt his fistful of anger, felt his whole body freeze at the sight of Amber in another man's arms. She was a woman he'd known for a mere week—yet she had somehow evoked fierce emotion in him. It was a confusing image to Nell. But her nephew was a grown man. It was not her business. Nor was the developing bruise on the side of his hand, its puffiness already beginning to turn purple.

After Jerry's call, she suggested to Charlie that he go back down to the guest cottage to shower and change clothes—and maybe get a little sleep before the chief arrived.

Now he sat on the leather couch in Ben's den, looking almost like the old Charlie—or at least the one they had come to know in this past week.

Sam had come back to the house with Ben after they checked out their boat. He knew the chief was coming and decided he'd like to stay. He'd been Charlie's surrogate older brother lots of times growing up, times when Charlie's older brother, Jack, wasn't around. Now seemed a good time to play that role again. And he figured he'd been around Amber enough this past week to be someone the chief would want to talk to eventually anyway. No time like the present, he told Charlie.

But rather than resent it as Sam thought he might, the grown-up Charlie seemed to welcome Sam's presence.

Nell moved in and out of the den while they began talking. She was finding it difficult to sit still. No matter how routine all this was—and how practical and nonthreatening Jerry Thompson was in his questioning—the process was still thick with tension and grief, an unsettling combination. But no matter, she listened carefully as Jerry began with Charlie, asking him to go back to the beginning, to how he'd met Amber on that freezing night just over a week ago.

A week. An eternity. Nell took a deep breath, released it slowly, and went to the kitchen to brew another pot of coffee.

Jerry took some notes, but mostly listened, except to pose a question that would take the conversation in one direction or another.

"What was Amber like? How would you describe your relationship with her?" he asked.

Charlie sat still at first, as if trying to figure it out for himself. Finally he untangled his thoughts and started in. "She was abrasive. I didn't like her at all the night I picked her up. She was this rude kid—woman, I guess, but young—and I was the grown man, years older—five at least—and wiser." His laugh was hollow, but he forged on. "I had no idea who she was and didn't really want to know. I had my own problems, coming to town the way I did."

"To help Dr. Virgilio," Jerry said. "That doesn't sound like a problem. She tells me you're doing a great job."

Had he talked to Lily already? Nell wondered. Why? Surely not to check up on Charlie—

Charlie went back to talking about Amber, avoiding discussing his unannounced reunion with his family. "Amber was like a boomerang. I dropped her off and never expected to see her again. But boom, the next morning there she was. It was as if she inserted me into her life—texted me at odd hours, called me for rides. This last week—it was like a year—ups and downs, arguments, even all-night conversations. Some days it was like I was at her beck and call. She'd show up unexpectedly." He looked up at Ben as if for confirmation.

Ben nodded and detailed the encounter last Sunday, when Amber had shown up at their house with Charlie's cell phone.

"She stole it from you?" Jerry asked.

Charlie shrugged. "It didn't matter. She gave it back."

"You said she expected you to be at her beck and call. That must have been irritating."

"It should have been. But it wasn't. I started liking it. I liked her. A lot."

"Romantically?"

Charlie glanced at Sam, then his aunt and uncle.

Nell felt sudden pity for this grown man whose cheeks were suddenly flushed.

"Yeah," he said. "She was volatile, but somehow it was okay. We had quiet, close moments. She'd drop the facade, and we'd talk about things on her mind—about her mother, why she had come back here, all sorts of things. I wasn't used to that, to having someone trust me that way. Amber could be rude and insulting—but also loving and sexy and someone I wanted to get to know, all in the space of a breath. Crazy."

Jerry leaned forward, his arms on his knees. "It's interesting that she confided in you so quickly."

"She didn't know anyone else here, not really, at least I didn't think she did. Except for the Gibsons, maybe. They were good to her when she was a kid. She never knew the Cummingses. They were family in name only."

Jerry nodded, as if the information wasn't new. Esther Gibson worked for him, and the police dispatcher was like family. He was surely familiar with that part of the story.

Charlie lifted up his coffee cup at the same time Jerry looked up from scribbling something on his yellow pad.

Jerry looked at him and frowned. "Hey, what happened there? Looks like you got a nasty bruise. That one's going to hurt." He reached out toward Charlie's hand.

Charlie looked at his hand.

"How'd you do that?"

Charlie took a deep breath. "Clumsy, I guess." He looked beyond Jerry and Ben, through the den window where the barren branches of the maple tree brushed back and forth against the side of the house. "I slammed it against something," he finally said.

"When was this?"

"Last night. I was angry at Amber. Or maybe with myself for letting her get to me. I wasn't sure. I'm still not sure."

"Go on."

"She had switched moods on me, just like that." He snapped his fingers on his good hand. "It had happened before. I should have brushed it off because I knew she was going through a hard time.

She did that off and on during the week when she was disturbed about something. I think she took it out on me because for some crazy reason, she knew I'd stick around. But last night, I let it get to me because I wanted to help her, you know? To be that guy who could make it better. I went off and took out my feelings on a rock down near the shore."

The room was silent for a minute that seemed to stretch into an hour. Finally Jerry went back to his yellow pad, scribbled a few notes, then looked up and said to Ben, "Amber didn't show up for the reading of the will, is that correct?"

"The first meeting we scheduled, yes, that's right," Ben said. "That was Sunday, the day she borrowed Charlie's car so she could do some errands and, or so we thought, get to the meeting. But she didn't show up."

Nell had almost forgotten. It seemed so long ago. At first they thought she had stolen the car, left town. But they were wrong.

"Do any of you know where she went that day?" Jerry asked.

Nell repeated what Amber had told her that next day. It was the first time she had visited her mother's grave, she had said. Time had fallen away.

"What about the rest of the week? What did she do?"

Ben explained about Monday's meeting, the one she attended.

"What was her reaction?"

"No one really knew at first. She left abruptly when it ended."

Charlie went through what he remembered from the week and Nell added confirmation to the parts she had played—finding Amber at the cemetery.

Jerry looked at Charlie again. "When she wasn't with you this week, where do you suppose she was?"

Charlie frowned. He shifted his shoulders as if his shirt were too small. A look of frustration flashed in his eyes. "She spent time at the Cummingses' office, like I said. They'll tell you that, too. She was going through the books carefully, figuring out her inheritance.

She was there late a couple nights and I picked her up. We'd go to the Gull for a beer. But when she wasn't there or with me—"

He shrugged again. "I don't know where she was." He lowered his head into his hands, and it was then that his body began to shake.

Chapter 17

Monday's winds were slightly tempered by the bright sunlight that flooded Sea Harbor, belying the icy horror that was slowly enveloping a town.

Nell and Ben were up early. They stood at the kitchen island, Nell refilling coffee cups and Ben checking messages on his phone. "Looks like a full day. Sam and I have a breakfast meeting at the club. Rachel and Father Northcutt want to meet sometime today, too." He looked up from his phone. "They want to talk about the will—and what happens to it now."

"What does happen?"

"We'll check the legal fine points. I didn't read the whole will, but I'm sure Rachel has been going over it carefully."

Nell nodded. Somehow a will that seemed important just a short week ago now was insignificant—except as a reminder that a woman mentioned in it was dead.

"You're distracted, Nellie," Ben said.

"I keep wondering about Andy Risso. I wonder if Jerry has talked to him. Why was he with Amber Saturday night? How did he even know her? And I'm sure from Charlie's perspective, it looked like he knew her well."

"If you saw him talking to Amber that night, others did, too. Maybe Pete, the other band members. Jerry will hear about it and talk to him. But it's not really so unusual, do you think? Andy had just been onstage. I saw Amber watching the band and listening to the music. She probably saw him up there, maybe liked the music and wanted to let him know."

That wasn't what Nell saw. Nor Charlie. But Ben was right. It wasn't out of the ordinary. It was so ordinary, in fact, that most people probably didn't notice. But she wasn't most people—and neither was Charlie.

Ben read his messages again, then slipped his phone back into his pocket. "Do you need me, Nell? Is there anything I can do here?"

"I don't know what," Nell said. That was the awful thing. What could they do? Except be there for Charlie.

He had held himself together as best he could the night before, not moving from the chair until after the chief drove away. And then he had collapsed—his emotions raw and profound. He'd sat with Ben and Sam for a long time, drinking black coffee, trying to make sense out of a senseless act. Trying to find answers to a death they still knew so little about.

Finally, much later, he'd walked back down to the guest cottage alone, his shoulders slumped, looking like someone who had no idea where he was or why he was going there.

"Are you surprised at Charlie's reaction?" Ben asked. He drank his coffee, his eyes moving toward the kitchen window as if to see down into the cottage. Then he turned back. "He knew Amber such a short time, yet this is tearing him apart."

Nell had had the same thoughts. But intuitively she understood. There'd been something there between Charlie and Amber—it was like what they had said that night at Izzy's shop—relationships—love—couldn't always be subjected to a clock. Something Charlie himself might not have completely understood. Aloud she said, "It's difficult enough having someone you know die. But this—this brutality—makes it almost excruciating. Charlie is feeling that."

Ben took his car keys from the hook. "Sure, it will be difficult for him. But we can't ease the way for Charlie. He's not the little boy you played touch football with in Kansas."

Nell allowed a small smile. "You're saying I hover. I'll try not to," she said. "But he's family, Ben. He'll need us. He'll need Izzy and Sam, too. I don't want him torn apart emotionally by rumors right now—and you know that will happen. So if I can protect him, I will—but subtly."

Ben kissed her on the forehead. "My wise wife. I love you. See you later."

Nell waved him off, then looked again at the newspaper that lay open on the island.

CUMMINGS HEIR FOUND DEAD IN PARK

Amber's name didn't even merit space in the headline, Nell thought. But maybe she was being unfair. Few people in town would have read an article that began with *Amber Harper,* no matter how big the font. Few people had ever heard of Amber Harper before now.

The article itself said little. Apparently Chief Thompson had been able to keep most of the details under wraps. What the town now knew was what Cass and Danny saw. Amber covered with new-fallen snow, the snow marred only by a narrow river of blood. Although the reporter made it clear that the wound was not self-inflicted, *how* it happened was not clarified. And the word *murder* was ominously absent.

Jerry had been vague the day before, protective of facts that needed a closer look before they threw them out for all to see.

But as Ben walked the chief of police out to his car, Jerry had nodded sadly.

It was murder. An awful one.

But although the reporter who was dutifully tapping words into a computer might have suspected it, she couldn't call it that; she didn't know it for a fact. So she had to concentrate on personal tidbits, like Amber's relationship to the Cummings family, and even that was scanty. A granddaughter who lived in another state, the article said, but Patrick, her father, was never mentioned. Nor was her mother. The fact that she had inherited one of the nurseries was covered in a brief history of the nursery chain and its founder, its success under the late Lydia Cummings's leadership. And a paragraph about Barbara and Stuart Cummings and their generous contributions to Sea Harbor.

Nell walked to the front door and checked the driveway to see if Charlie's car was still there. She knew he was working at the free clinic today, but she wasn't sure when. The BMW was gone. It brought unexpected relief to Nell. He'd be with good people in a wonderful place, helping others. Perhaps the perfect place for him now.

Before closing the door, she looked up and down the quiet, sunny street. It was deceptively peaceful. Inside homes, behind doors, people were checking Internet news, reading the *Sea Harbor Gazette* headline, some shocked, others hungry for details, talking about a woman named Amber Harper.

Before the day ended, the news would be spread everywhere, and then the rumors would begin in earnest. And maybe the worst part of all: the swell of fear would begin to build, to burgeon, to take over their lives.

Nell checked her watch. It was time to go. She put on her down coat, picked up a basket of scones, and headed to her car. First to Birdie's.

Then on to a sad visit to the Gibson house. And on the way, Birdie filled Nell in on the strange conversation she'd had with Amber Harper, just hours before she died.

Esther lived close to downtown Sea Harbor in a small square house with a porch housing snow-covered rocking chairs. She was waiting at the door.

Before Birdie or Nell could say a word, she welcomed them by collecting them as one to her ample bosom.

"She was a good girl," Esther said, pulling away. Her eyes were puffy and her face haggard from lack of sleep. "It's a nightmare that

I keep trying to wake up from. A horrible awful dream that won't go away."

She turned and tapped her cane along the narrow hallway. "Come sit."

Nell and Birdie followed single file to a room that opened up at the back of the house.

It was a messy room, with furry slippers sticking out from beneath the couch and newspapers scattered on chair cushions. A stack of small cloth napkins embroidered with tiny flowers and three empty teacups sat on the coffee table, next to paperback romances and a half-knit sweater. Embroidered pillows added color to overstuffed chairs. Esther's handiwork. Everywhere.

But what drew their attention were the brilliant, colorful knit afghans that hung over each chair and couch and the bright sunshine that poured through the wall of back windows. It was a room filled with Esther Gibson, warm and welcoming.

"You were gracious to open your home to Amber," Birdie said, looking around. "I look at this cozy room and I can imagine her right here. Feeling safe."

"Except she wasn't." Esther looked around the room, as if hoping she'd see Amber sitting in one of the chairs or standing near the windows in a pool of sunshine. Her eyes were damp and she shook her permed curls, held back from her face with a white comb. When she started talking, her thoughts were scattered, but the tension in her shoulders seemed to ease with the outpouring of words.

"When Amber was little, she spent time here now and then. As fond of her grandmother as I was, I hated her ignorance of the child. Out of friendship, I suppose, I tried to right the wrong she was doing to Amber. Father Northcutt made her realize her responsibility from the spiritual side of things, but he couldn't control her heart. Amber was frozen out of it. I kept in touch with Amber, off and on, after she left Sea Harbor. Some years more off than on."

"No matter, you gave her a place this last week. A week she sorely needed with people who cared about her," Nell said.

"But she was barely here, just to sleep. She gave me hugs as she came and went. She cared about us, I knew that. But like I told the chief, I didn't see her enough to even know what was on her mind, what her plans were, where she was headed next.

"I should have asked her. But she's grown up now. We'd wait, let her come to us if she needed us. Richard said she acted like she was out to prove something at first. But what would Amber need to prove?" Esther's face was filled with the awful wonder of what was going on right there in front of her, and of which she knew nothing. A young woman moving frantically through her days.

And then she was dead.

Birdie felt the pain in her voice. "Esther, what can we do for you?"

"Hold me together," Esther said. She dropped her cane to the side of the couch and lowered herself into it, urging Nell and Birdie to sit. "I made her come back to Sea Harbor. If she hadn't come back, she'd be alive."

Before either of them could respond, she raised her hands and shook her head. "I know, I know, I know. I couldn't have known what was going to happen, but it saddens me anyway. Let me be with my sadness."

"Rachel Wooten explained that it was important she come back. Lydia had stipulated she be here for the will," Nell said. "You did what you had to do."

Esther twisted an embroidered napkin with her fingers. "I also wanted her here because I secretly prayed Lydia would have finally done the right thing and left the girl something worthwhile. And it turns out she did."

"How did you convince her to come?" Birdie asked. "Amber was strong-willed."

"I'm not sure. Maybe I wore her down. A sweet nurse at Ocean View who had been lovely to Ellie had given me a box of her things after she died. Carly—that was the nurse—and I had gotten to know each other those later years. I shoved the box in the closet, hoping that Amber might come back to visit and I could give it to her. I suppose I could have mailed it, but the nurse said there wasn't much of value in it. Toiletries. Pictures of Amber I'd put in Ellie's room. A pillow I'd made. A vase—apparently there were always fresh flowers in her room. I told Amber about the box. Maybe the thought of having something of her mother's helped bring her back. Or maybe it was to find closure in it all."

"Did she open the box?" Birdie asked.

"I'm sure she did. I hadn't opened it—that was for her to do—but I had put it on her bed that night she arrived and I saw her pick it up and set it on a chair, as if there was something cherished inside it."

"Where is it now?" Nell asked.

Esther shrugged. "I don't know. It's not here. She might have thrown it away if there wasn't anything she wanted to keep." She frowned at her words, then said, "No. I would have noticed the box if it had been added to the trash. It was a decent size."

Nell tucked the thought away. Somehow she didn't think Amber would have thrown anything of her mother's away. Somewhere, she suspected, there was a box of Ellie Harper's belongings, as insignificant as they might be to others.

"People are intrigued that Amber didn't care about her inheritance," Birdie said. "Most people, when they find out they're a beneficiary, jump on the next plane."

"Amber wasn't like most people. She also didn't think Lydia would bequeath her anything worth traveling for. She thought it might be some sort of embarrassing token. And coming back here, to a place that had so many bad memories, was painful. Especially since her mother was no longer here. But in the end, maybe that's why she did agree to come. She had missed Ellie's funeral. Maybe it was to claim her mother's few belongings, to see the grave and put it all to rest? I suppose I'll be wondering for a long time. And in the end, it won't bring her back."

"Ellie's death didn't receive much attention," Birdie said. "It never came on my radar. That's unusual for such a prominent family."

"Lydia kept it out of the papers. Few people even knew Ellie existed, much less died. It was just a few years ago—three maybe. Father Northcutt conducted a small service at Ocean View Chapel, and then we buried her in the cemetery there. Her doctor, Father Larry, the Rissos, me—a couple of nice volunteers there who had watched out for Ellie."

"Jake was there?" Nell asked.

"Oh, yes. Jake doesn't forget people he likes, and he was very fond of Ellie. Patrick Cummings actually met Ellie in his bar. In fact, I think we were there that night. Back then, Richard and I rarely missed a Monday night at Jake's. Football, you know." She smiled as she slipped back into the memories of good times, easier times. "Stu Cummings was usually there, too."

"With Helen? Somehow that surprises me," Birdie said.

Esther laughed. "They'd been married half a dozen years by then—you know how that goes. Man's night out. Helen didn't usually come, though once in a while she'd surprise him, checking up on him, Jake would say.

"Anyway, Stu brought his baby brother in one night to celebrate Patrick's twenty-first birthday. Everyone was in love with Ellie—Stu, too. But when Patrick laid eyes on her that night, you could almost hear fireworks."

"Stu knew Ellie?" Birdie said.

Esther nodded. "Sure did. All Jake's customers did. And like I said, she was sweet to everyone, no matter who it was."

So Patrick, at least, had a brother he could confide in. Someone who knew the woman he loved. But she was saddened by the thoughts, too, wondering why Stu didn't go against his mother's wishes and create a better home life for Ellie's daughter.

"Like I said about Jake—he loved Ellie—and then her daughter, too. They'd take Amber out on that old boat of his and he'd tell her stories about her mom, what a good waitress she was. That crusty old galoot has a good soul."

Nell could imagine Amber out in the boat with Jake, listening to his tales. Then she frowned, replaying Esther's words, and was about to ask her to clarify when Birdie asked a question.

"Why didn't Amber come back for the funeral?" she asked.

"That was another regret of mine—and Amber's, too," Esther said. "I wasn't able to reach her in time. She had taken a temporary job on some cruise ship off the Florida coast and it wasn't until she got back to shore that she found my message."

"Ellie's death was sudden?" Nell was surprised. She followed the whistle of the teapot in the kitchen, brought it back, and filled the three dainty cups. Birdie unwrapped the basket of scones they'd brought and passed them around. "I thought Ellie had been in the nursing home for years."

"Unexpected is a better word, I guess, because, yes, she'd been a patient there for a long time. But she had been stable, her vital signs strong. Then one night she just up and died."

"What was the cause of death?" Nell asked.

"Most people with her condition die of a pulmonary infection or some other kind—and most die sooner than she did. Ellie was in good shape. The doc said her death was unexpected in that sense. But sometimes patients like Ellie die of no known cause. She had just turned fifty. It was a lonely death."

Lonely. And a death that caused barely a stir in the small town, Nell thought. Mother-and-daughter tragedies. One whose death went unnoticed by most of the world—and one whose death would not go gently into the night.

"Who was her doctor?" Birdie asked.

"Yours. Mine. Lydia's. Half of Sea Harbor. Our good friend, Alan Hamilton. He told me Ellie was as strong as he was. But sometimes that's how PVS patients die. It happens."

"Alan is a good doctor," Birdie said.

"That he is. And he had a wonderful bedside manner with Ellie. He'd sit and talk to her about politics, music, his dog."

"Did she ever respond?"

"Who knows? I asked him that often. He'd say, 'Are you asking the medical me or the other me?' The doctor in Alan said she didn't understand or hear anything. Yet she slept, woke. Yawned. She could swallow. And she'd blink now and again in a way that was unnerving—she couldn't have known me, but sometimes her eyes seemed to say something different. I got one of those looks the day she died. A light in her eye when I mentioned Amber. I swear it. Most of the medical folks said I imagined it."

But it was a happy memory. Nell was pleased Esther had one in her collection.

"Did you visit often?" Nell asked.

"Oh, I'm not sure what 'often' means. After Amber left, I went when I could. I felt I was going in Lydia's place, filling in. I liked Ellie. I swear she worked every shift, and she was always friendly and polite. Not exactly like Amber, but Amber might have been like Ellie if she had had her around to teach her. Anyway, after the accident, after it all happened, I'd visit Ellie, try to make her room a little brighter." She looked down at the embroidered napkin in her hand and held it up. Tiny flowers highlighted each corner. "I even made her a soft pillow and embroidered some flowers on the slip. Something to make her bed a little special, not so hospital-like." She fingered the roses on the napkin.

"When Amber was old enough, I'd take her with me—she was always with a nanny those days, before Lydia arranged for boarding school. We'd sit and read books at her mother's bedside."

Esther had leaned her head back against the high-backed sofa and partially closed her eyes. "I can't get my arms around anyone hurting Amber. It doesn't make sense to me. Oh, she was a rascal, that one. No innocence there. But she'd been gone from here for so long. So why? Why here? Richard and I were up all night trying to make sense of it."

"Jerry said he'd know more today, after he'd spent some time with the autopsy report," Nell said. "But no matter what they find, you're right, Esther. The death of such a vital young woman doesn't make sense."

Esther's voice grew stronger as she pulled out a reason that she could understand, no matter how painful. "It had to have been a drunken bum from the party—or someone who just wandered in and came upon her in those trees. Maybe a stranger doing something they shouldn't be doing, and Amber surprised him. Or someone robbing her. A tragic accident . . ."

Nell looked over at Birdie. Amber had told Birdie she had to meet someone that night. She tuned back in to Esther, who was trying to retrace Amber's steps, to find something to help her through her grief.

"Amber'd have fought back, though, wouldn't she? She'd never let anyone take advantage of her. She's a fighter. She'd have fought back."

And maybe she did. But she lost. Nell pushed against the image of Charlie's injured hand until it disappeared.

"Was Amber in touch with any old friends while she was here?" Nell asked. The image of Amber waving to the cyclist when they were leaving the cemetery flitted across her mind. Was that an old friend? Or perhaps she was simply waving to a stranger, the way one sometimes did when seeing a friendly face.

"Old friends?" Esther smiled sadly. "Amber didn't have any old friends. Boarding school was not a good match for her; she disliked it—and she didn't much care for the wealthy girls who went there. They had nothing in common, she told me once. I asked her what she meant and she just looked at me, that small face so like her mother's. Then she said with a sigh, 'I meant that they all had pets. I always wanted a dog that I could hug.'" Esther shook her head, the irony of Amber's words deepening the wrinkles in her kind face. "Imagine that," she murmured.

Birdie stirred a sugar cube into her tea. "So there were no phone calls for her here?"

"Calls?" Esther's frown lightened, as if Birdie had triggered a thought. "Yes. There was a call. But it wasn't for Amber, at least not directly. Last week Priscilla Stangel called me at the police station when I was working. You know her, Birdie. She manages Ocean View. Or at least she used to. She was calling from there."

"Of course I know Priscilla," Birdie said. "She's in my group—the Ladies' Classics and Tea Club."

Even Esther smiled at that. Most people in Sea Harbor knew or had heard about the infamous Sunday tea group, the "women of a certain age"—Sea Harbor's collection of grande dames—who met at the Ocean's Edge regularly. The group was decades old, as were its members, and at one time actually did meet over tea and crumpets and a discussion of the Great Books. But as the years went by the members unanimously agreed to replace the tea with sherry or Chablis, the crumpets with calamari. And the Great Books with gossip and "sharing wisdom," as one of their members put it. The staff at Ocean's Edge accommodated "their" ladies, still putting out the finest silver, the Spode china, and filling their Baccarat crystal wineglasses with the finest wine.

"I believe Priscilla primarily has social duties at Ocean View now," Birdie said. "Greeting people. She has a lovely handshake. Why did she call?"

"She thought she saw someone sitting in the room that had been Ellie Harper's for all those years."

"Is that unusual? Surely they haven't kept the room empty?" Nell asked.

"No, no, they haven't. But it happens it's vacant now because it's being refreshed or remodeled or something."

"Why was that information worth a phone call, and why you?" Birdie asked.

"Priscilla swore the woman looked just like Ellie. At first she thought she saw a ghost, she said, and then someone told her that Ellie's daughter was in town. So she decided it must have been her.

She told me guests needed to know someone there to be admitted. Did I know why Amber was sitting in her dead mother's room?"

Birdie chuckled. "It sounds like Priscilla's cataract surgery wasn't entirely successful."

"Well, that's what I thought, too, but of course I couldn't say as much to her. You know how she is. So I listened politely and told her she must have been mistaken and then I reminded her how excellent the security at Ocean View is and that no one could get in without a visitor's pass, everyone knew that. And I complimented her on what a wonderful asset she is to Ocean View. She called once more a day or so later, when I was at work, and left a message saying essentially the same thing—that she had spotted Amber again and that she was bothering the staff and I should do something about it—but I never followed up. I think she was still seeing ghosts and I didn't want to deal with it."

"You are the epitome of diplomacy, Esther, dear," Birdie said.

"Was that the end of it?" Nell asked.

"Yes. Amber had been to Ellie's grave; someone probably saw her there and Priscilla was confused. I thought about mentioning it to Amber, but when I saw her a day or two later, I decided not to bother her with something that didn't affect her, but might bring up sad memories. And good grief, the poor woman had had her share of those."

"That sounds like a good decision, Esther." Birdie patted her knee.

"I suppose," Esther said, although she didn't sound completely convinced that she'd done the right thing. Or if she had even remembered the phone call clearly.

"But as far as you and Richard were aware, Amber didn't reconnect with people while she was here?"

Esther shook her head. "I don't think she had any intention of doing that. She seemed focused on meeting with the people involved in why she'd come—Rachel, Father Larry. And of course she saw all of you. Jake. And the Cummingses."

"Maybe the one who actually got closest to her and knew the Amber who came back after all those years away—"

Birdie and Nell realized where Esther was going before she got there.

"Well, it was your nephew, Charlie, Nell. He was the one Amber seemed to want to see. The one who picked her up and dropped her off. I think—though of course we didn't talk about it—I think that maybe Amber was beginning to care for him, at least as much as Amber could care for anyone."

Birdie gathered up her purse as Nell cleared the table, taking the cups into the kitchen and thinking of Esther's words.

Charlie. The one who picked her up and dropped her off.

She retrieved their coats from the hall closet and when she returned to the family room to say good-bye, Esther was standing, leaning on her cane and smiling. She was somehow warmed by the company, or maybe her thoughts of Charlie and Amber. The comforting thought that maybe Amber had cared for someone. And that someone might have cared for her.

But instead of the sweet emotion on Esther's face at the thought of Charlie and Amber together, something else—a cold fear—wormed its way inside Nell. She was nearly thrown off balance by it. A feeling so strong she had to wrap her arms around herself to keep from shaking.

Charlie was the closest to Amber, not a husband, of course, but the one person she had let into her life. And in murder cases, who was it they looked at first?

Chapter 18

They headed next to Coffee's, where Cass said she'd be waiting in the booth in the far back section of the shop. The Monday ritual on the lobster company owner's day off. Strong coffee. Good friends.

"Izzy!" Nell said, surprised to see her niece sitting next to Cass. Four of Coffee's oversize mugs sat on the table, steam curling up from the cream-laden brew.

Nell rubbed her cheekbone, a nervous habit, wondering what would have brought Izzy from her shop on a busy Monday when the back room would be filled with college students learning frantically how to knit holiday hats and sweaters.

"Mae has the shop under control. Sam called." She pushed two of the mugs across the table.

Nell slipped into the booth beside Birdie. Her words were clipped. "Is Abby okay?"

Izzy nodded, then gave Nell part of a smile. "I love that your first thoughts are of her, Aunt Nell. I love that you love her so much."

"I love her, too," Cass said stoutly. "I'm her godmother, don't forget."

The gentle talk about a well-loved toddler was welcome—and a stark contrast to whatever message Sam had relayed to Izzy, the one that had brought her to Coffee's with a troubled look on her face.

"Sam was with Ben this morning," Izzy said. "Some planning

meeting about the summer sailing club. They got a call from Jerry asking them to come to the station when they had a chance."

"Why?"

"A couple of things. The news somehow leaked out about how Amber was killed. It was awful." Izzy traced the pockmarks in the table with her fingertip, then looked up and got the words out quickly. "She was stabbed."

Cass took over when Izzy's voice choked up. "Someone stabbed her with one of those heavy iron gizmos that were staked in front of the Christmas trees."

"The name placeholders," Birdie said softly. "Oh, my—"

The image settled in with a thud, vivid and awful. It would have been as lethal as a blunt knife.

"Jerry wanted Cass and Danny and the rest of us to know before the news started spreading. And there's something else." Izzy took a stabilizing breath and expelled it slowly. When she began talking again, her voice was businesslike, methodical. Izzy the attorney, needing to get the information out efficiently.

"It's no surprise that the police are wanting to talk to anyone who was connected to Amber. People she talked to casually that night, as well as people more closely connected to her—the Cummingses, Rachel Wooten, even Father Northcutt. Esther and Richard. And all of us. The police are thorough and won't give anyone an easy out. But they found a couple texts on Amber's phone that concerned Jerry."

"Texts?" Nell said.

"They were from Charlie. He sent them Saturday night."

Nell's face fell, though she realized she shouldn't have been surprised. He didn't know where she'd gone that night. He would have tried to reach her, to find her. To get her home safely.

"He was agitated—or drunk—when he sent them, at least as much as you can tell from texts. They rambled. But he said angry things. He said he was hurt, used. Jerry is concerned about it. It puts Charlie in kind of a bad place."

For a long minute they were all silent, each interpreting the news in her own way. Finally Birdie said, "Well, Charlie Chambers didn't kill anyone. We all know that. He will explain the texts and that will be that."

Birdie's tone of voice had difficulty matching her optimistic words, but they all nodded. That would be that. Of course it would.

"Charlie brought Amber to the park that night," Cass said. "They seemed fine. He was in a good mood when I saw him early on."

"Yes, he was," Birdie said. "But Amber was clearly distracted about something or other. I don't think it had anything to do with Charlie."

She repeated the conversation she'd had with Amber to Izzy and Cass. They all grew somber at the thought that Birdie was probably among the last to talk with Amber before she was killed—for sure the last among the knitters.

"She was sad and angry all at once," Birdie said. "I think she was trying to figure out what to do, some kind of dilemma in her head. Perhaps she thought talking it out with someone might help her clarify the issue." She paused, her voice sad as the conversation replayed itself. "We were to talk Sunday." Her words were soft with the irony and sadness of it.

"It's not surprising she wanted to talk to you," Cass said. "People are drawn to you, Birdie, even people you don't know very well. Strangers off the street. You better watch that. There's no telling who you could get mixed up with."

Nell smiled, but it was true. They were all drawn to Birdie's wisdom and fairness and compassion. It wasn't what she did; it was who she was. And the fact that Amber Harper had intuited as much made Nell silently appreciate Charlie's friend's sensitivity.

"You don't think she wanted to talk about Charlie?" Izzy asked.

Birdie looked off into the coffee-scented air and revisited the conversation in her head. "No, I don't think so," she said. "In fact, the way she treated Charlie that night makes me think she wanted to disconnect from him a bit, to maybe protect him from whatever was bothering her. I think she understood the feelings they shared for each other might not make him the most objective listener. She didn't really say as much, but it's what I thought."

"She was clearly preoccupied," Nell said. And then she fell silent, remembering Charlie's tension when he had stood beside her that night, remembering the fistful of anger she had sensed in her nephew.

"Charlie and I went looking for her a short while after that. We finally found her over near the gazebo." Nell paused, but just for a minute. "She was wrapped in Andy Risso's arms."

Chapter 19

Charlie's car was noticeably absent when Nell finally drove into her driveway just before dinner. A meeting in Gloucester had blessedly taken her a few miles away from the pall settling over Sea Harbor like a suffocating storm cloud. But now she was home—and there was still a murderer roaming free, and the cloud still hovered.

She realized when she saw the empty space that she was unexpectedly relieved. She wanted to see Ben first before she saw Charlie. Ben was her sounding board, the person who grounded her. Someone who would ease the anxiousness that had traveled with her to Esther's and to Coffee's, to Gloucester, and back.

She wanted to talk to him about seeing Andy Risso with Amber. And a hug that sent Charlie off in a huff so angry he nearly broke his hand on a granite boulder.

And Birdie's conversation with Amber had rained even more confusion into their thoughts.

She climbed out of her car, her thoughts as heavy as the bag of groceries she'd picked up on the way home, and glanced at a car parked at the curb in front of the house. Danny? She tried to read a mental calendar. Monday night. Was there something going on she'd forgotten about?

She hurried inside the house, the day's anxiety weighing her down with irrational worry. Danny was in and out of their house all the time; there was no need to be apprehensive.

He was sitting at the kitchen island, his long legs wrapped around a stool, a laptop open in front of him. A half-empty bottle of beer sat next to the computer.

Nell dropped her purse on the couch and hurried across the room. "What's up, Danny?" she asked, trying to hide the concern shadowing her face.

Danny looked up, pushing his glasses into a thick mess of sandy hair. "No worries, Nell. Ben took his car into the shop. I gave him a lift back. He'll be down in a minute."

From the floor above, she heard Ben in the bathroom, the sound of water in the sink, the familiar footsteps stomping across the bedroom and toward the back stairway.

Nell shrugged out of her coat. "I'm sorry for seeming fretful, Danny. I'm a little on edge." She walked around the island and gave him a good squeeze. "How are you doing? The past few days haven't exactly been a picnic for you."

"I'm okay."

"What have you been up to?" Nell set the bag of groceries down and poured herself a glass of wine.

Danny closed the lid of his computer and took a long swig of beer. "I worked in the bookstore some today, walked around town, then wrote in the library for a while. The peripatetic and oh-so-glamorous life of a writer," he said, trying to draw a smile.

Nell missed the cue and pulled out another stool, her face serious. "It's good to have this day over with," she said. "Get the news out there. Let people digest it. Then try to deal with it and move on."

Danny agreed. "You can feel the town tightening up, people looking at each other differently. Suddenly Amber Harper, a person lots of people around here had never heard of or seen before, is a bigger-than-life figure. Everyone knows someone who knows someone who knows her. And everyone seems to have seen her somewhere in the past week—at the Gull or in the bookstore or library or over at Cummings Northshore Nurseries—or hanging out with Izzy Chambers's brother."

And the last was the one most people would find most significant. "Each sighting is significant, true or otherwise," Nell said softly.

"People just trying to understand it all," Ben said, walking into the room.

He kissed Nell on the cheek. "I don't like what conjectures do to people, but I get it," he said, taking a beer from the refrigerator and snapping off the top. "It's self-protection against the ugly unknown enemy. People are relieved that Amber is an outsider. That way whoever did this is an outsider, too."

"And that means we're all safe," Danny said.

Ben's point, exactly. But Amber wasn't an outsider, not really—and the mind's way of making us feel safe was wrought with flaws. Nell moved the conversation on. "Izzy told us about your talk with Jerry."

"It was sobering," Ben said. "They waited until Charlie had finished at the clinic and then they called him in again. He's down at the station now. I offered to go along, but he'd already called Sam."

"More questions," Nell said, the fact obvious.

"Apparently Amber's phone was packed with texts to and from Charlie. The police needed a few answers. Especially about the ones he sent to her on Saturday night."

"We all know he was drinking that night," Danny said. "Cass and I saw him as we were headed to the Gull to meet Sam and Izzy and the rest. He seemed pretty serious about it, too."

"About?"

"The drinking. He had a beer in each hand. We tried to get him to come with us, but he said he had things to do and he wandered back toward the tent. Slightly wobbly but he seemed okay."

"Was he alone?"

Danny nodded. "That surprised us, too. He had come with Amber, but she wasn't with him. At least not at that moment."

"I wonder how many other people saw him," Ben said.

"And how many comments like that he made, words that could be twisted and turned to mean almost anything."

Ben looked down at his vibrating phone. "It's from Sam," he said. He stepped aside to read the text.

Nell was peering in the refrigerator with hopes of spotting left-overs. Lots of condiments. Cheese and half-and-half. She closed the door.

"It seems people are scattered all over tonight," Ben said.

"Who? Scattered where?" Danny finished off his beer.

"Cass and Birdie went to pick up some yarn at the shop and kidnapped Izzy on their way out. Birdie was lusting for one of the Gull's burgers, so they're indulging her and heading over to Jake's. Janie Levin is babysitting Abby, so Sam and Charlie are heading that way, too. He said Charlie handled his latest inquisition okay."

"Let me make a wild guess. There's a game tonight?" Nell asked.

Danny laughed. "Pats are playing KC. Sam is probably looking for a distraction for Charlie. It's not a bad idea."

"So, shall the three of us eat here in quiet and peace?" Ben asked, checking game time on his cell phone.

Danny looked at him. "You're a decent guy after all, Ben. Trying to save Nell from the greasy fries and leftover smoke in Jake's place."

"But I love Jake Risso," Nell said, getting up. "Even more than the delicious pickles and cabbage and half-and-half in my refrigerator, begging to be eaten. Please warm your car, Danny. I'm going to put on some lipstick."

The bar was only half-full, a relief to Nell. The noise was usually so loud its sheer force propelled her and Ben to the roof deck, not a comfortable place to be in December.

She smiled at Jake's unique and familiar holiday decorations—a corner tree strung with blue lights and hung with miniature blue suede shoes, sparkling guitars, and dozens of tiny figurines of the king himself in white jumpsuits, gold lamé jumpsuits, and a shiny Jailhouse Rock costume. Each year customers added to the collection and the tree got bigger and bigger. More crowded. And more interesting.

Tonight a swirling ball played "Blue Christmas." Over and over and over again.

Above them, Jake had hung a million colored icicle lights, the rows extending the entire length and width of the ceiling, all waving in the breeze of the ceiling fan. "Don't look up," Danny whispered as they walked in. "You'll fall over."

A round table near the bar offered a full view of three different television sets. Their group was already there, and the table filled with baskets of calamari and fried clams and pitchers of beer.

Nell looked over at the bar and met Jake Risso's tired eyes. He was taking orders and pouring drinks, a towel hanging over one arm, but he looked between the bodies at the bar, seemed to cheer up a little when he saw Ben and Nell, and waved. *Later,* he mouthed, and turned back to the customers, limping a bit as he made his way up and down the bar.

Nell looked around, her eyes adjusting to the dim light.

"Who're you missing?" Danny asked, catching her look.

"Andy Risso. I wanted to ask him something."

"Out of luck. Pete tried to talk me into taking Andy's place at a late-afternoon wedding reception gig they had today. *Me.* Who hasn't touched a drum since I was fourteen. I guess Andy was doing double shifts at a place where he volunteers and he couldn't make it. So Pete and Merry were handling the gig themselves, worrying about what a drumless Fractured Fish would sound like. I told them it had all the makings of a divorce for the poor couple paying them."

Nell chuckled. It was just as well he wasn't here. She wanted to talk with him, but the Gull might not be quite the right place, especially with Charlie sitting a few seats down the table from her, looking ten years older than he did last week.

She pulled her attention back to the group, to the chatter around her that expressed little of what was on anyone's mind. Ben had settled down next to Charlie and the two were discussing quarterback matchups and whether Tom Brady would play till he was forty. And every few minutes they'd lapse into silence, eyes glued to the screen as they watched a Brady throw, a Gronkowski catch. A fumble. A touchdown.

When Nell got up to use the restroom, Jake maneuvered his way out from behind the bar and stopped her with a hug.

"There's no joy in Mudville," he muttered, then shook his head in slow motion, his chest heaving slowly in and out and strands of thinning white hair falling across his sweaty forehead.

"Are you doing all right? Esther told us about your kindnesses to Amber. And to her mother before her. You knew Ellie?"

"Like a daughter. That's how my Marie felt about her, too. A daughter we never had." He glanced at the bar to make sure the other bartender was taking care of his customers and then grabbed Nell's arm. "Come ova here, Nellie," he said, and pulled her into the narrow hallway that led to the restrooms. "I bet you never noticed my rogues gallery in here, huh?" He raised bushy eyebrows at her, then gestured with both hands to the walls. They were lined with rows of framed photographs.

She'd seen the pictures over the years but had never paid much attention. The light was dim in the hallway and she didn't think they pictured anyone she would know.

"These go way back, all the way back to when Marie and I opened this place all those long years ago when Andy was just a twinkle in our eyes. Look here."

He pointed a stubby finger at a black-and-white photo in a gold frame.

The figures were blurry, but there was Jake himself, a young man then with a full head of dark hair, his smile familiar, his wide crooked nose unmistakable. His face was clean shaven and smooth. Well-muscled arms were wrapped around a woman about his same height, with blond hair the exact color and length of Andy's, with the same oval face and narrow nose, the same warm eyes and gentle demeanor. She and Jake were both laughing, the exuberance of youth wrapping them together in a hug so warm Nell had to look away for a minute, feeling the moment was intimate and should be private.

Behind the couple was the familiar green awning and gold marquee: THE GULL TAVERN.

Jake stared at it as if he had never seen it before—or perhaps because a long look would bring that day back, and along with it the woman he loved.

"Esther Gibson has told me wonderful stories about Marie. Your wife was well loved," Nell said, her eyes lingering on the young couple, then on Jake's face. "I wish I had lived here when she was alive."

"You'da loved her. Marie was a saint. Absolute saint. You ask Esther, Father Northcutt. Mary Halloran. You ask anyone. Damn good thing Andy took after her, not me. And they were so close, those two. You know what my boy does? He volunteers at the place that cared for her when she was in hospice. My boy, he does that. Makes him feel close to her, he says." Jake wiped the dampness from his eye with the back of his hand and hid his emotion behind a raspy laugh.

"Come on," he said gruffly, and turned Nell to another line of photos on the opposite wall. Again he pointed one out for her attention. This one was also in black and white, but taken with a better camera, with inside light. The figures were distinct.

Lined up behind the same walnut bar was Jake, a couple of other bartenders and waitstaff, and right in the middle of the group, next to Jake, a young woman with a sweet smile, her face tilted up in pleasure, as if working at the Gull Tavern was the most amazing job in the world. Her auburn hair was pulled back into a ponytail.

"That's her. That's our Ellie girl, as we used to call her. She was a prize, that one. Never without a smile or nice word for anyone, even for some of these weather-beaten fishermen who come in here, loud and rowdy, the whole bunch of 'em. They all fell in love with her, every single one."

Nell took a step closer and squinted at the image, looking for a resemblance to the young woman who had entered their lives this week, then so abruptly left. It was there in shades and nuances. Amber had her mother's finely chiseled face, her eyebrows and brown hair. It was clearly there, the mother-daughter connection.

But she realized with sudden sadness that what transformed Ellie Harper from a nice-looking woman into a beautiful one—and what her daughter had lacked—was a joyful, magnificent smile, one that seemed to embrace all of life's hopes and dreams.

She looked over at Jake and he mirrored her expression.

"Yeah, sometimes life serves up a pile of you-know-what. That little Amber, it was stacked up against her from day one. It ain't fair. Never was.

"When she was just a kid, barely knee-high to a grasshopper with these long brown pigtails, she discovered her mom had worked here. She'd sneak in here like she was invisible and I'd find her in this hallway, right here, staring up at this picture. Just staring at it, like memorizing it, or maybe trying to replace her mind's image of the woman in the nursing home who could never as much as give her a hug with this beautiful happy lady here. So I'd come stand beside her, tell her stories of that lovely lady who gave birth to her."

Jake sighed, then took hold of Nell's arm and walked with her back to the bar.

"I heard you might have introduced Patrick and Ellie?"

"Me? Nah. But it happened here. Patrick's brother, Stu, was a regular from the day he was legal. Not anymore so much, but when he was starting out, feeling his oats. Helen didn't like it much—she was more into martinis—so he'd come alone. Stu knew everyone, that one, quite a talker, just like he is now. And Ellie was as patient as a saint with him. Listened to his stories as if he were the only one in the bar. Then he brought Patrick in on his birthday to buy him a drink."

"And he met Ellie."

Jake nodded. "And worlds collided, as they say."

It was a romantic story. With a tragic ending that Jake was replaying as he talked. Nell watched the deep sadness fill Jake's eyes.

"Who could have done this to Amber, Jake?"

He shook his head. "I've been thinking and thinking." He knocked on the side of his head. "But nothing comes to me. Nothing. Amber didn't hurt anyone, didn't do nothing." He looked over at the round table where the others were sitting and talking, watching the game. He nodded toward Charlie. "He's a nice guy, Izzy's brother. I thought maybe, hey, maybe something is going on there, something good. And now—look at him. Miserable."

"Yes, he is, Jake. He's having a rough time with this—on all accounts, if you know what I mean."

"I know, I know. It's like they go for the husband or wife or lover first, like on the TV shows. People saw 'em together, so sure, they're going to poke at him. But Thompson is a good cop. A fair one. He'll figure it out."

"She was asked to come to Sea Harbor for the will, Jake, but why do you think she came? Was it for closure?"

Jake gave the question serious thought. Finally he said, "I think it depends on which day."

"Day?"

"It was like something was unfolding inside her last week, little by little. That night she came to town—she ended up in here, y'know. Maybe to see the photo, I dunno. Maybe because this was kinda her mom's place. So that miserable cold night after Charlie dropped her off, this is where she came, to Jake's."

He said it as a point of pride, that Amber had somehow sought comfort at the Gull Tavern. A place where she felt safe.

"But anyways, we talked late that night before I called Esther and said I was bringing her over for dry clothes and a good night's sleep. She told me she finally decided she needed to come back. She wanted to pick up her mom's few things. Sign the damn papers for whatever Lady Lydia was leaving her—those were her words, not mine. And then disappear.

"But then things seemed to change, day by day, and I'm not sure why. Charlie brought her in here almost every night last week. Sometimes it was real late, her looking like she'd been studying for some awful dreaded test. Charlie being attentive. Getting her a beer, a hamburger. I liked that she had someone who seemed to be taking care of her."

"But then her focus changed, like she was on a mission. Something happened, but I don't know what. Like she was putting pieces of her mom's life together, and she didn't want to leave town until the picture was complete. She was hell-bent on figuring out the company, *her* company, I suppose you could say, or something. But there was more to it. She started asking me lots of questions about Ellie—like she'd discovered something about her when she was rummaging through Cummings files, something that turned her attention more to her mother. She focused on those last years when I'd visit Ellie now and then. Who cared for her? How much did it cost? Who came to see her? What was it like, the day that she died? All kinds of questions, most of which didn't have answers, at least not from me."

Nell listened carefully, trying to imagine Amber's path those last days. Trying to make the questions fit together.

But the one image that stayed in her mind long after the others floated to the background was that of a young girl, a pigtailed little girl sneaking into a bar to stand in a back hallway, staring up at her mother.

Chapter 20

Charlie was scheduled to work at the free health clinic late the next afternoon. It left him with a long day. Or such was Nell's assessment that morning when she and Ben stretched their sleep-slogged bodies and prepared for their own day.

"I think I'll lure him out. That cottage is too small for the emotion bottled up inside him."

"He was quiet during the game last night," Ben said. "He barely talked. Sam's concerned. He thinks Charlie is blaming himself for Amber's death. Sam thinks there's something going on inside Charlie's head, something Charlie thinks he should have paid attention to, and if he had, maybe this wouldn't have happened. It might be good if he had something else to focus on. Those kinds of thoughts are useless."

Ben headed for the shower, leaving Nell standing at the bedroom window, rolling his words around in her head. A bigger concern than Charlie blaming himself, maybe, was other people blaming him. The suspicion lurked everywhere, embedded in every question Jerry Thompson had leveled at Charlie. Every note he had scribbled on his yellow pad.

Jerry had been open with Ben when they talked the day before—and fair. His suspect list was short, he said. But they were getting through it—talking to Cummings employees, especially the business-office people, with whom Amber seemed to have spent so much time.

And the force was not overlooking the fact of her unexpected inheritance and how it affected the Cummingses, he reminded Ben. They were turning over every possible motive they could come up with, including the fine points of Lydia Cummings's will.

He was sorry for dragging Charlie in, but he had to—Charlie's name came up in almost every interview. And for other reasons, too. The chief had paused then, uncomfortable with what he was to say next. But he pushed on. "Some of the same people who saw Charlie the night she died saw him drinking like a sailor. And he wasn't a happy drunk. His texts to Amber were proof of that."

Ben listened with a pained look on his face.

But the chief had moved on, assuring Ben they would get to the bottom of it. They would find the person, the murderer, he assured Ben.

But the reassurance brought little comfort—and wouldn't—not until his nephew Charlie's name had completely fallen off that list.

Nell looked through the bedroom window at the quiet guesthouse, the blinds drawn, the backyard scene idyllic. And then she imagined the other side of the shingled walls—and the troubled man boxed inside.

Nell waited until midmorning, then slipped on a heavy jacket and boots, collected a thermos of coffee and a toasted bagel, and went down to the guest cottage. Her footsteps crunched on the snow-crusted flagstones, and the frozen air stung her lungs. Bright sunlight warmed her cheeks. It brought all her senses alive—a startling sensation that felt cleansing and good. She knocked lightly on the door, not wanting to wake Charlie if by some stroke of luck he had been able to sleep in.

But he was up and dressed, as Nell had suspected he'd be, his hair still wet from a shower.

She set the coffee and bagel on the small table. "How about you and I spend some time together today? I need to go to the bookstore that Danny Brandley's parents run. You need an introduction. Then lunch with Izzy, maybe, if she's free?"

Charlie looked at his aunt with affection, but hesitated, shifting from one stockinged foot to the other. He shoved his hands in the pockets of his corduroys and looked directly at Nell, his eyes locking in to hers. "I'll be okay, you know," he said. "It was temporary, breaking down like that."

"I'm not offering to babysit, Charlie. I know you'll be all right. But I want to spend time with you, that's all."

Charlie knew it was more than that, but he nodded and agreed. "I could use some good books," he said.

They left an hour later in Charlie's car, dropping letters at the post office, then finding a parking place in the alley between Izzy's Knitting Studio and the Sea Harbor Bookstore. Nell moved to unsnap her seat belt and glanced into the backseat. It was littered with stained, dog-eared papers, wrappings from burgers, a candy bar, an empty Dunkin' Donuts cup. On the floor were a few books.

Charlie saw Nell's look as he turned off the ignition. "I know, I need to clean out this thing." He looked over the seat. "Amber wasn't the neatest person around. I think my backseat became her office or her trash can, not sure which." He took a breath and released it slowly. "Maybe that's why I haven't cleaned it up."

Nell nodded, remembering Birdie's affection for her first husband Sonny's belongings. A leather chair that still held the distinct cherry fragrance of his favorite tobacco. An old scarf, the first Birdie had ever knit for him, frayed and shrunk. And valued.

They both got out of the car and Nell looked once more through the back window. "What are all those papers?"

"Nothing, really. Things she printed off at the Cummings office, then tossed aside. Financial stuff. Salary records. She was a little obsessed."

"Salary records?"

Charlie shrugged. "Go figure. She thought their pay scale was screwy. Maybe she was looking to see if the owners got salaries, who knows? Amber actually liked to read financial records. She loved numbers. She told me the other day that she liked math because it gave her the sense that there was order in the universe, an underlying structure. And that made her feel safe."

The irony of Amber's comment hung frozen in the air.

Nell looked once more at the mess of papers in the backseat. "I suppose reading those things away from the Cummings office, when no one was looking over her back, was easier."

"Maybe. Garrett was there most of the time, she said. He told her he was going to start charging her for printing, but she reminded him that she owned part of the printers." He laughed.

Nell had to laugh, too. "It doesn't sound like she was trying to win friends and influence people."

"Nope. Not over there. But she had a soft side, Aunt Nell."

"I know that, Charlie. I saw the warm side of Amber the first day she came over to our house. And after that, too, even when she tried to hide it. I think it was because of you. You mellowed her, Charlie. You made her feel comfortable."

Charlie walked toward the bookstore door, looking at Nell sideways. "Even though she tried to steal my phone and chewed me out when I was late?" His smile was crooked, but Nell was happy to see it in any form.

"Yes, even though. And I wasn't the only one. Jake Risso has known Amber since she was little—and he saw it, too," she said. "The softness was there."

She walked through the doorway and waved at Archie Brandley. He was standing behind the computer, a pencil in his mouth and his glasses falling to the end of his nose.

"Archie, meet my nephew Charlie," Nell called out, then took Charlie by the arm and led him over.

Archie greeted him nicely, but with a slight reserve that Nell was sure Charlie didn't notice. But she did. It wasn't like Archie.

Archie had heard the rumors just like everyone else. And as much as he loved Izzy, her brother was an unknown in town. And a woman in his town had been murdered.

"Charlie's helping Lily Virgilio at the free health clinic."

"That so?" said Archie. "That's a fine place, the clinic."

"Yeah, it is. They're keeping a lot of kids healthy. It's a privilege to be able to help out some," Charlie said.

Charlie looked around the store, taking in the staircase to the second floor, the groupings of comfortable chairs, and the coffeepot perking near the window. And everywhere, from floor to ceiling, books. "This is a great bookstore you have here, Archie. Now I know what my friend Amber meant. She loved this place, one of the few things that hadn't changed since she was a kid, she said. She told me she nearly bought you out a couple days ago."

Archie warmed at that and held out a hand, shaking Charlie's. "Yeah, it's a damn shame what happened to Amber. She was your friend. I'm sorry for your loss, Charlie."

Nell watched the exchange, relieved that even after a few words, one could see through any rumors and fear and recognize who Charlie really was. A good man. Or at least that was what she hoped she was seeing in the thawing out in the bookseller's eyes.

"I didn't know you knew Amber, Archie," Nell said.

"Sure I did. When she was a little kid she'd come in here and hide in the kids' section reading every Nancy Drew and *The Secret Garden* and anything else she could get her hands on. Not that her grandmother couldn't have bought the whole darn store for her if she'd wanted to." He shook his head, his judgment out there in the air. Then he brushed it off and grinned at a memory. "One night I nearly locked the kid in. She was curled up and fell sound asleep. My wife, Harriet, found her when she was turning out the lights. Damnedest thing. I teased her about it the other day when she came in. Asked her if she still read Nancy Drew. She laughed. Then she hoisted some books onto the counter that were definitely not Nancy Drews. They were research types and I told her she should be getting some of those at the library, but she laughed and told me I shouldn't be saying that—it was no way to run a business, sending customers away."

"What kind of books was she buying?" Nell asked.

Archie scratched his head. "An auditing book, business reports, that kind of boring stuff. One other I can't rightly remember on some other topic, medical or something. She was trying to figure out her inheritance, would be my guess."

Charlie nodded. "Mighty heavy tomes," he said. "They're weighing down my trunk right now, probably be as good as sandbags if it gets icy."

Archie laughed and looked over as a young man headed to the desk. He held up a hand in greeting.

"Hey, Zack, my boy, I suppose you want a stack of superhero comic books?"

Nell and Charlie turned to see Zack Levin pulling out his earplugs to hear what Archie was saying.

"What's that, Arch?"

Archie repeated it and Zack grimaced in exaggerated fashion. "Archie, I grew up, didn't you notice? Jeez." He laughed along with the store owner and set a couple of Harlan Coben mysteries on the desk, then noticed Nell and Charlie. "Hey, guys," he said. He took a step toward Charlie and awkwardly clapped him on the back. "Hey, man. This really sucks. So sorry about Amber. She was way cool."

Charlie nodded, then moved the conversation to a more neutral place. "So, how're you doing, Zack? Things okay at the office, as they say?"

"Same old same old. Only not really. When Amber was there she gave me things to do. I felt useful. She picked up on the computer stuff in a second. In fact—" He looked around as if there might be a spy in the bookstore listening.

He lowered his voice and continued. "She could tell right away that O'Neal had cleverly blocked her out of some files. I couldn't even tell, but Amber picked it up."

"Blocked her out?" Nell asked.

"Yeah. It was his domain. He didn't like people poking around. Well, you saw some of that, right, Charlie?"

Charlie said yes.

"How did she solve that?" Nell asked.

Zack looked sheepish. "Well, I figured she was an owner, right? And I had all the passwords, since I was fixing computers, installing programs and things like that for them. So I told Amber I'd get the files for her. I figured Garrett was just trying to make it hard for her because they didn't like her around. He thought she'd get discouraged and leave. Didn't seem right. Jeez, it was her company. O'Neal was just a worker bee like me. Well, not exactly like me. He made big bucks."

Nell looked at Charlie. He didn't seem surprised at Zack's machinations. "Were you working on anything else with Amber?" she asked.

"I was helping her explore Internet banking for the company. Something fun."

"O'Neal didn't like it," Charlie said. "Amber said he was a Luddite."

Zack shrugged. "Yeah, it sent him off the deep end. They should join the twenty-first century, Amber told him."

Nell smiled indulgently at the conversation and kept it to herself that she refused to bank online. Cell phones were wonderful, but sending your checks off to some cloud somewhere? She would need more convincing.

Zack had warmed to his subject and went on, praising Amber's ability not to back down to the boss man. "She scolded him like she was the one in charge, not him. She said he needed to brush up on some things. But when he left the room, she told me it had nothing to do with being in the wrong century. It was something else completely."

"What was that?" Nell said.

Zack pulled out some bills and put them on the counter for Archie. "Oh, she didn't tell me. It was a surprise, she said. But from the look on her face, it wasn't going to be a happy surprise—at least not for O'Neal."

Chapter 21

Izzy ran out at the first honk, and they drove down Harbor Road to the Ocean's Edge restaurant—just a long enough drive for Izzy to chide Charlie about the smelly coffee cups and paper trash littering the backseat. She stacked the papers up neatly, shoved them into a portfolio, and set them on the floor.

"Sisters," Charlie whispered to Nell. The message that he liked having one was clear.

As he pulled into a parking space, Nell suggested she'd like a chance to look at the portfolio, grease and all. Charlie agreed and she reached behind the driver's seat, collecting the package and setting it on the floor next to her bag where she wouldn't forget it. Then she remembered the books, and said she'd be happy to take those off his hands, too.

She'd be happy to replace them with sandbags.

The Ocean's Edge was humming, the sounds of silver and dishes and glasses competing with the happy chatter of diners being well fed. Izzy, Nell, and Charlie walked in, shutting out the cold and welcoming the warmth from the large stone fireplace.

"It looks full," Izzy said, peering into the crowded dining room. The restaurant was a Sea Harbor landmark on prized real estate, the view over the ocean and harbor pier extraordinary, but it was the amazing chefs that brought people all over the north shore to the seafood restaurant.

Charlie read the blackboard sign in the foyer highlighting the luncheon specials, his stomach growling along with the words. "I don't even know what some of these words mean." He leaned closer and read out loud: *"Lobster-roe noodles, bucatini truffle crusted tuna?"*

Nell laughed. It was true the menu had become slightly more exotic since Don Wooten became the sole owner. But it had old favorites, too—lobster rolls, chowders, oysters on the half shell—even a steak sandwich. "You'll love everything. Great chowders and bisques, sandwiches. The fried oyster sliders are out of this world."

"That's if we can get a table," Izzy said, her eyes canvassing the crowded room. She was already feeling pangs of hunger that would settle for nothing less than the Ocean's Edge.

"For you? No question about it, Izzy," said a familiar voice behind them.

Izzy spun around with a start and grinned into the face of the restaurant owner.

Nell smiled. "Don, you never fail us, do you?"

"I save my favorite table for favorite guests," he said. He welcomed Charlie with a handshake and gave Izzy and Nell hugs, then motioned for them to follow him as he wove his way through the tables, leaning to the left and right to greet friends and neighbors and first-time diners, smiling and never losing his stride. He motioned to a tall, willowy waitress. "Arlene, you take good care of these special folks," he said.

The table was perfect, as promised, right next to the bank of windows and doors that would be open in the summer to the restaurant's wide porch. Today they offered an endless view of the water, as if the ocean were theirs alone. Nell never tired of it.

A basket of fried Ipswich clams arrived unbidden and Nell tried to find Don's eye to thank him. The restaurant owner was intuitive. As the city attorney's husband, he was keenly aware of everything going on behind the scenes this week, but he wisely concentrated on food today, not murder.

And she could see the relief on her nephew's face.

Izzy ordered her usual, the lobster salad, and Nell decided on the same. But they regretted it slightly when a long plate of fried-oyster sliders smeared with chili-lime aioli and topped with pickled onion and sprigs of arugula was set down in front of Charlie.

Charlie swooned.

Izzy looked into her brother's face. For a moment she said nothing, just enjoying the pleasure she saw there. And then she said softly, "See what you've been missing?"

The words were a surprise, even to Izzy herself. The emotion they carried was still thick and poignant. And it had little to do with food.

Charlie sat still, staring at the oysters, as if somehow they'd find a voice to help him out.

"Izzy," he finally said, finding her eyes. "Izzy, I know I missed a lot. But I couldn't come here, or to Kansas. Anywhere. I was a poor excuse for being anything, especially a brother or son. I didn't have much control over me, is how I saw it. And when that has an impact on other people's lives . . . well, then the best thing might be to bow out for a while." He stopped, fiddled with a fork, moved the tines along the tablecloth. "I needed to find the *me* that used to be, the one who teased you and pulled your hair and used my whole allowance to buy you the best Hello Kitty birthday present I could find. And then—then I need a reentry plan," he said finally.

The waitress named Arlene was back and the moment faded, then passed. "Okay, here's what I have," Arlene said. She put four tall elegant beer glasses on the table, one in front of each of them, then picked up a pitcher of beer from the tray. "This beer is from that nice man in the corner. It's a *gueuze,*" she added, clearly proud of her pronunciation. She explained while she filled the three glasses. "The man insisted they'd be perfect with seafood, but especially with the oysters, and he definitely knows his beer, I can vouch for that—he drinks a lot of it." She grinned and walked away.

Nell looked over to the corner and into the wide beefy wave of Stu Cummings. She nodded, lifted her glass in the air, and smiled back.

He wasn't alone. His wife, Helen, was there, and also Barbara and Garrett. A family gathering.

Charlie glanced over, too. He looked hard at the group. Nell couldn't read his expression, his face partially hidden behind his beer glass. But his eyes spoke volumes. Charlie Chambers clearly didn't like their beer benefactor—or anyone sitting with him.

Later, after finally pushing away plates that once held slices of airy lemon meringue pie and collecting the credit card receipt, Nell excused herself. She'd meet them at the front of the restaurant, she said.

She hadn't seen Stu since Amber's death, although Ben mentioned seeing him at the courthouse as he dropped some papers at Rachel Wooten's office the day before. Stu had been headed in to the attorney's suite and had seemed rushed, so the conversation consisted of polite expressions of sadness. It was her turn.

Nell headed over to the table where the Cummingses had been sitting. Stu and Helen were still there, Stu wearing an unusually sober expression. Helen, too, sat still and quiet beside him, nursing a martini, a worried look on her face. Garrett and Barbara were gone, their places cleared.

Of course they looked sad, Nell thought. It was a death in their family, a horrible tragic death. Amber was their niece, in spite of the way they might have addressed her in recent days. She had been quick to go to visit Esther, but the Cummingses had been affected, too, and that fact had nearly escaped her.

Helen spotted Nell first. She half rose, a smile fastened to her long, lean face.

"I don't mean to interrupt," Nell said. "Please, Helen, sit down."

Stu turned his head around to greet her, his hand outstretched. "Dear, Nell, you sit, too. Good of you to come over." He grabbed the back of an empty chair and started to pull it out.

Nell shook her head. "I just wanted to thank you for the beer, but mostly to tell you how very sorry I am—all of us are—about your niece."

For a minute Stu looked confused, as if not sure to whom Nell was referring, and then he quickly recovered. He nodded vigorously, a slight flush of embarrassment crawling up his neck. He ran a finger along the inside of his starched shirt, pulling it away from his neck. "Yes. It's a tough week. Awful. Terrible time. Horrible for that girl. We didn't know her that well, but she sure didn't deserve to die like she did."

"No, she didn't. She clearly had a difficult life—as did her mother."

Nell waited a minute to see if there was any acknowledgment of Amber's mother. A simple nod that yes, a beautiful young woman had had a tragic life.

Stu picked up his napkin and set it down again.

Helen drank the last of her martini and looked at her husband's discomfort. "Yes," she said politely, her face suggesting nothing more needed to be said. She fingered a broach on her lapel nervously.

"Please let us know if there's anything Ben and I can do—" Nell said.

Stu wiped his forehead with the napkin and forced a smile in place. "Thanks. Father Northcutt asked about a memorial service down the road, but we're not sure that's for the best. It might simply be prolonging a sad time. The family has already felt closure, I think."

"I don't know if any of us will feel closure until the person who did this is caught," Nell said. "It's tragic for a life to end that way, and awful for the whole town—the fear, the rumors, the way people look at each other. Chief Thompson is working day and night, but until he finds who killed Amber, we will all be in a kind of limbo."

Later, Nell wasn't sure what part of what she said had upset the usually genial Stu, but as she talked, his eyes narrowed and his voice rose a decibel louder than comfortable in the tasteful restaurant. "It better be soon, Nell," he said. "I hope the police know what they're doing. I have a business to run and they're everywhere, upsetting my staff, crawling all over the nurseries, as if the girl ever even set foot in them. It's upsetting. And makes no good sense. My unflappable sister, Barbara, is about ready to explode. She can barely get her work done, and says the files are a mess now. Garrett O'Neal is working fourteen-hour days getting things back in order."

Helen sat quietly beside him, a worried look on her face, but Nell noticed one strong hand reach out and rest on her husband's arm, as if calming him, protecting him from being too excited, wanting the conversation to end. Her grip was firm, and Stu finally sat back in the chair and took a drink from the water glass Helen pressed into his hand.

Nell was relieved when he stopped talking, aware that others sitting nearby could hear him.

But Stu wasn't finished. "You have to understand the upset this has caused to everyone in our family, Nell. We're wondering why they aren't out looking at Amber Harper's associates or friends. Who knows what kind of ruffians she knew? What kind of trouble she might have gotten herself into? That's where the focus should be, not at upstanding members of the community. I'll tell you this much: if they don't start looking, I will."

"Stu," Helen said, "your heart."

Nell lowered her voice, hoping Stu's blood pressure would lower along with it. She spoke calmly. "Of, course, Stu. Investigations are hard on everyone. And Jerry doesn't leave stones unturned. You know that. It's not just your employees. He's talked to all of us."

Stu took another deep breath and shook his head. "Sure, you're right, Nell. I know it's hard on you, everyone else. I know your nephew was her friend and they're probably checking him out good and hard. But sure, the police chief is a good man, like you said. All I'm saying is it's wicked hard on the staff, the landscapers, that's all. I just thank the good Lord my mother wasn't here to see the way the Cummings name is being bandied about, connected to a murder like this. She'd be mortified. Humiliated."

Helen looked up at Nell, a slight rebuke in her tone at upsetting Stu. "It's taking a toll on us. Tempers are short."

"Of course," Nell said. "And it's especially difficult for those who knew Amber." The conversation was uncomfortable, the focus not what Nell had expected it to be. She hastily repeated her offer to help—although it seemed a meaningless gesture now—then excused herself and walked away.

But the conversation stayed with her as she walked out to claim her coat—and it would linger into the day. Amber was Stu and Barbara's niece. *Flesh and blood*. A fact that seemed to somehow be missing in their distress over the tragic events. She thought of Izzy, Charlie, and their older brother, Jack. How intimate her tie was to each of them and would always be, no matter what they did or where they were. It didn't matter. They were family.

Charlie and Izzy were waiting at the front door, bundled up and ready to go.

The parking lot was busy, and they walked their way around the moving and parked vehicles slowly.

"Hey, there's my twin," Charlie said as they neared a crowded row of cars. He pointed to a shiny silver BMW, then admitted, "Well, not exactly a twin. Mine's used, rebuilt, a few years older. But hey, they say Bimmers are like fine wine—they get better with age."

It wasn't until they stopped to admire the shiny new version of Charlie's car that they noticed Garrett O'Neal and Barbara Cummings standing next to it, talking.

The two figures were shadowed by a Range Rover, their figures almost invisible in its height. The conversation looked serious, their faces close together. Barbara seemed to be controlling the conversation at first, her face unreadable, her demeanor controlled as always, but her body language registered displeasure. She had lifted her arm, a finger moving slowly in the air, a teacher getting a point across.

Garrett stood still, listening, nodding. Finally he wound his fingers around her wrist, gently pulling down her arm. He took her gloved hand in both of his, holding it still.

Barbara looked surprised at first. Then slowly took her hand back.

Garrett's voice was measured, his words slow and carried by a wind that whipped up off the water, carrying them the short distance to where Nell, Izzy, and Charlie lingered.

"I've promised you everything would be all right," he said. "It's under control, just as it always is. I know numbers backwards and forwards. Nothing gets by me. Nothing. You need to trust me more, have more faith in me."

"Faith in you?" Barbara's expression was curious now, as if she wasn't sure who this man was who was speaking to her.

He shrugged and opened the door for her, then stood there for a moment, one hand on the doorframe, looking at her intently through his thick glasses.

"What?" Barbara asked, frowning. "What is it, Garrett?" She kept her eyes on him as she lowered herself into the car. A boyish sort of smile slipped awkwardly across his face. "I take care of things, Barbara," he said. "Stu trusts me. Your mother knew I was the best thing to happen to Cummings Northshore. She knew I'd take care of what she built no matter what. I have. And I always will. I take care of things—for everyone. But mostly, I want to take care of them for you."

Garrett paused, as if wanting his words to sink in and take on meaning. Then he shifted from one foot to the other, his voice losing the firm tone of a minute ago, and an awkwardness creeping in. He pushed his glasses up his nose and finally spoke. "Barbara, I'm here for you, always. I think it's time."

Barbara looked up at him. "Time?"

"We should get married," he said. He moved then, blocking Barbara Cummings from view, closed her door, and walked around the car.

A minute later the car was off across the parking lot, its driver never checking the rearview mirror to see the three figures standing a few yards away, watching the car disappear in a plume of exhaust.

Chapter 22

"What do you make of it?" Nell asked Ben that evening. She uncorked a bottle of wine and poured them each a glass as she repeated the conversations she had had with the owners of Cummings Northshore Nurseries—one that she participated in, and the other overheard.

"I think all three of you were eavesdroppers, for starters," Ben said.

"Yes, besides that." Nell picked up a tray of cheese and crackers and headed to the fireplace.

Ben took a drink of wine and followed her across the room. He was always cautious about placing exaggerated significance in ordinary things, a temptation when looking for a murderer they were all desperate to find. At first he didn't comment when she mentioned Garrett O'Neal's cryptic comments about taking care of things. Instead he crouched down in front of the fireplace and piled some kindling and paper balls on the logs. He struck a match and lit the paper.

"Okay, here's what I think." He pushed himself upright, gazing into the red glow, fascinated as the paper balls exploded into flames. He moved to the couch. "Let's say that this is an ordinary day and you overheard two people who work together disagreeing about something or worrying about an office matter. I would say it means nothing. And frankly, from what you've told me, I'm not even sure it was a disagreement. Just an ordinary back-and-forth."

Nell kicked off each shoe and tucked her feet up beneath her. She watched the flames dancing against the blackened brick behind them. "Maybe you're right, but the thing is, it's *not* an ordinary day. No days are ordinary right now." She made room on the couch for Ben to sink down beside her.

"Are you thinking the conversation had anything to do with Amber's murder?" Ben asked.

"It's a possibility. Or something related to it. I think that's how we have to look at everything. Amber was not only related to those people, but she was messing with the business they owned."

"The business she owned, too," Ben reminded her.

"Exactly. And wouldn't it have benefited them if Amber was dead?" Nell said. "I know Stu seemed convinced last week that she'd sell it back to them. Now she's dead—and he seemed worried about things. But with Amber dead, he and Barbara are sole owners, right?"

"That'd be true if Amber didn't have a will. Then the property goes to next of kin. As sad as it may seem, that's Barbara and Stu. But if Amber had a will of her own, then that would dictate what happens to her share in the Cummings company."

"Did she have a will?"

"Rachel Wooten has someone looking into it."

"So alive, Amber wasn't a threat because Stu was sure he could buy Amber's share back. Let's assume he was right, although I don't think he really had any idea what Amber Harper was going to do."

"I'm with you there," Ben laughed. "But the truth is, even if Amber didn't sell it back, Cummings Northshore Nurseries is thriving. That company is making enough money to support half this town. It wouldn't have hurt them if she'd hung on to it. And Garrett is so tight with the books, I doubt if she could have done anything to harm the company. Besides, Barbara and her poker face would eventually have kept Amber in her place, don't you think?"

Nell didn't think that at all. "Amber was strong and opinionated. She might have wanted to change the way they did things, to somehow have a voice—even Esther was afraid she might want to do damage to the company."

Ben sat back, stretching one arm along the back of the couch, his fingers playing with her hair. He tugged a strand. "You're good at this, Nellie."

Nell smiled. In Ben's mind, she was good at trying to find motives and murderers as long as she was sitting in front of a fire with him at her side, both of them playing the armchair detective game. If she took it any further, he would have a problem with it. Nell left the muddy motive question wallowing on the coffee table. "You still haven't addressed my original question, Ben. Barbara rarely shows emotion. She's so levelheaded, composed."

Ben nodded. "True. She's a respected businesswoman. Careful and discreet when it comes to business affairs. And not very social. She keeps to herself."

"Yet she was displeased, and in a public place." She thought back over the conversation as she sipped her wine, then said with a chuckle, "I'm not sure which part of the conversation intrigued me the most—the beginning or the end." She filled Ben in on Garrett's parting words.

Ben's eyebrows lifted. "Now, that *is* a surprise."

"It was odd—I can't tell you why, exactly, but definitely odd. I almost felt sorry for him. I think he finally felt he had the right to ask."

"It almost sounds like a business proposal," Ben said. "People have wondered about that relationship behind closed doors for a while. Garrett is a huge asset to the company. He's quiet, but smart. And exceptionally good at what he does. What do they call the quiet Scorpios—the gray Lizard? I wouldn't be surprised if his birthday was in November. He knows financial reports backwards and forwards. In fact, that may have been what you were hearing. Barbara was concerned about something, maybe a late report or new insurance, taxes. Garrett was assuring her he had it all under control, just like he always does."

Nell thought about what he was saying. As always, it was logical. But was murder logical? Aloud, she said, "Ben, what happens next with the inheritance?"

"Rachel asked Father Larry and me to sit in on a late-afternoon meeting with Stu and a couple of others. So they'll talk about what we've talked about, but maybe have actual facts to lay on the table. Maybe they'll have found a will—or not."

She rolled her head on the couch cushion and looked sideways at Ben, and she could see that thoughts of wills and inheritances were leaving his mind with each sip of his wine.

She decided to do the same, finishing her wine and setting the glass on the table. She leaned her head against Ben's chest and snuggled there, her eyes on the fire, its warmth easing the tension of the week.

Ben's interpretation floated around in her drowsy thoughts. He almost always made sense. And he was known for his logic. But something was missing in his reasoning tonight—a missing or false premise? Or maybe he just had other things on his mind, like relaxing with his wife in front of the fire, going to bed early.

Ben had described Barbara Cummings as a discreet businessperson, a private woman. Nell suspected that to be true both in her personal and in her business life.

But no matter what Ben said, she felt certain the conversation reflected something more significant than insurance policies.

Nell felt sure of it, but she held her silence. For now, she willingly gave her mind and body over to the fire and to Ben's warm breath on her neck, to his arm around her—to the sound of his heartbeat against her ear, its slow regular beat hypnotizing her, blocking out all other thoughts.

. . .

Izzy had called the late-afternoon knitting class Holiday Help—and she made sure people knew that even those who only used fat needles and limited techniques were welcome. It was Izzy's Christmas gift to her customers.

With the help of our holiday elves, the e-mail they had sent to customers read, *you'll receive expert assistance on how to finish your holiday gifts before finding yourselves adrift in the New Year with yarn still dangling from your fingertips.*

"Elves?" Nell said to Birdie. She shook her head in mock dismay as she maneuvered the CRV out of Birdie's driveway and onto Ravenswood Road. "Did she really call us elves?"

"It was Mae," Birdie chuckled. "I'd recognize her purple prose anywhere."

"I hope some live bodies show up," Nell said. "Izzy said attendance has dropped off, especially at night. The same is true at the bookstore and other shops up and down Harbor Road. One of the busiest shopping seasons—and instead people are staying home behind locked doors watching reality television shows or ordering gifts online."

Birdie looked out the window as they approached the harbor area. Lovely festive decorations everywhere—but only a scattering of shoppers enjoying the twinkling lights. "Fear has power. Awful power," she said. "Nell, I know Jerry has a fine police force, but I think the investigation has stagnated. No wonder people are staying home. Someone is getting away with murder—and it might be someone who isn't finished with what he started."

The thought was sobering and uncomfortable, but Nell agreed. "Ben won't exactly come out and say that, but I think he feels the same way. The chief is under a great deal of pressure from all sides to put someone behind bars. Anyone, just to get rid of the awful fear. To have a face, a name, someone—" She stopped, her words stilled by worry.

Birdie followed the path of Nell's thoughts and stopped her. "Jerry Thompson is a thorough and fair man, we know that. He isn't going to arrest someone simply because he needs to put a town's collective mind to rest. Especially someone we know is clearly not guilty."

They drove in silence for a while, their thoughts wrapping Charlie Chambers in a protective shield and their minds jumping ahead, planning.

As they neared the yarn shop, Birdie rested one hand on Nell's arm and said aloud what she knew they were both thinking. "Nell, we're as close as Jerry to what is going on here, or closer. And we have a vested interest that transcends all sorts of rules. We need to put our thoughts out on the table and knit them together, see where they take us—and stop worrying about stepping on toes."

Relief spread through Nell instantly. Birdie's words unleashed feelings that had been bottled up for days now, ever since Amber had died and Charlie's life had changed. They'd all been doing the same thing, quietly, alone. Watching people, listening, coming up with conjectures that they'd held in the silence of their heads. It was time to say them out loud.

Nell pulled into the alley behind Izzy's car and turned off the ignition. She gave Birdie a long hug.

The shopwindows were lit up like Santa's Workshop, the light pouring from them warm and welcoming. A large display window in front matched the festive feeling. Mae's nieces had gone all out, creating a winter scene with mounds of snowy fleece covering the floor of the window, crocheted Christmas trees planted on the hilly surface. And across the "sky" above flew Santa's sleigh, pulled by reindeer wearing hand-knit hats in every color of the season.

COME KNIT WITH US, a sign planted in the "snow" read. Behind it stood a jolly elf, his green knit outfit decorated with tiny red snowballs.

Birdie focused on the elf. "Izzy didn't mention we needed to wear costumes. I suppose I could have dug up something."

Nell laughed and tucked her arm through Birdie's, guiding her through the bright blue door.

They were happily surprised to see people wandering around in the shop's main room. Fingers found their way into baskets of cashmere and wool and alpaca yarn. Lively voices admired the knit sweaters and hats decorating a Christmas tree in the center of the room. And everywhere tiny white lights spoke of a warm, safe place.

Birdie and Nell waved to Mae and her nieces, then made their way across the room to the back steps, lured by the chatter and the tender voice of Andrea Bocelli dreaming of a white Christmas.

"Izzy's shop," Nell murmured as she stood in the archway, looking down at the women gathering around the fireplace and the library table, the cozy corners of chairs. "It feels safe here. No matter what lurks in the darkness beyond this shop, there's no room for fear here."

At least that was her hope. She followed Birdie down the few steps, shrugging off her coat on the way.

Izzy stood over on the far side, encouraging people to find their niche—around the fire or table, the beanbag chairs and groupings near the window. She was clearly happy with the turnout.

Nell and Birdie stood in the back, watching Izzy work her magic, explaining things clearly but with the rush of emotion she was rarely allowed in the courtroom. Her passion had clear reign in the small yarn shop where the magical therapy of knitting happened daily. It was "the new yoga," she'd say as a sweeping calm settled over a group of beginners or old-timers, young or old, as they worked their needles, caressed their yarn, and breathed more deeply.

Tonight's group was a hodgepodge of young and old, singles and young moms, older moms and grandmothers and professional women balancing their lives by adding a respite to crowded days. Izzy explained that there were helpers scattered around—just wave a hand, she said. They'll be there to help.

Nell looked over heads and around bodies and knew it wasn't help with knitting that was most on their minds tonight—it was the warmth, the companionship that Izzy's back room offered, not to mention the happy sounds of carols, hot tea and spicy punch, and the freshly baked Christmas cookies that Margaret Garozzo had brought from her deli. It was a safe haven in a menacing world.

A touch on her arm pulled Nell's attention away from Izzy. She looked into the carefully made-up face of Beatrice Scaglia, a brocade knitting bag holding yarn and rarely used needles hanging from her arm. Helen Cummings stood just behind her, talking to Birdie.

The fact that Beatrice and Helen were friends never failed to intrigue Nell. Barbara, it seemed, would have been a better match for Beatrice, her commanding presence and authoritative ways not unlike the mayor's. But each to his own, and Helen was probably a lot easier to be with, more amenable to whatever Beatrice had to say. She was also more available, and a good source for what was going on inside the Cummings dynasty.

"Now, when does a busy mayor find time to knit?" Nell said to Beatrice.

"Nell Endicott, don't play games with me," Beatrice scolded. "You know I can't knit worth a tinker's damn. Someday when I get my rocker I'll have Izzy come over and teach me."

Nell chuckled. "Your secret's safe with me. And as long as you keep buying yarn here, Mae and Izzy will never tell."

Beatrice didn't fool anyone. The gatherings in the yarn shop's back room were her favorite place to get her political finger on the pulse of what women in Sea Harbor were thinking, talking about—and who they might be voting for. She was also not immune to catching any gossip or rumors circulating around. Nell suspected tonight her attention would be focused on talk of a murderer wandering the town she governed.

"I'm actually here because Helen asked me to come with her," Beatrice said. "She doesn't need a beginning knitting course but she did need a lovely dinner and drink at Ocean's Edge. So we simply combined the two. Women's night out."

"I suppose Stu is extra busy these days," Nell said.

"Of course he is, poor man. It's crazy, all that's going on over there. All the distress. Helen said she's just relieved that Lydia isn't alive to see it."

Nell was silent. The fact that Lydia might have caused it all seemed to have escaped the mayor.

"I understand Helen was close to her mother-in-law," Nell said. It wasn't a topic she particularly wanted to pursue, but she was finding it difficult to hear about the Cummingses' suffering when a niece of theirs lay in a morgue, unnoticed.

Beatrice nodded. "Helen was over there every day, even before Lydia got sick. Barbara didn't get along well with her mother, but Lydia and Helen seemed to have a good relationship, one that benefited them both. Helen confided in her, and Lydia liked that. Lydia listened to Helen's woes, her worries about Stu. Her fear of being alone."

"Being alone?"

"Oh, you know. Helen went from her parents' home to marrying Stu. She was, I suppose you'd say, a little naïve and not very independent. But there was probably more to it, especially in the early years of her marriage—Stu was prominent, wealthy, and there was probably a niggling fear that some glamorous woman might seduce him. Helen knows she doesn't have movie-star looks.

"But there wasn't any way on earth Lydia would ever have allowed a divorce in the Cummings family; her religion wouldn't permit it." Beatrice gave a small laugh. "Sometimes I think that's why Barbara never got married. It'd definitely have to be for life, and Barbara likes her independence, doing her own thing."

Beatrice paused, as if enjoying her own observation, then went on. "Knowing Lydia's strong commitment to marriage brought a certain comfort to Helen. She could worry with Lydia, then go home feeling better. But no matter—she's been a good wife to Stu, loyal to a fault. Sometimes I think without her at his side he really would have the heart attack Helen so often worries about."

As the crowd grew, Helen and Birdie walked over to claim the window seat. Nell watched Helen sit down next to Birdie. She was calm and composed, the way Nell was used to seeing Stu Cummings's wife. She wondered briefly who the real Helen was. The dutiful corporate wife? The one who sometimes handled liquor poorly? Or the one who had confronted Amber Harper, perhaps had threatened her on a public street?

She said, "You mentioned all the things the Cummingses are dealing with. What did you mean?" She felt sure it wasn't a prolonged grieving for their murdered niece.

Beatrice looked offended at the question. Her answer was clipped. "Finding Amber's murderer so they can get on with their lives running a successful company."

Nell followed her over to the window seat. "That's what all of us want, Beatrice."

"Of course it is," Beatrice said, but her words lacked their usual friendliness.

Helen looked up. "Nell, I owe you an apology for Stu's rant yesterday."

"No apology is necessary," Nell said. "Beatrice and I were just talking about what a tense time this is for everyone. Knowing a murderer may be walking free in our town—someone who has killed a member of your own family—is an awful thing to live through."

Helen took a deep breath and a sip from her coffee carafe, then spoke in the tone of a teacher. "The murderer is long gone, Nell. Stuart is right about this. The police are looking in the wrong places. It was probably an old boyfriend, maybe someone Amber jilted or hurt or cheated on—someone who followed her here and killed her. Then he disappeared across the country and left the police to turn the lives of all of us here upside down." She smiled, pleased at the perfect way she'd made her point, and she took another drink, carefully setting the coffee thermos on the floor beside her leg.

She pulled out her knitting as if she had solved the crime herself, and began to knit a row on a lacy angora scarf.

Birdie politely admired the pattern and offered help if it was needed—"That's why we're here," she explained, moving away from the subject of murder completely.

Nell looked around the room at the women sitting in small groups, sharing their lives. But as festive and welcoming as the room was, the chatter was more subdued than normal, and here and there Nell caught words that told her even knitting holiday gifts with good friends couldn't completely assuage the fear that traveled up and down the streets.

Helen's voice brought her attention back. "It's a terrible time," she was saying. "She should have taken Stu's offer and simply gone away. It would have been best for everyone."

Certainly for Amber, Nell thought, wondering at the odd way Helen was expressing herself. Her words were overly controlled, though coherent, and Nell wondered if they were bolstered by the coffee carafe in her hand. *Poor girl* certainly wasn't the sentiment she had seen on Helen's face outside the deli.

"Stu's offer?" Birdie asked.

"Stu and Barbara offered Amber a fair price for the nursery. It was more than fair. But she said she couldn't think about it."

Nell held back her surprise. She didn't know an offer had been made, though she had heard Stu mention putting one together. She wondered if Charlie knew.

"Maybe she thought by going through the financials she could force the price up," Beatrice said.

Helen sighed, her whole body looking tired. "Maybe. She claimed she had more important things to think about than the offer."

More important things? Nell looked over at Birdie. Their eyes met as they both replayed Amber's conversation with Birdie in their heads, their thoughts aligning.

Birdie looked at Helen. "I'm not sure money was that important to Amber. When she left town all those years ago, Esther suggested that she ask Lydia for an allowance—the sort of thing grandparents gladly do if they're able—but Amber refused to ask, even though she had little money of her own. And she forbade Esther to bring it up with your mother-in-law, Helen, who probably would have given it to her. Taking Cummings money wasn't a goal of Amber's."

"Then what was her goal? There was something wrong with that girl. No one walks away from money," Beatrice said, her voice incredulous that anyone would turn down honest money they didn't have to earn. A gift. "I'm sure she would have taken the offer eventually."

Helen fiddled with one of her knitting needles, pushing on a stitch with the tip of her finger. She uttered a slight yelp when the stitch slipped off the needle, then the next and the next until the entire row pulled free, curling like a red snake in her lap.

Helen's face fell, as if the lost stitches were worthy of great sadness.

Birdie held out her hand. "Let me," she said, taking the needles and yarn into her own lap and bringing the row back to life.

Helen watched nervously, sitting straight on the bench, her cashmere turtleneck elegant on the long-necked woman, her earrings and a collar brooch the color of her eyes. She looked startled when a phone pinged.

"That's yours, Helen," Beatrice said.

Helen pulled it out of her pocket, read the message, and stood up. "It's Stu. I need to call him." She excused herself, dialing her phone as she walked up the stairs.

"As you can plainly see, my friend has been unnerved by the pressure we're all under. She wants, like we all do, life to return to normal."

Nell watched her walk up the stairs, slightly wobbly near the top. "Helen is certainly a vigilant wife. I'm sure it's helpful to Stu, with the busy life he leads."

Beatrice didn't say anything at first; then she nodded. "Marriage is never easy. And having a formidable sister-in-law like Barbara isn't easy, either, but Helen handles it well, much better than I would." Beatrice glanced up the stairway.

"Is Stu all right?" Nell asked.

"I'm sure he is," Beatrice said. "We'll see. I think he's meeting with his sister and Rachel Wooten and some others. Trying to settle things now that the parameters have changed a bit."

Of course. Nell had almost forgotten. Ben was at that meeting, too.

Minutes later Helen reappeared, her stride more confident than when she left. She walked back, leaned down, and picked up her carafe, taking a sip.

If Nell had believed in teleportation, she would have sworn that in the few minutes Helen had been away, she had visited a fountain of youth and vigor. She was once again the strong woman, the swimmer Nell often admired over at Long Beach. The woman with the long stride who walked the Ravenswood Trails. A rosy blush replaced the sallow worried look that she'd worn before. Even her eyes had changed, now bright and clear.

"It's over," she said. "Our lives can return to normal."

Nell's breath caught in her chest and she pressed one hand against her heart.

Birdie pushed herself from the window seat, her eyes wide. "They caught the murderer?"

Helen looked at Birdie, surprised. "Murderer? The murderer isn't in Sea Harbor—he's far away by now. But we do know that Amber Harper didn't have a will."

Chapter 23

Ben was home when Birdie, Izzy, and Nell walked in an hour later. They had helped Izzy clean up after everyone left, and when a text on Izzy's phone told them Sam had taken several of Harry Garozzo's pizzas over to the Endicotts', they had piled in Nell's car and driven up the hill to 42 Sandswept Lane in record time. They were starving.

Sam and Charlie sat at the kitchen island in front of a laptop and several bottles of beer. Ben stood at the counter, uncorking a bottle of wine.

"So, is it true? Amber doesn't have a will?" Birdie asked, shrugging out of her coat as she walked across the room.

Ben nodded. "I figured you'd know. I was sitting next to Stu when he talked to Helen."

"Helen's excitement made us think that the police had arrested the murderer," Nell said. "She and Beatrice were on an entirely different wavelength than we were."

"It's their family business," Ben said cautiously, trying to tamp down the emotion.

"Business or not, somehow the priorities seemed skewed," Nell said.

"To us, maybe."

"You're way too understanding, Uncle Ben. So, what happened?" Izzy demanded.

"And what does it mean?" Charlie said, his voice agitated. "I still don't understand why this is even important. Is it going to help us find who killed Amber? Is it just a detour, something to divert attention? Who cares who gets the money or the company? Amber sure didn't."

It was the question that had bothered Birdie and Nell, too, as they watched Helen and Beatrice leave Izzy's shop. Somehow the unhappy facts that a relative had been murdered and a killer was roaming freely around their town were buried deep beneath the joy of an inheritance lost, a company regained. A husband happy.

Ben offered a brief explanation. "Since Lydia had willed the Sea Harbor nursery to Amber, it was hers to dispose of. We knew that, but it was a little more complicated than at first glance. The nurseries were legally connected in such a way that if Amber sold hers to someone else or somehow initiated poor financial policies, it could harm all the nurseries. It's what caused the uproar last week when the will was read. No one trusted her; she was an unknown. But it seems she didn't have a will, so according to Massachusetts law, her inheritance would go to the next of kin."

"Stu and Barbara," Sam said.

"How do we know she didn't have a will?" Birdie asked.

"Rachel had an investigator in Florida look into it. Amber actually had a lawyer there, which was a surprise. He worked for legal aid but lived in her complex and helped her out as a friend on a couple of things. He was zealous and tried to talk her into a will, but she laughed at him because she said she had nothing to put in it. And even if she did, she'd prefer that fate took care of it. She'd never have a will, she told him."

"That sounds like her," Charlie said quietly, nursing a beer. "She was like a bird, you know? Free—she said possessions tied you down."

He'd known her just one week, one short week. And in that time Charlie had read Amber's soul. Her aunt and uncle and grandmother knew her not at all. The thought made Nell happy and sad at once. She pulled the pizza cutter out of a drawer and handed it to Ben. "So the Cummingses didn't know they'd get the nursery back if Amber died until today?" Something was missing from this, something she'd heard, a stray piece of conversation. But hard as she tried, she couldn't pull up the memory.

"That's how it looks," Ben said.

Nell tucked the thought away. She wondered about the Cummings family, and how far they'd have gone to keep their company intact.

But surely she wasn't the only one wondering. Surely they were on Jerry Thompson's radar as he questioned people and gathered alibis. Surely.

And yet in her small world it seemed frighteningly clear that it was Charlie in the limelight. Not the Cummingses.

At least until more layers were peeled away.

It was time for serious peeling.

Chapter 24

Thursday was cold with a blustery wind, and Birdie offered to have Harold drop off some extra logs at the yarn shop so they could build a lovely fire that night. He'd been chopping firewood for weeks, she said.

It just might turn out to be a long knitting night, was Birdie's thought. One in need of warmth and yarn, of dear friends—and maybe even an extra bottle of pinot gris.

A large figure, slightly slumped, was walking out of Archie's bookstore as Nell got out of her car and opened the trunk. For a moment, in the shadows of the alley, she didn't recognize him.

He carried a bulky book bag under one arm. A puffy black jacket flapped open over his wide girth, and high-waisted slacks were shoved into large furry boots.

The figure was now unmistakable. "You'll catch your death of cold out here, Father," she scolded, abandoning the bags of food in her trunk and walking over to him. She smiled into his eyes, rheumy from the blast of cold air. "Button up."

She fastened several snaps on his jacket, then reached up and pulled his black furry hat down around his ears.

"You're like Mary Halloran," he said, chuckling lightly. "Mothering me to my grave."

"Now, who said anything about a grave? But you are looking tired."

The priest nodded. "Being my age does that to one."

That was true, but there was something else in his weathered face tonight. These past few days had aged the kindly priest. Nell looked into his face, trying to read something there. Secrets could do that to a person, their weight often more ponderous than life's ordinary tasks.

"Will there be a service for Amber?" she asked.

"Barbara and Stuart didn't want one. But I do. I'm going to ask Charlie and Esther to help. Ben said he thought Charlie would like that." His white eyebrows lifted in a question mark, seeking an opinion.

She nodded. "Yes, I think he would like that. And those of us whose lives Amber touched will want to be there."

"I didn't know the lass well, but she was a part of my days in that strange way life works sometimes. Her mother was a special person."

"You knew Amber's mother?"

"That I did. Ellie came to church regularly. She was a sweet young woman. Happy. Smart. Pretty. And so in love with Patrick Cummings. I'd see it on her face, and she'd share it with me in private—Stu knew, but otherwise they kept their little romance quiet, under the Cummingses' radar, if you know what I mean. Some girls would have flaunted it—Patrick was a catch—but Ellie didn't like attention in that gossipy kind of way. The pregnancy was a surprise to her, unplanned. She worried about it, and hid it well. But when she finally told Patrick, he was thrilled. They were two good solid young people, full of hope and life. Finding each other was a miracle, Ellie always said. She was so good for him, even got him coming to church now and then; she grounded him in a way that being Lydia's pride and joy didn't. When they told me about the baby and their marriage plans, I encouraged them to go to Lydia right away, to tell her. I knew Lydia would like Ellie. You couldn't help it. And imagine, Lydia's havin' herself a grandbaby. What great joy."

Nell imagined the rest of the story that was playing out on his face. His lips pulled tight, his shoulders rising and falling beneath the heavy jacket. She imagined what it must have been like to hear the news of the accident, the sound of all those dreams dying in a fiery crash.

The priest looked at her with a sad smile. "I was wrong," he said.

"But you may have saved one life—Lydia's. I know you helped her through those terrible days. And maybe Amber's, too. Where would she have ended up if Lydia hadn't respected your advice? Your wisdom?"

"Amber Harper." He said her name slowly, uttered like a prayer. The kind that required a refrain. A "pray for us" said in unison from a choir.

He pulled himself back together and went on as if the digression in the conversation had never happened. "After Amber's memorial, we'll bury her in a plot reserved for her next to her mother. Lydia thought of everything."

The thought was chilling. That somehow Lydia had the foresight to arrange a burial plot for Amber.

"Taking care of all those mundane things—things that required money but nothing more—was the best that Lydia could do. So that's what she did, knowing her limitations, and it eased her ethical struggle, her guilt. At least I prayed it did."

"Did her feelings change at all when she got sick?"

Father Northcutt considered her question. "In some ways. When she was dying, she began to think through her long life, something I suppose most of us would do if given the time. She'd done some good things, some not so good. She talked about Amber some, and she obsessed about Ellie, worried about her dying—"

"Ellie?" Nell asked. "She had died two or three years before that, hadn't she?"

The priest nodded. "Yes." He looked over Nell's head, as if Lydia were standing behind her, listening, watching the priest. He looked back at Nell. "Lydia knew she could bring Amber back to Sea Harbor by putting her in the will. I think it brought her a peculiar kind of satisfaction."

"So she did it to make up for things?"

The furrows in his brow deepened. And then he said, "Maybe a little of that, although she had made peace with her God about how she'd raised—or not raised—the girl. Those last days Lydia was very weak, and not always making complete sense. In her mind, Amber became two different people. She was 'that girl'—the person she had never really allowed into her life, the daughter of the woman who had killed her son. And at other times she became 'Patrick's daughter. So like her father. So smart.' Two Ambers. Lydia's tone of voice changed completely when she talked about one versus the other. I think in her peculiar way, she loved Patrick's daughter. And who knows, if love can be in one's subconscious, maybe she'd felt that way all along—her latest will, after all, was made some time before her illness confined her." He stopped talking, thinking back, as if to straighten out his thoughts for himself. Then he sighed, and murmured, "Of course," words that slipped out unbidden. "I remember now. Her will was made shortly after Ellie died."

Nell listened, the significance lost to her. Then she asked, "Do you think Ellie's death made her feel guilty about Amber?"

"No, like I said, she'd come to grips with all of that. Spiritually, at least. But those last days she did seem consumed about things. About Ellie dying. About her grown children, about the company—and somehow maybe she suspected if given the chance, Patrick's daughter might fix things. At the least, it would even things up."

"Fix things?"

He didn't answer. Instead he pivoted on his large black snow boots, looking around at the lampposts strung with Christmas lights, at the cars moving slowly along Harbor Road, a lone group of carolers walking past McClucken's hardware store, their young voices joined in "Silent Night."

He breathed deeply, taking it all in, then focused back on the woman standing in front of him, his eyes locking in to hers. "Lydia and I felt differently on some subjects. But here's the thing, dear Nell, we can't always control the world, now, can we? And we can't always absolve the sins of those we love."

He held her eyes for a moment longer, then smiled sadly and lumbered off to his small practical car, leaving her standing there, mulling over his words.

Chapter 25

Nell was the last one down the back steps, and Cass breathed a heavy sigh of relief. "I couldn't imagine you not showing, but when I walked in here and all I could smell was Izzy's awful coffee, I nearly had a heart attack." She walked over and relieved Nell of a heavy cardboard box. "I'm better now."

Izzy looked up from the fireplace. "Jeez, what a relief." She ignored Cass's irreverent retort and turned back, continuing to pile logs and kindling onto the grate. Harold had been true to his word and filled her iron firewood holder to the brim. She lit the bottom layer of kindling and sat back on her heels, waiting for the flames to curl up around the logs, licking them, coaxing them to pop.

Marvin Gaye was already humming through the speakers—"Ain't no mountain high enough." Izzy unfolded herself from the hearth and walked over to the long pine table, her shoulders moving to the beat. Anticipating the discussion ahead, she hoped Marvin was right.

Birdie read her look. "Mr. Gaye knows whereof one speaks." She lifted the heavy lid off Nell's slow cooker and leaned into the aromas.

The Endicott staples—garlic and wine, fresh cream and parsley—wafted into the room.

Birdie closed her eyes and breathed in the mingled odors. "Absolutely perfect for this chilly night." She took a spoon and stirred the chunks of tender beef. Rounds of carrots and onions and slivers of spinach, cilantro, and parsley floated in the thick caramel-colored sea.

"It's creative-thinking food," Nell said. "My version of it, anyway. Lots of wine and secret spices."

Izzy took a stack of heavy bowls from the cupboard and set them beside the napkins, butter, and basket of warm rolls. She began singing along with the CD as the singer moved on to "I Heard It Through the Grapevine."

Nell watched her niece, sensing the worry that lay just beneath the surface of the lyrics coming from her mouth. Although she and Charlie still had bridges to cross, he had worked his way, inch by inch, back into his older sister's life. His problems were now hers to solve, his worries hers to share. Charlie was fortunate. He had an amazing warrior on his side.

Cass filled her bowl and tossed a handful of croutons on the top, urging the others to follow. "Perfect choice of music, Iz. Pete tells me the harbor's grapevine is so heavy it's about to topple over."

"That's what happens when people are desperate for resolution," Birdie said. She carried her soup over to the fireplace and settled in with Purl curled up next to her. She turned to watch the glowing embers, dancing like fireflies around the logs. "There are more loose ends in this case than the first sweater I knit. And everyone, including the police, is tripping over them. I'd take the record mountains of snow we got last winter to the awful cloud that's hovering over us. Mae told me when I came in tonight that even her nieces—and they belong to the generation that knows they'll live forever—are hesitant to go out at night. They're trying to talk their parents into a trip to somewhere warm, and not because of the weather."

"Could the difficulty in finding the murderer be because no one is really invested in the woman who was killed?" Cass asked. "I don't mean to be crass, but the Cummings family probably doesn't care who did it. Relative or not, she wasn't important to people in this town."

"She was important to Charlie," Izzy said softly.

"That's true," Cass said. "And look where that's getting him. The police are watching him like a hawk."

Izzy caught her breath, the intake of air audible.

Nell looked over at Cass. She knew Cass's practical approach was an attempt to blur the awful image of seeing Amber's body. But her harsh words carried truth. It was Charlie's decision to pick up a hitchhiker on a blustery Massachusetts night—and then to let himself care about her. That was what got him in this trouble—the good things he had done. It wasn't the least bit fair, but somehow letting his kindness—and then his heart—get involved had stacked things up against him.

The police knew Amber had argued with Charlie that night. He hadn't tried to hide it—Nell hoped that counted for something. But his anger—the kind she remembered from his youth—had been forceful enough to nearly break his hand. And even Jake Risso had admitted that on Amber and Charlie's frequent late-night visits to the Gull, Amber had been tough on Charlie, especially after she'd had a few beers, sometimes teasing him harshly no matter who was around. It was her way, Jake had said. Kind of like a grade school kid teasing the guy she liked best. But it was embarrassing to Charlie. Guys don't like that. And Charlie was definitely a guy.

"I'm sorry for being blunt, Iz," Cass said. "I like Charlie. If I didn't have Danny following me around and if Charlie were a couple years older, I might go for him. He's a very cool guy and he sure as heck didn't kill Amber. I'd bet my lobster fleet on that. I'm just trying to put things out there so we can force ourselves to think the way the police are thinking. And then figure out what really happened."

"It seems obvious to me that the most likely people who might have wanted Amber dead were the Cummingses," Birdie said. "And I don't say that lightly. I like Stu and Barbara. But Amber was about to insert herself in their lives in an unpredictable way—something they didn't want."

"True. But killing her wouldn't have solved their problems if she'd had a will, and they didn't know if she did or didn't," Izzy said. She set a basket of rolls on the coffee table and sat down across from Birdie. "They lucked out, I guess, in a morbid way, finding out she didn't have a will."

Nell agreed, but that niggling feeling came back that she was missing something. "The chief told Ben that was a big point—the fact that they didn't know what would happen to Amber's share of the company if she died. It blurred motives a bit."

Birdie took a few sips of her soup, then set the bowl down. She lifted her wineglass, thinking about motives and wills—and playing devil's advocate. "If you think practically about the situation, most people Amber's age don't have a will. The Cummingses could realistically have assumed that Amber didn't have one."

Izzy jumped in, her lawyer voice intact. "But assumptions don't hold much weight when you're making important decisions. Stu and Barbara Cummings are very smart people and they couldn't just assume she wouldn't have a will. What if she did? What would that have done to their company?"

Nell smiled. She was echoing Ben. So alike, those two.

Birdie nodded, satisfied. Then she replayed Helen Cummings's happy state when she got the news that Amber had died intestate. "It was news they'd been eager to hear. At least Helen was. Indicating that they weren't sure when she died if she had one or not."

Nell's eyes widened, a sudden realization springing up out of her memory. "Wait," she said suddenly.

All eyes turned toward her.

"Maybe they *did* know Amber didn't have a will. At least one of them, anyway. Stu made a veiled reference at the club one night, shortly after Lydia's will was read. He said 'his sources' told him where Amber worked, that she was a waitress in Florida. I'm sure I heard him say that. It certainly sounds like he was looking into her past. Maybe he knew more than that?"

"And if his sources had discovered she didn't have a will before she died, the motive is back. Bingo." Cass scooped up the last remnants of soup.

Birdie raised one finger in the air as if to slow them down. "It might give us a motive. A beginning. *If*, in fact, it's true that Stu knew Amber didn't have a will. And if he knew, Barbara did, too. Although Helen was often in the dark about business affairs, Barbara told me she and Stu met nearly every day. They shared everything." She shivered at the thought of a person she had known for dozens of years being a murderer. "But motive doesn't equate to guilt."

"Rachel Wooten found out the name of Amber's lawyer friend in Florida," Nell said. "I could find out if anyone else had contacted him. At least it would be a start."

"All right, then," Birdie said, moving the conversation along. "When I think about Amber's short time here in Sea Harbor, it occurs to me how narrow this search is. It's concentrated on a will, a company. On one short week in Amber's life. But she had a lifelong connection to Sea Harbor, whether she currently lived here or not."

"True," Nell said. She set her soup bowl down. "I don't want to add confusion to our discussion—it's confusing enough—but I met Father Larry as I was coming in tonight, and he said some things we should think about. He knows all the players better than maybe anyone."

And confusing or not, the more facts—or memories—that they could pull apart, knit back together, make sense of, the better off everyone would be. Perhaps the entire town. But in the whole mix, what mattered most to Nell was helping her nephew Charlie escape the cloud that was shadowing his life. Charlie had been out of their lives for too long. He had been living in shadows. And if there was anything she wanted right now, it was to pull him out of that darkness completely and allow him to live his life.

She repeated the conversation while the others fell quiet, draining the bowls of Nell's creamy stew. Parts of the story they had heard before, but Father Larry's description added poignancy to Ellie and Patrick's romance. And parts of it were new—and perplexing.

"So he thinks Lydia thought Amber could help the company?" Birdie spoke the words slowly, trying to make sense of them. "It seems unlikely Lydia thought Stu and Barbara were incapable. They'd been helping her run the company for years."

"Perhaps that was the thing—she wasn't going to be around to help them," Izzy said.

"Father Larry wasn't guessing. What he said came from conversations he'd had with Lydia," Nell said. "Esther said something similar—that Amber was as smart as her father. Brilliant with numbers. So in a way, she'd be adding to the company what Lydia herself had provided. Lydia wasn't questioning her children's abilities, just imagining the company without her own abilities. And maybe, who knows, maybe it was even more than that. Father Larry said Lydia used the word *fix*, making things right—and it didn't make me think of bad management, but more about them as people. And perhaps Amber, too."

Nell began eating again, thinking about what she had just said. Even to her, her words were confusing.

"Perhaps she was forcing Stu and Barbara to do what she couldn't do—bring Amber into the family," Birdie said. "Making sure the sins of the father—or the mother in this case—would finally be righted."

"Maybe," Nell said. The explanation was admirable. But somehow it didn't quite fit.

"My ma thinks Father Larry carries around the sins of the world. I told her I thought that was sort of his job. But she said it seems especially heavy-duty right now."

"Heavy sins?" Izzy wondered rhetorically.

"It can't be easy," Nell said, thinking back to the worry she'd seen in the priest's face. She had always wondered about the burden priests must carry from hearing confessions. But it seemed to bring solace and relief to people as they passed off their burdens to the listening ears of the priest. *Good for the soul,* as the saying goes. *Forgiveness.* Was Lydia somehow wanting forgiveness?

"So Lydia willed Amber not just a piece of the company, but a piece of her family, in a way—" Birdie said.

"That was presumptuous," Izzy said. "She barely knew Amber."

"But Amber seemed to accept it," Birdie said. "She spent time looking into the business, from what Charlie says."

"Amber did exactly what I'd do if I inherited a business," Cass said. "She went to the office, looked through the records, and gathered up whatever information she could about the company. That makes sense to me. It's the only way she could make an informed decision on what to do about it. If I died and left my part of the Halloran Lobster Company to Pete—who has never in his life looked at a ledger—that's exactly what he'd have to do." The thought made her wince. "I'm sure Amber was much better at it."

"So maybe that's what she was doing," Birdie said. "But we're no closer to the murderer. Could she have found something odd, something about the company that they wouldn't want her to know? Or maybe being in the office, talking to people who worked there, she heard something?"

"I don't think Father Larry's message had much to do with the actual inheritance, although I can't be sure. But remember, he was Lydia's confessor. He was working very hard to say only what he thought he could. I think that's why it doesn't completely make sense to us," Nell said. "We need to fill in some blanks."

"One scenario," Cass said, leaning forward and using her finger to draw an imaginary picture on the low table. "Lydia knew Amber would get into the business end of things. She knew how smart she was. Maybe the business was screwed up. Maybe Garrett isn't as smart as everyone thinks he is. Or Stu or Barbara, for that matter."

"But Ben says the company is doing well," Nell said. "We're kind of going in circles. What would need to be fixed?"

"Companies can appear healthy to outsiders, even when there

might be something going on inside," Cass said. "There're all sorts of things that can be done to make you look good. Creative accounting, among other things."

The thought sobered them, and they set it out there. An internal indiscretion? Something Amber spotted?

"If the company was having problems, having Amber inherit part of it was probably the last thing Barbara or Stu wanted—no matter what their mother thought," Cass said.

"Zack Levin—Janie's brother—is an intern over there. He said Amber was going through lots of things, comparing reports, tax forms, checking ledgers, payrolls," Nell said. "It made sense, since she was a part owner."

Cass got up to refill her bowl. "Maybe she discovered the staff wasn't being paid enough. And Amber might have wanted to change that—somehow that seems like something she might want to do. But it would affect the company's bottom line."

"That does sound like something she might do," Nell agreed.

"Dessert," Izzy said, stopping the flow briefly. She had baked chocolate chip cookies that day, huge and chunky, a skill she was diligently perfecting now that she had a sweet toddler to impress. She cleared away the soup bowls and set a plate of the cookies on the coffee table, and without a word, knitting baskets and bags were magically unearthed. In minutes half-finished yarn ornaments—snowmen, lobsters, sailboats, and fish—were lined up on the table alongside skeins of soft merino wool in all the joyful colors of the season.

"Have the police talked to Andy Risso?" Birdie asked. She was attaching a yarn hook on her completed whale, smiling at her handiwork before adding it to the basket of finished ornaments.

Cass nodded. "According to Pete, the police talked to all of them—him, Merry, Andy. Amber had hung around the gazebo that night, listening to the Fractured Fish play. She'd been nice, Pete said, though not very talkative. They told the police that she was alone at the time and seemed to be worried or sad or something. But she had liked the music. Andy said she helped him carry some equipment to the dolly."

"So, that was it?" Izzy asked.

"They saw Andy hug her. But he hugs everyone, Pete said. Not a big deal."

That was true, Nell thought. Andy was a hugger; there was nothing unusual in that. But the embrace Nell had witnessed when he and Amber stood near the drum cases seemed more familiar than Andy's usual greeting. Certainly more emotional.

Nell pushed aside the image and concentrated on casting off the last row on her boat's sails. The tight stockinette stitches were perfect, and the sailboat would be stiff enough when she was finished to hang proudly from the tree.

"Charlie said he didn't see Amber again that night, not after he stormed off, grabbed some beers from a stranger's cooler, and almost ruined his hand." Izzy's tone held a rebuke and sympathy at the same time—a sisterly response.

"She seemed to have been swallowed up in the crowd," Birdie said. "When we left, it was bigger than when we came. That tent was bursting, people warming themselves beneath the heat lamps and spilling out onto the paths through the trees."

"Were the Cummingses still there?" Izzy asked.

"I'm sure they were," Nell said. "Since this was their idea, Stu and Alphonso felt a responsibility to hang around."

"Amber told me she had to talk to someone that night," Birdie said. "She was looking at her watch when she said it, as if it had been planned." She replayed the event in her head. "She was upset. She talked about bad things happening. She seemed pressed to do something about it and thought that talking it over with someone might help. I suppose what she said would fit with what we've talked about tonight—with messy books and a company that might have problems—but somehow . . ." She shook her head, trying to feel the emotion she'd felt that night. The distress on Amber's face. "Somehow I don't think it was about her inheritance."

"Then what?" Izzy pulled a skein of pure red wool yarn from her bag. A perfect hat for her snowman. With barely a glance down she began looping the yarn onto her needles, pulling it in place. And then the next and the next.

Nell watched her. Loop after loop. That was what they were doing. Were the loops too loose? Maybe all of them, including the police, were walking down the wrong road. She tuned back in to the conversation and wasn't at all surprised when Birdie answered Izzy's question by mirroring her own thoughts.

"If not the inheritance, then what? I'm not sure, but somehow I don't think Amber was anguished about the nurseries that night. Intuition, maybe, but we were going to meet the next day—and I certainly know nothing about Cummings Nurseries."

"Birdie is doing exactly what we need to do," Izzy said, picking up on the thread. "We're not thinking outside the box—it's all been about her inheritance, who it affected, and why. That's logical, sure, and a place to start. But maybe we're not seeing things right in front of us. What else did Amber do that week?"

"She went to the cemetery to see her mother's grave. But what else? Where was she when she wasn't at the office?" Cass asked.

"She could have gone back to the grave site," Birdie said slowly, her mind replaying the conversation she'd had with Amber the night she died. "She talked about her mother. Ellie was on her mind, and in a ponderous way, I thought. A troublesome way."

"Maybe she was coming to grips with her mother's dying and not being able to be here before she died. Maybe she was putting together the pieces of her mom's life, the things she had missed out on—the things her mother had missed out on—and wanted the picture complete before she left."

But the truth was, none of them had any idea what it was like to be Amber, a grown daughter of a mother she had never known in an ordinary sense. The woman who had given her life but, except for a few early weeks, had never been able to hold her, to take her to a park or bandage scraped knees. To express her love.

But maybe, when they had followed her footsteps to find her murderer, they would discover some pieces of that life as well.

Chapter 26

"Cass said she could get away from the office for a couple hours and she insisted on going along with us," Birdie said. She stepped out of her furry boots and followed Nell into the kitchen. "I told her we'd pick her up at her office."

Nell handed Birdie a mug of coffee. "Cass acts tough, but she can't erase what she and Danny saw that morning. I'm glad she's coming with us."

Birdie looked at an arrangement of holiday greens on the island. "That's a lovely display, Nell."

"A sweet girl at Cummings Nursery put it together for me. It'll be fine outdoors, she said. The place looked festive and humming with business when I picked it up. I think Stu's complaints over the police questioning his employees were a bit overblown."

"The master doth protest too much?"

"Maybe. Although I don't know how his pestering the police would help anything." Nell poured a generous stream of half-and-half into her coffee. "Do you?"

"No. But it could be that Stu is like any business owner and truly wants people out of his hair—what little he has left—so he can get on with growing his empire."

Birdie sipped her coffee and looked out the window. It was another cold December day, but sunny, without a cloud in sight. The early snow had all but disappeared, and from the warmth of Nell's kitchen, one could almost imagine it was a spring day instead of a few weeks before Christmas.

"What's wrong, Birdie?"

"I sat in Sonny's den for a longtime last night, wrapped in a blanket, cozy and warm and looking at the moon—and thinking about the whole Cummings clan, including Amber, Lydia, Ellie. It's like a Shakespearean play. So many relationships to sort out. Even Garrett O'Neal—an outside who's an insider."

And Charlie, Nell thought. An outsider, too. But certainly a part of the drama. An outsider who was an insider.

"I went over everything we had bandied about in the yarn shop—imagining each piece of the puzzle as pieces of yarn. Trying to figure out how one works with the other, and how they make a whole."

"And?"

"And I got a giant headache, drank a glass of warm milk, and went to bed. But before I did, I felt confident that we have almost everything we need. Almost. There is something that Amber said to me the night she died that is trying to make itself heard, but when I focus on it, it slides away, just beyond my reach. But we'll reach what we need eventually. And then we'll untangle the mess."

"Are you saying that you think the murderer is in that pile of yarn, in that web of relationships?"

"Or on the periphery where we might not see him yet. But connected. Yes."

They put the arrangement of greens in the trunk and picked up Cass at her office near Canary Cove. Halloran Lobster Company was housed in a low modern building right on the harbor waters. Cass had built it on land she'd inherited from an old fisherman.

Driving into the parking lot, Nell reflected on the irony of it. Cass and Amber had both come into inheritances. Cass had used hers to expand her company, to build a much-needed office, and had given some of the land to the town to build a children's park and memorial garden. Nell wondered what Amber would have done with hers. Sold it and used the money to benefit herself and others? Gone to school? Or stayed in Sea Harbor and become a part of the Cummings empire? Nell tossed out the last possibility almost before it entered her mind.

Cass came out and climbed into the backseat, chewing on a bagel. "We're starting to walk the road. That's what Danny calls it in his mysteries. Following Amber."

Birdie nodded. "She's the one with the answers, Catherine."

Nell drove to the edge of town and up the winding road she had traveled just a few days before, the road Amber had traveled. The road to Ocean View. The familiar trademarks were there, the trees lining the road and a couple of miles later, the tall iron fence and the carved OCEAN VIEW sign that indicated they were close. She drove past the guardhouse and along the tall security fence surrounding the campus to the cemetery at the top of the hill. The wooded area was crisscrossed with winding pathways, memorial benches, and narrow road signs that allowed visitors to find the memorials, to be alone in secluded spots.

Birdie spotted the hawthorn tree and Nell pulled over to the side of the narrow road, turning off the engine. In the distance they spotted several joggers, a bicyclist here and there, and heard the sound of a motorcycle.

They sat in quiet for a few minutes, looking out at the evergreens, the tended pathways. The carefully manicured hedges with their tops trimmed off even as winter was making itself known.

Nell looked over at Birdie. She had shifted in the car seat and was looking back the way they came, toward the Ocean View campus, just visible through the trees. "What do you see?" she asked.

"Something Amber and I had talked about that night at the harbor party. I'd almost forgotten about it—it hadn't been important at the time—but seeing Ocean View today brought it back."

Cass leaned forward with her elbows on the back of the seat so she could hear.

"Amber asked me about a plaque in the main lobby of the nursing home. She wondered about the inclusion of the Favazza family name on it. I explained the family connection, then congratulated her on her excellent memory. What child remembers names on a plaque she saw years ago?"

"I suppose it's unusual but not impossible," Nell said. "Amber left Sea Harbor when she was, what? Sixteen or seventeen?"

"Yes. She was just a teenager."

Nell and Cass listened.

"I suppose an observant visitor to the lobby might remember the frame or plaque itself, probably not the names on it unless it was your own family or friend. But here is where it falls apart. The plaque Amber described—the ornate, showy piece—was put up at the sixtieth-anniversary celebration of Ocean View, the year they remodeled the lobby. I was there. I remember. And that was seven years ago."

There was quiet in the car.

"There was an old framed list years ago," Birdie went on, "but it was stuck in a hallway somewhere where no one would notice it. Amber described the glitzy, gold-edged one that hangs in the lobby now."

"So Amber was there. Priscilla Stangel wasn't seeing a ghost," Nell said softly.

Birdie nodded. Then she turned and explained to Cass what Esther had told them. "We all thought Priscilla was mistaken. She's older than sin and can't see well."

Cass glanced back to the edge of the Ocean View property. "But how could Amber have gotten in? That fence would be almost impossible to scale."

"And why would she want to go inside?" Nell added. But she'd no sooner asked the question than she thought she knew the answer.

"Maybe visiting the place where her mother died would bring some comfort to her, since she wasn't here when Ellie died."

"Yes, I guess that makes sense. Except Priscilla left a later message saying something about Amber bothering the staff, asking questions, and keeping them from their work. She suggested Esther keep her from returning," Birdie said. "But she somehow managed to get in—and I'm not sure how that happened—I can't imagine people there not being courteous to her. The Cummingses spent a fortune on her mother's care—and it's really a lovely place, if a little extravagant for my taste."

"If she went back a couple times, maybe she was wearing out a welcome," Cass said. "But we still don't know how she got in."

They mulled that over, the questions of "why" and "how" hanging heavy over any reasonable answer.

"If she had mentioned to Esther that she wanted to visit Ocean View, she probably could have arranged it," Nell said. "I wonder why she didn't."

Their breath was slowly fogging up the windows of the car, reminding them of why they were there, and Cass suggested they continue the discussion later. She hopped out of the car and took Nell's evergreen arrangement from the trunk, and they made their way over to the small monument.

Esther's stone planter was there, but the squirrels had done serious damage to the arrangement she had planted some weeks before. Nell pulled a plastic bag out of her purse and they gathered up the remains. Cass lifted up the holiday arrangement from the Cummings Nursery and set it inside the vase, tucking some chunks of nearly frozen soil around the sides.

They were so intent on their job, the roar of the motorcycle coming around the path from the other side of the cemetery was a dull sound in the background, blending in with the squeal of gulls and winter wind whistling through the pines.

It was the voice that startled them to attention: "Who would ever have imagined that you three wonderful ladies liked to play in dirt?" he asked.

Cass spun around, dropping several of the silver bells she was attaching to the evergreens. "Jeez, Andy," she said. "What the h—"

"Andy, what a nice surprise," Nell said.

"Well, my goodness. What are you doing here, Andy Risso?" Birdie asked. "And why in heaven's name are you carrying a helmet?"

Andy looked down at it, then feigned a stern reply. "It's the law, Ms. Favazza. Don't you get any ideas of riding your bike without one."

Birdie laughed and looked behind him to a Harley parked near the side of the road, just behind Nell's CRV. "I'd forgotten you ride one of those. I asked Sonny to buy me one, once. It was the only request he ever denied me."

Andy loved it. "Come next spring I'm taking you out on it. Be ready."

"Do you ride up here often?" Nell asked.

"Oh, sure. My mother's buried right over there—" He pointed through the trees. "I like coming over and visiting her. Sometimes it's just me and her here. It's nice. We talk—"

Nell felt a startling wave of déjà vu as Andy grabbed a handful of blond hair and snapped a rubber band around it.

She looked toward Ocean View, then back to him. And then she felt several missing pieces land together with a heavy *ka-chunk*.

"You volunteer at Ocean View," she said, more to herself than to those standing around looking at her. Jake was so proud of his son, she'd heard it in his voice when he told her about it.

Andy picked up her words and looked at Nell, surprised. "Yeah. Long time now. They have a hospice floor and they were good to my mom when she was a patient. Pop and I spent a lot of time there back then. I saw how it mattered to patients when they had visitors. I even thought it mattered if they didn't know I was there." He looked over at the monument with Ellie Harper's name on it. "Like Ellie. The nurses would kid me about it, but sometimes I thought she knew I was there."

"You visited Ellie," Birdie said.

"Sure. Pop came with me sometimes. Sometimes I'd go in on my break when I was volunteering. Ellie was like a member of our family. She worked at the Gull. Then after the accident, Pop kind of adopted Amber. Lots of the shopkeepers knew her. She was a floater, sort of roamed the town more freely than most kids her age. And she'd end up in our place a lot. Sneaking in. She was kind of like a little sis."

They took her out in their boat, Esther had said. *They.* She meant Andy and his dad. Of course. She should have put those pieces together right away. Andy was like a big brother. Someone Amber knew and trusted and would hug tightly if she was worried or upset about something—exactly what she was doing the night she died.

Andy was still looking at the monument, and then his gaze shifted to the empty space next to it.

The three women had been so intent on sprucing up Ellie's grave that they hadn't noticed it before, but the area next to Ellie's had been marked off with chalk, outlining the dimensions of a casket. The hole that Amber's body would be lowered into.

Nell rubbed her arms. Beneath her down coat she felt a sudden chill that rivaled the cold around them. It traveled in all directions, circling around her.

Cass walked up and tucked an arm around her waist.

Andy glanced at them, then looked back at the monument at the top of Ellie's grave. "I'm glad Ellie didn't have to know the gruesome way her daughter died."

His jaw was set, his usually gentle eyes lit with anger. "It's an awful thing." He shook his head as if denying it would negate the horror of it.

"Amber visited her mother's grave last week," Nell said, watching his face. "We picked her up, gave her a ride home."

"I know. I saw you guys leave."

It was the answer Nell expected. And the explanation for how Amber was able to bypass Ocean View security. "I'm guessing you managed to get her inside Ocean View without a pass."

Andy stared down at his boots, a lopsided smile on his face. Then he said, "Sure I did. She had the right to come in and revisit this place. It was her mother's home all those years. All the life she had with Ellie—at least what she could remember—was at Ocean View. So I got her a pass the first time. I just explained to the director that she needed some closure. He's kind of a hard-ass, but he said okay."

"The first time?"

Andy nodded. "It was soon after she arrived, a Sunday, I think. She had come into the bar the night before, that night she arrived in Sea Harbor. Nasty night. I came in late after our gig at the community center to help Pop close up, and there she was, as if she never left. Cold and wet and skinny. She told Pop and me what brought her back, how ambivalent she was about the whole Cummings will. What she really wanted, she said, was a look at the place where her mother died. She wasn't even sure why, but could I call someone over there and get her in? She knew going over there might be upsetting, but she thought she should do it, that it'd be a good thing in the end. I agreed with her. I was going to be out there the next day anyway, so I called and arranged it."

"That was the day she missed the meeting with the lawyer."

"Yes. She didn't mean to, but once she found the suite her mother lived in, she couldn't get herself to leave. It upset some staff, I think. They didn't quite understand.

"And then, a couple days after the will was read, she wanted to go back again. She was more insistent that time. She wouldn't tell me why, but she said it was very important and she was so determined I figured if I didn't get her in, she'd try to scale the fence and end up in the hospital—or jail. She didn't want a tour guide. Just wanted to walk around. I could see how much it mattered to her, so

I snuck her in. Not anything I'm proud of, but it seemed so important to her and I figured it wouldn't hurt anything or anyone to go in a couple times. It was hard to say no to her, you know? I'd get her on the grounds, then go off and do my volunteer gig, leaving her to do whatever. I didn't see her once I dropped her off, so I didn't really know what she was up to. At first I thought she was still coming to grips with her mother's death."

"But it wasn't that?"

"Maybe it was in the beginning. But her intent seemed to change a couple days later. I'm not sure why. When I asked her, she said she had lots of questions about her mother's care here."

"What kind of questions?" Nell asked.

"She was vague. Her mother's care, medicine, her doctor, visitors. The cost of staying there and who paid for it."

"She must have known who paid for Ellie's care," Birdie said.

"She did. But she said it wasn't Lydia; it was the company itself. I'm not sure why that made any difference, but she seemed to need answers."

"She spent time in the Cummings business office," Nell said. "Maybe she saw some invoices or checks."

"I heard Garrett talking about what a pest she made of herself over there," Andy said with a short laugh. "No surprise. But it made sense. She wanted to know what she'd inherited. Maybe she wanted to know how 'her' company's money was spent."

"That's logical, but a little strange to obsess on a single expense like that," Cass said.

"Yeah. It wasn't just that, though. Her whole obsession with Ocean View was strange. And I don't think it had anything to do with seeing her mother's room and putting things to rest—she was so mad at the Cummingses. Rightfully so, but I tried to get her to let it go. What good did being mad do? Somehow she seemed to want to blame them. But I'm not even sure for what. They had spent a ton of money making sure Ellie had the best care."

"Do you have any idea what she did at Ocean View?" asked Cass.

"I heard from several staff members that she was asking questions. Bothering the nurses about what it was like when her mom died, was she in pain, how long did it take—questions that made the staff understandably uncomfortable. It had been three years since Ellie died and there's always turnover in those places, so some of them didn't know what she was talking about or who Ellie Harper was.

"But some did, and at first they tried to be nice. Then the last time she went—it was that Saturday, the day she died. I had a shift that day, so I drove her over with me, but I had to leave early because we were rehearsing for the harbor gig that night. When it was time to leave, I couldn't find her. So I left. Later I heard that someone found her trying to find some files or something and told the director. He had security show her the door, literally, and threatened to call the police if she ever returned."

"What do you think she was looking for?" Birdie asked, trying to conjure up the look on Amber's face that night. It was sad and angry and determined. A mixture of disparate emotions that didn't reside comfortably on the young woman's face.

Andy shook his head. "I don't know. But when I saw her at the harbor party later that same night, she was clearly upset and very angry. She started crying when she saw me—something Amber didn't do easily. She said it was wrong, all wrong."

Nell frowned. "Wrong?"

"I don't know what she meant. Something was tearing her apart in a way that being thrown out of a nursing home wouldn't have done. I think whatever it was she was looking for at Ocean View—she thought she might have found it."

Chapter 27

Ben found the Ocean View story interesting and troubling. "I wish she had felt more confident with us so she could have asked us to help," he said.

"I suppose when you are on your own at such a young age, you are less likely to depend on others." Nell stood at a cutting board chopping onions, her eyes watering.

"True enough. From what Andy said, it sounds like Amber thought there was a connection between Northshore Nurseries and Ocean View, something other than the fact that Lydia paid the bills."

"I don't know. At the least the bills led her over there. And being there disturbed her."

"Hospital—medical places—can be off-putting, I suppose, especially if your mother died there."

"On a slightly different note, you were right about something," Ben said. "I did as you asked—got the name and number and put in a call to Amber's lawyer friend in Florida. Stu hadn't let any grass grow under his feet. He tracked the guy down the day Rachel told him Amber was in his mother's will. He knew from day one that his niece didn't have her own will. He knew before Rachel did."

"Which means he knew without Amber around there'd be no fuss about the nurseries, no threat to the company."

Ben nodded. "It's strange that he pretended otherwise—that's not like Stu. But it served a purpose, I guess. He avoided casting suspicion on himself."

"But it's out there now. The suspicion, I mean. Unless Helen is a top-notch actress, which I doubt, she didn't know about it. But Stu did, and he probably told Barbara." Nell tossed the onions into a frying pan and wiped her eyes with a tissue. "Will you pass that information along to Jerry Thompson?"

"I'll mention it, although Jerry is going to wonder why we're digging into this."

Ben had given in begrudgingly to Nell's request to find the Florida lawyer. *"Let the police do their job,"* he'd insisted when she asked. But he'd obliged, just as Nell knew he would, and she also knew why: it kept her from doing it herself and being more closely involved in a murder investigation than she had any right to be.

"I've been thinking about Stu a lot," she said. "Even if he had done his own investigating, you were right about the more important fact. I don't think it matters if Stu knew she had a will or not."

"You didn't feel that way last night."

"No, I guess I didn't. Or maybe I thought it was a loose thread that needed to be tied off no matter what significance it had, just so we would know. But I don't think Stu Cummings would kill anyone, especially not over something his mother had decided to do. It would be an act of defiance, and I don't think he would do that. Father Northcutt told me once he was truly devoted to his mother. He didn't go against her wishes."

"I agree," Ben said, repeating what he had said the night before. "Stu may not have liked what his mother did, and he may even be relieved now that he doesn't have to deal with Amber being a part of the company, but he wouldn't have killed her for it."

Nell added chunks of red and orange peppers and asparagus to the bowl and mixed in a stream of olive oil. She turned as she stirred and said with a slight smile, "Thank you for not saying 'I told you so.' But there's another, more practical reason he couldn't have killed Amber."

"And what's that?" Ben's eyebrows lifted as he took the olives from the refrigerator.

"Stu was too visible at the harbor party that night. He spent the whole evening meeting and greeting and making people feel comfortable. Making announcements. It was his party, in a way—he was the host. And remember what he had on? That fire-engine red down jacket. He looked like Santa himself, minus the beard. It would have been next to impossible for him to have slipped into the wooded area without being noticed."

Ben listened, holding back a smile. Using Stu's girth and attire as an alibi might not hold up in court, but it was a convincing argument.

He started taking martini glasses from the cupboard and lining them up next to the shaker. "So we agree that Stu probably didn't kill Amber. But I think you have more reasons for changing your mind than you're letting on, Nell. I think it's more than puffy red jackets." He looked across the island, his eyes locking in to hers. *Tell me,* his eyes said.

But Nell looked away. There was more. Things that seemed far removed from Stu Cummings. She hadn't had enough time to sort through her thoughts about their visit to the cemetery and talk with Andy Risso. They were still frayed, like a poorly knit sweater, filled with images of Amber wandering the halls of Ocean View, trying to find the mother who had died without her.

Her thoughts were muddy, too muddy to share with Ben just yet. He'd try to clean them up with practical surmises, things that she didn't want to hear right now.

She, Birdie, and Cass had talked nonstop on their way home from the cemetery. And then they'd sat in Birdie's den for another hour, sipping herbal tea and eating Ella's chicken wraps, replaying Andy's words, sorting through images, trying to find reasons for Amber's actions. They were following her, and she'd taken them to a nursing home.

Why?

As the last crumbs of their sandwiches had disappeared and their tea had gone cold, the decision was made. If they were truly going to follow Amber's footsteps, they'd have to get across that fence themselves—and they sincerely hoped it wouldn't cost Andy Risso his volunteer job to get them there.

"Nell?" Ben said, bringing her back to the kitchen and the fragrant odors coming from the stove.

"Sorry." She smiled, changing the subject. "Do you know if Charlie's coming tonight?"

"I think so. I saw him around noon. He said he had a midday shift at the clinic but would come over afterwards. He dropped off a portfolio with some papers in it and a few books of Amber's he said you wanted. He was about to toss the papers in the trash when he remembered. They're in the den."

"I must have brain overload, I guess. I completely forgot about those papers. I'll look at them later. Thanks. The papers, but also the box that Esther had given Amber. She kept meaning to ask Charlie about it, but the thought usually came when she was in the shower or some other inopportune time. If Amber had thrown it away, she might have mentioned it to Charlie."

"I checked the book titles," Ben said. "They were interesting."

"Oh? Archie said they were mostly business, financial manuals. That doesn't sound interesting at all, at least to me." She smiled, her ongoing feud with math a running joke.

"Yes, there were a couple of business-related books—running a business, financial statements. Not exactly bedside reading. Seeing them made me wonder if Amber was actually thinking about running the Sea Harbor nursery that she'd inherited. And thinking about that reminded me . . ." Ben's voice grew husky, and he frowned at his own emotion, but went on. "It reminded me that Amber had just finished business school. She was smart, healthy, vital. A whole life ahead of her. And then in an instant, her dreams and ambitions, her chance for loving someone, for giving life, for experiencing getting older and wiser—all of that was cut off because someone decided to end her life. Just like that. Robbed her of a future. In one cruel moment."

Nell looked over at the anger and sadness that mixed together in her husband's pained face.

And her heart swelled with all the things she loved about him.

She hid her own emotion in the heat of the oven, checking the pork tenderloin, sprinkling wine into the pan. She spread the vegetables out on a cookie tin and slid it onto the bottom rack beneath the tenderloin, then closed the door.

Ben had busied himself mixing a small batch of martinis, the icy silver shaker held tightly in his hands as he brought his feelings under control. "These are for you and me, babe," he said, smiling at his wife as he poured the mixture into two chilled glasses.

Nell moved to his side, took her glass, and touched its rim to Ben's. Their eyes met in a toast that didn't need a single word.

"Okay, then," Nell said, setting her glass down and moving away from the shared emotion before the others arrived. "Back to the book. Archie said there was one that had nothing to do with financial gobbledygook. What is that one about?"

Ben thought for a moment, one ear tuned to a car pulling into the drive. "It was a medical text or manual. Mayo's maybe? Amber didn't mention health problems, did she?"

Nell's surprised response was shattered by the sound of heavy boots, light ones, and the tip-tapping of Red's nails on the hardwood floor. She wiped her hands on a towel and hurried across the room to capture Abby in a hug. Recently little words were coming out of her perfect heart-shaped mouth, and Nell knew without question Abby was telling her grand-aunt how much she loved her. Danny, Cass, and Birdie came in before the first set of gloves and coats were piled in the den, and the Brewsters arrived shortly after.

Cheese and crackers, stuffed mushrooms, and a basket of rolls filled the island while Sam and Ham Brewster headed toward the fireplace to pile on a few more logs in the hearth.

Cass had her iPod out, searching for the new Sam Smith album, hurrying to get it in place before Danny had a chance to plug in his old eighties favorites.

Jane Brewster handed Nell the salad she had made, and Nell gave her oldest friend a hug. "I needed that, and you need one, too," Jane said, her full head of streaked gray hair swirling freely around her face as she looped one arm around Nell and drew her over to the sink.

"How is Charlie doing?" she asked.

"He'll be as happy as all of us when this nightmare ends. I suppose that's how he is."

"Lily Virgilio came into the gallery today. I don't think she's going to let Charlie leave. She said he's absolutely amazing with the kids—they completely forget they're in a doctor's office when he starts with his magic tricks and crazy songs. He's a wonderful help to her and Janie Levin—Lily actually looks more rested since he arrived. Working her own practice and the clinic was a load."

Nell smiled.

"But after singing Charlie's praises today, Lily looked concerned. At first she was hesitant to say anything, but she knew I'd see you tonight, so she talked to me."

Nell's heart immediately skipped a beat. "She was concerned?"

"Charlie had a three o'clock shift this afternoon, and he didn't show up for it. Lily wasn't worried about the shift—it was easily covered. But it was so unlike Charlie that she was concerned. Something important must have happened to keep him from the clinic, she said. And she just wanted to be sure he was okay."

Nell looked out the window. The guesthouse was dark.

Across the room, Ben was mixing martinis and listening to Danny and Cass, his face full of laughter.

He had said Charlie was coming after his shift.

But he didn't show up for his shift.

"Hey, sweetie," Jane said, tilting her head as she peered into Nell's face. "I didn't mean to worry you. Charlie's a big boy. And responsible. I'm sure he's fine." She handed Nell a hot pad. "Check your pork tenderloin. It smells ready. I'll toss the salad."

Nell walked to the stove and pulled out the roast, her mind going over possibilities. But none came readily to mind.

Izzy walked over with a sleepy Abby on her hip. "Aunt Nell, Abby tells me she wants her favorite great-aunt to read *Goodnight Moon* to her." She rubbed her nose into Abby's soft curls. Abby's eyelids drooped.

Nell's worry washed away momentarily as she lifted the sweet baby from Izzy's arms and cuddled her close. Abby nuzzled down, one tiny fist rubbing against her curls.

Izzy looked at Jane, who had taken over at the stove. "What's up, Jane? I could see Aunt Nell was stressing about something, not her usual way on Friday nights."

Jane smiled. "You're a wise and perceptive niece. Abby and *Goodnight Moon* will hopefully take care of some of that." Jane pulled out the tray of vegetables and turned the oven off. She turned to Izzy. "Did you happen to notice if your brother's car is in the driveway? I didn't look when we came in."

"No, it's not there. Sam talked to Charlie earlier today. He is coming here after work."

Jane hesitated for a second, then said, "Something must have come up, because Charlie didn't make it to the free clinic today."

Izzy's eyes widened. She looked across the room, spotted Sam, and waved him over. "Where's Charlie?" she asked him, her voice carrying a slight edge.

"Am I your brother's keeper?" Sam asked, attempting to lighten the tone.

The look on Izzy's face erased his smile. "I told you earlier—he's at the clinic. But he's coming here later." As he talked he checked his watch, then his cell phone for messages. He looked at Izzy and Jane. "What's going on?"

"Sometimes I think you know Charlie better than I do, Sam," Izzy said. "He didn't show up for his shift. Would he miss a shift at the clinic?"

"Maybe, if there was a reason."

"But he'd have called Lily or Janie to let them know, right? And where would he go? What would keep him from work?"

Nell walked back into the kitchen, her face noticeably more relaxed after just a few minutes of Abby's tonic. "Any word from Charlie?"

Izzy shook her head.

Sam was already tapping numbers into his phone.

They waited. Sam's brief voice message suggested Charlie give him a call as soon as he got the message. "No worries, just wondering if you're coming over for your aunt's amazing dinner. You miss one, you might never get invited back," he joked.

Izzy was typing in a phone message before Sam finished, her words more terse: *Charlie, call me.*

"He could have forgotten about the shift. He's had a lot on his mind these days," Sam said. "We all forget things."

Nell half listened to the excuses. She began taking out the rolls, whisking together a citrusy orange sauce for the meat while Jane helped, slicing the tenderloin into juicy slices.

Charlie was fine.

When Ben came over to her side, he reinforced her thoughts. "Don't worry, Nellie. Everything is being blown out of proportion these days." He put one arm around her shoulders. "We see evil and suspicious faces all over the place. We wouldn't be thinking twice about Charlie taking some time for himself under ordinary circumstances."

Nell leaned slightly into his side and said, "Dinner's ready. Uncork the wine and call the troops."

Ben was right, she thought. None of this would be a concern, not if less than two short weeks ago Amber Harper hadn't walked into their lives. And then—been murdered.

But she had.

And sometimes worry was real.

Chapter 28

Charlie didn't call, but he finally answered Izzy's text.

It was after Cass and Danny had taken Birdie home—the weariness of the week weighing on all of them. The Brewsters had called it an early night, too.

Finally it was just the sound of the humming dishwasher. Sam and Ben were drinking a scotch in the den and Izzy was trying to decide whether to leave Abby at her aunt and uncle's for the night or to wake her and take her out in the cold.

But mostly she and Nell were stalling, hoping to hear a car drive into the driveway.

Finally the text came. *I'll be there soon,* it read.

In less than ten minutes, they heard the car drive up and a door slam.

Charlie walked in, kicking off his boots at the door. He greeted them as he walked across the family room, shrugging off his jacket, his attempt to appear normal in place. But he didn't look normal.

He looked like the lone survivor of a grueling boot camp, his hair matted down when he pulled off his hat, his cheeks raw from the cold. He was disheveled, weary, and looking as if he'd lost his best friend.

"Where've you been?" Izzy said, her eyebrows pulled together in a harsh scowl, her worry hidden beneath the scolding.

Ben and Sam had come out of the den at the sound of the door.

Ben poured his nephew an inch or two of scotch and put it in his icy hand. "You look like you need this. It'll warm you," he said.

Nell walked to the microwave to heat up a plate of leftovers. Izzy stood near the island, her arms wrapped around herself as if Charlie had brought a blast of cold into the kitchen—one unrelated to the weather outside.

Charlie straddled a stool and rested his arms on the island, leaning forward, but his eyes were on his sister and when he spoke, it was to her.

"I didn't mean to worry you."

"Well, you did." Izzy held his look. She repeated her question.

"I've been a couple of places. The last one being a walk around the shoreline for as far as I could go. Around boulders, up that hill on the point, along the sand. The back shore."

"In this cold?" Nell asked. "At night?" The shore was long and winding, rugged in places, and not a place for an evening stroll in December.

"No wonder your cheeks look like they're going to fall off," Izzy said. "And before your ridiculous ocean hike? Where were you then?"

"The police station," he said. He took a breath. "Tommy Porter called me and asked if I'd stop by the station today on my way to work. I suppose 'asked' is not entirely appropriate, but he's a nice guy. He asked."

"More questions?" Ben asked.

Charlie nodded. "They had come across a text message on Amber's phone that somehow had been misplaced. Actually she had deleted it—that's why they hadn't seen it earlier. But when they received the records from the phone company, they found it. It was a message from me."

"And?" Izzy picked up her coffee mug, cradling it in hands that had suddenly grown cold.

"It read 'I killed a man.'"

The silence in the room was deafening. Finally Sam spoke,

stepping in as if he were Charlie's older protector. *Don't touch him,* his body language said.

"Morgan College," Sam said.

Charlie nodded.

Sam clenched his jaw and shook his head. "You didn't kill anyone, Charlie." He looked at Izzy, then back to Charlie.

Charlie took a long swig of scotch, his eyes narrowing as it went down, stinging his throat.

"I finally get it," Sam said, his voice sad. "It's why you left. Dropped out of college. Dropped out of our lives. It was that damn football game."

It had happened at the end of his last summer before his senior year, at the small Colorado school where Charlie had gone to play football, not entirely to his mother or father's liking. But he was getting a free ride. And then there was the promise of skiing from November to April—Charlie was in heaven.

And he loved playing football; he was good at it. Even pickup games during late summer when they'd be getting ready for the fall, playing whenever they had the chance, everyone wanting to be first string when the real play began. Sometimes frat guys filled in to make the extra team. It usually worked well. There were always assistant coaches around—school rule—to keep the games instructive and safe.

Charlie looked over at Sam. "You were there that weekend, Sam. Remember how hot it was? But a little heat doesn't stop football players—not tough guys like us—and I was 'the man,' the one who took the ball carrier down, the one who saved games." He said the words facetiously, his dislike for "the man" clear. He looked around at the others. "Sam had stopped in at Morgan, just to check in on me and to say hi. He was doing a photo shoot in Aspen, but stayed around for some of the game."

"You're into detail, aren't you?" Sam said quietly, his memory of the day hazy and not completely in sync with Charlie's, but clear enough to know where Charlie was headed. "It wasn't your fault."

Charlie looked around as if anxious to get it over with, to explain his life away in two minutes. To lay it out on Nell's island, for better or worse, something he should have done years ago.

"We were crushing the other team that day—mostly frat guys—when one of them started calling our quarterback names, you can imagine the kind, maligning this really great guy simply because he marched to a different drummer than the frat guy did. He wouldn't stop. On and on, goading our guy, sexual slurs. I could feel my blood rising, my face getting hot, that awful boiling feeling I used to get when my temper was winning out over my mind. I knew the frat guy would be receiving the next pass, and I was ready for it. The ball went up, his arms went up to catch it, and I barreled into him with all I had, pummeled him to the ground. My teammates were ecstatic."

Nell looked at Sam. He hadn't taken his eyes off Charlie, as if his look might help him through it.

"Then everyone got quiet. I couldn't figure it out for a minute, then looked down. The guy didn't get up. He stayed right there on the ground, convulsing, his body flopping uncontrollably."

Nell stopped herself from going over to him. It wouldn't help him finish.

"An ambulance took him to the hospital. It wasn't until later that the coaches got the results. A separated vertebrae, they told us in the locker room. He was paralyzed.

"But after a few days, no one talked about it anymore. Not the coaches, not my teammates, not other students. It was like it never happened. I was supposed to forget about it. The season started, life went on. It was no one's fault, they said, a football injury. It's too bad, but it happens."

"They were right, Charlie. It was no one's fault," Sam said.

"You knew about this?" Izzy said, looking at her husband.

Without waiting for an answer, she turned to Charlie. "Did Mom and Dad know?"

"No. And don't give Sam that evil eye. He was headed to Aspen that day and had to leave before the game was over. Lots of times guys don't get up right away. Drama on the field. Sam went off to Aspen after the guy was taken off to the hospital, and the game actually went on. It wasn't until later that we knew the extent of it. And like I said, even the guy's family didn't blame anyone. No one." He swirled the amber liquid in his small glass until it became a small whirlpool. His voice dropped. "They left all the blaming to me."

Nell thought back to any hazy memories she might have of that time, of Charlie's time in Colorado. Her sister, Caroline, had called, upset when Charlie had dropped out of school without a word to anyone. He spent the rest of the year as a ski bum. Caroline and Craig thought he was just getting something out of his system. But then, it seemed, he dropped out of life. Moving around. Odd jobs here and there. Sending cards occasionally, e-mails. But missing family holidays, celebrations, Izzy and Sam's wedding. "We could have helped," Nell said softly, but Charlie chose not to hear.

"I got into some strong stuff, my own cure to forget it all. I was pretty useless for a while. Woke up every night sore and achy, like I had just played a football game. I'd stumble around, then fall back into bed, not feeling anything. Going home to Kansas City or seeing you, Iz—or Jack and you, Sam—it was beyond what I could do. I simply couldn't hack it. I had flunked out of the family, is how it felt. The youngest. The mess-up. I'd e-mail Mom that I was okay. Just out exploring the world. I even got a job on a freighter, made some good money, and bought myself the used BMW as if it would prove I was worth something." He laughed at his own foolishness. "But jobs never lasted long because I'd fall back into darkness and have to claw my way out, messing up along the way.

"It was a girl in Idaho, of all places, who finally forced me to do something. She worked in rehab at a small hospital and we hung out with some of the same people. One night she told me what I already knew—that I was a disgusting human being and of no use to the world. I should either kill myself or shape up, she said. Just like that. We were friends—and for some reason I actually thought about what she said. For a week or so. Frankly one of her choices was way more appealing than the other. I don't know for sure why I didn't go that route. But I didn't. I decided to pull myself together. Rehab, anger management. The whole shebang.

"Angel—that was my friend's name, if you can believe it—managed to get a good deal on the treatment. I had some money, that inheritance we got from Dad's aunt, Iz. And maybe Angel told them I was a charity case, who knows?"

Charlie's story had flooded the room, filling every corner and crevice, and while Nell heated Charlie's now-cold food, they played with their drinks and tried to arrange his story in their minds, following the journey that had taken him from them. And wishing at every turn he had turned to his family for help.

Nell set his plate back in front of him and he managed a bite before Izzy asked something they were all wondering.

"Nursing school," she said, the need to fill in the gaps overriding the emotion they were all feeling. "How did you end up there? Dad had you signed up for Harvard law when you were in preschool."

"Yeah, go figure," Charlie said.

Nell handed him a glass of water and he drank it gratefully. Then looked at his sister and finished his story.

"At the end of rehab the director plugged each of us into a supervised volunteer program. Mine was working on a playground—kind of like a counselor—with some tough young kids. They spent most of the time shooting baskets, playing hard and banging up knees, heads, bloodying noses, even a sprained ankle or two. I surprised myself by liking it as much as I did. It guess it doesn't take a shrink to figure it out—all that shame for the tackle, all the guilt. It made me feel, I don't know—useful, maybe? I liked fixing the kids up, tending to their cuts and sprains, keeping them calm, and making them laugh. While I was there, the supervisor told me about a nursing program in that godforsaken town. She said they actually needed students to keep their grant money, and she thought I'd be good at it." He stared down at his hands for a minute, then looked at Izzy. "And you know what, Iz? I was. I am."

Nell's emotions were bottled up so tightly in her chest that she found it difficult to breathe. As Charlie's journey unfolded in her kitchen, her sister's youngest child appeared in her memory—the playful one, charming teachers, carefree. His grades never as good as his older brother's and sister's because he didn't study much, but no one cared, because he was Charlie.

Izzy climbed onto the stool next to her brother. "But you didn't let us know, when we could have helped, or even when things were getting better. Why, Charlie? I want to shake you. Beat you up." *Hold you close.* Her eyes were damp.

He picked up his fork but held it still beside the plate, looking into Izzy's eyes. He swallowed hard, as if there were something stuck in his throat. A lump as big as his fist. "Because I wasn't sure I'd make it. I didn't know if I'd fall back into hell. I didn't want to take anyone with me—and I didn't want those who loved me and whom I loved to have to watch." He was holding himself together as best he could. But beneath the surface was a battered young man, ready to cave in upon himself.

His eyes begged his sister to understand.

Izzy looked at her younger brother, certainly no longer a baby brother. And she wrapped her arms around him, hugging him tight.

Chapter 29

Charlie was spent, his shoulders slumped, his body as weary as if he'd just run a marathon. But there was a lightness to him that Nell had not seen in the weeks he'd been living in her backyard.

"What did you tell the police?" Izzy asked. It was her lawyer's voice, crowding out the emotion.

"Not the whole made-for-TV movie I just told all of you. Amber had texted me really late one night right before she died. She was filled with thoughts of her mother, obsessed with the fact that she was alone in that bed at Ocean View. She was blaming herself, regretting she hadn't stayed here for her. She kept saying she could have protected her. She was tossing all sorts of crap on herself, and telling me I wouldn't understand, not with the charmed life I had."

"So you jarred her out of it by dropping a bomb." Ben said.

He nodded. "But it was real, too. For a long time I felt like I *had* killed him. I stole some years from him, for sure. His parents would never let me see him, so I didn't know until an old coach tracked me down for some silly reunion—it was just a year or two ago—and incidentally told me the guy went through a lot, but a couple dozen surgeries got him back on his feet. He was married with a couple kids."

"You explained this to Tommy Porter?"

"And Chief Thompson. But I could see through their eyes what a prosecutor would see."

An angry kid who grew up to be an angry man.

It was a perfect Saturday morning outing.

Ben and Sam, with Abby bundled up in a carrier on his back, were taking Charlie to the yacht club to introduce him to the *Dreamweaver,* their prized sailboat.

Nell could have questioned their good sense, since the sailboat was in storage, the sails were removed, and the warehouse the club provided was cold and drafty. But she knew exactly what these men in her life were doing—distracting Charlie from the ponderous weight he was carrying around. Weekends were long, and for Charlie, Saturdays would be especially painful for a long time.

She waited ten minutes after they left—just in case Ben forgot his phone or came back looking for a pair of gloves—before gathering up the papers and books in his den and heading out the door.

Izzy was in the drive, and together they headed over to Birdie's. Cass would meet them there.

Birdie had lit a fire in the fireplace and cleaned off the round oak table in Sonny's den. They settled around it, gratefully accepting hot glasses of tea from Ella.

"The Cummings business office, the cemetery, and the nursing home. The Gibsons' house, Charlie's car, and the Gull. Unless we've missed out on chunks of Amber's time, these are the places she went in her short week in Sea Harbor."

Birdie had pulled scraps of purple yarn from her tapestry bag and placed them like snakes in the center of the table. Colorful stitch markers defined the Gull, the rectory where the will was read, Ocean View, Harbor Park, and Cummings Northshore Nursery. Amber's journey.

"Amber found something or did something or saw something she shouldn't have along this purple route that made someone want to kill her."

"All we have to do is find it," Izzy said. "A breeze." She pulled back a thick hank of hair and fastened it with a band. "I'm ready."

Birdie and Cass had been filled in on Charlie's journey, at least the parts that mattered in a police investigation. Bits and pieces would be shared later, in the way close friends did.

"They have nothing concrete on Charlie," Cass said. "Phone calls and e-mails will verify his explanation. But no matter, Charlie needs to be off their radar completely."

"And someone needs to be taken off our streets and out of our lives," Izzy said, the emotion in her voice showing how personal the quest had become.

Beyond the mullioned windows of the den, the sky was a bright wash of color, as if a child had taken wide sweeps of watercolor to it. Waves of powdery purple and pink were vivid against the blue Saturday sky. "The yarn color of Amber's path matches the sky," Nell observed. "I think that's an omen, Birdie. A good one."

She reached down and picked up the portfolio containing the papers from Charlie's backseat. "May the good-omen fairy guide our way."

But could a collection of ketchup-smeared printouts lead them to a murderer? Perhaps not. Yet they were of interest to Amber—and that made them eminently interesting to them. And hopefully significant.

Nell pulled the printouts out of the folio and passed them around. Food and coffee stains blurred some words, some numbers, but not enough to make the sheets useless.

They smoothed them out on the table.

"Phew," Cass said. "These smell like greasy french fries."

"Charlie's car became Amber's office and their diner."

"This shows me more than anything that Charlie was falling in love with Amber Harper," Izzy said.

"That he let her mess up his car?"

"Yes. He was always fastidious about cars. And I know he loves that BMW. When he was sixteen my dad got him a new Subaru. Only Charlie, by the way. Jack and I shared a used *gold* Chevy Blazer. Charlie was so protective of his car that he never took the plastic coverings off the backseat."

Cass laughed. "You Kansans. Pete and I shared a clunky beat-up truck my dad hauled lobster traps in. And I mean we *shared* it—with a crew of fishermen."

Izzy smiled and turned back to the array of printouts in front of her. "Somehow I feel like Amber herself is asking us to straighten this mess out. She started it for us, but somebody has to finish it."

Nell's thoughts exactly. She put on her glasses and picked up a dog-eared sheet, then several others with the same head. They were year-end summaries. Amber had used a highlighter and Nell's eyes went to a bright yellow streak through a headline: SALARIES.

Charlie mentioned that Amber looked at payroll. Something she was going to address, was his surmise. Low-wage issues, maybe. But as Nell scanned the sheets she saw that the nursery staff—gardeners and landscapers—made very fair salaries, and the cashiers, too, all above minimum wage, all nicely compensated. One star for Barbara and Stu Cummings.

She ran her finger over the rows. Then spotted the Magic Marker at play again. This time highlighting the word *Bonuses.*

Again the managers of the various stores fared well, the owners, too. And then she stopped, surprised at a hefty bonus listed after a name close to the end of the list.

She leafed back to salaries and double-checked. No wonder Amber was concerned. As an owner, she might not have approved. But Barbara and Stu apparently had.

Nell pulled the sheet aside and passed it around the table. "Amber singled this out. I see why, except that bonuses are up to the company leadership, right?"

Birdie read it, and nodded with interest. "It's high. Nice for the person getting it. But maybe something Amber didn't like or think equitable."

Cass and Izzy looked at it, too, frowned, then placed it in their "pay attention to later" pile.

Minutes later Birdie assembled her handful of printouts and sat back in her chair, sipping her tea. "I wish my Sonny were here. He loved numbers. But the fact is, I don't. If there are hidden liabilities and incorrect asset valuations and all those other things Sonny used to talk about, I will never find them. I don't even know what they mean. I've always agreed with you, Nell—you and Fran Lebowitz. There is no algebra in real life."

Nell chuckled, happy that Birdie had brought it up. There were certainly more useful things she and Birdie could do. She looked over at Cass and Izzy, barely able to pull their eyes away from their numbers. "I'm sorry, you two; Birdie's right. You both run businesses. You need to be the ones to go through these. You even seem to be enjoying it, which is beyond my comprehension—but I admire it, I do."

Cass laughed. "You're mathophobes, both of you. Give me those." She grabbed their sheets and went back to the ones in front of her. "This is interesting. Cummings Nurseries are doing well. Amber should have been pleased about that. It makes me wonder what she was looking for. I do see some oddities in the accounting. Strange accounts that Amber highlighted. Things that maybe got her attention and she needed to check through more carefully. She had pulled old financial reports, too, not just the most recent ones."

"Any red flags?"

"Not sure." Cass looked at the scattering of papers. "But we still have a lot to go through. It's fun—a little like reading someone's diary."

"Each to his own," Birdie said primly.

"But, Birdie, before you fink out on us completely, I think you and I should go over some of these payments. You'd know the names of the companies even better than I do. Look for anything that seems out of line. Companies that wouldn't be offering services to a place that sold trees and plants, that sort of thing. Or maybe ones you've never heard of."

Nell looked at her and frowned. "Cass, what are you looking for here? We're following Amber, remember."

"True. But who knows what she found that she might not have been looking for? Things that made her think people were doing things they shouldn't be doing. Isn't that what she said? Bad things."

Birdie shoved her chair closer to Cass's and began looking down the line, making notations, at times her silvery eyebrows lifting in surprise.

While Birdie conscientiously worked through the printout, Izzy ran her finger down a row of numbers, her eyes moving from one column to another and back again. "There's always a chance for simple errors in these things," she said to anyone who might be listening. "But even though bonuses are always up to a company, big discrepancies get your attention. Like at those big Wall Street companies. I can see why Amber was intrigued with these."

Ella walked into the den carrying a tray, her interruption and the coffee, fruit, and warm cinnamon muffins a welcome break. They happily shoved back chairs and set papers aside. Ella poured coffee, warning them not to spill it on the rug, and retreated as quickly as she'd come.

Izzy picked up a muffin and nibbled on its edges, resisting eating the sugary top first. She glanced again at the top sheet on her pile and tapped it with one finger, leaving another grease spot. "There's an expense on this ledger that stunned me. It's not a red flag, but definitely startling." She lifted the paper up. "It's a year-end summary of expenses from a few years back. Amber highlighted a line on it." She passed it to Cass, then watched while her friend's eyes widened in surprise.

Nell took it from Cass, held it out for Birdie to see, and together they scanned the page. "Oh, my," Nell said, her tone matching Birdie's wide eyes.

"A year's 'residency' at Ocean View," Nell said, "is that what they call it—residency?" She looked at Birdie.

"Yes, it sounds better than 'nursing care.' I knew it was expensive to live in Ocean View's homes, but I had never seen the figure for long-term nursing home patients. This is quite amazing." Birdie held the paper up close and read the fine print. "Ellie had a suite—a very nice one apparently."

Cass was awed. "It better have been. You could buy a house with a full-time nurse for less than that. I can't get my arms around this kind of expense. Who can pay for things like this?"

"It seems Cummings Northshore Nurseries could. And did. For almost thirty years," Birdie said.

They were silent as they all did the math in their heads. No one was able to utter the final figure out loud. It was more than most of them would make in a lifetime, Cass whispered.

Most of Sea Harbor, Izzy said.

Nell looked at the sheet again and shook her head. "It's literally a fortune. The exorbitant price of guilt, in my mind, although Father Larry doesn't see it that way. He said Lydia was at peace with everything she'd done. She wanted nothing to do with Ellie—so she didn't visit. Not once, all those years. But she spent a fortune on her care. That made it all right, at least in her mind."

"Tit for tat," Cass said. "It's certainly a different way of looking at what people need. I suppose Barbara and Stu supported it. It relieved them of any responsibility for Ellie. Or did they visit her? Maybe they did, just to see where those large chunks of cash were going."

Nell looked at the summary sheet again. "The family business apparently could shoulder that expense, but imagine less able people?"

"Which is most of the world," Cass said. "It's bigger than most mortgages, for sure."

"I remember the relief when Ben and I paid off the mortgage on our Beacon Hill brownstone," Nell said. "We were young, and not having to pay that amount every month was huge for us. Ben broke out the champagne."

Izzy laughed. "Sam doesn't know it yet, but he's taking Abby and me to Spain the year we pay our mortgage off," she said. "For a month."

Cass looked up. "Think about it. Suddenly, the day Ellie Harper died, Cummings Northshore was no longer paying this enormous amount of money. It was enough to make a significant difference to the company's bottom line. I can't imagine they mourned Ellie's death any more than they did her daughter's."

They were silent, processing the somber, sad thought.

"I wonder if Amber had that same thought," Birdie said quietly.

"She had the same information we have," Cass said. "With one difference."

"Yes, an important one. She loved the woman whose death freed up that money," Nell said. She got up and carried the tray back to Ella's kitchen, her thoughts filled with the Cummingses' generous care of Ellie Harper—and all of its ramifications.

Cass looked up when she returned. "If we're walking in Amber's shoes, we need to think her thoughts—or what she might have been thinking. And I think this is an important one, at least to consider."

They all agreed. But the thoughts were muddled, tangled, and first they needed to get through the facts and figures at hand.

Birdie picked up one of the books found in Charlie's car.

"Are these the books that Amber bought at the bookstore?" she asked.

Nell nodded. "Ben put them in the car this morning and I haven't had a chance to look at them." She walked over to the den bar and poured a glass of water.

"Well, we don't want these—" Birdie pushed the two business books across the table to Izzy and Cass. "That leaves this."

Birdie turned the book over and looked at the cover. "Well, look at this."

Cass and Izzy looked up.

Nell walked back to the table and took the book from Birdie's hands. She slipped on her glasses and read aloud: *"The Permanent Vegetative State: Medical Facts, Ethical and Legal Dilemmas."*

"Her mother's condition," Cass said, more to herself than the others.

"We're getting to know Amber through what she left behind," Birdie said. "She was consistent in how she went about things. She wanted to examine her inheritance, understand it, explore the company's standing, its health, I guess you'd say. And now the same with her mother."

"Except the company was alive, and she had some control over it," Izzy said. "Her mother was dead."

And there was little she could do about that.

Nell opened the book. Some pages were dog-eared; others had pencil marks. There were a couple of loose pages printed from a computer, folded and tucked inside. She looked at one chapter heading that had a coffee spill in the center of the page. "Causes of Death in PVS Patients."

"Andy said her mother's death was very much on Amber's mind those last days," Cass said. "She must have been trying to understand it."

Unfolding a sheet printed from a Web site, Nell read, "Pathology of dying."

"I suppose this is what Andy was referring to," Birdie said. "Amber was going overboard, trying to understand something that didn't have an explanation. Maybe it's something each of us would have done, walking in those shoes."

Nell looked over at Izzy. "Didn't Charlie mention something like that, too?" The weight of Friday night's conversation was ponderous in Nell's mind, coming back in bits and pieces.

"Yes, something about wishing she'd been here to care for her?" Izzy said, unsure herself.

Nell didn't think that was exactly it. It would come back, most likely in the middle of the night.

"It was unusual that Ellie lived as long as she did," Birdie said. "Maybe that was on Amber's mind."

"Or maybe she was making up for not being here at the time, trying to get all the facts in place so she could put some closure to it," Izzy said.

Nell frowned. "I'm not sure. I think we may be missing some pieces." She looked over at the printouts filled with numbers and columns. "I'm not sure Amber was looking for closure." But what was she looking for in this tangle of numbers? Or in trips to a nursing home where her mother no longer lived?

Birdie looked at her yarn trail, still in the center of the table. "It's clear to me. We need to go on a road trip."

Chapter 30

It was Saturday, not a good time to be visiting offices. But Birdie thought it was worth a try. They'd had that good omen from the sky, after all.

The business office of the Northshore Nurseries was a nondescript brick building hidden behind the nursery's acres devoted to trees and bushes. The outdoor acreage was scanty in the winter months, but the young and hearty oaks, maples, and hawthorns still populated some of the fenced-off areas behind the nursery building itself, and another lot, bustling today with business, was filled with Christmas trees waiting to go to a good home.

Nell drove through the packed parking lot, slowing for people coming out of the nursery shop carrying poinsettias, garlands, and cellophane-wrapped mistletoe. She drove back along a drive that led her to a small parking lot in front of the brick building. A tasteful sign above the door indicated they were in the right place: CUMMINGS NORTHSHORE NURSERIES BUSINESS OFFICE, it read.

"As many times as I've been to this nursery, I never once walked into this building," Nell said, pulling into an empty space.

"That's good," Cass said. "It probably means you always paid your bills. I ordered some plants for our new office building once and somehow the bill got lost. Garrett O'Neal had someone calling us hourly until I sent someone over to pay it. He also charged us a sizable late fee. Conscientious fellow, that Garrett."

"I hope he's conscientious enough to be working on a Saturday and can give us some idea of what Amber was doing here," Birdie said. "Her printouts have left more questions than answers."

"To you, maybe. I think there's plenty there. And I think Amber saw it, too."

Izzy peered through the blinds and knocked lightly on the door. "I see a light."

A shuffle inside produced a friendly face peering through a slit in the door blind. Immediately the door opened.

"Hi, guys. Whatta you doing here?" Zack Levin grinned at the visitors.

"Well, Zack Levin," Birdie said, a smile filling her small face. "What a devoted intern you are, working on a Saturday."

"Hey, I'm hourly. I love extra hours. And they pay me more for Saturdays." He grinned again and ushered the four of them inside. "What brings you all here? You owe us money?" He laughed.

Nell smiled. "We were hoping to talk to Garrett O'Neal," she said. She looked around the outer room. It was filled with printers, faxes, computers, desks, and file cabinets. A receptionist's desk was near the door, a beautiful poinsettia plant beside it.

"Hey, sorry," Zack said. "Garrett's not here. But I am. How about I give you a tour?" His face lit up.

"Sure," Izzy said. "Let's go for it, Zack. The cook's tour."

"Cook's tour? Hey, we have a kitchen," he said. And he led them there first, showing them the small room equipped with shiny stainless steel appliances.

The rest of the rooms were equally as impressive, the whole building proving to be larger than its modest exterior. Several executive offices were tastefully decorated, and the conference room boasted a bar, an oval table big enough for the city council, and a wall filled with Canary Cove artists' works. Above the bar were dozens of wooden award plaques honoring the company.

"They have meetings here for all the managers—all the branches. Board meetings. We're the hub," Zack said proudly.

He pointed to two large office suites, one on either side of the conference room. "Those are the owners' suites," he said. "Pretty cool. Though Stu—he lets us call him that—isn't here a lot. He moves around, checks on the other nurseries, goes to meetings. His sister"—he nodded to the other suite—"is here most of the time. She's sort of the inside worker bee. He's the outside guy."

"Barbara," Nell said, more to herself than the young man standing next to her.

Zack nodded. "Yep, she's the boss around here. I was afraid of her when I first started working here—she has that big face and doesn't talk much, but she's okay. She plays fair and brings cookies sometimes. She lets us be, do our jobs. Trusts us. She's busy, managing all the different places. Works really hard when she's here. But locks her office door at five, and doesn't expect us to work late, either. I asked her about it once and she said, 'We all need our own lives. You, me, everyone.' She kind of smiled then, sort of mysteriously, and I imagined hers, a secret life. Cool."

Zack looked through the glass door of her office. "Some of us wonder what she does at night, but hey, you don't ask your boss that, right?"

"Probably a good decision, Zack," Cass agreed.

"Yeah, I thought so. But I did hear one of the maintenance guys laughing about it one night when I was working late."

"Laughing about what?" Cass said.

"Running into Barbara one night. He says she's not the homebody we all imagine her to be. Who knew? But I'm glad—she needs to have fun, too." He turned and walked toward another office on the other side of the kitchen.

"And that's Garrett's place." Zack pointed to the smaller office. "He's a different breed. Seems calm, but a little hyper about his domain. He's here a lot. Comes in at night. Kind of freaks out if people mess with his files. And he'll do anything for his boss. He never calls her boss, though. It's like he wants us to see them as a couple."

"Oh?" Izzy said.

Zack blushed. "Yeah. He's devoted to Ms. Cummings. And she goes along with it, which is what none of us can understand. But hey, maybe she sees something there that we don't. And he's happy, so what the heck, right? And he's a smart dude for sure. He knows the company books inside out."

Nell thought about the tangled relationships that existed everywhere once you scratched. She looked back toward the kitchen, imagining the staff's break sessions. How interesting it would be to be a fly on the wall.

"So, where's your office, Zack?" Cass asked.

"You making fun of me, Cass?" he asked, playfully poking her arm, a leftover familiarity from the summer he'd spent helping her and Pete repair lobster traps. "But actually I do have one—well, not really. It's the computer room where we keep the server and other equipment." He pointed to a corner room, then started walking toward it, waving for them to follow. They dutifully did, then stood at the door, smiling at a wall of humming machines.

"Posh, Zack," Cass said.

Zack laughed, and walked them back to a small, nicely appointed waiting area, separated from the rest of the main room with plants. "Too bad Garrett's not here—but hey, maybe it's something I could help with? I've been here awhile. I sort of know my way around."

Birdie hesitated, then said, "We were hoping to talk to him about Amber Harper."

"Amber," Zack said slowly. He rubbed his chin where a slight shadow of a beard was trying to grow.

"We thought maybe Garrett would have some idea of what she was looking for here. We talked to him once about it, but sometimes things come back to you later, after you've had time to think about it."

Zack was quiet, listening. Then he looked around as if Garrett—or Amber herself—might suddenly appear. "Garrett didn't like her messing with things, but what could he do? The police didn't ask much about what she was doing here. They figured like most people here did, that Amber was here to find out what she'd inherited. It was only Garrett who had a problem with that."

"What did you think, Zack?"

Zack shifted from one foot to the other. He rubbed his chin again.

"I thought she was looking into the business she now owned part of," he finally said. "But other stuff, too. I don't know. Once she started looking through things, her focus seemed to shift. Almost like she didn't care too much about her inheritance, but she just didn't like some people here. She connected them to her mom, to the awful life she had—or didn't have, I guess you'd say, right?"

Without waiting for an answer, he led them back into the room with the humming machines and reached one skinny arm down behind the server as far as it could go. He pulled out a stack of papers, one or two escaping the loose clip and floating back beneath the large machine. He shook his head, then pushed the clip more firmly in place.

"Here," he said. He rolled up the printouts and thrust them into Birdie's hand. "Amber wanted these files, and she didn't have the password. She knew I was in here on Saturdays so asked if I could get them for her. She had some other things she had to do and couldn't come in that day."

They looked at the papers in Birdie's hand.

"It was her company, you know," Zack said quickly, unsure of the looks on their faces. "She had a right to them, even if Garrett didn't think so."

Birdie patted his hand. "Yes, she did," she said nicely. "Thank you, Zack."

They were the printouts that stayed behind the server, gathering dust. The ones he never had a chance to give Amber on Monday, as they'd planned.

Because by Monday, Amber Harper was dead.

Chapter 31

Cass had to go home. Danny was waiting for her. They had started taking long walks along the shore together. Sometimes early in the morning, like the morning they'd found Amber's body beneath the newly planted trees. Sometimes whenever they could fit them in. Walking along the water, she said, was healing, and was helping them both wash away the image that had taken an unwanted hold on their lives.

Walking along the water was time with Danny, time that was becoming increasingly important to the way she lived. To *who* she was, she had confessed to Izzy and Nell earlier. Walking along the water with Danny was as vital a place in her life as Nell's dinners and Ben's martinis and Thursday night knitting.

But she'd take the latest printouts with her and get to them later. There might be nothing there, she said. Zack had been caught up in the drama of it, and as best she could tell, he might have had a crush on Amber Harper. But then, maybe she'd find something that Amber had seen. Something askew.

So far, the financial records they'd looked at that afternoon at Birdie's home hadn't led them to Amber's murderer. But these might be different. And until the murderer of Amber Harper was behind bars, they wouldn't count anything out.

. . .

Nell and Birdie had other plans.

"Mind if I join you?" Birdie asked the wide familiar figure sitting alone in the Canary Cove shop.

Birdie sat down before Henrietta O'Neal could answer her. But her neighbor loved company. Birdie knew they'd be welcome. The real question was whether they'd manage to get away from her talkative friend before Christmas.

Henrietta looked up and beamed. "And Nell is here, too. How grand." Then she lowered her voice to a whisper, shielded her mouth with a pudgy hand, and said, "The tea would be much better with a shot of whiskey. But it will do."

Finding Henrietta in Polly Farrell's Tea Shoppe would have seemed like a coincidence, except Birdie didn't believe in coincidences. The fact that she and Nell had stopped in after dropping Izzy and Cass off—and had found Henrietta sitting alone—was part of some grand plan.

Nell got up and carried back a tray with a teapot, cups, and an assortment of tiny cakes. "The British may have something on you Irish, Henrietta," Nell said, sitting down opposite her. "High tea is lovely."

Henrietta waved away Nell's words with one chubby hand, her lined face crinkling into a grin. "Polly's as Irish as I am. She just pretends to be an anglophile, God knows why." She waved her cane at her friend behind the counter.

"You have the shop to yourself," Birdie said. "That's nice."

"It certainly is because I fit better when it's just me. I tell Polly all the time to make this place bigger. Five tables? What is she thinking? And these rickety chairs are barely able to hold me. But that's my teasing her, that's all. I love this place and Polly knows it."

Henrietta popped a piece of cake into her mouth and looked at Birdie and Nell over the top of her rimless glasses. "Now tell me the truth, what's going on in the lives of the likes of you?"

Birdie laughed. "That's a mouthful, even for you, Henrietta."

"It's about the beast, isn't it, now?"

"The beast," Nell repeated. "A perfect word for a murderer."

"That's what he is. A beast prowling our town. It's shaming us all, that we haven't found him yet. The Cummingses must be beside themselves."

"I suppose you get Cummings updates from Garrett. He's right in the thick of things, isn't he?" Birdie said.

"I don't see much of Garrett." Henrietta shook her head. "And when I do he doesn't talk much, never has. But it's a fine thing the Cummingses hired him, isn't it? The youngest of seven, he is. A poor place to be in a family as aggressive as his—especially with the others going off the way they did and making themselves rich. Every last one of 'em, though who knows how they got to the top?"

"Henrietta, what are you talking about?" Birdie asked.

Henrietta slapped the air with her hand and her eyes crinkled with laughter. "I do go on, now, don't I?" She took a sip of her tea. "I never much liked Garrett's appendage of my husband's family. He's my late husband's nephew. My husband didn't much like Garrett's father, or his wretched children. Garrett was the smartest in the lot but lost out on the high achiever gene. Too quiet for his own good, was how his father put it, although my Michael and I laughed at that because the father was the same way; he and his son Garrett were two peas in a pod."

"I suppose quiet isn't the best trait to have in a big family."

Henrietta's blue-gray curls bobbed in agreement. "He's as polite as a teacher's pet—and smart, like I said. But sometimes being with him is like being with a rock. What goes on in that head behind those big glasses? I try to see him now and again, but I don't see him often, that's my rule."

"He seems to be doing well at the Northshore Nurseries," Nell said.

"Yes, he makes a boatload of money now. You saw that snazzy car, I suspect. I could hardly fit in the backseat. Horrible car."

"Henrietta, you're awfully cranky today," Birdie said.

With that, the round woman tilted her head back and laughed mightily. "You're right, Birdie. Life is too short to be cranky, though living as long as I have has given me some rights to an ornery mood now and again. But I shouldn't speak ill of Garrett, like him or not. It isn't who I am, now, is it?"

In a way, it was who she was. Henrietta held such strong opinions about things that she was often cranky. Often found carrying signs to protest a building or a candidate running for office who hadn't met her criteria. But she also had the remarkable ability to wash it away with a smile as big as the moon, and a heart that matched it. Sometimes.

"Does Garrett enjoy his work?"

"I'd say he likes it enough that they'll have to carry him out on a gurney, that's how much."

"And Barbara?" Nell asked, her eyebrows lifting.

Henrietta chuckled and patted Nell's hand. "I know what you're asking. It's a strange relationship for sure. I always thought he should find himself a quiet little gal over in Lanesville, but there is something about the formidable Barbara Cummings that has a hold on that man. He's crazy about her. I'm sure of it, even though he doesn't say much, though things seem to be changing a tad. Just the other night I took him to dinner and he had a few drinks, something I've not seen the man do before. Frankly I was glad to see it. He loosened up a little—quite frisky, if you can believe it. He told me he was going to ask Barbara to marry him. The man is head over heels in love with that woman. Now, I don't agree with her politics—and her leisure activities are not of interest to me, though I'd love to challenge her in a game of canasta sometime. I'd beat the pants off her. But she is most definitely powerful and smart. I asked Garrett if he thought she'd say yes." Henrietta paused for effect, then went on. "'The time is right,' he said. Barbara needed him."

"Needed him?" Birdie repeated.

Henrietta's head was nodding again. "Needed him. Yes. And

I've no doubt she does. The man is a genius with numbers. But need him for romance? Who knows? But that night, Garrett's eyes, even behind those thick glasses, were like a puppy's. If he's right and they go for it, then good for them, and I'll do as Father Larry does, toast them with the finest Irish whiskey. I'll 'God bless 'em'. . . I suppose."

Nell felt suddenly uncomfortable with the conversation. Who was to say why people married, why they coupled? What they saw in each other? It was a mystery, plain and simple, and if Garrett O'Neal and Barbara Cummings could bring to a life together one pinch of what she and Ben had in their life, well, as Henrietta said, 'good for them.'

A young man in the door waved at Henrietta and she pushed her tea aside. "There's Jason come to fetch me. I am off to dinner." Henrietta's driver was one of her grandsons, a nice young man who was paid an enormous amount of money to drive Henrietta around, a fact that brought great relief to the town of Sea Harbor. Henrietta behind the wheel of a car wasn't a pretty sight.

"One question, Henrietta," Nell called out just before Henrietta reached the door.

She turned back, leaning on her cane. "And what's that, Nell?"

"I'm just curious. Why did you want to play canasta with Barbara Cummings? It's somehow a scenario that's hard for me to imagine—but a greatly entertaining one for sure. I want to be invited." Nell laughed.

Henrietta's grin turned her face into a happy maze of wrinkles. "Garrett claims Barbara is quite the cardplayer, but has she ever played canasta with North Shore's 1966 canasta champion? I don't think so!"

Henrietta swung her cane in the air and twirled it around and gave a whoop of laughter so robust that it rolled out the door along with her square body, startling a man across the street.

Chapter 32

Priscilla Stangel had come through for Birdie, just as Birdie knew she would. Old friendships rarely fail one.

Sundays were wonderful days at Ocean View. Full of activities, people visiting. And most certainly a tour could be provided. It would be her greatest pleasure to show her friend around.

Cass begged off, wanting to spend time with Danny and with a stack of printouts. "The ones that don't smell," she'd said.

Nell stopped at the closed gate and spoke into the intercom, giving the faceless man in the stone gatehouse her name. He came out, his uniform crisp and neat, and checked her driver's license, then Birdie's and Izzy's. Finally he allowed a small smile and handed Nell a map of the campus and three passes enclosed in plastic. A minute later the black gate rolled open and Nell was waved through.

Nell looked over at Birdie. "I feel like I'm about to enter Fort Knox. How did Andy ever get Amber inside?"

"There's an employees' gate near the laundry building. Everyone who works here is given an electronic pass because they don't always have a guard on duty over there," Birdie said.

The main building was in the center of the complex, the grounds much like that of a fine New England college campus. Winding paved pathways crisscrossed across spacious lawns, all leading to smaller buildings and homes tucked into wooded areas. Massive pine trees were lined with tiny white lights, park benches covered with a dusting of snow and ropes of green. It was a winter fairyland.

They made their way to the main building and up a fan of steps leading into the spacious lobby.

"This is beautiful," Nell said, her voice hushed as if she wasn't sure they belonged there. People passed them by, coming and going, some carrying flowers or gifts, and all of them bundled up against the cold.

Inside, they spotted Priscilla Stangel immediately. She was standing near the half-moon reception desk. She wore thick-lensed glasses, her back slightly stooped, her hair as white as snow. She wore a strand of pearls, a soft wool suit, and practical shoes—fitting into the elegant, spacious lobby as perfectly as if an artist painted her there.

They enjoyed watching her for a moment as she greeted people, some who embraced her, probably remembering her from earlier years.

"She's a legend," Birdie whispered. "For better or for worse."

Priscilla squinted over the top of her glasses, then recognized Birdie and came over, her gait slow but her steps sure. She hugged her friend warmly and greeted the others. "I'm so pleased Birdie has brought you by. I love showing off my Ocean View."

Birdie had filled them in on Priscilla's venerable career as director of the whole organization. Thirty-five years, Birdie had said. And over those years, she had entertained the Ladies' Classics and Tea Club with hundreds of rollicking Ocean View stories—always told discreetly, of course, never revealing names that could possibly embarrass a potential benefactor.

"Can you believe I thought of retiring?"

Birdie couldn't, although she knew the board had urged just that. Ocean View was Priscilla's life, and she blessed whatever board member finally had the humanity to urge the others to keep her on, even in a job that was a slightly sophisticated version of a Walmart greeter. It kept Priscilla alive—and she loved it.

"There are a lot of things going on today, lots of visitors in from out of town," Priscilla explained. "I'm going to be busy, but I'll give you the mini tour and then set you free with your map. There are lovely volunteers everywhere to answer questions."

The setup was perfect. One worry had been escaping from Priscilla's watch to do some looking around on their own. Priscilla was giving it to them on a silver platter.

As they walked through the lobby and around the public areas, Nell brought up the question that needed clarification first. "Is this the building Ellie Harper lived in?"

Priscilla didn't seem surprised by the question. "Oh, yes," she said. "Ellie had one of the suites. Elegant. It was the China Rose Suite." She grasped a polished wooden railing and began walking up a flight of stairs, wide enough for a bridal party. "I was so very sad to hear about her daughter. That poor girl—" Her voice dropped as one's did when one was talking about a tragedy.

"Yes, it's awful," Izzy said. "Amber Harper was a good friend of my brother's."

Priscilla's head nodded as she continued walking up the stairs. It wasn't clear to any of them if she heard.

At the top she caught her breath and faced them. "I thought I saw the girl here one day. It frightened me. Ellie was here for so long—we all knew her, tended to her. I saw this figure in the room that used to be Ellie's and I thought it was Ellie's ghost—the similarity was jarring. The nurses explained to me later that her daughter was in town, that that's who was sitting in the chair. I knew the daughter must be staying with Esther Gibson—Esther used to bring her in here, you know. I called Esther and suggested she ask the girl not to return. And then I saw her again, and I called again. I regret it now. But she shouldn't have been here. This is a place to visit the living, you see. She knew no one here. We're very careful with who comes and goes."

Priscilla moved on, through a wide archway into an elegant sitting area, as posh as the lower level but with a more assisted feel—

walking bars attached to the walls, wheelchairs, and young helpers escorting people to comfortable wingback chairs. A well-dressed group, some with oxygen tubes and in wheelchairs, was gathering around a large-screen television. Soft music played in the distance and a uniformed man tended a polished walnut bar, serving lemonade, coffee, tea, and cocktails. It was a country club atmosphere with nursing home assistance.

"Was Amber being disruptive?" Birdie asked. Her voice was matter-of-fact.

Priscilla looked up. "I'm responsible for people coming and going," she said, a hint of defensiveness creeping into her soft voice. "I need to know who is here. Who is visiting."

"Of course you do," Nell said. "I know you do a wonderful job. I'm sure you saw to it that Ellie had excellent care."

Priscilla pushed her glasses up her nose and smiled graciously. "She had the very best care. Dr. Alan and Father Larry were here religiously. The nurses used to tease that she had more male visitors than anyone on the wing. And every single week someone brought her the most beautiful fresh flowers."

Fresh flowers? Was that a Lydia touch? Owning a nursery, it would have been an easy gesture, Nell thought, but somehow she didn't think Lydia was the sender.

"The nurses were kind to her, loving," Priscilla added.

"Are any of the nurses who cared for her still on staff?" Izzy asked.

The question seemed to challenge Priscilla, but finally she said, "No one that knew her from the beginning like I did. They're all gone. But there are some who were here during the last few years of Ellie's life. Some volunteers, too, perhaps." She began to mumble names softly, pulling them out of her memory one by one. *Patty. Erica. Carly.* "Someone could check for you, of course. I instituted a very exact record-keeping system when I was director."

They held back smiles. Birdie had shared the tale. Priscilla was fastidious at keeping records, and that included the Ladies' Classics and Tea Club. She recorded every book they read—back when they actually discussed them—every wine they favored, every appetizer and piece of cake they ate, and she also dutifully recorded the names of waitresses and waiters who served them at Ocean's Edge. No one knew what Priscilla did with her information, but somehow, somewhere, there was a stack of yellow legal pads that recorded the Ladies' Classics and Tea Club activities for all posterity—and it was continuing to grow.

They could only imagine the kind of record keeping she had instituted at Ocean View.

Priscilla pointed down a wide carpeted hallway. "Our suites are in that wing."

"So that's where Ellie lived?"

Priscilla nodded. "China Rose." She smiled.

"May we look at it?" Birdie asked.

"Normally I would say no, even to you, Birdie." Priscilla smiled. "But China Rose is empty right now. We're always updating and remodeling. Everything at Ocean View is up to date, you know." She looked up at a large clock on the wall. "I'll need to leave you for a bit, but there are nurses around, people to answer questions." She pointed them in the right direction, hugged Birdie again, and bade Izzy and Nell good-bye. Then slowly she made her way back to her position in the lobby, graciously greeting every person who came through the door.

They walked down the hallway, a wide and welcoming area, the walls filled with fine art. Halfway down they came to a nursing station with polished wooden secretary desks, flowers, computers, and comfortable chairs. A pleasant-looking young woman took off her glasses and walked over, offering to help.

"Carly," Izzy read her name tag out loud.

The young woman smiled, then subtly checked the passes pinned to their coats.

"I'm sorry," she said, embarrassed that they'd seen her checking. "We're careful about who comes in and out. Those are security rules."

"Is there a need for that here?" Birdie asked.

Carly lifted one shoulder and laughed. "Not really, but sometimes we get people who aren't visiting someone or who don't have passes like yours. So we're careful about it."

Birdie nodded. "Is it possible to see the China Rose Suite?"

Carly looked surprised at first, then led them to the end of the wide hall. The door was open and Carly explained that the suite was almost ready for occupancy again. It was the loveliest suite on the floor.

"It's very beautiful," Nell said, walking inside. A wall of windows looked out over the grounds and in the distance, just visible above a band of sweet bay magnolias, was the sea. She walked over and looked out at the vista Lydia Cummings had paid for. She wondered if it had brought Ellie any feeling, and comfort or pleasure.

Carly walked up beside her. "It's beautiful, isn't it? A woman lived in this room for a very long time, and every day we moved her so she could see this view."

"Ellie Harper," Nell said softly.

"I thought maybe you knew her. There was something in your face when you walked into the room."

"I didn't know her, not really, but I feel like I do."

Birdie and Izzy had come over to the windows and looked out.

"Did you know her, Carly?" Birdie asked.

Carly nodded. "I've always worked in this department. And Ellie Harper got to me, somehow. I had a job offer a few years ago over in Danvers, closer to where I live, but I turned it down. I couldn't leave Ellie. Doc Hamilton felt that way, too. He talked to her all the time. I would hear him, so I decided I'd talk to her, too. We had great long talks, Ellie and me. My boyfriend would laugh, but I could tell, he felt the same way. He loved Ellie, too. Her cast of admirers."

Carly looked at the bed as if Ellie were still in it. "She had good friends. Sometimes patients like Ellie are left completely alone, but she must have been quite an amazing woman to have endeared herself to people the way she did. Loyal friends. Do you know every single Monday morning I'd come in and there'd be the most beautiful bouquet of flowers here?"

"Did Ocean View do that?" Birdie asked. "An expensive touch."

"Oh, no. They don't do that. There wasn't a card. Someone brought them on Sunday nights and they stayed beautiful all week long until the next arrangement arrived."

"Have you been here a long time?" Izzy said. "You aren't very old."

Carly laughed. "Old enough. I came here right out of school. I was with Ellie about nine years, I guess. I was with her the day she died, or at least most of that day. When I came in the next morning, she was gone. It was very sad for those of us who knew her over the years. She'd become a part of our lives in a strange but very nice way."

"I hope that last day was a happy one," Birdie said.

"I think it was. Doc Alan was here that morning. And her friend Esther. Risso. Those people were so loyal. I think Father Northcutt was here that day, too, and one or two others. I didn't know her night visitors because I didn't regularly work nights.

"When I left that day I gave her a kiss. I don't know why, I just did. She looked beautiful that day. I could almost imagine what she looked like when she was young. I plumped the pretty pillow her friend Esther gave her, tucked her in, and kissed her good night."

Carly's eyes filled and Nell felt a surge of gratitude for this sweet woman who had loved Ellie Harper.

Carly excused herself and for a while they stood alone in the lovely room that had been Ellie Harper's home for nearly her whole life. And they imagined Amber, sitting on the upholstered couch by the window, Esther beside her, reading the young Amber books.

On their way out they stopped by the nurses' station again. Carly had her back to them, checking the computer. "Carly, were you here a week or so ago?" Nell asked.

Carly turned. It was as if she had been waiting for them, for the question. "When Ellie's daughter showed up, you mean?"

"Yes."

"I wasn't here when poor Priscilla Stangel saw her sitting in the chair and thought it was a ghost. She came a couple more times, but our paths only crossed once. It was a Saturday and I had taken the night shift for someone. I sometimes did that. Apparently she'd been here awhile that day, and one of the nurses called security and they were making Amber leave as I came on duty. Physically escorting her out of the building. I felt awful when I heard what was going on, so I rushed out and walked down with her. I liked her right away. She reminded me of what Ellie might have been like, feisty and strong. We stood outside together, just the two of us, and I told her about my time with her mother, about her friends, the flowers."

"Why did they make her leave?"

"Some of the nurses were new and didn't know her mother. They were freaked out by her questions. It was understandable."

"Do you know what she was asking about?" Nell asked.

Carly fiddled with a pencil, rolling it between her palms. "What any daughter in her position would want to know. How did her mother die? Was she alone? What was her last day like? Was she in pain? Amber had every right to ask those questions. She wasn't here when Ellie died. She needed to be as close to that day as she could, to live through it, hour by hour, with her mother. I understood it. It's exactly what I would have done if Ellie had been my mother. And I would probably have wondered, just like she did, why my mother died suddenly, without any sign of wearing down. Even though it sometimes happens with PVS patients, I would have wondered. So I tried to answer every question I could."

They heard the compassion in Carly's voice. And could almost hear Amber pressing for answers.

Carly was quiet for a minute, as if weighing whether she should say more. Finally she did.

"And that's why I said yes."

"Said yes?" Izzy asked.

"She asked me if I could find some records for her, and I said yes. I owed that to Ellie's memory. I told her I'd get them that night, and I'd give them to her the next day, on Sunday."

They were all quiet, going back through the days, but it only took seconds to mentally put the calendar in order, only a few seconds to figure out what had happened between that visit and the next day.

Ellie Harper's daughter was murdered.

Chapter 33

They made one detour on their way home from Ocean View, a pleasant diversion from the tension of the day.

"I think Esther's knitting needles are what get her through those long shifts at the police station," Nell said. "She knit some ornaments for our Harbor Green tree and asked me to pick them up. I think she has at least a dozen. She's putting us to shame."

Esther Gibson was home as promised, but not alone. She and her husband, Richard, were sitting in the family room playing poker with Alan Hamilton and another good friend, Claire Russell. "It's our Sunday ritual," Esther explained as they walked back to the family room.

Nell felt a sudden, grateful rush. She'd been hoping to run into Doc Hamilton—and here he was. Birdie's good omen was still working its magic. Hopefully it would stay with them, the wind at their back, until the "beast" was behind bars.

And hopefully that would be soon.

"We're interrupting your game," Birdie said, eyeing the poker chips stacked at each place. She looked over at the doctor and said, "I don't mean to insult you, Alan, but they're beating the pants off you."

Alan looked at her and joked right back—"Good thing Esther doesn't allow strip poker in her little casino."

"Excellent thing!" Birdie said, with such punctuated enthusiasm that they all burst into laughter.

"Sit, sit," Esther said.

"All we have is beer and bottled water," Richard said. "Any takers?" He pointed to a makeshift bar.

Izzy went over and grabbed water bottles for Nell and Birdie and one for herself.

"So, has this been going on long? This little clandestine gambling casino?" she asked, perching on the arm of the couch.

"Blame it on Richard," Claire said. "He's pretty good at it. They say he's taking Reno by storm."

"Richard, I'd never have guessed," Birdie said. The retired fisherman was quiet, usually letting Esther take the lead in conversations. Being a cardsharp didn't fit his profile.

Richard laughed at Birdie's surprise, but then confessed, "Esther keeps me on a tight leash. Reno's a special occasion. Usually I go to some of the casinos around here—but it's just for fun and with only a couple of fifties in my pocket. Esther's rule. That's it. When it's gone I come home. It's fun. Same expense as going out to dinner and a movie." He grinned, warming to the subject. "Some guys joke that playing the slots is a sure way of getting nothing for something. Not true for me. I have fun with my buddies, drink a few beers. That's what I get. I stay away from folks I know out there who take it too seriously."

"Who's that?" Claire asked. The landscaper had turned Nell's backyard into a paradise for Izzy's wedding, and she had been a cherished friend to all of them ever since.

"Oh, you know, other folks around town," Richard said. "You get to know each other. You'd be surprised, some Sea Harbor folks have made a bundle off the slots, the cards. Lost a bundle, too. Not me." Richard laughed again.

Esther filled in. "Gamblers are friendly folks. Our Reno trips are mostly because we can stay in a friend's lovely home and I can sit on the fancy porch and smell the trees and enjoy the free meals the casinos give us. We drink wine there, not beer. It's uptown."

Richard snorted, his beer foaming over the rim.

Esther fussed at him and grabbed a box of tissues. "Enough talk about Reno. See what it makes you do?"

Nell pulled up a chair across from the doctor. "Alan, were your ears burning today? A nurse at Ocean View sang your praises to the sky."

"Ah, that's music to my old ears," the doctor said, tiny laugh lines spreading out from his clear blue eyes. He took off his glasses and forked his fingers through his hair, strands of silver showing among the brown. "Better than those who want to cook my goose, right?"

"I can't imagine anyone wanting to do that, Alan," Birdie said.

Nell agreed. Doc Hamilton had been the Endicott family physician for years and the man didn't have a mean bone in his body. She was happy to see he and Claire had linked up together recently. Two interesting, wonderful people. It was nice when they found each other.

"What were you doing at Ocean View?" Alan asked.

Birdie sat down on a chair Esther pulled up. "Following Amber, you might say. Walking in her footsteps."

They put their cards facedown and turned her way. Birdie went on. "Amber had been pouring through the Cummings financial papers." She looked over at Esther. "Esther knows all about that, so you may, too. We're just trying to figure out what her thoughts and emotions were that last week, why she did what she did, went where she went and why."

Alan nodded. "Trying to help put an end to this difficult time," he said solemnly. "I knew Amber stopped over at Ocean View. I ran into her one day. She was being rather abrupt with one of the nurses."

"Amber could be abrupt," Esther said.

"I was glad to see her. She didn't remember me, of course, but when she realized I had been her mother's doctor, she became more open. I tried to reassure her that her mother had had good care at Ocean View, and that her life there was peaceful. She asked a lot of questions about that last day, but that's understandable."

"I'm sure it was comforting to her to talk with you," Nell said.

"I think what she really wanted me to do was turn back the clock so she could have been there holding her mother's hand that night she died. Or better yet, have protected her—she kept saying that. It's hard sometimes—especially when the deceased isn't sick in the usual way—to understand how they could be alive one day with strong vital signs, then dead the next. It was really difficult for Amber to accept it. But it happens."

"Did you tell her you visited Ellie often?" Izzy asked.

"Yes. She was glad that her mother had friends who came—Esther, me, Father Northcutt, Jake, a few others. She said she wanted to thank them, all those people who had 'filled in' for her, as she put it."

Amber's surge of gratitude surprised Nell. Not that she wasn't polite, but somehow she wouldn't have expected it to be a focus for her. But maybe she wasn't giving her credit. Amber returned to Sea Harbor older and wiser. And, perhaps, with a sense of gratitude for the good things that had been done for her mom.

"We met a nice nurse over there that said she assured Amber of the same thing. Her name was Carly . . . Carly something," Birdie said. She felt inside her coat pocket. "She gave me her card. I have it here somewhere."

"Carly Schultz," Alan said.

"That's it."

"She's a great nurse. She became attached to Ellie."

"She said you visited Ellie the day she died," Nell said.

Alan rested his head back and Nell could see his mind going back over the years to the day Ellie died. "The day, yes," he said, nodding. "I wish I had been there that night instead so she wasn't alone. Carly felt the same way. Esther here, too."

Esther nodded. "It was hard for Amber—it would be for any one of us. But she hadn't seen her mother in years. Details were important to make up for that."

"Larry Northcutt had been there that day, too," Alan said. "He and I relived that day a couple months ago when we met at the Cummingses' home, of all places. It was shortly before Lydia died. Lydia was quite ill by then and often requested visits with Larry. Confession was good for the soul, she'd say. Maybe it was, because she fell asleep peacefully while we were still there. But confessions must be hard on priests, because Larry looked old, less than peaceful. The two of us sat for a while talking quietly while Lydia slept.

"The conversation turned to Ellie Harper and the care Lydia had provided for her. And we talked about being there the day Ellie died.

"Father Larry didn't say much, which was unusual—you know him, he's never at a loss for words. But he seemed preoccupied with the woman in the bed. He looked over at Lydia a couple times. Bowed his head slightly. Maybe in prayer? Yet he seemed to be listening to me at the same time. Then he turned away from her and spoke softly, as if to keep his words away from her. His words were odd, especially since he'd just heard her confession, but maybe I heard him wrong. He said something about helping Lydia forgive. But I must have heard wrong, because that's what priests can do, right? They're the ones who grant forgiveness?"

Nell looked out the window, listening to Alan's story and remembering one of her own. A cold Thursday night when a burdened Father Larry stood outside the bookstore and talked about sins, and about forgiveness. Was it someone else who needed forgiveness?

Alan had switched the topic, uncomfortable with the puzzling memory. "Ellie's death that night was a surprise, but it was probably a blessing, as people say. In spite of that, though, it was difficult for those of us who had spent so much time with her. She had a hold on people, even then."

"Knowing she died in her sleep probably brought some comfort to Amber," Claire said.

Richard got up and brought back a couple of beers. "It's the way I want to go," he said.

They all agreed, and Birdie, noticing that Richard was frequently looking down at his cards, also agreed that it was time for the four of them to get back to their game and confiscate the rest of Alan's fortune.

Esther chuckled, got up, and took a cloth bag of knit ornaments from the shelf.

"Don't forget these," she said, handing the soft ornaments to Izzy and telling her to be careful not to drop the bag.

"We're going to need more than just one tree for your ornaments, Esther." Izzy laughed. "A forest maybe."

Esther sat back down and picked up her cards, fanning them like a pro, her mind already moving on to her next bid, but she smiled at the comment.

"Esther, one more interruption," Nell said. "I promise we'll leave then. Did you take flowers to Ellie regularly?"

Esther looked up and set her cards down again. "You heard about those beautiful arrangements? No—I brought a vase in case it was needed. But those flowers arrived like clockwork."

"They were beautiful. I assumed Lydia sent them," Alan said.

Esther shook her head. "No, it wasn't Lydia. I asked her once. She said it was a foolish, expensive gesture. And she was quite adamant." She looked back at her cards, then up once more. "Is that it?"

But before anyone could answer Esther was spreading her cards out on the table. "Royal flush," she called.

In Esther Gibson's world, knitting and poker went a long way in easing the pain of difficult days.

The texts came in as they drove away from Richard and Esther's and headed home.

Cass had left it on all their phones, explaining that if any of them planned on feeding her that night, they were out of luck. She and

Danny were having dinner with her ma, but she needed to talk to them ASAP. She was off the next day. Monday early, Izzy's back room? And would Birdie please bring some of Ella's cinnamon rolls?

The sun was already slipping away, the sky filling with darkness. They all agreed that packing another mind-taxing session into their day would probably not be fruitful, no matter how anxious they were to put it all together—and to find out what Cass had found.

"If texts were like voices," Birdie said, "we'd have an inkling." But the blandness around words on a tiny phone screen provided few hints.

"We're this close," Izzy said, her thumb and index finger a yarn-width away from touching.

Nell and Birdie nodded, their emotions tangled as tightly as Purl's basket of play yarn. *Close.* But only if they were seeing things correctly, if their intuition and patching together the pieces Amber had laid out for them all fit neatly together, piece by piece, stitch by stitch.

Only if Amber's footsteps were truly leading them to the end of the road and not off the end of a shaky pier.

The woods were truly dark and deep.

And they had at least a mile to go before they'd sleep.

Chapter 34

"I think we are following Amber as closely as we can," Nell said. "It's the fork in the road that we need to concentrate on." She handed Izzy the bag of Esther's decorations and poured herself a cup of coffee with a thank-you nod to Birdie.

Birdie had not only brought Ella's cinnamon rolls to the Monday gathering, but had asked Harold to stop at Coffee's for a carafe of his Colombian dark roast. Coffee perked by Izzy might not start them off on the right foot.

Izzy came down the stairs with napkins and her laptop. "I don't know if we'll need this," she said, "but it's a quick connection to the world."

She set it on the table and walked back a step to check the calendar posted near the bookcase.

No classes until the afternoon. The shop would be quiet.

At the sound of Cass coming through the shop, Birdie peeled the foil off the cinnamon rolls and Izzy hurriedly made a place on the coatrack for her parka. "How was dinner with Mary?" she asked.

"Corn beef and cabbage," Cass said. "And it's not even St. Pat's Day."

She carried a stack of papers, covered with highlighter, that she put down on the table. "Where do we start?" she asked. Then she spied the cinnamon rolls, rotated her eyes upward as she gave thanks for Ella Sampson, and pulled out a chair. She grabbed a napkin and a couple of the yeasty rolls.

Nell began by filling Cass in on the journey to Ocean View. The snippets of conversation. And Carly Schultz.

"An ally," Cass said, and Nell nodded.

Birdie, in the meantime, had pulled out her purple yarn and configured a map on the table. "Here's the problem," she said, pointing to a spot where the yarn-road forked. "This one goes one way, and this goes another. But which way leads to the murderer?" Her question hung in the air, unanswered.

Amber's footsteps were not easily followed. The foci were clear: the Cummings business office and Ocean View. But the sinking feeling that when they got a hairbreadth away from where they were going, the path might end or split off in another direction, was always present.

"That won't happen," Izzy said. "Sometimes patterns make no sense, not until you get further along. That's what's happening here. One step at a time."

They would stay with the pattern; they wouldn't give up.

Not until the murderer was found. The "beast," as Henrietta so eloquently put it.

Nell thought about Charlie. He'd seen the light in the kitchen that morning and stopped in before his early shift at the clinic. He was slowly reclaiming the man he was—the man he was becoming. She loved the light in his eyes when he played with Abby on the floor, the way his face softened when his sister teased him or gave him a hug. And the way his whole body came alive when he was on his way to help little kids with vaccinations and strep tests at the Sea Harbor Free Health Clinic. But the darkness would come back when things were quiet and thoughts became too heavy. When a police car went by or a siren broke the night silence. A shadow that wouldn't be stripped away completely until Amber's death was resolved.

Soon, my dear Charlie, she vowed silently. *Soon this will end.*

She got up and refilled her coffee mug, then settled back at the table with the others, drinking coffee and sugaring up with Ella's pastries.

Cass looked at the pile of papers on the table. "I feel like I'm on a moving sidewalk and we're not getting off until we've figured it all out. It's coming together somehow. I think we're close."

Izzy nodded and looked over at her aunt. "This reminds me of that afghan we knit for you and Uncle Ben," she said. "It had those panels, separate pieces that had to be knit separately, then finally sewn together before we could see what it was going to look like."

"Or see where our mistakes were," Birdie said. "Yes, Izzy. It's very much like that." She looked across the table at Cass, then at the folders she had brought. "And you look like you're sitting on one of our panels. Let's get it out before you explode."

Cass licked the sugar off her fingers, then wiped them with a napkin. "Amber wasn't just trying to get her arms around what she inherited when she went through the business files. At least not once she got started. I can tell from her notes that she spotted things right off the bat, checks and balances that didn't balance. And she probably became intrigued by what she was seeing, just like I would have. Underneath the sheen, Cummings Northshore Nurseries had some secrets." She looked down at some notes she'd scribbled on a yellow pad, then went on.

"Amber was a savvy, smart woman. I wish I had had a chance to know her. After going through all this, a part of me thinks that once she got into the puzzling parts of the Cummings accounting, her focus changed. She hated the Cummingses. Maybe what she wanted to do then was to put someone in jail. A sense of justice, maybe? And she might have found the way to do it."

She passed a packet of papers to each of them. Neatly clipped together, the information arranged in neat columns. Cass had done her homework and then some.

"It's almost as if Amber was the project leader here, and she's handed it over to us to check all the facts, make sure there's proof of the things she found. You'll see what I mean when you go through it. What she found were suspicious billings—lots of them. Her notes indicate further documentation was needed. Maybe she ran out of time, or moved on to something else once she went to visit Ocean's Edge. I don't know. But what's missing is verifying the false reports. That's what Amber didn't get around to doing."

"I'm not sure I understand," Birdie said.

"Bogus companies were billing Cummings, and Cummings was paying the bills. Those billings were the ones Zack gave us that had been password protected."

"The ones hidden behind the server?" Nell asked.

The slip of a smile revealed Cass's pride in what she'd pulled together. "Yes."

The room fell silent as Izzy, Nell, and Birdie carefully read through the lists Cass had prepared. Copies of documents, checks, and bills, along with some notes from Amber, and plenty of notes from Cass.

Five sheets in all. "And there's more," Cass said. "Amber went back several years, examining everything from salaries to expenses. Some of it, I think, was truly to access the company, part of which was hers—just as all of us thought. And then she turned to assessing how that company spent its money." She looked at the list of allegedly bogus companies. "And finally, seeing some of the past expenses the company had because of Ellie's care at Ocean View, Amber's attention turned to the nursing home."

Izzy stared down at the ledger sheets. "Why would they do it? I have expenses. I pay people. I have no reason nor desire to make up additional billings."

But before her words were out they all knew why someone would do it. And Izzy knew why she loved Mae and the twins and her accountant. They had no interest in paying fake yarn companies and somehow benefiting from it. None at all.

Nell stared at the papers. Barbara had to have known if Garrett was embezzling money from the company. Garrett, her constant companion. Garrett, who wanted to marry her. She thought back over the days, the conversations, random comments that revealed people's private lives in a new light. Garrett O'Neal's new BMW.

A purl row with knit stitches thrown in haphazardly in the middle.

It didn't line up perfectly, but it would soon.

At one point, Nell looked over the top of her glasses at Cass and pointed to a comment Cass had made on one of the sheets. "Reno?" she asked, her voice more amazed at the coincidence than shocked. They'd been talking about Reno just hours before.

Birdie said there were no coincidences. She wondered if it held true in this case.

"A company in Reno is billing Northshore. Check out what the company in Reno does," Cass said.

Nell did. "They make green therapeutic devices. They're expensive, the green devices."

"Very," Cass said facetiously. "When no one answered the phone, I checked the company address on Google Earth. It happens to be a beautiful vacation house outside Reno, Nevada. The original sales description on Zillow says it has four bedrooms, three baths, and an amazing deck that overlooks the mountains and nearby casinos. I suspect the only green thing they make there are margaritas."

They went back to work. One by one billings were checked, accounts checked by phone or Internet, company names looked up and crossed off, their brains kept alive by too many cups of Colombian roast.

"It's creative accounting at its finest," Izzy murmured. She highlighted another company that seemed to have a paper existence, its product manufactured only in someone's mind. And Northshore Nurseries dutifully sending it monthly payments.

No one even noticed when Mae came in, nor when the store opened for business. Nor when the shop began to buzz with greetings and conversation, the clink of change, the heavy door opening and closing. Not even the laughter of children playing in Izzy's magic room filled with toys and books.

When they finally came up for air, they noticed a tray of deli sandwiches at the end of the table and a fresh pot of coffee.

"Saint Mae," Izzy murmured.

It wasn't yet noon, but they'd started early and accomplished much.

And they were starving.

Birdie stood and stretched, then settled back at the table, a concerned look on her face. "Do you think this is what Amber was looking for?"

"No. I think it's what she found," Cass said. She passed the sandwiches around and began unwrapping a turkey on rye.

Nell rubbed her eyes. Numbers swam in front of them and asked the bigger question, the one that hovered there in the air, wobbling. Not sure if it had an answer.

"Do we think this is why Amber was killed?" Birdie pressed.

They had facts and figures.

But could one easily jump from figures on a sheet of paper—even from embezzlement—to murder?

People had killed for less.

But something didn't feel right. The yarn was still tangled, loose.

"There's a big piece missing in all this," Izzy said. She finished her sandwich and began to scoop up Cass's papers and put them back in folders. "How is any of this connected to Ocean View? Or is it? Charlie said that except for visiting her mother's grave, Amber was totally focused on the financial records that first day or two. But then her attention shifted to the nursing home."

"And she didn't finish what she'd started here," Cass said, pointing to the folders.

Nell had been thinking the same thing. And then she thought of the afghan and the panels. Each one different until you saw them together.

Birdie spoke up. "Amber went back several years in comparing figures and she saw the checks written out to Ocean View in the ledgers. Lydia also sent donations, it seemed. She was generous. In fact, Amber had highlighted a check to Ocean View whenever it came up. They were all reminders of Ocean View and that the Cummings money had paid for her mother's care—all legitimate. All generous."

"And possibly that's the only connection," Nell said. "It reminded Amber of her mother. And maybe she was through with examining the Cummingses' affairs and needed to move on to what was really important to her—visiting her mother's grave and where she'd spent her last days."

But they all knew it was more than that. Nothing in Amber's behavior had been a gentle quest to say good-bye to her mother. She had promised her mother something, a promise she wasn't taking lightly.

Birdie remembered her final conversation with Amber. "She was on her way to collecting enough financial information to act on it if she wanted to. To do something to the company—which was now partly her company. She could have chosen to be vindictive—or not," she said. "That could have been what she wanted to talk to me about. She mentioned something about making decisions, doing the right thing. Exploring different ways of handling something. She had options—"

Until she didn't.

"But it doesn't sit right, does it?" Izzy asked. "The Amber you described that last night seemed more anguished. Would fake billings have done that to her?"

"And Charlie has insisted all along that money wasn't something Amber paid much attention to."

They all agreed; it didn't sit right. Something was off-kilter. A row that needed to be pulled out and restitched.

They looked down at the folders on the table, filled with facts and figures about the Cummings Northshore Nursery, figures that hadn't been intended for anyone to see.

They didn't know how it fit into the big picture. But they knew they couldn't discount it. At least not yet.

"Remember what Amber told Charlie about math?" Izzy asked. "She liked it because things added up. It gave her the sense that there was order in the universe. Math made her feel safe."

The irony of her words settled in with an echoing thud.

There was nothing in any of this that made anyone feel safe.

Chapter 35

"There's a class in here at two," Izzy said, collecting their sandwich wraps and coffee mugs. "We need to leave shortly or we'll be here for the rest of the afternoon teaching intarsia."

"I don't know Intarsia," Cass joked. "And I have no intention of spending my day off teaching her."

The day was wide-open for all of them. They had tacitly canceled meetings and appointments, and Mae's nieces were there the rest of the day to help in the shop. There were no excuses to get off the moving sidewalk Cass mentioned, not until they encountered the "beast" at its end.

The sound of a text message came from Izzy's phone. She looked down, then smiled.

It was from Charlie, Nell knew. She could tell by the look on Izzy's face whenever she was reminded that she had a younger brother back in her life.

Izzy looked up. "I think some wise spiritual guide is in our lives today, helping us reclaim Sea Harbor. That was from Charlie. He's at work but suddenly remembered something he'd forgotten to tell us. He has a box of Ellie's things that Amber left with him. She gave him orders to keep it safe."

Nell brightened up. "That's wonderful. Esther thought it might have gotten thrown out."

"Charlie says he'll be back at your house soon. Do we want to meet him and take a look?"

"Did he say what's in it?" Cass asked.

"Esther wasn't sure." Nell explained where the box had come from. "The nurse at Ocean View said it's mostly personal items, photos, jewelry. Esther didn't think it was important."

Izzy tapped her phone absently, thinking. Then she said, "If Amber thought it needed to be kept safe, there must have been a reason. It's important."

There was an immediate flurry of activity as they cleaned the table and gathered purses and keys.

Izzy went up to have a word with Mae while Cass headed for the coatrack, glancing over at Nell. "One thing. Do you have any of that apple crisp left in your fridge?" She pulled out her keys. "Brain food." She smiled.

When they walked in a short while later, Charlie was standing at Nell's stove, frying an egg. A good-sized cardboard box sat on the island, its flaps closed. ELLIE HARPER was printed across the side in bold black magic marker. And below, Esther Gibson's name and address.

"Late lunch," he said, pointing to the pan. "We were busy. I didn't have time to eat."

Nell smiled.

Izzy looked at the box, then over at her brother. "You're okay with us going through this, Charlie?"

He nodded, sliding the egg onto a toasted bun. "Amber brought it into the cottage one night and we went through it together. She wasn't into 'things' and I thought she'd tell me to throw it all out. But she went through it carefully, piece by piece. It seemed like it took forever. I kept saying 'what?' when she would hold something up, examining it like it was gold. But she didn't say much. It was as if she was seeing her mother in every single piece." He carried his plate to the counter.

"It somehow seems disrespectful to be looking at her mother's things. Ellie's things. Someone we'd never met, a stranger, really," Birdie said.

"She doesn't seem like a stranger, though," Nell said. "I've come to like her. And her daughter, too—" She smiled at Charlie. "I think whatever Amber did that last week she was doing for her mother. To make things right, somehow." She pulled open the crisscrossed flaps on the box, and the others all gathered closer.

The top layer held pieces of clothing—a robe and nightgowns, clearly laundered, folded neatly, and packaged in sealed plastic bags. A sweater. Nell took them out one by one.

"I wonder who bought her clothes?" Cass asked.

Lydia, they guessed, or Ocean View itself with an allowance from Lydia?

"My money is on Esther Gibson," Nell said, and they all agreed that was the most likely scenario. Kind, generous Esther Gibson.

When they came across a hat, soft as feathers and knit with yellow cashmere yarn, their guess was confirmed. Esther had worked the hat without seams for comfort, and used the softest cashmere Izzy sold. It was loose and lovely. A perfect head covering to ward off drafts—and to make one look pretty.

Nell felt a catch in her throat and set the hat aside.

The photo frames also had Esther's touch—brightly painted ones framing a small girl who got bigger with each new frame. Amber as a baby. As a toddler. As a preteen. Charlie looked at the pictures for a long time, then set them back beside the box.

Close to the bottom of the box was a pillow wrapped in tissue paper. It was just slightly smaller than a bed pillow but soft, with tiny folds—the perfect size for cushioning one's head. Birdie lifted it out and held it up to the light.

"Esther again," she said, and touched the embroidered flowers that circled the cotton covering.

"It's lovely," Nell said. She looked more closely at the white cotton fabric. "That's a shame. It's torn." She pointed to the side where the fibers were pulled loose, exposing the lining beneath.

"Amber noticed that, too. She looked at that pillow for a long time," Charlie said. He took it from Birdie and turned it in his large hands, then set it on the island. "It seemed to upset her, but she wouldn't say why. She was becoming a little unglued those last couple days, as if things were unraveling for her. And looking through this box seemed to make it worse, though she insisted it was what she needed to be doing. She stayed with me that night and she had horrible dreams. She sat up once, still asleep, and threw the bed pillow on the floor, screaming. I woke her up, held her. And then she cried, hard. And she didn't stop."

He picked up the pillow again and stared at it. "But this pillow here, she couldn't stop looking at it."

"Esther did a beautiful job," Birdie said.

Charlie nodded. "But I don't think that's why she was looking at it. Not that she was unappreciative, but it was something else." He turned it over and touched a soiled spot on the back with his finger. A three-year-old smudge.

"She asked me what the dirt was. 'It's three years old,' I told her. How would I know? And she calmed down a little then.

"She had a bunch of articles explaining how people died—they're stuck in one of those books I gave you, Aunt Nell. She was trying so hard to understand her mom's last hours, I think. Amber was so smart and things were a little easier for her if she could completely understand them. She wondered if I'd ever seen anyone die in nursing school, what it looked like."

Charlie took a deep breath, then continued. "I had seen one person, an elderly lady, die in her bed. There was some edema fluid on the sheet—I think I was trying to impress her a little, mentioning terms I knew."

They looked at the pillow for a long time, and then Birdie took it carefully from Charlie's hands and set it back in the tissue folds.

It was only then that Izzy noticed the last remaining item in the cardboard box. A square tapestry jewelry box.

She took it out and opened the lid, then set it on the counter so they could all look inside.

Nell lifted out a women's wristwatch, silver and dainty. A watch that had long ago stopped telling time, perhaps rescued from the accident and never worn again, moving along with its owner from a hospital to a nursing home. Tiny diamond earrings were enclosed in a small plastic bag.

"Patrick," Izzy guessed, imagining the story as it might have unfolded. "He couldn't give her a ring—not yet—so he bought her these beautiful earrings."

Earrings her daughter should be wearing right now. Cherishing the gift to her mother from her father.

Birdie took out the last piece, a sealed plastic container holding a beautiful oval pin. The size of a silver dollar piece, the edges solid gold, the center a circle of ivory.

"It's elegant," she said, holding it in the palm of her hand and looking at it carefully. "And valuable, though the pin is bent."

She passed it around for all of them to see as they tried to fit it into Izzy's romantic story.

"Maybe it was something she had on the night of the accident," Nell said, but without much conviction. The stories they'd gathered about Ellie Harper held images of a freshly scrubbed, beautiful woman, comfortable in jeans and shorts and flannel shirts. Not unlike her daughter.

Nell rubbed the oval with the pad of her finger. And then she frowned and put on her glasses, peering at the worn letters on the back of the brooch. She held it up to the light. And then her frown deepened as she passed the pin around, from Izzy to Charlie to Cass to Birdie.

They couldn't fit it into the story. It didn't make sense to them.

But perhaps it might to someone else. Birdie slipped the pin back into the plastic wrap and pulled out her phone.

Chapter 36

Birdie's karma or good omen or whatever it was had not forsaken them. Izzy claimed it was the spiritual guide she had called upon.

Nell said that *whoever* it was who stepped in to help them along the way, she was grateful.

And grateful to Carly Schultz, too.

Carly answered her phone immediately when Birdie called. Mondays were always slow and she had a break coming up. She'd like nothing better than to visit with her new friends.

Charlie watched them head for coats and scarves. He gulped down the last of his milk and looked at Nell. "I'd like to go along," he said.

Nell stopped short, then walked over and gave her nephew a hug. "Of course you should be with us," she said. "Don't forget your hat."

The route was now familiar to them, up the winding road to the iron gate. Carly had sent word that she had visitors coming; it wouldn't be a problem getting in.

But Nell held her breath anyway, and didn't completely relax until the gates had silently rolled open and they found themselves inside. And then they shut behind them.

Carly was waiting inside the lobby and greeted them with hugs as if they'd known each other for a long time. She included Charlie and Cass in her hugs, too, not even acknowledging that they hadn't met before. She was thinking about moving to Sea Harbor from Danvers, she told them as she led them off to the lunchroom. And meeting all of them was adding significant weight to the "pros" side of her pros-and-cons decision chart. They were right up there next to her Sea Harbor boyfriend, she said.

They settled at a quiet table near the window with Cokes and hot tea.

Birdie mentioned seeing Doc Alan the day before and the nice things he had said about Carly.

"He's the absolute best," she said. "Everyone loves him."

"He thought one of the reasons Amber had come over that week was that she was grateful to everyone who had helped her mother and wanted to thank them."

None of them had completely bought Alan Hamilton's kind explanation for Amber's unannounced visit to Ocean View, if it could be called a visit. The last week of Amber's life was not one she wanted to spend on pleasantries and being grateful, they felt sure of that. And the further along they got in following her footsteps, the more certain they were that nearly every move Amber made that last week was to reach a goal.

And that goal was finally becoming clear to the determined friends. Perhaps—if the good omen or guide or whoever she was stuck around—she could help them reach it.

Soon.

Carly listened and nodded now as they drank their tea and talked about Amber's gratitude. "She thanked me that day. And Doc Alan. The priest. And I suppose that's why she wanted to know anyone who had been with her mother that day. To thank them."

She looked up then and spotted another nurse across the lunchroom. "Oh, wait, there's someone who knew Ellie. You might want to meet her."

She waved her hand and called to an older woman examining the sandwiches displayed in the glass case, "Georgia, over here."

The genial-looking woman waved back and lumbered across the room, then shook hands as Carly introduced her to her new friends.

"What can I do for you?" Georgia asked.

"They're here because they knew Ellie Harper. Or her daughter, actually. Charlie here and Amber were good friends."

"Ah, our Ellie, she was a darling. Carly and I loved her. There was something about her, something that reached out to us."

"Georgia mostly worked nights while Ellie was here."

Georgia nodded. "And sometimes nights are long around here. Very quiet, usually. So often I sat with Ellie, knitting hats and scarves and what have you."

"I suppose you enjoyed Ellie's beautiful flower arrangements, then," Birdie said. "For the life of us, we can't find anyone who owns up to having sent them."

Georgia laughed. "They were beautiful. We miss them. Came like clockwork, every week. I have my suspicions, but no proof, mind you."

"The mysterious night visitor," Carly said knowingly.

"A night visitor?" Nell asked.

"Carly has a bit of drama in her," Georgia said. "But it's true that occasionally Ellie had an evening visitor. As crazy as it sounds, though, I never saw the person to talk to."

"But security here is so tight," Cass said. "Surely someone did."

"It's different at night, but of course there would have been security guys around. No one like Priscilla, though, who would definitely have known," Carly said. "But visitors at night are fine, no rule against it, though they have to sign in."

"Carly's right," Georgia said. "But this was kind of mysterious. There was an older nurse who no longer lives around here who confirmed that someone came in and sat by her bed occasionally. She suspected that the security guards were a bit richer after those visits, if you get my drift."

Georgia paused, looking as though she had something more to say, but then seemed to think better of it and excused herself to grab a sandwich before her shift ended.

"Now, what were we talking about?" Carly asked.

"I think we were talking about Amber wanting to be sure everyone who helped her mother was thanked."

"That's it," Carly said with a snap of her fingers, her eyes lighting up. "That must be why she wanted those files—so she wouldn't miss anyone."

"What files?" Nell said. "Didn't you tell us Amber was bothering the nurses about medical files, her mother's medical records?"

"Oh, no. She asked a lot of questions along those lines. But what Amber wanted to look at were the *visiting* records for that week. The log-in books. No one ever looks at those things, no one, but sweet Priscilla is dutiful about keeping them. Apparently she has been for years and years. Some poor volunteer spent a whole summer inputting them. And to this day, Priscilla insists every guest sign in.

"But I don't know why the nurses were skittish about giving them to Amber that day. Maybe they were busy and just didn't want to take the time. Or maybe . . . well—" Carly looked embarrassed.

She smiled and shrugged. "I think Amber was a little demanding with some of them. But she only wanted to thank people who had cared about her mom, and that's all good, right? Maybe find out a little more about how peaceful her mother was that day. She had every right to do that. They should have helped her."

Carly took a drink of her Coke, then looked up and said with conviction, "And that's why I said yes."

"You were going to get her the visitors' log-in?"

"No. I mean yes. I printed them out for her."

And then they realized what Carly was saying.

"But never had the chance to give them to her," Birdie said gently.

Carly nodded, sadness clouding her eyes.

"Do you still have them, dear?" Birdie asked.

"Maybe. Oh, no, I don't. I shoved them in my locker. It was a holy mess, and I finally cleaned it out a couple days ago and threw everything away. I'm so sorry. Was it something you'd want to see?"

"We might," Nell said. "Would it be too much trouble to print out another?"

Carly checked her watch, then shook her head. "Not now. The business office is locked up tighter than a drum."

Nell hid her disappointment beneath a new topic. "There's another thing we wanted to talk to you about, Carly." She explained that they had gone through the box of Ellie's belongings that Amber had left with Charlie.

Carly remembered the box. "Yes, I was the one who took care of that."

"The box was packed with such care, Carly. We knew it was probably you."

Carly blushed. "I think I even remember what was in it," she said. She thought for a minute and then said, "There were clothes, but I don't remember them really, except that Esther Gibson had bought her some nice things. I just wanted her daughter to know that. That's why I put them in the box. Esther wanted Ellie to feel pretty every single day. But what I remember most are the diamond earrings. Esther had told me the story about Patrick and Ellie—and I knew they must have been given to her by him, by Amber's father. When I packed them away that day, I imagined Ellie's daughter wearing them. The thought made me happy."

"There was a pillow, too," Charlie said.

"I remember. That beautiful pillow that Esther gave her. We kept it on her bed, tucked it in with her at night. It was always with her, kind of like a child's blanket, you know?"

"And this? Do you remember packing this?" Nell pulled the plastic bag from her purse.

Carly looked through the clear plastic, frowning uncertainly at the jewelry. "No, I don't think—"

Then suddenly her eyes lit up and she pulled the brooch from the bag, running her finger over the mother-of-pearl. She turned it over. "Oh, sure, I remember it now. At first I thought this was a design on the back, and then one of the other nurses said they were initials. But they weren't Ellie's initials, so we figured they were her mother's maybe," she said. "So I put it in the box. But let me tell you where I found it. It was the strangest thing."

And then Carly Schultz leaned forward, and, as if telling good friends about a movie she'd recently seen, she told Izzy, Nell, and Birdie why it was the strangest thing.

Another piece. But not a *ka-chunk*. Not yet. Not until they saw the list.

When they finally walked out the door of Ocean View, Nell's head was spinning. It felt like midnight, though her watch said just a little after five. The winter sky was unusually dark at the early hour, with only a sliver of moonlight lighting the trees. Lamplights in the parking lot guided them to Nell's car, where they piled in, turning up the heat immediately.

Nell maneuvered the car toward the guardhouse and stopped, waiting for the iron gate to open.

While they waited, Charlie took in the manicured surroundings of Ocean View, then leaned toward Nell and pointed to a painted sign just outside the entrance.

Ocean View Cemetery.

"Amber will be there, next to her mother, right?"

Nell nodded. She checked her watch again. All each of them needed was a quick shower and time to dress before the eight o'clock caroling. It would work.

"It's a short detour. Should we drive past?" Although Charlie had been there once before, she suspected he needed to see it now, knowing it would be where Amber would lie.

The others were fine with it, as long as Nell kept the heat on high.

The gate opened, and once again Nell made her way down the narrow, winding road that led back to the carefully tended Ocean View Cemetery.

The wind whistled through the trees as she pulled the car slightly off the road. A lamplight nearby offered little light, but Nell remembered exactly where Ellie's grave was—beneath the old hawthorn tree.

"Come," she said. "Let me show you."

They left the car running and the others talking quietly in the backseat, processing the day. "It's close, just around that curve," Nell said.

She thought she heard an animal howling, the sound of a wolf perhaps, and stopped for a minute, peering into the darkness. She simply wasn't used to being in a cemetery in the dark, she thought, and began walking again, this time nearly colliding with Charlie's back.

He had stopped dead still in the middle of the path.

"Charlie?" she said, her eyes adjusting to the darkness. "What's wrong?"

He turned partially toward her. "Shh," he whispered, a finger to his lips. Then he wrapped an arm around his aunt and brought her to his side, one hand pointing ahead of them.

If it hadn't been for the shiny down jacket reflecting the single beam of moonlight, they might have stumbled directly on top of the man. But Charlie had heard the noise, too, and had stopped on the path.

A short distance ahead, unaware that he wasn't alone, a broad figure crouched down on one knee on the unforgiving ground beside Ellie Harper's grave. His body rocked back and forth, arms wrapped around his chest, holding himself together. His head was low, cradled in his hands, and his body leaning toward the raised mound beside him.

And pouring out of the shaking form, rolling across the gravestones and up to the night sky, was the unbearable keening of a man in the deepest depths of sadness.

Chapter 37

Charlie and Nell sat in near silence on the drive home, processing separately what they'd seen. Or *heard*.

They'd waited on the trail just long enough to know there was nothing they could do to help, and that making their presence known would be intruding on a fiercely private moment. Then they had quietly turned and walked back to the car and driven off. Only when they were well on their way to drop the others off did Charlie turn and tell Izzy, Cass, and Birdie what they'd seen.

Or what they thought they'd seen.

"Someone was crying at Ellie's grave?" Izzy repeated.

"Who?"

"It was dark," Charlie said. "And we only saw the back. Everyone kinda looks alike in the winter anyway. Big jackets. Hoods. Hats."

Nell was silent. The sound still echoed in her head. It had been raw and frightening, and she worked with it now, trying to interpret it. Grief and anger, the deep anguish of guilt or sin—strong emotions sometimes collided and twisted together. They were often difficult to separate.

She turned into Birdie's circle drive and idled near the front door.

"Nell, you couldn't tell who it was, either?" Cass said. "You should have sent Birdie to look. She knows everyone."

"With these eyes I might have mistaken him for Ellie's tombstone," she said, climbing out of the car. She waved good-bye, said she'd go get gussied up and see them in a couple of hours, and disappeared up the steps.

After dropping off Cass and Izzy, Nell and Charlie headed up Sandswept Lane.

Nell was relieved to see the house lit up; Ben sometimes overdid it, but tonight the glow inside warmed her before she even opened the door.

Charlie headed for the guest cottage, promising to meet them later.

Nell waved him off, then glanced at her phone as she walked through the door. An unfamiliar number appeared on the screen.

Nell answered to hear the friendly voice of Georgia, the nurse they'd met earlier that day at Ocean View.

"I hope you don't mind the call," Georgia said. "I got your number from Carly Schultz and needed to get something off my mind."

Nell assured her it was fine, but Georgia's tone puzzled her.

"I didn't mention this today, but I had talked to Amber Harper when she came to Ocean View. I recognized her right away. She looked a lot like sweet Ellie."

She went on then, quickly, as if her break was about to be over and she needed to get something out.

"I'm worried that I might have caused her distress, or encouraged her in a way I shouldn't have. But no one was paying attention to her, answering any questions—probably because they didn't have any answers. I might not have had any answers, either, but I had an opinion and I shared it with her. I was on duty the night that Ellie died. I checked on her at eight o'clock that night. Her color was good, her breathing, her vital signs. In fact, she seemed in better shape than she had a couple weeks earlier, when she looked a little sallow. So I told Amber what I told the doctor and the director, the priest—and anyone else who asked me about that night. I told her that her mother was in fine shape—for Ellie, anyway. And that I agreed with her that there was no reason her mother should have died."

Nell's mouth dropped open, but before she could say anything in response, Georgia thanked her for listening, then politely excused herself, saying she had to get back to work and hung up.

Ben was on a call when Nell finally took off her coat. She was glad for the opportunity to collect herself, to jump in the shower, and to be alone for a few minutes as she tried to process Georgia's call.

At first she wasn't clear on what the nurse's message was. But as water sprayed down on her face, she replayed it in her head without her own emotions intruding. It was something she sometimes found difficult to do.

Georgia's only regret in speaking openly with Amber seemed to be that she might have caused her distress. Could she have? Charlie had talked about Amber becoming obsessed with her mother's death, and she wondered briefly if Georgia's talk might have contributed to that obsession. Opinions can be bolstered by numbers, certainly. And if she had done that, it was clear the nurse was sad—and sorry. Nell hoped that the nurse would forget about the incident—she certainly had nothing to do with Amber's being killed.

But her call had added clarity to what might well have ended Ellie's daughter's life.

From downstairs she heard the sounds of Ben shaking a martini. She glanced at the bedside clock. Good planning. They'd have a little quiet time together—before a not so quiet evening. She dried her hair, dressed quickly in a soft blue dress, and hurried down the back stairs.

"What's all this?" Ben greeted her, motioning to the things littering the island. "A man can barely make a martini in the middle of this mess." He kissed her on the cheek.

"You'll manage." Nell kissed him back.

"Hmm," Ben said, then handed her a martini and pulled out a stool for each of them. "I suspect there are things sitting here that we need to talk about?"

Nell looked at the box and realized suddenly that she didn't know where to start. So much had happened. But Ben Endicott was the best listener in the world, and now and then, he even had the amazing ability to straighten out strands of purple yarn.

Nell pointed to the yellow pad and the summary sheet Cass had given each of them and started in. She'd taken the big stack home for Danny to see, but would bring it over the next day for Ben to take a look at.

When Nell had finished, Ben had a look of quiet disbelief on his face.

"I don't know how to reply to all this, what to say first. You've covered a lot of ground today."

"Ground" didn't begin to describe it in Nell's mind.

"Nellie—" he began, a familiar look appearing in his eyes.

She nodded. "It's okay, Ben. Don't worry. We're not going to get hurt. That's already been done."

Ben swirled the liquid in his glass. He glanced over at Cass's notes. "Do you think Amber's next step before she was killed was to confront the Cummingses about what she'd found? Maybe take this to the police?"

"I don't know. She almost seemed to lose interest once she'd figured it out and moved on to something else. I think it was more than that. There was a reason she became so interested in Ocean View.

"Amber was goal-oriented," Nell went on. "We thought all along that walking in her footsteps would lead us to her murderer. And I think that's what is happening. The problem is she walked to two different places and we've been trying to find the connection between the two. We're getting close, but maybe not in the way we thought." She paused and considered her words. Maybe not in the way we thought. *Of course. That's exactly it.*

She shook her head. It happened like this so often—just thinking out loud to Ben made something that had seemed murky to her earlier suddenly become crystal clear in the telling.

Ben looked over at the box that held Ellie Harper's material possessions. And a lot more. It was a whole story in a box.

"Ben." Nell pulled his attention back to the yellow pad. "Do you think what Amber discovered at Cummings Northshore would be a motive for murder?"

Ben nursed his martini for a while, thinking of the company he'd known to be strong and solvent and successful. The accounting problems had been a surprise. The reasons for them an even bigger one.

Finally he said, "A motive? Maybe. Do I think that's why she was murdered?"

They both thought of what that meant. And who the players were.

"These findings show that there is something going on over there that shouldn't be. It's definitely troublesome. But it's not clear how it would all pan out."

"So," Nell said.

Ben laughed. "So what you're asking me to do, Nellie, is to concur with you. You already know what you think. And you probably know what I think, and you knew it even before we began this back-and-forth."

"Of course," she said. The comfort of knowing Ben's thoughts and inclinations matched hers was dimmed only by the fact that they still didn't have all the panels matched up. But they were only one small stitch away.

Ben went out to heat up the car while Nell put on her coat and gloves.

As she clicked off the lights and walked out to the car, she realized she hadn't mentioned the man at Ellie's grave site to Ben.

She stood with her hand on the car door for a minute, glancing up at the sliver of moon. The same moon that had lighted the way to Ellie's grave a few hours earlier. She remembered the sound, hearing it all over again, the awful anguish that echoed in her head.

Maybe she hadn't said anything to Ben because it was too hard to describe.

But maybe it was because she simply wasn't ready to talk about it.

No matter how dark and cold it was, Nell was certain about whom she had seen kneeling at Ellie Harper's grave.

And finally, at last, she understood who had killed Amber Harper—and why.

They solved the parking problem by texting Danny and Sam that they could all park in the alley next to Izzy's yarn shop. The red-brick historical museum was just across Harbor Road and a short walk through the small corner park.

"We certainly clean up nicely," Birdie said, stepping out of the backseat of Danny's car. She looked admiringly at Cass's slinky, short dress. "You won't catch many lobsters in that, Catherine."

"Or maybe she will?" Danny said, his eyes doing a Groucho Marx imitation.

Izzy and Sam drove up a few minutes later, pulling up next to Archie's bookstore. "Sitter problems," Sam explained. "Izzy had forgotten to run the sitter's résumé past Homeland Security."

Izzy smiled smugly, knowing her husband was very impressed with the fact that she'd transformed her tired, frumpy body into a tall, shapely one in a holiday red blouse and formfitting skirt. "I look great," she'd said to him. "And I know it. Eat your heart out, Sam Chambers."

Charlie stood next to Sam, laughing the hardest. Getting to know a grown-up sister was even more fun than he had imagined it could be.

Nell watched them all, enjoying their antics and glad they had come. No matter what they were wearing, she thought, or how tired they were, this might be exactly what they needed. A touch of Christmas. One evening of setting aside what they knew to be true: that a murderer was about to be taken off the streets.

But in the process lives would be turned upside down.

And when she pulled Birdie, Cass, and Izzy aside, and they walked together through the small park so close that people thought they were trying to keep warm, Nell told them the whole truth about the figure at the grave site that day.

Like so many homes on Cape Ann, the Sea Harbor Historical Museum had been built a century before for a wealthy sea captain. Over the years it had been many things before finally being added to the historic registry and resuming its Colonial roots. It now housed exhibits, an impressive library, staff offices, and a paneled hall for events, where tonight's party would be held.

"It's a Christmas jewel," Birdie said, looking up at the electric candles in each window and the garlands that circled the pillars beside the door.

Two college-aged girls dressed in elf costumes opened the double doors and welcomed them inside.

Immediately they were swallowed up in the fairyland the committee had created—a giant tree that reached nearly to the ceiling, filled with lights and ornaments. Instead of bringing toys to the event, everyone filled out donation cards to purchase new toys and placed them on the tree—already heavy with the red and green envelopes.

Passing out the cards were Mr. and Mrs. Santa Claus, sitting in red velvet chairs and looking every bit the regal beneficent pair. The gentle and congenial Gibsons. Nell laughed and she and Birdie immediately headed over to Esther, not nearly as anonymous as she thought she was in her well-used costume.

"How did you know it was me?" she said as Nell leaned over and gave her a hug.

Birdie answered. "Maybe because you've worn the same Mrs. Claus dress at every Christmas event for the last twenty years, my dear?" She turned to Richard and gave him a hug, then frowned. "Santa, that beard has to go. It smells like mothballs. Surely you can afford a new one."

Richard laughed heartily, practicing his *ho-ho-hos*.

And then Nell had a niggling thought—a piece of the yarn that hadn't been woven into the whole quite snugly enough. Intuition had given them an answer that afternoon, but knowing it factually would tighten the stitch. And, as Izzy often said, criminals weren't convicted on women's intuition. Maybe they should be, but it didn't often stand up in court.

"Speaking of money," she said. "I hope we didn't ruin your poker game the other day."

"How can you ruin a poker game? I robbed Alan blind—eighteen dollars and fifty-two cents. And then he turned around and robbed me right back. Claire and Esther gave up on us."

Nell and Birdie laughed.

"So, how does family room poker compare to the Reno casinos? That's big-time, Richard," Nell said.

Esther broke in. "It's the redeeming piece in all of this poker and slots and blackjack thing. We go twice a year, something we can only do because one of Richard's local casino buddies lets us use his place. It's a small world, Nell." She leaned in and whispered conspiratorially, "Always assume someone you know is around the corner because they probably are. Imagine, finding someone from Sea Harbor right there in Reno."

Esther described the house and its generous owner, and said it was a wonderful opportunity. They should all go together sometime. They might even want to try the slots.

And the house is magnificent, Esther said: four bedrooms and three baths. And an amazing deck that overlooks the mountains and is close to their favorite casino. Imagine that.

Imagine that. Nell felt another piece of the puzzle slip into place.

It landed with such an echoing thud she was sure Esther and Richard must have heard it.

The stitch was pulled tight. And without asking, though Esther called it out to them as they walked away, they knew who owned the magnificent home. "Friends of yours," Esther said, who would be happy to have them as guests, even if they didn't like the casinos all that much.

Nell and Birdie bottled up the conversation and carried it across the room where the well-dressed elves were now passing out tiny sausage and shrimp puffs and champagne. Nell wasn't shocked or even completely surprised at Esther's revelation, nor was Birdie.

But they at least understood a "why" that had been floating around for days. Although Esther and Richard, Claire, and Alan Hamilton played poker for eighteen dollars and fifty-two cents, for others it could be a dangerous addiction. An addiction that could ruin people's lives—or make them do unsavory things to pay their gambling debts. It was something people sometimes died from—or even killed for.

While Birdie went off to greet an old neighbor, Nell stood alone, enjoying the quiet in the middle of a jovial, noisy crowd. Sometimes it was the best kind of quiet, being surrounded by noise and not being a part of it.

She noticed Barbara Cummings, her red tailored suit a nod to the season, standing beneath one of many sprigs of mistletoe that hung from the ceiling. Several women, including Mrs. Esther Gibson Claus, stood with her, talking. Nell noticed Garrett O'Neal seeking Barbara out, spotting her, then standing back against the wall close to the group of women. His red bow tie was perfectly tied, his hair carefully combed, rimmed glasses hiding thoughts and emotion. Finally he moved to Barbara's side, one arm grazing hers.

Barbara seemed not to notice his presence, her posture erect and still.

A convenient couple, someone had called them. Perhaps that's what it was, at least for one of them.

But the thought made Nell enormously sad.

She looked beyond them and spotted Stu Cummings and Ben standing together, talking quietly. Stu looked worn, his congenial smile seeming to be an effort. When people crowded in, the two men moved away to a quieter spot behind the enormous Christmas tree.

In the next minute, as if somehow planned, Jerry Thompson joined them.

Birdie was back and handed Nell a glass of champagne. "Sam and Izzy are heating up the dance floor," she said. "I think all the tensions of today are being exorcised effectively."

Nell nodded. Exorcised but not gone. She nodded across the room to where Beatrice Scaglia, Barbara, and Helen Cummings stood with a group of council members. A waitress passed by, accepting their empty glasses and replacing them. Helen reached for another as Barbara looked over, spotted Nell, and nodded in a brief hello, then turned away.

A rebuff? Nell turned and followed Birdie across the room, her heart heavy, to where Father Northcutt sat alone on a couch, watching a toy train circle a small tree.

"You look like you could use this, Father," Birdie said, handing him a glass of champagne.

"Now, how did you know I was sitting here thinking about a glass of bubbly?"

"I just knew," Birdie said.

His smile was sad, but, as always, warm and welcoming.

"One of the nurses told me she met you lovely ladies today at Ocean View," he said.

Nell nodded. "They think highly of you over there, Father."

"Oh, my, highly can be overrated, Nellie."

"Your presence to those patients means a great deal. Even those like Ellie Harper—"

"My sweet Ellie. She was a pleasure to be with, even though her life was not a real life, not lying in that bed for all those years."

"Not a full life, surely," Birdie said. "Not like ours. I can't quite imagine it."

"It's hard to understand, isn't it?" His head nodded, his meaning not clear. But he went on. "Sometimes death is a release. Even when it's unexpected. I understand how people have trouble with that, a conflict between moral imperatives, now, isn't it? An ethical dilemma."

Izzy and Cass had walked up as Father Northcutt was thinking out loud.

Ethical dilemma.

Birdie looked at the others. The words rang out as they listened and heard, not Father Larry's words, but Amber Harper's.

Amber's quandary the night she asked for Birdie's guidance. Exploring the right thing to do with the information she had.

Birdie gazed at the kindly priest. Finally he looked up and met her eyes. "Sure and we all know it, Birdie. This has to be reconciled. Too many people's lives are on hold because there is still a crime unsolved, justice unserved. And a motive that may not be honorable." He looked around the room, then down at his hands, arthritis taking hold of his fingers as the lives of people he cared about took hold of his heart.

A group of parishioners moved in to share a word with their pastor, and the women moved away, taking the priest's words with them.

"It's very sad," Birdie said. "But we're here tonight for other reasons, not to be sad. There will be time for that." With forced brightness, she suggested to Cass that they take to the dance floor.

"Birdie Favazza, no one's asked me to be their dance partner since high school. But let's go—what's that crazy thing you say—cut a rug?"

But before they could move through the crowd, a familiar voice called out their names from the other direction. They turned around and looked into the smiling, excited face of Carly Schultz.

Behind her was Andy Risso, lifting his shoulders and palms as if to wonder how this had all happened. How did all these people who were important to him know one another?

Carly looked beautiful, her short blond hair bouncy, a bright green and red dress short and saucy. She hugged all four of them as if they'd been friends for a long time.

"Andy's my boyfriend," she said proudly, tilting her head toward him.

"This is the boyfriend?" Nell asked. "Our Andy?"

"Of course. The one who visited Ellie with you sometimes." Birdie clapped her hands, delighted with the connection.

"We met at Ocean View. All the older patients love Andy, so I said to myself, 'Hmm, I think those ladies have good taste. Maybe I should give him a look. So I did. And sure enough, they were right." She laughed, a full and happy sound.

"Well, we like him, too. You have absolutely wonderful taste, Carly," Nell said.

"Don't get too full of yourself, Risso," Cass warned. "I could tell Carly stories, you know."

Carly giggled. "I couldn't believe it when I saw all of you across the room." She looked at Nell. "I was going to have Andy take me to your house on our way home."

"Oh?" Nell said, but somehow she knew exactly what Carly was going to say.

Carly opened her purse and pulled out a single sheet of paper, folded twice into a small, neat square. "I think it might smell like my perfume," she said.

Nell assured her that the perfume would only make it sweeter. She took the folded paper and slipped it into her purse. *Thank you, Priscilla,* she said silently. She patted the purse gently as if pushing a final puzzle piece in place.

Cass watched the couple as they walked away, Andy's arm holding her tight. "Who knew? Do you think our magic brings these things about?"

"No," Izzy said. "If it did, you and Danny would be married." She pointed to the lobby and suggested they find a quiet spot.

"What did she give you?" Cass asked.

"The visitors' log from Ocean View the day Ellie died."

"She must have sensed our disappointment earlier today and talked a security guard into letting her into the office," Birdie said. "She's a lovely girl. Andy is fortunate."

Nell took a deep breath and pulled the paper from her purse, then slowly, carefully unfolded it, smoothing out the wrinkles. Izzy took out her cell phone and clicked on the flashlight, carefully scanning the names.

Ellie had had a banner day for visitors the day she died, just as they had been told. Beginning with her doctor in the morning, her priest. And her friends.

And then a final visitor that night. The one who had ended Ellie Harper's well-tended life with one swift movement.

A plump pillow with tiny embroidered roses placed carefully over her mouth.

Chapter 38

Father Northcutt got the call a second before Cass's phone pinged. And then Birdie's.

Mary Halloran had covered several bases, hoping someone at the party would answer.

"Come," she said.

They all got the call, and no one asked "Come where?" It was December novena week and Our Lady of Safe Seas Church stayed open long hours. Mary Halloran would be there picking up stray bulletins, filling the holy-water fonts, and making sure people were orderly and didn't fall off the prie-dieux. A December novena always brought in some homeless folks, which was why Mary insisted that Father Northcutt hold it in December—a nice reason to give people a warm place to go. And who knows, maybe they'd even light a candle or two while they were there.

The church was just a few blocks from the historical museum, but Birdie suggested she find Father Northcutt a ride and the others run on ahead as fast as they could.

Cass's mother needed them.

Their breaths plumed up into the frosty air as they raced through the small park and around the corner to the church. They pushed the heavy carved doors open and stepped into the stillness of the ornate church, its enormous ceiling rimmed in gold, the rows of old wooden pews polished to a high sheen.

Before them was the long center aisle, which led to the solemn sanctuary at the front.

They stood eerily still, not sure whether they were alone. The pews were empty, the low lights along the walls casting shadows onto the side aisles.

A sound in the distance drew their attention toward the front of the church, where they spotted Mary Halloran standing alone on the top sanctuary step, talking out loud.

"Who's my ma talking to? God?" Cass whispered.

They walked tentatively down the aisle, knowing instinctively that quiet was the best way. With one hand beckoning to them and no words, Mary Halloran urged them forth. Her eyes were focused elsewhere.

As they approached the steps, they followed Mary's look to the right, into a small recessed grotto where a life-sized statue stood on a small rise, her arms outstretched. Also standing on the platform and holding one of the statue's hands was Helen Cummings.

In her other hand she held a knife.

She wobbled slightly, her eyes nearly shut. "Don't come near me," she pleaded, her head turning just enough to know there were several other people besides Mary Halloran watching her. She recognized Nell, and her face contorted.

"A security guard told me what you were all up to," she said, this time looking back at Mary. "I found out they got the sign-in sheets from Ocean View, the smarty-pants. Snoopy, like the daughter was. Amber should have left it alone, Mary. She should have. I told her that, that night at the Harbor. That's all I wanted—to meet with her, to talk for just a few minutes. To explain. That's all." Her head began to move back and forth with the rhythm of her words.

"The past is always best left alone, I told her. She was quiet, but for a minute, I thought she was listening. I thought she understood that her mother was better off. Her mother had no life in that bed. But I had a life. A life with Stuart.

"But Amber just stared at me. A hard stare. It was painful to watch, so cold, and then she turned away from me, shunning me. And I knew she hadn't heard. Or understood. She started to walk away from me, down the path. To walk away and ruin all our lives—"

Her voice grew husky, deeper, and from where they stood, it looked as though tears were streaming down her face.

"I couldn't let her go off like that, you know. She had her mother's things. The pillow. My beautiful brooch. It must have stuck to the pillow that night. But when I couldn't find it, I remembered where it must be. Ellie had no one here; it would surely get thrown out. Then her daughter came back to ruin my life—all our lives."

She looked out at Nell now, and her voice dropped to almost a whisper. "I didn't want to hurt Amber—I only wanted to make her understand. But I could see in her eyes that she didn't."

A banging of doors and a ruckus in the back of the church shattered the silence and for a moment, Helen lost her balance, her head leaning forward and one foot flying awkwardly in the air. But her hand held tight to the statue's, and she managed to regain her footing.

Birdie followed Father Northcutt down the aisle. But it was Stu Cummings who created the commotion, his heavy footsteps taking him to the front of the church in seconds. He stood near Nell.

"Helen, get down from there," he ordered. "You'll hurt yourself."

Nell looked over at him. His words were strong, his stance firm, and in his eyes was a pain so deep that she looked away.

"Why did you come, Stuart?" Helen said. Her voice shook as she looked at her husband. "Please go away. I did it for you. It was all for you. It was the only way you would stop visiting her, a dead woman! But you kept going. Your mother told me it would stop. But it didn't. Some nights I followed you, Stu. I knew from early on, from those nights in the Gull when she'd serve you beer. I saw how you looked at her when she was with Patrick. And then a miracle happened—the accident—and it solved everything."

She shook her head. "But it didn't. She was still there, in that room filled with your flowers. Where you sat at her side." Her head dropped. Finally, with great effort, she lifted it and focused on Stu.

"You cared for me, Stu. All these years, you cared for me. But you loved her."

"Helen," Stu tried again. But his voice was choked and the word fell to the floor.

As if suddenly waking up, Helen's voice grew stronger. "Watch me, Stu." She waved the knife in the air. "Soon you'll have two dead women. Will you love me then?"

Nell looked away, just in time to miss seeing Helen Cummings fall to the floor, the knife slipping away as her head hit the marble, where she fell into a sound, unconscious sleep.

One she wouldn't wake up from until safely behind bars.

Jerry Thompson showed up with Ben and the others at the same time as an ambulance and police car. No one knew for sure what was happening in Father Northcutt's sanctuary.

Stu slumped down in one of the pews, his head in his hands. Nell sat down beside him. She had decided not to tell him she had seen him at Ellie's grave. He'd had enough sadness in one day to last the next one hundred.

But she understood now the mixture of sounds that carried his emotions earlier. Love and guilt, sadness and pain.

Suddenly she felt enormous sadness for Stu Cummings. She leaned over and wished him peace. Then silently followed the others out of the church.

They left the church as solemnly as if leaving a requiem Mass. And without an actual plan, they straggled into the Endicott kitchen a short while later.

Charlie put on coffee while Sam pulled several beers out of the refrigerator and uncorked the wine.

Ben brought out a bottle of scotch.

"It's over," Birdie said. "This time it really is."

But there was no joy. Lives were wounded, upended, and an unstable woman would never live in her comfortable world again.

"Amber was so sure her mother didn't die naturally," Ben said.

Nell shared with them the call she'd gotten from Georgia, the night nurse. "That little bit of encouragement might have been all she needed. No one else would listen."

"Don't you think her doctor, or Father Northcutt, maybe, wondered, too? But because Ellie's life was so limited, it wasn't something that would be looked into. The only one who might was a daughter who regretted not being here when her mother died." Birdie looked out the window into the night. "There's nothing happy about any of it. It's all so sad."

"I think we were right that Amber probably suspected Barbara, at first, thinking she did it for the money," Cass said. "Amber knew so much from the Cummingses' financials. It was like reading a diary for her. She knew how much money they'd save if they didn't have to pay for her mother's care; she knew about Barbara's gambling debts, her need for money; she knew about the bonuses Barbara paid Garrett to continue his doctoring of the books—"

"I think Garrett would have done it for love, if Barbara would have given him that," Nell said.

Ben poured the scotch. "Well, I think the gambling and embezzlement issues are going to be taken care of outside the law," he said. "Garrett did it for Barbara, not himself, not really. And the truth is that it's the family itself that would bring charges. Stu won't do that, not if Barbara gets treatment and Garrett shapes up. They're damn lucky."

Cass puffed up. "Yes, they are."

Danny patted her on the back. "Good job, Sherlock."

They laughed, tired, weary laughs that sent them to finishing drinks, rummaging around for gloves and keys and coats, and heading into the night for well-deserved long winter's naps.

Chapter 39

Father Northcutt had been true to his word, allowing Esther and Charlie to plan a suitable memorial, something to remember the woman one of them had known nearly her whole life, and the other had known just a week. A week that would have a lasting effect on Charlie Chambers. A week spent with a woman who had helped him open his heart from its long slumber.

They gathered together in the sanctuary of Father Larry's church late one afternoon, just as the last rays of sunlight poured through the stained-glass windows, casting colorful bands across the marble floor. Lined up along the steps were all of Esther's framed photos of a young Amber. A pot of wildflowers sat beside them, flowers that Esther Gibson seemed to have miraculously produced in the middle of winter.

No one knelt or sat, instead choosing to stand in a semicircle, arms looped around shoulders and waists, memories filling the space. After a brief prayer by Father Larry, Jake and Esther spoke of the little girl they had known and loved—one who had grown into a young woman who would have made her mother proud.

Izzy stood next to Charlie, her arm entwined with his. She looked at him, wondering whether he was going to speak.

Instead he smiled and gave her a brief hug, then walked over to join Andy Risso and Pete Halloran, who were both standing near Esther Gibson.

Andy pulled a drum stool from behind him and sat down as Pete picked up his guitar, then began strumming until the two had captured the beat. Esther grinned at Charlie, then wrapped one plump arm around his shoulders, and in the next minute the unexpected quartet filled the sanctuary in true Jimmy Cliff fashion with "I Can See Clearly Now (The Rain Is Gone)."

Before they'd finished the final verse, everyone had joined in, sopranos and baritones alike, heads thrown back as they cast away the winter with song, welcoming the sun and assuring Amber Harper—and themselves—that it was going to be all right.

Chapter 40

The crowd in the Harbor Green a week later was the largest Nell could remember. A joyous gathering of children and parents, elves and carolers, and the ever-present Fractured Fish.

Esther Gibson had brought out her Mrs. Santa Claus costume again and sat on the gazebo stage beside the band, passing out lollipops with the promise that Mr. Santa Claus would be coming into Sea Harbor on Christmas Eve.

Charlie carried Abby over to the stage. Her eyes were bright, watching the twinkling lights hanging from the gazebo roof and delighting at the snowflakes landing on her mittens.

"See this lady, Abby?" Charlie whispered into his niece's ear. "She magical."

Esther's smile spread across her lined face as she reached out and lifted the toddler onto her lap. "And so are you, my love," she said to Abby, bouncing her a bit.

Izzy stood nearby, beaming, as Abby reached up and touched the soft white ball at the end of Esther's furry red hat. Her daughter's world was filled with enchantment.

In the next minute Abby turned and reached for Uncle Charlie to take her back, to play his finger puppet games with her and sing her silly songs.

And he did, finding it difficult to be away from his niece for long. His niece, his family. His town. Charlie's world.

Izzy puffed with pride as she looked at her brother kissing the top of her daughter's head. "He's in hot contention with Red to be her favorite playmate," Izzy had told everyone that morning when Charlie announced his plans to stay in Sea Harbor.

"Doc Virgilio is short staffed, so I'm going to hang around for awhile," he'd explained, but his arm around his sister and his eyes on his niece spoke to reasons that didn't need a lot of words and had little to do with how busy Lily's clinic was. There would always be a place for Charlie there, she had told him.

"There you are," Charlie said now, carrying a wiggly Abby over to her mom.

"Come on, you two," Izzy said. "Let's go look at the ornaments."

Together they walked down the path toward the magical trees. They had been transformed that day by teams of zealous workers, hooking tiny ornaments to fragrant trees, bending their branches, and turning them into works of art. Tiny hand-carved wooden fishermen, boots, and clay running shoes the size of a thumb, with crocheted headbands and water bottles.

Abby squealed as they stopped in front of a tree filled with knit fish and whales and tiny sailboats in reds and blues, greens and yellows. "Daddy boat," Abby insisted, pulling Nell's version of Ben and Sam's prized Hinckley sailboat from the branch and cuddling it in her hands.

"Our tree's the best, right?" Izzy whispered into her daughter's ear.

She looked up at Charlie. "Abby thinks we're awesome."

Charlie laughed. "Yeah. I think so, too. But I dunno. Have you seen the blood pressure cuffs and stethoscopes on ours?"

The sky was beginning to darken, and an expectant feeling hovered over the fairyland of trees. "Time to get back," Izzy said.

Once the sky was dark, the tree lights would be lit. And the holiday season would truly begin. They wandered back along the path, finding the rest of their crowd gathered near a fire pit.

Father Northcutt sat on a bench next to Ben and Sam. "It will take more than a week to bring us all back to that safe and gentle place," he said. "But this is certainly a good start."

Dozens of benches circled an enormous fire pit that the Sea Harbor firemen were protecting. The crackling flames sent wafts of warmth their way.

"These weeks have taken a toll on you, Father," Sam said.

"Added a few gray hairs maybe," Father Larry joked. Then he grew somber, his smile fading. "Helen justified it all, you know. Mercy killing, she called it. But it wasn't that, for sure. She never visited Ellie. Only that once. There was no mercy in her act, only jealousy, and a good deal of fear, I suspect. There was good in Helen, but there was also the other."

"And Lydia suspected," Nell said quietly, finally understanding the cloud that had weighed down the priest all these months. She sat on an opposite bench, her elbows on her knees, wanting to clear the sadness in his eyes. "You carried all that, Father Larry."

"Ah, it's what we do, Nellie." He looked into the fire, the flames dancing off his glasses and warming his cheeks. "At first I was surprised at how hard Lydia took Ellie's death. Some people called it a blessing and maybe it was. Who knows? These are difficult things to figure out. But I wondered about Lydia. And then she shared one day that she had an inkling—that was all it was, an inkling—of what Helen had done. It weighed heavily on her. At times I thought it hastened her own death."

Abby's spinning laughter drifted over to where they sat. Charlie and Izzy, with Abby on Charlie's shoulders, joined them and the mood drifted up into the flames above the fire pit.

Izzy looked at the light dusting of snow and rubbed her mittened hands together. "It's almost time," she said.

"For what?" Cass said. The words came out quickly, as if she was bewildered at Izzy's comment.

Danny pulled her down next to him on a bench.

"The tree lighting, of course," Izzy said, looking at her friend curiously. "Isn't that why we're here?"

"Oh, that," Cass said, and looked over at the gazebo where Pete, Merry, and Andy were tuning up. On the top step, Alphonso Santos tapped the microphone to life, and around the park, people hustled toward the action, children standing on picnic tables and benches. Waiting.

Alphonso brought them all to attention. "It's almost time," he said in his deep baritone voice. "But first—a hand for the tree decorations and the amazing teams that have turned this park into a fairyland."

The crowd cheered wildly.

"But there's a slight change in procedure and I hope we don't have disappointed tree trimmers tonight. I don't think we will. Our conscientious judges have spent hours looking at the magic you've performed here. And they've come up with not one—but thirty-two winners!"

The crowd screamed and Alphonso held up one hand to hush them.

"It's the truth. Thirty-two entries. All winners. And I don't know if you'll believe this or not, but some Santa somewhere in this town looked at all the donation sheets and added a fistful of dollars to each one. Each bid sheet—" Alphonso put on his glasses and looked down at a small scrap of paper. "Yes, that's what it says here. Each one totaled the exact same amount. And need I say, a *huge* amount—one that will keep all our children healthy and the Sea Harbor Free Health Clinic in business for a long, long time."

The crowd cheered again, families clapping, too, but in the next minute the fidgety children began calling for lights.

But Alphonso wasn't through.

"So it didn't seem to be a year to pick a winner, this Santa said. We'll save that for next year. But you need to know this: this year every single person who donated time and thought and love during a dark, difficult time to making these trees beautiful is a winner. That's what Santa said. And who was I to argue?"

Alphonso looked over to the edge of the gazebo, where the mayor of Sea Harbor, Beatrice Scaglia, was standing. Next to her, a short, hefty man in a red parka looked a little like the Santa of whom Alphonso spoke.

Beatrice Scaglia stepped back and let the light shine on Santa as Alphonso held his hands out and directed attention that way.

"My thanks to my close friend and our benefactor, Stuart Cummings." And then he added in a voice that said more than his words, "Stu, you're in our hearts."

Stu bowed his head as the crowd cheered, clapping their support of a generous man who was traveling through dark days—and letting him know that he wouldn't be making that journey alone. It wasn't how Sea Harbor worked.

As the clapping died down, Beatrice stepped up beside Alphonso on the stage, her eyes damp. She took the switch from Alphonso's hands and smiled out at the expectant crowd.

Pete gave the nod, and as the band filled the air with "It's Beginning to Look a Lot Like Christmas," Beatrice flicked the switch and thirty-two trees turned Harbor Park into a blaze of holiday light.

All around people oohed and aahed, and a band of carolers began singing along, urging the crowd to join in.

"What power," Cass said, looking up as the snowflakes seemed to listen to the song's message and began falling more freely.

They all sat together, the joy on Abby's tiny face warming them more than the fire or lights could ever do.

Janie Levin and Tommy walked by, the lights reflecting off their faces. "Zack just told me he got his job back," Janie said. "Stu gave him a raise, too, and the promise of a job when he gets out of school. An early Christmas present."

"Christmas present!" Cass jumped up. "That reminds me. I have yours." She looked down at Danny.

Danny lifted his eyebrows suspiciously.

"No, really," she said. She looked up then as the snowflakes began to fall in earnest, their dancing magical as they fell on lifted faces.

"Perfect," Cass said, flakes collecting on her dark eyelashes. "I ordered the snowflakes."

"That's my gift?" Danny asked.

"Danny gets an early gift?" Izzy teased. "What about us?"

Cass shushed her. She looked around at the circle of people who filled her life. "I have gifts for all of you, too, but they'll have to wait until Christmas."

"So Danny's special?" Izzy persisted.

Cass nodded. "Yep," she said.

As if intuiting where the attention was, Abby pushed herself off Charlie's lap and toddled over to Danny. He picked her up immediately and cuddled his goddaughter tightly, but his eyes were on Cass.

"That's okay, my Abby doll," Cass whispered. "You're a part of this, too."

And then Cass bent down on one knee onto the frozen ground, and she looked up into Danny's face.

Snowflakes floated down on her cheeks and nose and went unnoticed.

"Okay, this is it, Brandley," she said, and nervously pulled a small box out of her pocket.

Izzy gasped.

Danny frowned. "What . . . ?"

But it took Abby to move the action forward. She took the box in her chubby hands and lifted off the top, gleefully pulling out a braided circle of purple yarn. She held it up into the light of the trees for her godfather to see.

"Wing," she said.

And then she helped her godmother slip it onto Danny's finger.

His wing finger.

Izzy, Birdie, and Nell pulled out tissues.

The men shook their heads in happy disbelief, clapping one another on the back.

Father Northcutt uttered, "God bless 'em."

And Danny, Cass, and Abby hugged and hugged and hugged.

Nell's Sailboat Ornament

My thanks to talented designer Linda Dawkins for generously sharing her sailboat pattern with the Seaside Knitters. Linda lives on a farm in South Africa with her husband, children, and many pets and other animals, inspiration for some of her beautiful patterns.

Materials

Chunky yarn for the boat
8 mm needles for this chunky yarn
2 double-pointed 4 mm needles to knit the I-cord for the mast
Green yarn (or color of your choice) for the sail
Needle for sewing parts together
Pipe cleaner

Boat Pattern (Knit 2)

Cast on 10 stitches in chunky yarn.

Row 1: Knit.

Row 2: Increase into the first stitch, knit across the row, and increase into the last stitch (12 stitches).

Row 3: Knit.

Row 4: Increase into the first stitch, knit across the row, and increase into the last stitch (14 stitches).

Row 5: Knit.

Row 6: Increase into the first stitch, knit across the row, and increase into the last stitch (16 stitches).

Cast off.

Finishing

Sew the two knit boat pieces, right sides together, on the sides and underneath.

Turn inside out so that the right sides are on the outside.

Turn inside out again and pick up 4 stitches in the middle of the boat with your double-pointed needle and attach the yarn for the mast.

Knit an I-cord for about 4.5 to 5 inches for the mast.

Push a pipe cleaner into the top of the mast. If it is difficult, push a long, thick wool needle down at the same time to guide the pipe cleaner. Trim the pipe cleaner once it has reached the base of the boat. Cast off the I-cord and sew the top closed.

Sail

4 mm needles

Cast on 12 stitches.

Row 1: Knit.

Row 2: Knit row, knit 2 stitches together at the end of the row (11 stitches).

Row 3: Knit.

Row 4: Knit row, knit 2 stitches together at the end of the row (10 stitches).

Row 5: Knit.

Row 6: Knit row, knit 2 stitches together at the end of the row (9 stitches).

Row 7: Knit.

Row 8: Knit row, knit 2 stitches together at the end of the row (8 stitches).

Row 9: Knit.

Row 10: Knit row, knit 2 stitches together at the end of the row (7 stitches).

Row 11: Knit.

Row 12: Knit row, knit 2 stitches together at the end of the row (6 stitches).

Row 13: Knit.

Row 14: Knit row, knit 2 stitches together at the end of the row (5 stitches).

Row 15: Knit.

Row 16: Knit row, knit 2 stitches together at the end of the row (4 stitches).

Row 17: Knit.

Row 18: Knit row, knit 2 stitches together at the end of the row (3 stitches).

Row 19: Knit.

Row 20: Knit 1 stitch, knit 2 stitches together (2 stitches).

Row 21: Knit.

Row 22: Knit 2 stitches together.

Bind off.

Sew the sail onto the mast and sew in all ends.

Designer's note: Just think how many colors you can use to knit these little boats. Oh, my—the possibilities are endless!

For more about Linda and photos detailing the finishing of the sailboat, please visit: http://www.naturalsuburbia.com/2011/07/boat-knitting-pattern-tutorial.html.

Nell's Easy Pork Tenderloin

(perfect for a wintry Sea Harbor night)

Serves six

Ingredients

¼ C good olive oil
¼ C soy sauce
¼ C packed brown sugar
2 cloves garlic, minced
1 T fresh grated ginger
3 T Dijon mustard
Kosher salt
Ground black pepper
3 pork tenderloins, about a pound each

Directions

Whisk together above ingredients and pour into a one-gallon sealable bag (or use an oblong glass dish and pour over tenderloins, then cover) and refrigerate overnight or at least 3 hours.

Preheat oven to 400 degrees.

Remove tenderloin from bag, discard marinade*, and pat dry with paper towels. Sprinkle meat with salt and pepper.

Heat 3 T good olive oil in ovenproof pan or skillet and sear all sides of the tenderloins until brown (about 3 minutes total).

Put pan/skillet in oven. Cook, uncovered, until meat thermometer inserted in the thickest part reads 140 degrees (about 10–12 minutes).

Transfer to a platter, cover loosely with foil, and let rest 10 minutes before slicing into ¾-inch pieces.

*Sometimes Nell adds ½ C white wine to the marinade, cooks it down, and serves it with the roast.